Jane O'Reilly would like to say that she's the secret love child of Wonder Woman and grew up on a tropical island in the Pacific, but in reality she grew up in the north of England where it was quite cold and if anyone had any super powers, they kept them well hidden. After university and a brief and very misguided spell as a teacher, she decided it would be better for everyone if she stayed at home and looked after her children. She wrote her first novel when her youngest was a baby, and has published numerous contemporary and erotic romances with Harlequin Escape and Carina UK. But what she really wanted to write was a book about a space pirate in which she could blow things up . . .

Find out more at www.janeoreilly.co.uk

By Jane O'Reilly

The Second Species Trilogy
Blue Shift
Deep Blue

DEEP BLUE

BOOK TWO
THE SECOND SPECIES TRILOGY

Jane O'Reilly

piatkus

PIATKUS

First published in Great Britain in 2018 by Piatkus
This paperback edition published in 2019 by Piatkus

1 3 5 7 9 10 8 6 4 2

Copyright © 2018 Jane O'Reilly

A CIP catalogue record for this book
is available from the British Library.

ISBN 978-0-349-41663-2

Typeset in Baskerville by M Rules
Printed and bound in Great Britain by Clays Ltd, Elcograf S.p.A.

Papers used by Piatkus are from well-managed forests
and other responsible sources.

Piatkus
An imprint of
Little, Brown Book Group
Carmelite House
50 Victoria Embankment
London EC4Y 0DZ

An Hachette UK Company
www.hachette.co.uk

www.littlebrown.co.uk

For Patrick

CHAPTER

1

8th October 2207

Vessel: The *Alcatraz 2*. Prison ship
Destination: N/A
Cargo: N/A
Crew: N/A
Droids: Unknown

Jinn didn't know how long she'd been out for. It could have been a matter of minutes; it could have been days, or even weeks. She awoke to darkness, to a silence that was unfamiliar and yet somehow not; to a smell that she couldn't quite place, a chemical tang that left a strange taste in the back of her throat.

But at least she awoke.

Opening her eyes, she tried to take in her surroundings and tried not to panic. She was in a hospital. The white walls and the smell and the equipment that dotted the room all told her that. But which one? Two deep breaths, then she tried to get off the bed. But she couldn't move. Her arms, legs and torso were bound with rubbery white straps that flexed when panic finally took hold and she fought against them. Her movements set a series of lights flashing and an alarm sounded, a hideous wail that seemed to scratch at her head from the inside out.

Jinn twisted in the bed as the alarm continued to scream. A droid came over. She felt the sharp sting of a needle and then there was nothing.

When she woke again, she knew better than to move. Cautiously, she turned her head, the only part of her that wasn't strapped down. There were other beds, lots of them, and the men in them were all strapped down, too, just as she was. When she saw them, Jinn knew where she was.

She was back on board the *A2*.

Her mouth curved into a small smile and she relaxed back into the bed. *Excellent*. The plan had worked. She hadn't been sure that it would. She kept as still as she could, focusing on her breathing and the weight of Tellurium in her forearms. *Come on*, she willed it. *Come on. Work*.

At first there was nothing, then she felt the all too familiar rush of heat into her hands. She lifted her head, trying to see, but the straps that bound her to the bed tightened immediately, pulling hard across her thighs, her chest, to the point where it became difficult to breathe. The room began to spin. She had no choice but to stop, though she gritted her teeth in frustration as the alarms sounded again, no doubt summoning more of the droids with their drugs, their oblivion.

If she was going to get free, she was going to have to think. She would have to outsmart whoever had designed this prison. The droids came, and so did the drugs and the darkness, and this time she dreamed. She was in her mother's apartment in the Dome. Ferona was there, dressed in pale blue truesilk, looking exactly as Jinn remembered her. Her mouth was moving but Jinn couldn't hear the words.

And then there was pain, so much pain, and she touched her hands to her stomach, and when she lifted them her palms were wet with blood, and Ferona was laughing, laughing, laughing.

Jinn woke with a gasp, her heart thundering.

Only a dream, she told herself. *It was only a dream*. She'd gone to her mother's apartment. That was how she'd ended up here. But the rest of it wasn't real.

She willed the Tellurium out of her system again. She willed it to travel down, in thin, seeking wires that forced their way through the medibed and into the computer system that controlled it.

Her body jolted as she became part of the circuit, but the straps that held her down didn't respond. Jinn moved a little against them. Nothing. She let out a shaky breath, her heart still racing from the shock, then she redirected the Tellurium. But she must have triggered a warning system in the bed somewhere.

A medical droid that had been working on the other side of the room rushed towards her. *Shit*. She wouldn't let it drug her again. She wouldn't. The bed shocked her as she struggled against the straps, making her scream out with pain and frustration. The droid moved closer, hand raised, needle ready.

And then it was flying back across the room. It disappeared into the darkness. A man moved towards her. He was half-naked and filthy, and when he spoke his voice was a low, rough whisper. 'I'll get you out of here,' he said. 'But try anything stupid and I'll break your neck.'

He dropped to one knee at the side of the bed, and a moment later the straps that held her down slid away. Jinn scrambled off the bed and into a crouch at the side opposite to the man. Blades out, she looked him over. Dark hair hung knotted and tangled down his back, and he had the lean, hungry look of someone who hasn't had enough to eat for far too long. His face had sharp, elegant lines, and his eyes were yellow-green. He was familiar under the dirt. 'I know you,' she said. 'You were here before. You're Jozeph Li.' She remembered watching him chase after the *Deviant* as it raced out of the docking bay, remembered leaving him behind when she'd first escaped from this place. It seemed so very long ago.

'Talk later,' he said. 'We need to get out of sight.' He pointed at the ceiling, and then he leapt straight up and disappeared. Where in the void had he gone? Jinn followed his path up into the darkness. At first she saw nothing, then her eyes gradually adjusted.

There was a hole in the ceiling where one of the Plastex tiles had been removed. It wasn't big. But it was big enough. She scrambled up onto the bunk, but the hole was still a good two metres above the top of her head.

'Jump!' Li called down to her. 'Hurry!'

'I can't get up there!'

'You can. Trust me.'

Jinn took a deep breath. She bent her knees. She closed her eyes. The muscles in her legs, which had at first seemed heavy, shocked her with a sudden explosion of power. She flew up, up, and then strong hands were on her waist, pulling her forward. She stumbled, collapsing onto her hands and knees inside a dimly lit, poky space.

Something was different.

She'd been modified. She knew it all at once, just as she'd known where she was. She'd been too busy trying to get away from the droids to notice before. She felt it now, though. The sensation was all too familiar.

'Am I green?' she asked as Li scrambled to put the roof tile back in position.

'What?'

'Am I green?!'

'No,' he said. 'You're whiter than a bloody snowflake.'

Jinn pressed her hands to her face, then sat back. Her legs felt strange. In fact, her entire body felt strange. But she wasn't Type Two. She wasn't toxic. She wasn't Type Three, either. She couldn't hear anything but the thundering of her heart and the hoarse rush of her breathing.

She'd been able to jump a height that should have been impossible. She willed out her blades, willed them back in again. The Tellurium reacted with a speed she'd never been able to generate before. It was as if her entire body had been upgraded, and suddenly she knew.

She *knew*.

There was only one thing that could have done this. 'I'm Type One,' she said. She scrambled back, away from Li. Type Ones had increased strength and incredible powers of healing. They were also highly aggressive, and that was not something she ever wanted to be.

'You're an incomplete Type One,' Li said.

'What do you mean?'

'You only went through the first stage of the process. They don't administer the final dose of serum until you're in one of the cages down in the hold. Too dangerous.'

'So I'm not aggressive.'

'Not unless you choose to be.'

Jinn dropped her head to her knees and rested it there for a moment. The first time she'd been here, she'd seen the people being held in those electrified holding cells. One of them had nearly killed her. But that was what you got when you spliced Sittan DNA into human cells: something different. Something that wasn't human anymore.

She wasn't that. She didn't really know what she was yet, but she wasn't that. Looking around, Jinn quickly took in her surroundings. They were in a maintenance tunnel a couple of metres wide and about the same high. When she got to her feet, her body felt different. She hadn't noticed it before but she was noticeably taller. The lack of light hardly bothered her at all.

It felt very odd.

But it didn't matter. There would be time to think about it later. Right now she had a job to do.

'I need to get to the control deck,' she said.

'What for?'

'I've got to take the ship offline,' she said. That was why she was here. That was the plan. Go to Earth, get sent back to the *A2*, stop the government from sending the people on board to Sittan. Stop more people from signing up to the programme that would see them genetically modified and traded as slaves to their alien neighbours. 'Once I've got control of the freighter, Dax and the others . . . '

'Dax is gone.'

'What do you mean he's gone?'

'He was here,' Li said. 'They checked him over, gave him the final dose of serum and then they loaded him on a transporter. He's gone.'

'No,' Jinn said. He couldn't be. 'He's on the *Mutant*, not here.'

But the memory came flooding back. It hadn't been a dream. She had gone to Earth. She had been arrested and taken to her mother's apartment in the London Dome. Then Dax had come after her, and Ferona had ordered a droid to shoot her right in the gut, a potentially fatal wound. And so Dax had surrendered. He had done it for Jinn, to keep her alive, because Ferona had told him Jinn would be left to die if he did not. 'Why didn't you help him?' she asked Li, desperately.

'And risk getting caught?'

'You helped me!'

'You didn't have four security droids standing over you 24/7. Look. You escaped from this place before, which means you can escape from it again. You want to help Dax? Get those friends of yours to come and get us.'

'I need to get a message out.'

'That might be a little difficult,' Li said. His shoulders slumped.

'Why?'

'All the terminals have been removed.'

'They must have left the central unit to keep the life support running,' Jinn said. 'I should be able to hack into it. It's on the control deck.'

It took them about thirty minutes to reach the control deck, which was located three floors up. But when they got there the central computer had been removed. Two smaller units had been fitted instead, and she couldn't access either of them. She tried anyway. Beside her, Li said something rude. She knew how he felt.

Think, Jinn, think.

Cut the power. Reboot the system. Bypass the seals on these two units.

She wasn't outdone. Merely delayed.

The easiest place to cut the power would be down in the cargo bay where the main generator was housed. There were other places but they would be difficult to reach and time was now of the essence.

She forced open the doors of the control deck and trekked along the passageways that led down to the bottom of the ship. Although the control deck had been changed, nothing else had. There were still trails of bilehore slime crossing the walls and the ceiling. Still the tucked away corners where prisoners who had once occupied this ship had built the closest thing they could to a home.

The vast chamber was just as she remembered. It was still too hot and it still stank, though at least this time she didn't have to deal with the shock of what it contained. But somehow with that element missing, the details of it hit her that much harder. The vivid yellow of the arcs of electric charge that ran the length of the cages. The smell of sweat and burning flesh. The noise.

Lowering herself onto her stomach, Jinn edged along the walkway. The air was stifling, filled with the smell of hot metal and human filth. At the end of the walkway was the familiar spiral stairway that led down to the lower floor. She crawled to it, then slowly made her way down the stairs.

The generator would be down on the deck where the droids could easily reach it, to ensure that it was maintained. She pushed up into a crouch and watched their movement for a moment until she spotted a repair droid. It scuttled around the cages then over to the wall where several flashing control panels were housed. Pipes ran away from them, each one as thick as her arm.

There. That had to be it. Keeping her low position, Jinn moved to the bottom of the stairs as quickly as she dared. It was even hotter down here. The challenge now was to reach those controls without getting too close to the cages. Wiping away the sweat that ran into her eyes, Jinn pressed her back against the wall and carefully made her way across. The droids ignored her for the most part, busy with the men inside the cages.

She edged further round the edge of the space until eventually she reached the intersection of power cables on the wall. She reached out, touched them, whipping her hand away as the heat of the metal scorched her bare flesh. She could hear the power crackling inside the metal pipe that ran floor to ceiling, and knew she'd found the sweet spot. All she had to do now was inflict enough damage on it to take it out. The system would compensate for the damage and reboot, picking a pathway that avoided the broken pipe, and, in so doing, would reset the main unit on the control deck. But she'd have to make it quick. Sooner or later, the droids were going to notice what she was doing, and she very much doubted they would like it.

Jinn set her blade to the pipe, counted to three, and sliced clean through it. Electricity sang through her body as she severed the wires inside. For a moment there was nothing but blackness and a terrifying sensation of numbness. Her body quickly recovered. She could feel it healing from the inside out, a rush of warmth and sudden drop in energy. She leaned back against the wall and breathed deeply as the heat subsided and the exhaustion fled as quickly as it had appeared.

And it was a good thing that it did. The instant she'd severed those wires, the electro cages had switched off. Darkness filled the space now together with the sound of scrambling footsteps. There was yelling and screaming. Droids clattered around in the darkness.

Then the emergency lighting switched on.

'Bloody supernova,' Jinn shrieked, pressing back against the wall. The prisoners were tearing each other apart. She had never seen such violence, such eager brutality. Screams of rage and pain filled the air, together with the unmistakable tang of blood.

At the bottom of the stairs, she saw Jozeph Li snap the neck of a man who had his teeth in his arm. He threw the body aside, a look of distaste on his face. Jinn sprinted towards him. 'Let's go,' he said.

Jinn didn't need to be told twice. They made it out of the cargo bay, just, and made it back to the control deck in record time. Jinn pressed her hands to the ports on the now unsealed units. The Tellurium pushed out of her fingertips and connected with the computer. She searched, found the channel she was looking for. It took several seconds too many to make the connection, time in which her heart threatened to stop and her stomach to empty.

When Theon's face filled the screen, Jinn didn't know whether she wanted to laugh or cry. 'Theon,' she said. 'He's gone.'

'Yes,' Theon said. 'I know. I take it you're in need of rescue.'

'Like never before. How quickly can you get here?'

'How quickly can you get the docking bay doors open?'

Jinn instructed the system to open the doors. 'It's done.'

'Be ready for us,' Theon told her.

She turned to Li. 'I won't leave you behind this time,' she said.

'I'm counting on it.'

She disconnected from the computer and willed out her blades. 'I'm ready.'

'What *are* those?' Li asked her.

'Another time,' she told him.

'I'll hold you to that,' he said, and they sprinted back into the bay, knowing that this was their only chance of escape. At the far end, the airlock hissed open, and the nose of a small white transporter slid into view, but it was so far away, too far away.

And between them and the transporter, a group of security droids were tangling with some of the Type One males. It was hard to tell which side was winning. Blaster fire peppered the hold, bouncing off the walls, ricocheting in all directions, sparking small fires all over the place. 'Run!' Li shouted. They ran faster, faster, until they hit the wall and kept on moving, up the side of the cargo bay and onto the ceiling, just as she had done with Dax once before, only this time she wasn't being carried.

The speed was all hers. There was no time to try and

understand it now, because they were close to the transporter, so close. But not close enough. A huge male darted in front of them, knocking Jinn to the floor. His eyes were wild, his pupils little more than narrow slits. A blaster shot caught him in the shoulder and he roared, but didn't get out of her way.

Jinn flipped onto her stomach, scrambling away from him. A strong hand hauled her to her feet. 'Theon!' she gasped.

'Get to the transporter,' he said. 'Go. I'll keep them back.'

She opened her mouth to argue with him, but he was already gone, spinning away from her, tackling another Type One before he could grab her.

Jinn didn't need to be told twice. She broke into a sprint, flinging herself at the half-lowered ramp. Jozeph Li wasn't far behind, his booted feet hitting the ramp and making it shake. He grabbed Jinn by the back of her shirt and hauled her further up the ramp, further still, until she was on the floor inside the belly of the transporter.

She stayed there for a moment, trying to catch her breath. 'Theon!' she screamed. 'Come on!'

But he was too deep into the fray. And above the noise of the men, she heard something else. An alarm. A very distinctive alarm, one that sent a shiver of fear down her back. It was a sound that anyone who had undergone pilot training knew only too well. The self-destruct had been activated.

Jinn scrambled to her feet, dashed through to the empty pilot's seat of the small ship and dropped into it. She plugged in. Her retinal screen came on almost instantly, and she fired up the drive. If they stayed, they died. All of them. Theon ... she saw Theon on the screen, fighting his way through the crowd of men and droids, trying to get to the transporter. They grabbed his arms, his legs.

And then they tore him apart.

'No!'

But he was gone.

The alarm had changed, warning all on board that they were

into the final count. Through a haze of tears, Jinn connected with the onboard computer. How she managed to fly them out of there, she wasn't sure, but she did. She flew onwards, onwards. The *Mutant* was just ahead. She docked with it quickly, leaving the little transporter and sprinting to the control deck where Eve and Alistair were waiting.

'He's gone,' she said. She could barely believe it. 'Theon's gone.'

'We know,' Eve said. Her eyes were bright, and her face was wet. 'We heard it . . . his comm . . .'

'They're monsters, all of them. They activated the self-destruct. It's . . .'

The force of the sudden explosion rocked the ship. The brightness of it filled the viewscreen, a flash of pure white light that was just as quickly swallowed by darkness.

They sat there in silence, in stillness. Jinn was too shocked to speak. She had escaped it by seconds. She had escaped it because Theon had sacrificed himself, giving his life in place of hers. All of the men on board were dead, killed by their own actions. They had been completely out of control. Her plan hadn't been a plan at all, it had been a disaster waiting to happen.

'So where to now?' asked Li, as the final traces of the explosion faded away.

'Dax has been taken to Sittan,' Jinn said. 'And we're going to go and get him.' She walked to the pilot's chair and sat in it. 'I won't leave him to die on that planet. He deserves better than that.'

And so had Theon, and the men on board the *A2*. She had let them down. She had let them all down.

She wouldn't do that to Dax.

CHAPTER

2

30th October 2207

Intergalactic Senate, Kepler System, Sector Five, Neutral Space

Ferona Blue had been at Kepler for less than three hours. Her skin still felt tight from the five jumps it had taken to get there, and her stomach refused to settle. But none of that bothered her. She had more important things to think about. She waited as her personal droid zipped her into an elegant feathered dress, then smoothed down the bodice, enjoying the firm hold it had on her.

'They're here.' Swain came into Ferona's quarters almost at a run. Sweat gleamed on his forehead and he rubbed at it with his pocket cloth, a sure sign that he was nervous.

'And?' Ferona asked him. She turned, letting her skirts swirl around her ankles, then sat down at her vanity table so that the beauty droid could fix her hair.

'I didn't see any of them,' Swain replied. 'I only saw their transport landing.'

Ferona closed her eyes for a moment. She tried to find her calm, really she did, but it wasn't possible. She picked up a brush and hurled it across the room. It smacked against the wall and clattered to the floor. Fortunately, it was solid silver and didn't break. 'You were supposed to greet them!'

Swain flinched, and that annoyed her even more. She should have brought Lucinda, her other assistant. Lucinda never flinched. But Lucinda was needed on Earth, where she could keep an eye on President Vexler, so Swain had been her only option. And he was completely out of his depth.

When the senate had agreed to vote on whether or not to allow human ships to pass through alien controlled space, they had scheduled it for an Earth month later. Then the *A2* had been destroyed, the Sittan had asked for the vote to be delayed, and Ferona was desperately trying to keep the empress onside.

'Do you want me to go back?' he babbled. 'I can go back. I can greet them now. It won't take long.'

But he made no move towards the exit. Instead, he made a great show of wiping his face again, then folding the silk square and tucking it neatly into his pocket.

Ferona gritted her teeth. 'No,' she said. The Sittan empress didn't think much of her male assistant anyway, and right now Ferona shared that sentiment.

Swain's relief was obvious as he moved across to the floating refreshment station and programmed himself a bag of vitamin water. Half of it was gone before he noticed Ferona's irritated gaze on him and hastily ordered her a slender glass of Koffee. There was food available on Kepler, but Ferona didn't eat it. She didn't trust the other senators not to slip something into her meal that would render her unable to participate in talks – having done it herself on several occasions – so she always brought her own.

She took the glass of darkly steaming Koffee without thanking Swain, sipped at it delicately and considered the situation. The Senate talks were due to commence in a little over two hours. The Sittan party had cut it very fine, but there was still time for a personal greeting, though now that Swain had failed to do the groundwork Ferona would have to make the initial move herself and that wasn't how she had wanted to do things.

Three shipments of Type One males had been sent to Sittan

in the past week. Ferona was desperate to know if the empress was happy with them. There was no reason why she shouldn't be – five hundred additional units had been included in the shipments, taking the total to two thousand. It would have been an unexpected bonus, one she was sure the empress would have appreciated.

And it had made a very clear, very important point.

The destruction of the *A2* had not stopped the programme.

Setting down her half-empty glass, Ferona swept on her senatorial robes, ankle-length and white, and checked her appearance in the holomirror that beamed up from the floor with a tap of her foot on a pressure plate. Her hair was neat, curled up at the base of her neck, and the gold-feathered dress was simply perfect peeking under the hem of the heavy robes. Deeply satisfied with herself, if not with her assistant, she strode to the exit.

Swain quickly followed her as she'd expected he would, and the two of them snapped on breathing masks as the door to her quarters closed behind them. Kepler was a very wet planet. The acidic mist that lingered everywhere caused lung damage if inhaled in any significant quantity. The sea rippled and churned three hundred metres below, deep green cresting up into high white peaks that slapped against the narrow base of the tower. Her quarters were in a glossy bubble held safely out of the way of the waves.

Their transport, a blunt-nosed little boat, hovered at the edge of the deck that ringed her quarters. Three thick cables kept it anchored in place. It could work both in air and water, though Ferona had no desire to test it at sea. It felt flimsy enough in the air.

She stepped into the boat first, Swain following and taking the controls. As soon as they were seated, the cables retracted and the boat was set adrift. Swain quickly began to pedal. The steady hum of the paddles was somewhat reassuring, though the pace was plodding at best as he steered them away from their quarters and towards the Sittan pod.

The communal areas, including the large debating hall, were housed in a vast central bubble supported by a dozen lean white legs. Each race had their own pod arranged in a circle around it. The Sittan pod was a fifteen-minute drift in their precarious little craft. She felt a twinge of nervous anticipation at the thought of seeing the empress, and pressed a hand against her restless stomach.

Earth was dying, driven into an ice age by scientists who had believed they could fix global warming. They'd succeeded in cooling the planet, that much was true, but with average temperatures of thirty below, plant life had been decimated and now oxygen levels were falling. Humans had moved into huge heated Domes built on the remains of the capital cities. More had been forced to dig down underneath them, living in squalor below the surface, surviving on government handouts. All of them, in the Domes and below, were running out of time. The public believed that what they saw was the whole truth, but they didn't know that waste from the Kaelite ore used to power the Domes had contaminated the water supply. There was nothing left on Earth for humans now.

But a new planet had been found. They had called it Spes, after the Roman goddess of hope, and early probes had sent back details of the surface and the atmosphere and shown them to be clean and lush and habitable. It was a chance for the human race to start over. The only problem, a small, silly, bloody impossible problem, was that in order to get to Spes, Earth ships would have to pass through sectors of space controlled by their alien neighbours. The Sittan and Shi Fai in particular did not want thousands of dirty human ships passing close to their home planets, and had turned a deaf ear to all pleas for help.

While the other politicians had spent their time wringing their hands and despairing, making pointless speeches and empty promises, Ferona had found a solution. A way to make a deal with their alien neighbours, offering them something in return for safe passage across their space. The Second Species programme. The Sittan wanted human males strong enough to survive their arena, and the Shi Fai wanted human females immune to their toxic physiology. The technology to create them had already existed. All Ferona had needed to do was set up manufacturing on a larger scale, and the deals had been done.

Type One males for the Sittan, and Type Two females for the Shi Fai. She considered it to be a fair exchange given what was at stake. She also privately felt that the human race would benefit from a little pruning back. In reality, it would be impossible to take everyone on Earth to Spes. It was vital to make sure that those who did go were the very best, the most likely to survive and make good lives for themselves. And that was not the Underworld workers who had signed up for the Second Species programme in their thousands, tempted by the promise of a future they would never see.

'I hate this planet,' Swain muttered. 'And this boat.' He angled the prow to avoid a group of strange looking creatures that jumped from the sea. They had fishlike bodies with wide, flat heads and skin the colour of tarnished copper. They flapped long translucent fins and growled at the boat.

Swain docked the boat quickly if not smoothly, holding it steady as the cables spooled out and automatically connected them to the landing platform. It had been the Lodons who had originally created this place, when they had first encountered the Dra and had wanted to thrash out the finer details of their relationship on neutral ground.

As that relationship was now symbiotic, and the Dra lived inside the bodies of the Lodons, Ferona couldn't help but wonder what those discussions must have been like. It was a hundred and sixty years since humans had made first contact with their alien neighbours, but over a thousand for the Lodons, and not every race they had encountered had been invited to join the Senate. Humans were part of a very privileged group. The dozen races that now formed the Senate were the best that the galaxy had produced. They had the highest levels of intelligence and planets rich with resources. Ferona suspected that this also made them the most likely to go to war, and that the Lodons had created the Senate as a way of forestalling that, but she kept that thought to herself.

Swain alighted from the boat first, holding out a manicured hand to Ferona as she climbed the narrow steps up onto the platform. A large, shining bell had been suspended from the roof, and she picked up the double-ended hammer that lay underneath it and struck the curve. The Sittan didn't go in for droids and vid screens. They preferred pomp and ceremony.

Ferona, who had packed her own quarters with as much modern tech as it could hold, found it rather silly. The mesh that concealed the entrance shimmered slightly and two of the empress's guards stepped out onto the platform. Swain took a step back. Ferona didn't move. She refused to be intimidated by the blood-red uniforms they wore, or the narrow blades that hung down from each hip, or the blazing yellow eyes that said they would cut the flesh from her bones and enjoy it.

'Senator Blue,' the taller of the two said. She dipped her head slightly, never taking her eyes off Ferona. As she straightened her neck, a row of spikes emerged on each side, each one needle-sharp and the length of a little finger.

'Grenla,' Ferona replied, acknowledging the leader of the empress's personal guard. Even in her heeled boots she barely reached the shoulder of the Sittan female.

The mesh shimmered again and the hanging slats were pulled aside, tapping gently against each other. There was a scent of incense, something dark and earthy overlaid with the pungent taste of smoke, and Ferona tried not to breathe too deeply as she walked carefully through to the room concealed within.

The empress was sprawled on a low couch, licking the ends of her bejewelled, clawed fingers, which currently held a half-eaten piece of juicy orange fruit. It was less than an hour before talks were due to resume. They would be debating issues that potentially had a galaxy-wide impact. The empress had turned up late, hadn't bothered to attend the earlier talks which had settled a squabble between two races warring over farming rights on a small moon that orbited both of their respective planets, and was lounging around as if she had all the time in the universe.

Ferona held her hands palm-up at waist height, as was the Sittan way. 'Empress Talta,' she said. 'May the Mountain find you strong and well on this blessed day.' The translation device clipped to the left collar of her robes instantly translated her words into Sittan. She preferred that to the Universal tongue which was clumsy at best, and didn't always carry the nuance of what was said. Nuances were very important when dealing with aliens, especially the empress, who was always happy to take offence over the smallest of slips.

'Senator Blue. I don't recall arranging a private meeting.'

'You didn't,' Ferona said. 'But I wanted to pay you a courtesy visit. I trust that the ambassadors are serving you well.'

'As well as can be expected.' The empress sniffed, dark nostrils flaring. She dropped the half-eaten fruit into a tall metal urn at the side of her couch and held out her hand. An attendant immediately rushed over with a cloth and began to clean it.

'I am pleased to hear it,' Ferona said. 'Did you notice that we sent an additional five hundred units this week?'

'It was noted, and the Sittan people thank you for your generosity.'

'I think you will find the next consignment even more to your liking.'

The empress sat up. 'In what way?'

'Our scientists have found a way to modify the formula slightly,' Ferona said. She clasped her hands in front of her, relaxed her shoulders, even though she could feel the zing of tension and the rub of sweat on her back, partly due to the heat generated by the fire pit that blazed in the centre of the room, partly a reaction to the flash of the empress's pointed teeth. 'It enhances maturation rates. These males are younger, stronger and more aggressive.'

'I see,' the empress said. She got slowly to her feet. A jet black robe was brought to her and slipped onto her muscular frame. 'I am glad to hear that the project is still progressing, despite the recent . . . setbacks.'

'The explosion at the *Alcatraz 2* was unfortunate,' Ferona replied. She was prepared for this, had practised her answer. 'But the new facility is larger, better equipped, and, as it is closer to the jump gate, has allowed us to cut transport time considerably.'

'Do you know yet what caused it?'

'A group called Humans First is believed to be responsible,' Ferona told her. 'They don't agree with genetic modification and think that we should accept the genes we are given at conception. It was an attempt to put an end to the Second Species programme. And it failed.' She smiled widely.

That much at least was true, even if the rest of it had been a complete pack of lies. Humans First weren't responsible, although they were a pain in the neck. Ferona knew exactly what had caused the explosion. Somehow, the men on board had triggered the self-destruct. There had always been a possibility that something would go wrong on board the ship, and so she'd had a failsafe built in and she couldn't say she was sorry that it had been used. The *A2* had been well past its best. Fortunately, Dax had already been modified and had been on his way to Sittan. He hadn't been among the men killed when the prison exploded. He would die on Sittan instead.

The empress had requested him and Ferona had delivered him, something she was deeply proud of. He had been a difficult man to track down. She had intended to modify her daughter in the same way, though not for the Sittan, which was why Jinn had been on board the *A2* when it was destroyed.

Jinn's death kept Ferona awake at night more often than she would care to admit, but she was sure that the feelings would fade in time. It wasn't that she was grieving, as such. But it had been such a waste. There had been such potential.

'I look forward to the arrival of the new fighters,' the empress said. 'I am sure they will not disappoint. How many are there?'

'At the moment, we have eight thousand awaiting transport.'

The empress's yellow eyes gleamed with avarice, and Ferona knew she had her.

'There will be more,' she promised. 'This is only the first consignment.' She smiled again, though this time it took a little more effort. Two thousand was a miracle, given that a new facility had had to be built from scratch. The men were no longer volunteers. She'd had to start paying them to sign up for the programme to counteract the drop-off after the *A2* had been destroyed, and that had been a bitter pill indeed.

'Excellent,' the empress said. 'I believe it is time for us to make the crossing to the senate hall.' She shuddered. 'I do so hate this planet. It's so wet and unpleasant.' Then she turned and walked away, heading through the doors at the other side of her quarters and out onto the boat beyond, leaving Ferona to scramble for her own transport.

It would all be worth it in the end. When the human population settled on Spes, they would have access to almost unlimited natural resources. They would have everything they needed. And they would have cemented strong relations with the Sittan.

Ferona lost herself in the dream of it as Swain piloted the little boat over to the main meeting hall where all the senators gathered to thrash out their differences. She imagined blue skies and towering trees, and water that flowed freely over the land. She imagined walking through a garden of real flowers, picking fruit from a tree. She would be able to walk outside without freezing to death, without poisoning her lungs with toxic air. It would be paradise.

Senator Hann was waiting for her in her box when she arrived, dirtying it with his damp, musty smell. Swain flicked on the privacy screen as Ferona acknowledged the Shi Fai senator and his assistants with a nod of her head. 'Hann.'

'Senator Blue,' he replied. 'I have come to thank you for your most recent gift. We are delighted to have received it.' His voice came through the little translator box that hung on a silver chain around his neck and bounced against his protruding belly.

'You are most welcome.' Ferona gritted her teeth. She harboured an intense dislike for the Shi Fai, an innate sense of disgust from which there was no escaping. Physically, they were repulsive. Hairless and stocky, they had fleshy bodies and moist skin patterned with dark purple veins that curled around three large eyes. Tentacles protruded where their mouth should be. The senatorial robes hid a lumpy, awkward body. And they smelled. It was their way of communicating with each other, through the use of pheromones rather than sound.

The problem was that she judged them by human standards, and they were not human. Neither were the Sittan, to be fair, but at least they weren't repulsive. But the Shi Fai were useful. Their technology was organically based, completely different from anything humans possessed, and their planet produced many resources useful to all other alien races. Faidal was the original source of the Silver Rice plants used as a source of cheap food by the majority of humans. Although the rice could be grown on Colony Four, the plants needed replacing every three years and only the Shi Fai had the seeds.

'We look forward to receiving our next shipment.'

'I look forward to sending it to you.'

Ferona was hugely relieved when the little senator bade her farewell and made his way across to his own booth. 'Spray the freshener,' she hissed at Swain. He quickly pulled a bottle from his pocket and misted the air, and within a few seconds she could breathe again.

'Do we have enough women for the next shipment?' she asked Swain.

'Not yet,' he said.

'Set up recruitment centres in the Underworld Cities,' she told him. 'Lower the age limit. Offer something for the families of women who volunteer. We must keep the Shi Fai onside.'

'Consider it done.'

Ferona settled in to her seat as Swain flicked the privacy screens off and the debates began.

CHAPTER

3

30th October 2207

Vessel: The *Mutant*. Battleship/carrier hybrid
Destination: Sittan
Cargo: None
Crew: 4
Droids: 7

'Ow!' Jinn dropped the laser cutter she'd been holding and sucked her burned finger. The cutter hit the floor with a clatter, bouncing away into a corner somewhere out of sight.

The gravity generator whirred, groaned, its little red lights blinking slowly. The stupid thing had been stuttering for the past forty-eight hours. At random intervals it would turn off and everything that wasn't strapped down would float, including the crew. The first time it had happened they'd had no warning. Bodies had smacked into steel. Curses had been spat out, and blood had drifted in odd, wobbling droplets.

It had been even worse when the generator had powered back up a couple of minutes later. There were a lot of sharp edges on the way down, and Jinn was pretty sure she'd hit all of them.

After she'd picked herself up and checked on the others, she'd strapped herself into the captain's chair, Dax's chair, and checked the system. The main computer had reported an unexpected fluctuation in the power supply to the generator, and predicted a 0.5 per cent chance of reoccurrence.

Either the computer was crap at maths or it was also malfunctioning, because they'd had five more episodes over the next eighteen hours, lasting longer each time. They couldn't keep going as they were. They needed to get to a repair station. But until then they'd have to live with whatever temporary fix they could manage.

Jinn inhaled and wiggled the fingers in her right hand, forming her Tellurium into a blunt tool. She stretched out her hand and hooked the cutter. Then she carefully moved it closer. She'd managed to replace the power coupling which seemed to have stopped the generator from powering down completely, but it was only working at 80 per cent capacity.

They had some gravity, but not the amount they were used to. They weren't floating, exactly. It was more like being drunk. Every movement felt loose and soft. A normal footstep turned into a clumsy, awkward jump, and, when you fell, you fell just slowly enough to see the pain coming.

'Any progress?'

Jinn turned her head to see Eve slowly approaching. She was wearing a thick padded jacket and gloves and her movements were cautious. 'Depends on your definition of progress,' she said. 'I've replaced the power coupling, but the computer isn't telling me anything we don't already know.'

'Like that the grav system is on its last legs, you mean?'

'Pretty much.'

Moving slowly, Eve placed a sealed water bag on top of the generator and eased it forward, careful not to put herself too close to Jinn. Jinn retracted her tech, picked up the bottle and gratefully took a mouthful. Her clothes were soaked with sweat. She felt damp, lightheaded, strange. It wasn't just the heat. It was the Sittan DNA that had been spliced into her cells.

She hadn't wanted the modifications. She hadn't agreed to them. But they had been done to her anyway, and now that alien DNA was part of her. The changes she was experiencing were unpredictable, her body strange and uncomfortable even before the gravity had failed.

'Theon could have fixed this,' Eve said.

Jinn rubbed her eyes and looked at the broken generator. 'Yes,' she said. 'He could.'

But Theon was gone. She still felt the pain of the loss. The only thing that kept it from overwhelming her was this ship and the fact that there was so much to do. The *Mutant* had lost the rest of its crew months ago. When the government had announced what it called a 'programme of intergalactic cooperation' and declared that everyone who signed up would have their debts and criminal records expunged, as well as getting guaranteed places on the ships to Spes, Dax's crew had collectively decided it was a better deal than they were currently getting.

Jinn couldn't blame them. The politicians had done their job well. They had managed to make trafficking and slavery sound reasonable, even desirable. They had made life on the alien planets sound like a six-month holiday, and the Second Species modifications sound straightforward and easy. The small print had quietly mentioned that the procedure had an unfortunately high mortality rate, but who read the small print?

Dax did. She missed him. 'How far are we from Sittan?'

Eve kept her gaze steady. 'Five days if we jump. Twenty-seven if we haul straight space.'

'That long?'

Eve nodded.

Jinn carefully put the water bag down. Twenty-seven days.

It felt like forever. It already felt like years since she had seen Dax, since she had breathed his scent, touched his skin, heard his voice. It was six weeks since she had seen him on the vid screen in her mother's apartment in the Domes, when he had turned himself in, freely, willingly, for her. When she had woken up on the *A2*, he had already been altered, was already gone. She was desperately clinging to her memories, terrified they would slip away and she would lose what little she had left of him.

She had to get to him. But if she was going to do that, she had to figure out a way to fix the damn ship. Jinn turned her attention back to the broken gravity generator. The parts she'd replaced gleamed under the bright glow of the hover light she'd set up to illuminate her work. But the control panel on the generator continued to flash in that same slow, steady way. Whatever was wrong with it, she couldn't fix it with what she had. There was no way they'd be able to make it to Sittan without having it repaired. It simply wasn't safe to jump without reliable gravity. 'Where are the others?' she asked.

'Li is doing some maintenance work on the water recycler,' Eve told her. 'Alistair is on the control deck fiddling around with the light settings or something.'

Jinn deactivated the welding helmet she'd been wearing. 'Time for a group meeting. I'm not going to be able to fix this, and we can't continue as we are.'

Eve's expression was grim as the two of them walked across the docking bay to the elevator at the far end. Once inside, she tugged a strap loose from the sleeve of her jacket and tied herself tightly to the hand grip on the side of the car.

Jinn leaned back against the opposite wall and wrapped her fingers round the grip. Five days, if they jumped. Twenty-seven if they didn't. Since Dax had gone, the others had looked to Jinn to lead them. Nothing had been said, not openly anyway, but they each had their roles, their strengths, and they seemed to think hers was the ability to make the difficult decisions.

The elevator slid smoothly to a halt and the doors eased open, spilling them out onto the control deck. The floor sloped down to the seats in front of the huge viewscreen. The captain's chair was positioned on the left, the navigator's to the right in front of the screen, and, between them, a seat for the pilot. The lights were low, shading the deck in darkness.

Alistair was sprawled in the comm. chair, playing idly with a puzzle ball. The spinning disc floated several centimetres above his palm. He touched a finger to a small blue disc on the underside, moved it to the equator. The ball flashed as the disc dropped into position. The game responded almost immediately, swapping a red square for the disc. The ball folded in on itself, then opened up again.

'How many times has it beaten you now?' Eve walked over to where he was sitting. He looked up at her, and then slowly vacated his seat, moving carefully out of her way.

'Thirty-four. Today.'

'And you're still trying?' Jinn asked.

He shrugged, tucking the game disc into his pocket. 'Strategy,' he said. 'I make it think I'm weak. It's more likely to make a mistake that way, and then I'll beat it.'

'Or you're just a masochist,' Eve pointed out.

'That, too,' he said. Then he angled his gaze at Jinn. 'I've fixed the cooling problem. Programme was running at half-speed. Judging by the look on your face, I'm guessing we won't be back to normal gravity anytime soon.'

'We don't have the parts,' Jinn said. 'I don't even know what parts we need. But we don't have them.'

Alistair frowned. 'That's unfortunate.' His modifications had given him intensely powerful hearing, making him Type Three. He could detect the firing of neurones in the brain, the movement of neurotransmitters. Whatever a person thought, whatever they felt, Alistair knew. A tiny implant installed behind his right ear enabled him to drown out the noise from other people's heads when he needed to, and only deal with the noise inside his own. Still, even with it turned off, a decade selling high-end skimmers and transporters had given him an uncanny ability to read people. 'So we're going to have to stop for repairs?'

Jinn flopped down in the captain's chair. It was far too big for her, custom-built to accommodate Dax's bulk. She could feel the width of his shoulders and the strength of his arms when she sat in it. 'It's either that or spend all our time tied to our seats, hoping nothing else decides to break.'

The doors to the elevator slid open again, and Li strolled onto the control deck. He moved to the nav chair, yawning and combing his hair back with his fingers before knotting it up on the back of his head. A greasy boiler suit, too short in the arms and legs, covered most of his heavily muscled body.

'We need a repair station,' Jinn told him. 'Do you know if there are any in this sector?' She didn't have the knowledge, having spent very little time outside of Earth-controlled space, but Li was well travelled. He had even spent time on Sittan. If there was a repair station nearby, he would know.

'Jump or straight haul?' he asked.

'Straight haul,' she said.

He brought up the charts. It only took him a few seconds to pinpoint their location. 'The *Riva* is closest,' he said. 'But it's risky. Puts us right back at the edge of Earth-controlled space.'

Jinn shook her head. The last thing she wanted to do was get caught by agents, which was a real possibility if they used a station anywhere close to Earth. 'No,' she said. 'We need somewhere else.'

His fingers flew, and the chart changed. He swiped it left, then right, then jabbed it with his finger. 'There,' he said.

'Computer, enlarge map.'

The image expanded in front of Jinn, a holographic representation of their location and the surrounding system. The *Mutant* flashed as a small green spot. The repair station was mapped out in red. Jinn knew it immediately, and for the first time in forty-eight low-grav hours, she felt a glimmer of hope.

'The *Articus*,' said Eve.

'Yes.' It was in the wrong direction, but it was deep enough into neutral space that it should be reasonably safe. More than that, she knew it. And she knew someone with a workshop tucked away on the lower level who might just be able to help them.

'It's eighteen days straight haul, or three if we jump the Crimson Twins at gate 117,' she said. 'If we jump, and the generator fails on us while we're in the hole, we might not make it out the other side.'

'Can you handle the jump?' Eve asked.

'Yes,' Jinn said. Now that she'd been modified, she no longer bled every time she plugged into the flight computer. She could work for hours without rest, without food. She was growing stronger by the day. She could make the jump.

'Then do it,' Alistair said.

'All right,' Jinn replied. 'Strap in,' she told them. 'And hope that grav generator holds out.'

CHAPTER
4

1st November 2207

Vessel: The *Mutant*. Battleship/carrier hybrid
Destination: Sittan
Cargo: None
Crew: 4
Droids: 7

The grav generator didn't hold. It blew up at precisely the same moment as they exited the jump, the resulting explosion thundering through the ship. Jinn focused on the image on her retinal screen as the final vestiges of colour faded and they left the jump hole behind. At least the grav generator had decided to blow at the end of the jump, and not during.

She pulled in air, forced it out, and disconnected. 'Everyone okay?'

Alistair groaned and pressed his hands to the side of his head. 'I'm going to have the mother of all headaches.'

Jinn twisted round in her seat. Eve's expression was grim, but she gave a nod, indicating she was all right. There was no sign of Li.

'Li?' Jinn yelled. 'Where are you?'

'In the cargo bay.' His voice came through the onboard comm.

'What in the void are you doing down there?'

'Keeping the air recyclers functioning,' he said calmly.

'Are you hurt?'

'I'm not dead.'

Jinn took a moment to catch her breath, then unfastened herself from her seat and pulled herself across to Alistair. His face was washed out to grey, his eyes screwed up tight, arms wrapped tight around his head. 'I'm fine,' he said. 'I just need a minute. And some blockers.'

She turned on the comm. 'Li? Can you bring some blockers up here? There should be some in the med bay.'

'I'm on it.'

There was no point regretting the jump, because she couldn't undo what had been done. But Jinn did find herself wondering if she'd have made the same decision before she'd had the Second Species modifications spliced into her DNA. And that made her think of Dax. She wondered where he was, what he was doing. If he was still alive.

She had to believe that he was. He'd been a Type One for a long time, and she'd seen him survive things that would have killed a normal man. But he had been as she was now – an incomplete Type One.

She wasn't ready to think about what he might have become.

Li made it back to the control deck, a box of pain shots gripped in one big hand. Eve sat rigidly in her seat and watched as Li dosed Alistair with everything they had.

After too many long minutes, he started to relax. Li lifted him from his seat and floated them both towards the exit. 'I'll take him down to the med bay,' he said. 'Let the medidroid assess him properly.'

'I told you, I'm fine,' Alistair slurred.

'Shut up and do as you're told,' Eve told him. She waited until Li and Alistair had left the control deck before adding 'idiot'. Then she turned to Jinn. 'So now what?'

'It's only a couple of hours straight haul to the *Articus*. Less, if I push it.'

'So push it,' Eve said. She put her hand to her mouth and gnawed at her thumbnail anxiously, but didn't move from her seat.

'I intend to.'

A quick mental command turned her retinal screen back on. An image of their route filled her mind, the blackness of space overlaid with a grid of sharp glowing lines. Jinn took in it, her quick mind assessing, calculating.

She flexed her fingers, feeling the wires that extended from her palms into the ports underneath each hand. She checked the status of the phase drive. Good enough. It powered up with just the slightest touch of her mind, roaring into life like a snarling animal, echoing her own feelings. Frustrated. Angry. Impatient.

And so she let it fly.

For the next hour it filled her completely, the adrenaline rush taking over her body. She couldn't tell where she ended and where the *Mutant* began. It was wonderful. Only a few months before she'd been so close to giving all this up, her body no longer able to cope with the vast amount of nanotech that circulated in her bloodstream. The tiny robots which connected together to form her prosthetics had been killing her from the inside out. She'd been initially modified to cope with the standard amount of Tellurium. After a difficult first few years off planet, she'd had additional tech injected, enough to allow her to form the Tellurium into twin blades. By thirty she'd been living on borrowed time.

Meeting Dax had changed all that.

What had been done to her on board the *A2* had changed her further, altering her DNA beyond the pilot mods she already had. She was stronger, faster, and her healing rate had increased far beyond anything a normal human could manage. She was also taller, heavier, and uncomfortably reckless.

She flew on and on, blood surging through her veins, the burn in her hands a pleasure now, and as she flew she thought about the Second Species programme, and how humans had ended up in this position. It could so easily have been avoided. All they'd needed to do was step back from the edge of the cliff when the damage that was being done to Earth's environment first became apparent in the twentieth century. If they had just been a little less greedy instead of walking right up to that edge and then suicidally jumping off it, they could quite easily have stayed on Earth forever.

Sometimes Jinn wondered if perhaps humans had outstayed their welcome in the universe. They were, after all, architects of their own destruction. They had trashed their home planet and made it uninhabitable. Killed countless species. Killed each other. She wasn't entirely sure they deserved a second chance. That said, she wasn't ready to give up yet either. She was certain that, if the chance was there, they should take it. That something could be learned from the mistakes of the past.

The *Articus* came into view, nothing more than a pinprick in the distance at first, then growing larger, taking on shape and colour and detail. It was exactly as she remembered it. A pocket of human existence far enough away from Earth-controlled space to be independent, and small enough to be ignored by the other species that frequented this sector of the galaxy. The repair station was built around a narrow shaft with a solitary central disc studded with vessels of all shapes and sizes. There were transporters, cruisers, short-haul freighters. There were also plenty of empty ports, more than she remembered seeing the last time she had been here. The *Articus* was too small for ships to dock internally, so they clung to the outside like blades in flesh as repair droids moved over them, chewing away everything that was rotten and replacing it with fresh new parts.

For the first time in what seemed like ages, Jinn felt a little less afraid. This was a place for pirates, for bandits and thieves and mercenaries. It was a place in which she belonged. She slowed their speed as they grew nearer, angling the *Mutant* so that it followed the slow rotation of the repair station.

She held steady as Eve contacted the *Articus* docking authorities and paid the charge. The conversation was fast, brusque, impersonal. 'Have a nice day,' the *Articus* employee said without even a hint of sincerity before he disconnected.

The docking arm locked onto the *Mutant*, the powerful electromagnetic connector holding them fast, filling the control deck with a faint buzz that softened the silence. There was a second smaller thud that signalled a spacewalk linking to one of the exit doors.

Jinn disconnected, turning her palms over and watching as the wires pulled back inside her skin, the small puncture holes closing up almost immediately. The cuff of her shirt was dirty, and she could feel it sticking to her back. She needed a long, hot session in a chemicleanse, but it would have to wait. If people didn't like the way she smelled they could just stand further away.

She gripped the armrest of her seat. 'Computer, restraints off.'

The computer obeyed and her body lifted clear of the chair. Fortunately it was a slow drift. She'd had experience in zero grav as part of her pilot training, but it had been a long time ago and her skills were rusty. She propelled herself forward, swimming off the control deck and down to the lower level which housed all the now empty personal quarters.

She met Li and Alistair floating along one of the corridors. Alistair was still pale, but at least he didn't look like he was about to pass out. He gave her a wonky smile. 'Told you I was fine.'

Jinn made a mental note to send him to one of the medical centres on the *Articus* for a proper assessment before they left. He was too jacked up on pain blockers right now to know if there was any permanent damage or not.

Eve remained behind. Her voice came over the internal comm. 'I'll catch up with you,' she said.

'Okay.' Jinn propelled herself forwards. She quickly learned how much of a push was too much, how she could move herself forward with nothing more than the air from her lungs.

But progress through the ship was slow, partly because Alistair couldn't quite control his movement. In the end, she got hold of him by the back of his shirt and pulled him along with her. He closed his eyes, let her drift him into the airlock at the junction between the *Mutant* exit door and the spacewalk that would lead them onto the *Articus*.

Li slipped in with them as they pushed their way inside the airlock, the door of the *Mutant* closing slowly behind them, sealing them in. Then the gravity increased and they sank to the floor. The door on the other side of the airlock opened.

'I hate this part,' Li said.

'Why?' Jinn asked him.

'I like to have something more substantial than Plastex between me and certain death,' Li said. This from the man who had survived the fight cages on Sittan and had the tattoos across his shoulders to prove it.

'Scared?'

'Yes,' he said, with a decisive nod of his head and a flex of those shoulders, hidden now inside a snug black jacket.

The sealed tunnel was made from clear, rigid Plastex, allowing them a 360-degree view of their surroundings. All around her, Jinn could see the other vessels, so many different colours, so many different shapes. They were beautiful even though most of them were old and a little worn. She saw a lean Hoyle jet and a fabulous class one yacht and felt a pang of envy.

Jinn would quite happily have stayed on the walk a little longer, but Li didn't hang about. The three of them were across the spacewalk and on the *Articus* in less than a minute. They waited for Eve to join them before moving off. She was wearing the long, hooded cloak that she always wore when she left the *Mutant*, hiding her face from the crowds. Now that the government had made the Second Species public knowledge, Eve had even more reason to be cautious. So did the rest of them.

But at least they weren't green.

As they started to walk away from the docking bay towards

the lift tubes that would take them either up to the stores or down to the workshops, Jinn couldn't help thinking about the last time she'd been here.

Dax had given her a way to cope with her tech, and she'd given him herself in return. It hurt to be here without him. 'Come on,' she said to the others. 'Let's get this done. I don't want to spend any more time here than we have to.'

Grudge's workshop lay on the lower level of the central ring, in among stores selling engine parts and all the other bits and pieces needed to keep a space vessel functioning. The *Mutant* had originally been his ship, and he would know how to repair her. Jinn could only hope that he would agree to do it. Without Dax to vouch for them, there was no guarantee they would be welcome. But Grudge was the only engineer here they could even remotely trust.

They moved quickly through the *Articus*, keeping close together, not wanting to invite trouble. It was oddly quiet. Gone were the stalls and the street vendors selling fast food and cheap clothing.

'Where in the void are the cleaning droids?' Alistair asked, kicking away empty beer bottles and discarded food wrappers. His movements were loose, not entirely controlled, his voice a touch too loud. 'I know this is a rough part of the station, but I don't remember it being this bad.'

He tripped over something and nearly crashed into Eve.

His gaze dropped to the floor and he shoved his hands into his pockets. 'Sorry,' he said.

'Don't be sorry,' Eve told him, her skin flushing deeper green. 'Just be less ... high.'

The few shops and bars down on this level were open but none appeared to be particularly busy. The huge vid screens that soared overhead, advertising beauty products and medical enhancement services, were stuttering and cracked, though they still played their endless messages suggesting that the road to happiness was paved with spent credits. Everything was grimy and neglected.

And there was a smell, sour, distinctive and oddly familiar, though Jinn couldn't remember where she had encountered it before. Her visceral reaction to it was too sharp for her to believe that it meant anything good.

She picked up her pace. The sooner they got to Grudge's the sooner they could get the *Mutant* repaired and the sooner they'd be away from here. 'This place is giving me the creeps.'

Li moved alongside her. 'Something is not right here,' he said. 'I agree.'

The tall man kept his steps light, but his whole body was tensed, and he was watching the street.

'We need to be ready for trouble,' she said.

'I'm always ready for trouble,' he replied, his heavy biceps flexing. 'Isn't everyone?'

'No,' Jinn said.

Li looked puzzled. 'Then what do they do when it arrives?'

'Panic,' she told him. Jinn turned her attention to the others. 'Alistair, are you picking anything up?' She could tell from the way his walk had changed that the pain blockers were already starting to wear off. He touched behind his ear, deactivating his implant. 'No,' he said. 'Nothing except this blasted headache.'

Eve looked at him. 'You need to get to a medical centre,' she said. 'We should have done that first.'

'It's nothing,' he said. 'I just need more blockers.'

'Eve's right,' Jinn told him. 'You need to get yourself looked at. And the sooner the better.' And if she'd been thinking straight, she'd have made sure that was their priority. But she'd been in such a rush to see Grudge she'd convinced herself that Alistair could wait.

'Yes,' Alistair said. 'I think you're right.' He staggered a little, pressed his fingers to his temple. Jinn caught his arm, held him steady. Even through his jacket she could feel that he was burning up. Shit, she *should* have put him first. These people always came first. Dax had taught her that.

But there was no claiming back the time that had been wasted.

'Eve, go with him,' Jinn ordered. She knew Eve would argue if she tried to send anyone else. 'Are you armed?'

Eve pushed her jacket aside, revealing a little close-range blaster resting at the side of her hip.

'Good,' Jinn said. 'Don't be afraid to use it. There's something going on here, and I don't like it.'

They synced the personal comm. units attached to their sleeves and then they split up, Eve and Alistair heading off in the direction of the elevators that would take them to the higher level and the medical centres. Jinn's comm. link blinked in her peripheral vision as she and Li made their way along the walk-way. They passed closed workshops and abandoned snack stalls. Interestingly, a pop-up weapons store appeared to be doing a roaring trade.

Her hand strayed to the blaster strapped to her upper thigh, and she gave herself a moment to sense her tech. The warm tingle in her palms reassured her that it was there, waiting, should she need it.

By the time they reached Grudge's workshop, Jinn felt a deep sense of unease.

The entrance to the workshop was closed. The once pristine heavy alloy doors were thick with grime, and one of them had a new and large dent in it. Jinn walked up to them, reaching for the intercom.

'Wait,' Li said.

She didn't get the chance to ask him what for. He grabbed her around the waist and threw her straight up towards the ceiling. Air rushed past, blood thundering in her ears. But her reflexes were surprisingly sharp. She caught hold of one of the beams that crisscrossed the ceiling, swinging for only a moment before hooking her legs over it and pulling herself up. Li landed on the beam opposite. He pressed a finger to his lips and pointed down.

They had to be fifteen metres up. It was a long way to fall. She swung one leg over so that she was sitting astride the beam and gripped it tightly. It was better, though not much. She locked her legs together at the ankle, and then looked over the side.

There, in the doorway of the workshop, were a couple of people she identified as ore seekers. Both had the thin, angular build, the circular plates at the side of the neck that would extend to form neat breathing masks, the grafted metal fingers that would allow them to climb their way through the underground caves of Colony Three. Hunting down the pools of chloroplatinic acid was a highly dangerous job. The platinum extracted from it was used to build phase drives among other things, and it fetched a high price. But that didn't explain what they were doing here. She glanced across at Li. His expression was grim. Jinn slowly moved one hand to the blaster at her thigh. Despite the prosthetics and the breathing masks, eventually the acidic vapour started to affect the brain. Ore seekers were known to be paranoid and trigger-happy. She held her breath until the two of them had made it to the end of the walkway.

Grudge stepped out of the workshop. He looked around, and then he looked up. When he saw Jinn, he stilled. Then he raised an eyebrow. 'Jinnifer Blue. What a pleasant surprise. I assume you're in trouble.'

'Always,' she called down.

'Come on, then.' He turned, disappearing back inside the workshop. He left the door open.

'Can we trust him?' Li asked.

Jinn swung her leg back over the beam. 'Looks like we're about to find out.'

Carefully, she turned onto her belly, and slowly lowered her weight until she was suspended over the walkway. She flexed her fingers and took a deep breath. Then she let go.

Long seconds passed as she dropped, unable to breathe, unable to do anything but anticipate the impact. When it came, it was as if she'd dropped no more than a metre. She tucked into a roll and snapped to her feet. There was no pain in her feet or her thighs.

Li hit the deck with a bang. He dropped to a crouch and then straightened up. He pushed her inside the workshop before she could say anything. The thick door swung closed behind them. He waited just in front of it, leaving Jinn to follow Grudge through the workshop.

As she looked around, it quickly became apparent that the security doors weren't the only thing that was new. The last time she had been here, the place had been stacked ceiling high with dismantled ships and dismembered droids. Phase drives, complete and in parts, had lined one wall. Now, it was almost empty. Roof-mounted cannon guns swivelled in her direction.

About halfway across, Grudge stopped. He turned to face her. His hair was still grey and the mining prosthetic attached where his right arm should be was still ugly. But he looked older, thinner, and more worn.

Jinn gestured to the workshop. 'What happened to all your stuff?'

'Sold it,' Grudge said. He came to stand in front of her, looked her up and down. Set a hand to her jaw, moved her head from side to side, then took her wrist and examined the Tellurium bracelet that circled it. 'You've been modified. Type One, I assume?'

'How can you tell?'

He snapped his arm up as if he was going to punch her in the face. She caught his fist before it could make contact, and then stared at her long, pale fingers wrapped around his hand in disbelief.

'That's how,' he said. 'And the man with you? A replacement for Dax?'

'No,' Jinn said. There was no replacement for Dax. 'I was sent to the *A2*. They modified me there. Li was already on board. He helped me escape. He was part of the original programme with Dax and the others. Something of a loner, I think. Dax said he refused to stay with the rest of them when they left Earth. Went his own way.'

'And now he's with you. Where is Dax?'

'Sittan.'

'So the reports are true. And Theon?'

Jinn let go of him. She couldn't hold his gaze. 'Gone,' she said.

'Ah,' Grudge said. 'The *A2*?'

'Yes. He ... I let the men on board out of their cages. Theon held them off so I could get to the transporter before it self-destructed.'

'Then he died a good death,' Grudge said. 'The death he wanted for himself.'

'It wasn't a good death,' Jinn said. 'There's no such thing.'

'Sometimes there is,' Grudge told her. 'I need a drink. Want a drink?' He turned away from her and strode to the rear of the workshop and into the mid-section of a transporter that had been turned into a home. It contained a battered table and a few chairs. A bed was folded up against one wall. The chemicleanse in the corner looked new, and there was a remodelled Autochef mounted next to the table, as well as a bank of vid screens showing every inch of the workshop and the walkway outside. On closer inspection, Jinn noted that the walls were reinforced carbonite, and the door was made of aluminium alloy thicker than her arm.

Grudge walked to the Autochef and ordered two tankards of a fruity smelling, frothy drink. He rubbed at the back of his neck as it worked. 'I suppose the question, then, is what are you going to do about Dax?'

'I'm going to Sittan to get him.'

'I assumed as much.' He picked up the first full tankard and held it out to Jinn. Then he picked up the second and downed half of it in one go. 'Did they do something to him, on board the *A2*?'

'Gave him the third dose of serum.'

'Then he'll be changed.'

'Probably.' There was no point in trying to deny it. She drank a little of her own brew, barely tasting it. It went down easily enough. 'But Dax isn't like the other men they're modifying. Even as a kid I doubt he was like them. Plus they spaced out the serums. That could have made a difference.'

'And you're hoping that will be enough to keep him human.' Grudge finished his drink, slotted his tankard in position for a refill.

Jinn shrugged. 'It's all I've got. What about you?'

'You know, this used to be a safe place to live. Not a great place, but a safe one. We didn't have any trouble. The Security Service left us alone, and the aliens didn't bother coming here. We all got along. A dealer called Darkos took care of most of the security. We paid our dues, and he made sure no one had any trouble, kept the place clean. But out of the blue, the droids stopped patrolling. Then the bounty hunters turned up and cleaned us out, and some of the scumbags who live here decided to trash what was left, apparently just because they could.'

'What happened?'

'I don't know,' Grudge told her. 'No one does.'

'Haven't you tried to find out?'

'Repeatedly,' he said. Then he pointed at Jinn with his prosthetic arm. 'So. What have you done to my ship?'

'You mean my ship,' she said. 'How did you know that was why I was here?'

He raised an eyebrow.

'Gravity generator is blown,' she admitted.

'How blown?'

'Completely. I tried to fix it, but I could only get it to maybe eighty per cent capacity and then, when we jumped to get here, it gave up completely.'

'Power coupling?'

'Replaced it,' Jinn told him. 'That's how I got the eighty per cent.'

'I see.' Grudge lifted his own drink, took a deep swallow. 'I may know where there is a replacement generator.'

'I thought you'd been cleaned out.'

'I have. But others weren't so unlucky.'

'Are these others people I want to deal with?'

Grudge looked amused. 'Darkos has spares in the lockup in his workshop.'

'The bounty hunters didn't empty it?'

'Just because Darkos decided to stop protecting the rest of us doesn't mean he decided to stop protecting himself.'

'You need security agents ...' she began, but, even as she spoke, she knew it was pointless. Worse than that, it was a mistake.

'Do you think the Security Service cares about a place like this?' Grudge asked her.

'No,' she admitted. It carved a sharp wound into her heart, knowing that those back in the Domes, those who claimed to care so much, cared so little. But she wasn't one of them, not anymore. She wasn't entirely sure what she was. She downed her drink, flexed her fingers, felt the warm weight of her tech.

'Take me to Darkos,' she said. 'Let's see what he's got.'

CHAPTER
5

1st November 2207

The *Articus*. Repair Station, Sector Four, Neutral Space

Bryant was dying. He'd been dying for so long now that it had actually become quite tedious, the constant waiting and wondering if it was going to be today. Stretched out on the velvety red sofa of his grubby living quarters, he was busy thinking about the unfairness of life when someone poked him hard in the ribs.

'Bryant, you need to get up.' The voice filtered through his clouded brain with the rough scratch of a boy just into his teens.

'Don't want to,' he told it. 'Leave me alone.'

But the voice kept pushing and the jabs to his ribs kept coming. He forced himself upright, no mean feat given the way his head felt. The movement caused an explosion of pain that had him gasping for breath as what felt like shards of broken glass moved through his gut and then settled themselves into new and unpleasant places.

Euphoria addiction was a bastard.

'Davyd,' he said. He scrubbed at his eyes, trying to clear his vision, and brought the boy into rough focus. Davyd had been using Darkos' grooming droid again. His dark hair was cut very short, and there were swirls shaved into one side. 'What time is it?'

Davyd moved to the Autochef, programmed it. 'Twenty-five thirty.'

Bryant blinked, slowly. His eyes were gritty and sore, and his eyeballs felt too big for their sockets. He leaned over the end of the couch, groping for his drug gun. His fingers closed over it. Stupid thing was empty. Davyd took the gun from him, loaded it, then handed it back. He didn't turn away as Bryant yanked up his shirt and fired the liquid into the bruised patch on the left side of his belly.

The Euphoria worked quickly. Within minutes, he was on his feet. The pain was still there, but he no longer cared about it. He almost didn't care that he'd just shot up in front of the boy, or that Davyd had loaded the gun with shameless ease. A plate of leftover food sat on a low table next to the couch. Bryant picked it up and began shovelling it in with his fingers. 'Where are the others?' he asked, through a mouthful of cold, congealed stew. 'Still in the compound?'

'Of course.'

Bryant acknowledged that with a nod. 'Good,' he said, chewing loudly. It tasted like salted rubber. He ate it anyway because he was hungry and he couldn't be bothered to get anything else. There was plenty of food available, so he had other options, but options meant work and that was beyond him.

The flourishing business that Darkos had created, trading flesh, drugs and pretty much any other form of illegal that would generate a quick profit was no longer running, and Bryant couldn't say he was too sorry about that. Darkos had been a scumbag. Fortunately, he hadn't put up much of a fight, and the recycling unit had taken care of his fat, pasty corpse. He'd also been a hoarder. They could hole up here for years if they needed to. There was food, fuel, drugs, everything they could possibly need. Bryant refused to think about anything beyond these walls. There was little point.

In his clearer moments he'd watched enough of the newsfeed to know that Caspian Dax was now on Sittan. The pirate was being hailed as a global hero after he'd allegedly volunteered to join the Second Species programme. There was even a thirty-second sound bite of him asking others to do the same.

Bryant wasn't fooled. He could read between the lines well enough to know that the story being spun by the media was government-approved. He wondered what had really happened. He also wondered what had happened to the rest of Dax's crew. Where was his former co-worker Jinnifer Blue, and that green bitch who had poisoned him? Not that it mattered. There was no chance of finding her, not now, and Bryant had found that if he took enough Euphoria, he almost didn't care about that either.

Stretching the kinks out of his back, he strolled over to the balcony that ran along the far side of the room and overlooked the workshop below. He could see the other boys playing with a flyball, trying to catch the small, shiny sphere as it darted through the air.

Droids patrolled the perimeter of the workshop. Three were on permanent watch at the entrance. The opposite wall of the room housed a bank of vid screens, linked to the cameras that covered every centimetre of the workshop, as well as the walkway outside. A sharp pain stabbed in his abdomen, and he gritted his teeth, waiting for it to pass. It took longer than it should have.

His addiction to Euphoria was growing. There was no point trying to deny it. Still, thanks to Darkos, he had more than enough to keep him going for however long it took for the poison in his system finally to finish him off. As well as the stash in the safe there was a room hidden away on the highest level of the building that contained not only enough Euphoria to make the entire population of the *Articus* high for a month, but also a manufacturing unit and storage drums of the raw ingredients.

Davyd moved to stand beside him. Unlimited access to the Autochef had done the boy good. He no longer looked half starved, but the dark circles around his eyes hadn't faded, and Bryant wondered how well he slept. 'Are you dying?' Davyd asked him. The question was posed so casually, as if the boy was asking him if he wanted another drink.

'How the fuck should I know?'

But he did. Every day when he woke up he was surprised to find himself still alive. He existed in a place that was closer to death than any sane person would want to be, and he didn't know how to escape it. He didn't know if he wanted to escape it. What was the point in living? He'd lost his position with the Security Service. He'd stolen. He'd killed. He couldn't return to Earth, not now. Even a Dome brat had to face the consequences for murder.

Ever since he'd met Caspian Dax, his life had been on a downward spiral. He hated that fucking pirate and his crew. He hated Jinnifer Blue even more. How could she betray everything Dome dwellers stood for and throw her lot in with that criminal?

Bryant could barely bring himself to think about the freaky green woman who had poisoned him with nothing more than the touch of her hand on the back of his neck. He rubbed at that patch of skin.

Sometimes he thought that maybe it was time to let go, to finally slide from this half-life into the complete peace of death. And maybe he would do it, too, if Davyd didn't stubbornly refuse to let him, and if he wasn't such a coward. He didn't want to go knowing that he had done nothing, achieved nothing, that no one would remember him.

Mostly, he was afraid that it would hurt.

'There's someone outside,' Davyd said. He stood facing the screens that linked to the security cameras that surrounded the workshop. 'Look.'

'The droids will deal with it,' Bryant told him. He was tired already. He started back towards the sofa, legs growing heavier with every step.

'I think . . . I think it's the woman,' Davyd continued.

'What woman?'

'The one from the newsfeed. The one with the white hair and the implant on her face.'

Bryant turned so abruptly that he felt dizzy. He moved in behind Davyd, dwarfing the Underworld boy, and scanned the screens. 'Computer, enlarge screen four.'

It stretched out, filling the space previously occupied by ten smaller images.

And there she was. He wouldn't have believed she was real if Davyd hadn't spotted her first. A bigger wave of dizziness swept over him, rushing from the floor upwards. He wobbled. Davyd caught him and steered him into a chair. His skinny fingers dug into the thin fabric of Bryant's shirt, stabbing into bruised skin, but Bryant didn't care.

'Open the gate,' he told Davyd. 'Let her in.'

'But . . .'

'*Do it!*'

'Yes, sir,' the boy said, before darting forward to the control panel mounted in the wall just below the screens. He stabbed in a code. The panel flashed. On the screen above, Bryant saw the gate swing slowly open. He saw Jinnifer Blue hesitate, but only for a moment.

And then she walked into the workshop.

He was on his feet again almost immediately. He stumbled towards the door and onto the glider that took him gently down to the lower level. His bare feet slapped against the mosaic tiles that patterned the floor, his open shirt flapping against his torso. Bryant moved at a speed he hadn't managed in weeks, and kept it up until he stumbled to a halt in the middle of the yard.

Four security droids surrounded her and the man she was with, weapons raised and pointed at their heads. For all his faults, Darkos had known how to protect himself. The droids were top of the line. Although roughly humanoid in shape, they had four arms instead of two, and no face to reason with. Weapons were integrated into the two upper arms. Joints worked in every possible direction. They were still running on the same programme that Darkos had used, only Davyd had changed the command codes to put Bryant in charge. The droids would protect him without him even having to order them to do it.

'It's you,' he said, unable to keep the stunned desperation out of his voice. 'It is you, isn't it?'

For a moment he wasn't sure. The face was the same, and the hair, but she was much bigger than he remembered, and her eyes gleamed an astonishing cerulean blue instead of pitch dark.

Her gaze slid over him, working from the ground up before dropping back down again. Then it zeroed in on his face. 'Bryant?' She made to move a little closer. The droids moved in and stopped her. 'What in the void are *you* doing here?'

'I could ask you the same question,' Bryant said. His right eye twitched and he rubbed at it, then quickly tried to fasten his shirt. His skin prickled with embarrassment.

'Where is Darkos?'

The question came from the man. Bryant didn't recognise him. He was short and square, and his arm had been chopped off and replaced with some fuck-ugly metal contraption. Underworld. Bug. Irrelevant. Bryant's brain fired out those conclusions in three quick shots. 'Darkos is dead,' he said. 'I killed him.'

'I see,' said the man, and then fell back to silence.

'Do you?' Bryant asked him. A muscle cramped in his gut, and he held his breath, waiting for it to pass. Then he turned his attention to Jinnifer Blue. Shame made him angry. 'Is she with you?'

'Who?'

'You fucking know who! That green bitch, the one who was with you on the *Europa*.'

'I don't see why that's any business of yours.' She looked around, taking in the courtyard, the workshop. 'I need a gravity generator. I understand there might be one here.'

'I wouldn't know,' Bryant told her. He could still hardly believe that she was here, she was real.

'Then you won't mind if I take a look.' She started forward, gaze fixed firmly on the storage units at the rear of the yard.

The shot came from the droid on his left.

Jinn staggered back as it caught her in the shoulder, her torso twisting with the force of the impact. The front of her khaki-coloured jacket stained dark with blood, and a knife sprang out from the palm of her right hand. 'You shot me!'

'Technically that droid shot you,' Bryant told her, certain now that he had the upper hand, although he was unnerved by the sight of the knife in such close proximity. Last time he'd seen her blades, she'd been further away, and he'd had a weapon in each hand.

She shrugged out of her jacket and looked down at the wound. The shot had been fired at close range and it showed. She pinched the gaping edges of the wound together with her free hand and inhaled sharply, glaring at him. When she dropped her hand away, what had been a hole was now nothing more than a purple mark on her skin.

Bryant blinked. 'How did you . . . ?'

'I'm Type One now,' she said bluntly. 'Unless you're planning on cutting my head off, this is just a waste of time.'

Bryant just stood there and looked at her. He didn't understand it. 'How in the void are you Type One?'

'Because I was sent back to the *A2*,' she told him. 'I have to admit, this time it was my own fault. But I still haven't forgiven you for the first time.'

'I only took you to the *A2* because you deserved it!'

Her eyebrows rose a little. 'Careful, Bryant.'

'It's the truth. Everyone I took to that place did. No one on board was innocent.'

'And you're a hero, I suppose. Look at you. You're pathetic. What is it? K? Euphoria?'

Bryant's mouth twisted. 'None of your damn business.'

'Euphoria, then,' she said. 'Oh dear. You really are in a mess. Not feeling quite so smug now, are you? Just another junkie, like all those Underworlders you used to hate so much. At least they had an excuse. You got what was coming to you, Bryant, and I can't say I'm sorry.'

'That's not fair!' Bryant wailed. 'I'm fucking dying, and you get made over into a superhuman?' He shook his head vigorously. 'I don't believe this.'

'It is what it is,' she told him. 'Call off your droids. I'm not going to hurt you. All I want is a gravity generator. Apparently you have one.'

One of the boys darted in front of her, putting his short, skinny body between Bryant and Jinn. 'Stop it!' he shouted. 'Leave Bryant alone!'

Jinn straightened up and stared down at the kid. 'Who in the void are you?'

Bryant tripped forward and grabbed the boy by the shoulder, pulling him out of Jinn's reach.

She raised her eyebrows and folded her arms. Then she shook her head, and her stance seemed to soften. 'I'm not here to start a fight with you, Bryant. As soon as I've got what I came for, I'll leave. I need a Mark 3 unit, the one with the supercharged pressure conduits.'

'What's it worth?'

'I'll pay market rate,' she said.

Bryant let go of the boy, gave him a push in the direction of Darkos's living quarters. 'Get out of here,' he ordered the rest of them. 'You too, Davyd.'

'But . . .' came the scratchy voice from behind him.

'*Now!*' There was the scuffle of sulky feet and mutters of complaint, but they did as he said. He couldn't blame them for delaying. This was the most exciting thing to have happened in weeks.

'Who are they?' the man asked him.

'Part of Darkos's inventory,' Bryant told him.

'I see,' the man said again, and this time Bryant got the impression that he really did.

He could sense Jinnifer Blue watching him, her gaze sharp on his skin, and he was suddenly very aware of his scabby feet and crumpled shirt, and the fact that he hadn't used a chemi-cleanse in days.

Maybe there was a gravity generator here. Maybe there

wasn't. It didn't really matter to him. But one thing did. 'Your poisonous green friend,' Bryant said to her. 'The one who touched me back on the *Europa*.' The one who had started him down this road. 'Is she here too?'

'She might be. What do you want with her?'

'I need information.' His heart had started to pound. His hands were twitching more violently now, and he shoved them into his trouser pockets. 'She might be able to help me. The medic told me that if I could find out what I'd been poisoned with, they might be able to create an antidote.'

'Give me the generator,' Jinn told him. 'Whether or not she wants to talk to you is up to her.'

CHAPTER

6

The 5th day of the fifth turn

Karakai Arena, Fire City, Sittan

Sittan was a planet without mercy. Scorched by the heat of three low-burning suns, the ground was a maze of cracked, broken obsidian. Sharp dust covered everything. It tainted the air, coated the curving walls of the buildings, blew in through open doors and insinuated its way through gaps too small to see. Water was a scarce commodity. What little there was ran oily and thick, winding its way down from the higher ground and feeding the springs that boiled under the city.

Since he had arrived on the planet, Caspian Dax had learned how to hide from the heat, how to breathe through the dust that threatened to destroy his lungs with every inhalation. He had learned how to live with pain beyond anything he had experienced before. He had learned that, on this planet, sacrifice was everything.

In the Karakai Arena, where the floor smoked and the smell of sulphur hung heavy in the air, Dax had discovered just how far he was willing to go in order to survive. The first kill had been easy, something which had shocked him. The others had been easy, too, and they hadn't shocked him at all.

In the distance, the black spear of the Mountain overshadowed everything. It saw every death, watched every drop of blood that fell with still, silent censure. It was the source of the empress's power, or, rather, the lava that flowed from it was. But the Mountain was unpredictable and capricious.

And it had been dry for too long.

The Sittan believed that the Mountain would reawaken if they fed it with enough blood, and so they killed and killed and killed. But Dax didn't think that any of the young Sittan males who entered the arena truly wanted to die. They wanted what awaited the few who survived. Only those males were allowed to bond with the females, to take ownership of land, to father children.

But Dax wasn't Sittan. The only prize that awaited him when he won was another day and another fight, and that was all he wanted. The Mountain was just as dead now as it had been when he'd arrived and he didn't expect that to change anytime soon. No amount of blood could make a volcano erupt. That was just superstitious nonsense.

The bottom line was that the Sittan liked violence. Oh, they believed that their violence had a purpose, but that wasn't their sole motivation. They liked violence so much that they had run out of their own males to kill, and so had started killing human males instead. Dax was okay with that. He had no reason not to be. He shared their DNA, and so he shared their hunger for violence, deep and insatiable.

Thousands of Sittan stood in the tiered levels that surrounded this showground of pain, their favourite place to gather and be entertained. They were uncloaked, dressed in the close-fitting black that concealed some of their skin and none of their weapons. The males were massive and brutal, with sharp-cut muscles and a thick line of ebony hair that ran from the base of the skull to the small of the back. Their females were lithe, supple, beautiful, lethal, the empress the most exquisite of all. The paired males sat at the feet of their females. The unpaired ones loitered and preened, flexing their arms and displaying their facial spikes in the hope that a female would notice them.

But the females wanted blood. They wanted to see it flood the arena, wanted to see it rush from wounded flesh. They wanted to see death. The Mountain had to be fed, and only male blood would sate its hunger. It was dry because the blood it was being given disappointed it. The males would have to do better.

Dax scrubbed his hands over the rough hide of his trousers, up over the hard planes of his stomach, his chest. He turned his face to the sky and roared a warning, there under the burning heat of those three bright suns.

Someone was going to die today.

But it was not going to be him.

The seventeen black stripes tattooed across his left shoulder paid testimony to that. Seventeen stripes for seventeen kills. Twenty-three on his right shoulder, for the males who had been weak enough to surrender before he dealt the final strike that would take them from this life into the next. They had been dragged from the arena by their trainers, broken and bleeding and shamed.

Dax flexed his fingers and considered his opponent. The Sittan male was bigger than the others Dax had already fought. He was dressed in snug breeches that ended at the knee and little else, exposing acres of bright blue flesh. Every bare centimetre was decorated with an intricate pattern that had been carved into his skin. The spikes that covered his head were fully extended, his close-set yellow eyes gleaming with aggression, with cunning, with the smug satisfaction of someone who believed that they had the edge. The stripes on his shoulder said that maybe he was right. Somewhere inside Dax's mind, a soft voice cried out *Caspian. Be careful.*

The Sittan's skin and black hide breeches gleamed brightly as he swaggered, flexing his muscles for the crowd. If he'd been smart enough to show fear instead of arrogance, Dax might have considered him a worthy opponent. Instead, he looked and found him lacking.

Then the bells sounded and the fight began.

Dax didn't waste a second. It took him only a moment to charge the Sittan down, to bang a shoulder into his gut and knock him to the ground. He didn't try to grip his opponent's flesh. It would be too greasy to hold, like trying to wrestle a slimefish.

The Sittan grabbed him by the throat, and they rolled together across the floor of the arena, the sharp black sand biting into Dax's skin. It mingled with the oil, creating an abrasive, greasy mixture that scraped and scratched.

The fighter snarled, baring barbed teeth the colour of polished steel as he pinned Dax down. Dax knew from experience that they could bite through bone. He'd lost a chunk of his shoulder that way. Those head spikes were also vicious. They could rip through skin, through muscle. But the Sittan had vulnerable areas. It had taken a while to find them, but he'd been determined. The soft slits on either side of the neck, which were used for breathing. The genitals, which were positioned between the legs, similar to his own. The eyes, if a man was desperate enough.

'I am going to kill you slowly, human,' the Sittan snarled at him, in low, guttural tones.

Dax responded with a smile. He had realised early on that if he was going to survive here, he was going to have to be smart. Strength wasn't enough when everyone had it. So he'd learned, and he'd learned quickly. He could feel the hot burn of the black sand against his bare back, as the suns scorched his eyes. This was a dangerous position to be in, a vulnerable one. The chest markings had warned him. They indicated a wealthy family, and that meant training. It meant this fighter would use tactical skill as much as brute force. He would be clever. He would be ruthless. He would do whatever it took to win. But what he didn't know was that Dax would do more.

The soft voice in Dax's head drove him on. She came to him now, as she always did at these moments when death drew near. She whispered his name. *Dax.* He didn't know who she was, or even if she was real. But the need to find out had kept him alive through every fight, every wound, every spilled drop of blood.

With a sharp twist, Dax broke free. He punched out at the Sittan and caught him in the side of the neck. The Sittan twisted his head, digging the spikes into the thick flesh of Dax's forearm. Blood gushed. The crowd roared. Dax rolled, shoved to his feet, his forearm burning from more than just the wound.

The cheating bastard had put something in the oil. Now he didn't just want to kill the Sittan, he wanted to make him hurt. As the two of them circled each other, Dax touched his left shoulder, where the seventeen stripes interlocked. His message was clear. There would be no surrender.

And so it began. The crowd and the heat and the memory of the other fights were forgotten. All that mattered now was victory in this one. They crashed together time and time again, using teeth, fists, feet. Dax's chest burned as his skin ran hot with sweat, as blood slicked his palms, dripped into his eyes. Whatever the Sittan had put in the oil made the edges blur, made his pulse unsteady, but it didn't bring him down. Fists met stomachs, faces. A kick to the side of the head left the Sittan reeling, the spikes on that side of his head snapped into pieces. He responded with a punch to the face that had Dax spitting teeth.

The broken pieces lay on the black sand. Dax stared at them, spat more blood, more shattered shards of tooth. They would grow back. But it made eating difficult in the short term, and he hated that. He looked up at the Sittan. 'Yield.'

The Sittan laughed. 'To you, filthy human?'

'It's the wise choice.'

The Sittan laughed. 'I am not like the others,' he said. 'I will not be swayed by words. I am not afraid of pain.'

'You will be,' Dax told him, running his fingers through the sharp black sand. 'You will be.' He slipped his fingers deeper into the sand, ignoring the pain that screamed through his hands as the tiny grains of obsidian dug their way in through the cuts in his skin. Sittan hide was thick, almost leathery, much tougher than the soft, weak skin that covered his own body. But he needed the sand to give him grip.

'Never in this lifetime,' the Sittan snarled. And then he threw himself forward, and Dax knew that this time they would not break apart until one of them was broken. They were no longer playing, no longer testing the limits of the other. Flesh smacked against flesh, hands fighting for hold, feet slipping into the sand. Fingers found vulnerable places and dug in hard. Dax roared in agony as a blow struck his kidneys, then another smacked his left ear. He responded in kind, knuckles bruising, the thin skin splitting as he rained punches down on the chest, the abdomen, of the Sittan. But he couldn't get close to the neck, to the genitals, and the Sittan scored hit after agonising hit. Dax let him.

This one was clever. This one understood. It knew his anatomy, knew the truly vulnerable spots that the others had never been able to find. The Sittan hooked an arm behind his thigh, and, in one swift move, dumped Dax flat on his back. His vision swam, the arena spinning away behind him. He tasted blood. And he heard the voice again, soft and female and so very familiar. She lingered on the edge of his memory, always there, always just out of reach. *Get up*, she said. *Hurry*.

Dax rolled just as the Sittan planted a knee where his face had been. He staggered to his feet. It wasn't difficult to make his disorientation look genuine. 'Surrender,' the male said.

Dax dropped his gaze. He held his breath. And when the male moved in to strike the final blow, he grabbed his knee and twisted. His gritty fingers slithered over oiled hide, but it was still enough to make the Sittan lose his balance. More than enough to make him bare his teeth and lose his judgement. In the corner of his eye, Dax could see the empress sitting atop her throne of carved volcanic glass. He could feel the fascinated scorch of her gaze. It woke him up. It burned the exposed flesh of his back as he pinned the Sittan down. 'I don't surrender,' Dax told him. He had done that once before, though he couldn't remember when, or why.

He only knew that it had been a mistake.

The Sittan punched him in the throat, a blow that would have killed a normal man. His chest heaved as he fought to breathe, even the oxygen-rich air of Sittan not enough for his starving lungs. The thump of Dax's knee between his legs had the warrior roaring, but it was more from anger than pain. This fighter was padded as well as oiled.

'You cannot win, human,' he snarled. 'But if you beg, I will consider the quick death.'

'You think you can kill me?' Dax pulled back. He let the male up, angling his hips and swinging his leg. The kick caught the Sittan full in the chest. The following punch caught him under the chin, knocking his head back. His remaining spikes lengthened, narrowed, and he charged Dax down, but his strength was fading.

Dax dodged the first punch the Sittan threw. He took the second against his shoulder where the scar of a bite had left the flesh hard and tender, because the Sittan was so desperate to deliver it that he left himself open. Dax took his chance. He responded with a kick to the abdomen, then another, then another, laying pain on top of pain. The Sittan staggered back, clutching his belly, screaming in agony. Around them, the crowd surged. All of them were on their feet now, all of them screaming the chant that Dax had heard too many times before.

End him.

Dax was ready. But the glint of a blade took him by surprise. He had only a moment to see it, to understand it, before the Sittan plunged it deep into the muscle of his thigh. A memory flooded his mind, a memory of a woman with a blade. He staggered back. The hand he dropped to his thigh came up wet, hot, bloodied. It seemed there were still some things to learn.

'I offered you the quick death,' the Sittan told him. He flexed his wrist, the light glinting on the second blade concealed in that hand. Weapons weren't allowed in the arena. It was hand-to-hand, fists and feet and teeth as weapons. Tainting the oil was considered poor sportsmanship, but it would be overlooked. A blade was another matter. A fight like this was as much about the mind as the body. About the ability to overcome fear, to overcome pain, to work with what you had and nothing more. Death came slower that way. Killing was harder.

'You're afraid,' Dax said. He switched his focus away from the brutal wound in his thigh and back to his opponent. 'You're not sure you can win.'

'Of course I can win.' The Sittan brought his arm forward in a flash-quick strike that slashed across Dax's stomach. The wound wasn't deep, but it burned. Oh, how it burned.

'There will be no glory if you end me with a blade.' Dax feinted, dodged the next slash of the knife.

'No one will care when you're dead,' the Sittan snarled back. 'The Mountain will have you.' He swung again, and this caught Dax across the face, slicing neatly across his cheek. 'And killing you will bring me everything I ever wanted. She wants you dead now. I'll be rewarded. I'll be free of my family.'

There was an eagerness in his voice, a desperation that overruled all the training, all the skills the warrior possessed. That was his weakness. That was Dax's way to end this. He straightened up, never taking his gaze off the Sittan. 'Then do it,' he said, exposing his bare, vulnerable flesh, inviting the creature in. 'Take what you want.'

The Sittan's yellow eyes burned with hatred, with greed, with the hunger for victory. He threw himself forward, the blade in his fist. But he was tired and he was uncertain, and he was far too afraid of death.

'Forty fights,' Dax said, as he dodged the blow, as he grabbed the Sittan by the throat and shoved his free hand beneath the waistband of hide breeches made slippery with oil. 'Seventeen kills,' he said, as he shoved his hand deeper, as he found the Sittan's genitals, as the sharp black sand lodged in his palm cut deep into soft, vulnerable flesh.

The Sittan howled.

Dax squeezed harder. He squeezed until the Sittan's eyes went dark, until his hands fisted in agony. He dropped the male to the ground, and put a foot on the arm that held the knife, kept it there. As the Sittan thrashed, he turned his gaze to the royal seats, where the empress lounged in her throne. Her expression said that she was bored. She rested an elbow on one bent knee, long, curving claws stroking over one sharp cheek.

'Finish it,' the Sittan snarled, his voice low, harsh.

If Dax had been less animal and more human, he might have refused. He might have stepped back, might have let the Sittan warrior live, even though it would have been a life of shame and degrading work in the mines below the palace.

But genetic engineering had stolen that option from him. Slowly, he moved his hand from the Sittan's groin to his throat. He pinned him down as he thrashed and twitched, as his skin darkened, as his eyes bulged and his heels kicked deep into the dirt. He tightened his grip as the rush of victory hit him, as the Sittan went still, as the light in his eyes went out.

The crowd surged. The roar was deafening. Kulaks exchanged hands, marking bets won and lost. Dax straightened up, lifted his fists to the air and accepted the victory. He turned, slowly, letting all of them see the damage the Sittan had done to his body, the bruises, the sweat, the broken skin and the blood. He traced the gaps in his mouth with his tongue. Three missing teeth. His hands were shredded, his thigh and his gut throbbing in memory of the blade that had sliced so deep into his flesh.

The knife lay close to the Sittan's outstretched hand, half buried in the dark sand. Without taking his eyes off the crowd, Dax moved closer to it, closer, until it was hidden under the press of his foot. He wanted that knife, and he intended to have it. It would be useful when he was sent back to his cell under the arena.

He stayed where he was as the body bearers entered the ring, as they grasped the arms of the dead Sittan and dragged him along the hot black sand. His broken body was loaded onto a cart, ready to be taken to the crater at the top of the Mountain.

Dax didn't move as the empress was carried into the arena, her throne lifted by a quartet of males, all young, all brutally strong. But he looked at her as she marked his shoulder with another black stripe. He didn't try to speak to her. He'd learned on his first day what happened to males who spoke to a female without invitation.

She moved in front of him, regarded him steadily through soft yellow eyes that slanted slightly up at the corners. Her mouth was full and red, her skin perfectly smooth. He could almost have thought her beautiful, if it wasn't for the fact that she was the colour of the sapphires wealthy Dome women decorated their fingers with back on Earth. She had curving hips and three full breasts, and Dax sensed she was curious about what it would be like to be pleasured by a human. To be pleasured by him.

She traced the wound on his belly with her finger, dug a claw into the split flesh. 'Where is the knife?'

'What knife?'

'The one he used to try and kill you,' she said.

'There was no knife.'

The empress smiled, and it was a hot, wicked thing. His head started to throb. She dug her claws in a little deeper and he let her push him back.

'Ah,' she said. 'There it is.' She gestured to one of her guards, who stepped forward and picked it up. It quickly vanished beneath the folds of her scarlet cloak.

The empress pulled her claws out of his gut and stroked them down the side of his face. 'Why lie? You have nothing to gain.'

'Because I could,' he said. Because all of this was a game, and he was bored with it. Killing had become as normal as eating, the need for violence just another hunger to be sated.

'I wonder what else you can do.'

'Plenty.'

Her eyes gleamed. 'Is that so?' She beckoned the guards closer with a flick of her hand. They moved in to surround him, the tips of their razor sharp spears pressed against his exposed flesh.

Dax didn't move. The tips of those spears were dipped in a long-lasting narcotic. It wouldn't do any permanent damage, but it would make him viciously unwell for several days.

He prepared to be taken back to the holding area under the arena. He didn't have the knife, which was a shame, but he was sure he could find another way to amuse himself.

The empress gestured to the tallest of her guards, a powerful female called Grenla. 'Take him to the palace,' she said.

'The palace?' Dax couldn't hide his surprise.

'Yes.' The empress leaned forward. 'I want to see exactly what else you can do.'

CHAPTER

7

The *Articus* was a very different place from the thriving repair station Eve had first come to as an anxious eighteen-year-old on the run from a medical facility back on Earth. She preferred not to dwell on that part of her life. She'd learned to cope with the more difficult aspects of the Second Species modifications. It had been easy, relatively speaking. She hadn't suffered from the raging bouts of uncontrollable aggression that had characterised Dax's early days of the change, or the pain that Alistair had endured until Theon had designed his implant.

In her dreams, Eve still saw herself as she had been, caramel-skinned and happy, or as happy as anyone could be growing up in Underworld New York. Even in the Underworld Cities there were those who had more and those who had less.

She'd had more.

Alistair had less.

Eve's parents had been from the other end of the city. Both had been teachers at the school. A respectable profession, with regular wages. Their lives hadn't been a day-to-day existence, stretched between the bimonthly food handouts.

Alistair's father had been a drunk. Eve could still remember her parents talking about it, when the man had traded his rations for alcohol yet again, leaving Alistair to fend for himself. Alistair would stubbornly turn up at school dirty and hungry. Some of the other kids would taunt him about it. Eve hadn't joined in, but she hadn't stopped them, either. She'd never spoken to him until he'd sat next to her in the waiting room at the Medipro office.

It had been the first time she'd ever left the underground city. The Medipro building had been both breathtaking and fascinating, housed as it was in a long, low bunker on the surface. Such an adventure. It had turned into a nightmare when the supposedly safe treatments they'd been given had taken effect.

Theon had got them out. Without his help, they wouldn't have survived beyond the first few weeks, but he'd managed to keep them alive and keep them from killing each other long enough for them to make it here.

It wasn't the life they had planned for themselves. But in the end, Alistair had made the most of it. He'd found himself a good job on the *Europa*, selling luxury ships. He'd had a home, a nice apartment in the residential centre. He'd made something of himself, unlike Eve. She'd remained on the *Mutant*, while he'd . . . he'd . . .

Gone somewhere he could get away from her and be with normal women.

'This place is a dump,' she said, annoyed with him. With herself. With life.

'It's better than the *Mutant*.'

'You always hated space travel.'

'It makes me itch,' he said. 'Space is too big, and spaceships are too unreliable.'

They had been walking for over an hour, slowly circling the *Articus*. They'd found the one remaining medical centre, where a medidroid had scanned Alistair and given him blockers. It was nothing that rest and time wouldn't heal. No bleeding in the brain, or anything else that might prove fatal, though the droid had warned him to avoid a repeat of the incident. Next time, he wouldn't be so lucky.

'The *Mutant* is still better than this,' she said, gesturing around them.

'It's not the nicest place I've visited,' Alistair agreed. 'But I don't remember it being as grotty as this.'

Neglect covered everything, slimy and gritty. Alistair checked the weapon holstered at his hip one more time.

'Keep touching that thing and you'll shoot yourself in the foot,' Eve told him. 'You won't look half so pretty with a prosthetic leg, you know.'

'Some women find that sort of thing attractive.'

'I guess you'd know all about that,' she said. 'Plenty of women on the *Europa*.' She folded her arms and kicked away a pile of discarded food cartons that hadn't made it into a recycling unit. It had been a spiteful, unnecessary comment, but she hadn't been able to hold it in.

The air stirred slightly around them, courtesy of the huge fan in the roof that pulled out the used air. It was filtered and cleaned before being released back through vents in the floor. Remnants of previous visitors littered the walkway, food wrappers, burned smokes, a couple of used drug guns, an abandoned comm. link. Normally cleaning droids would have removed all of it, but those were no longer functioning here. It made for a grim, intimidating atmosphere.

Eve moved closer to him, not touching, but closer than she normally dared.

Alistair moved away.

'Did you move away from the women on the *Europa*?' she asked.

Alistair exhaled slowly. 'Please don't do this.'

'Why not?'

He didn't look at her.

'So did you?' she persisted.

'Did I what?'

'Did you move away? Or did you let them touch you?'

'Do you really want me to answer that question?'

She folded her arms, her jaw tight. He had. Of course he had. And why wouldn't he? The *Europa* was full of beautiful, pale-skinned Dome women who would happily slum it with an Underworlder as pretty and charming as Alistair. And he needed affection, craved it. Deserved it. They walked on in silence for a while. Eve spent the time thinking miserable, furious thoughts.

'There's something wrong here,' Alistair said softly. 'It's too damn quiet.'

She kept her gaze pinned to the floor and concentrated on not crying, on making her voice normal. 'I thought you liked quiet.'

'Not like this.' He hunched his shoulders and shoved his hands into his pockets, glancing around as if something had spooked him. 'This place used to be busy,' he said. 'Remember? When we first came here I thought it was the most exciting place I'd ever seen.'

'When we first came here, it *was* the most exciting place we'd ever seen,' Eve said as her comm. unit buzzed. It was Jinn. 'What's up?'

'Can you come to Darkos's workshop? It's on the upper level. Unit 3721.'

'Is there a problem?'

'Remember the agent from the *Europa*?'

She certainly hadn't forgotten. 'What about him?'

'He's here,' Jinn said.

'What?'

'Here, alive, and asking for you.'

'He can't be.'

'Well, he is.'

Eve took a moment. She breathed in. Breathed out. She was close to the edge of the walkway, and she leaned her weight against the sticky wall. He was alive. A weight lifted from her that she'd barely been conscious of carrying. 'What does he want?' Alistair stopped walking. She caught his gaze. She wanted to take his hand, but that wasn't an option.

'Five minutes of your time. But I have to warn you, he doesn't look pretty, and he's so high on Euphoria he can barely stand upright.'

It didn't matter. He was alive. 'All right,' she said, and ended the call.

'Eve?'

'He's still alive,' she said. 'The agent I touched. He's alive. I didn't kill him.'

'I heard,' Alistair said cautiously.

Eve straightened up, though her whole body was trembling. 'Don't you understand what this means? I touched him, and I didn't kill him. Jinn said he's a mess, but he's alive.' Her heart skipped a beat. Ever since she'd been modified, she'd known what she was. But maybe, just maybe, things weren't as bad as she had believed.

She saw concern in Alistair's expression 'What?'

'It's just . . .'

'Don't,' Eve told him.

'Sorry,' he said, and she knew that he meant it. It didn't help. 'You're right. It's great news. The best. Come on. Let's go and find out what he wants.'

The workshop Jinn had gone to was somewhere on the upper level. A couple of touches to her personal comm. and Eve located it, the workshop showing as a little red dot on the map. She pulled her cloak around her and started to walk. There was a bank of elevators not too far away and she headed for it.

'Eve, wait.'

She kept moving.

'Eve, please.'

'What now?' She glanced back at him over her shoulder, the glance quickly turning into a full body twist when she saw his expression. 'Are you feeling okay? Are the blockers wearing off?'

'I'm fine,' he said. 'It's not that. It's . . .'

'What?'

He stared at her, blue eyes gleaming in his pretty face. 'Be careful,' he said. 'He used to be an agent. We can't trust him.'

'I'm always careful,' Eve told him.

The elevator door pinged open. Eve was about to step inside when something lean and long-tailed shot out. It swerved around Alistair, before scrabbling into a crack at the edge of the walkway and disappearing. Eve shuddered.

'It's fine,' Alistair said. 'It was just a hag rat. They're harmless.'

'They're still revolting.'

Fortunately no more appeared when the doors closed and the elevator started to move. 'Upper floor,' Eve ordered.

It went down instead of up.

She leaned back against the wall, the soles of her boots pressed hard against the floor. The elevators on the *Articus* were designed to move cargo as well as people, so the cart was wide enough that she could put a comfortable space between herself and Alistair. The sides were dented and scratched, the handrail loose when she tried to grip it. A dozen lights pitted the ceiling, but only three of them were working.

The elevator dropped again, then jolted to a halt that made the lights flash off for several anxious seconds before switching on again. 'Next time we're taking the stairs,' Alistair said grimly as the doors creaked open. No one got on, though the doors didn't close. The waiting stretched. Neither of them moved. 'Upper level,' Alistair reminded the cart.

Still nothing.

'Stupid thing must be broken,' Eve said. Still, she gave it a few more long seconds before she pushed off the wall and walked out.

At first, she heard nothing but the hum of the air recyclers and the crackle of a busted vid screen. And then ... then there was something else. A strange ripple of sound that didn't belong in the grubby, empty space of the lower level.

'What in the void is that?' Eve asked.

Alistair glanced across at her, and she didn't like what she saw in his face. It didn't surprise her as much as it should have when he pulled the blaster from the holster at his hip and armed it. 'I don't know. But we need to get to the workshop.'

'I don't think we'll be getting there in that heap of junk,' Eve said, gesturing back at the elevator. She could feel her skin prickling as she pulled her own weapon from its holster. The sound had stopped again, leaving the itch of paranoia behind.

Maybe they had imagined it. This place was creepy enough to make you crazy.

'Agreed,' he said. He looked right, left, then gestured straight ahead. 'If memory serves me right, the emergency stairs are that way.'

'Stairs,' Eve muttered as she fell in alongside him. 'It's like we're back in the dark ages.' But the glide carts didn't come down this far, so they didn't have any other option. They moved closer together, not close enough to touch but close enough to feel the defensive need behind it. They picked up speed. The giant fan overhead continued to whirr, a constant whop whop whop that stirred the air as all around them the *Articus* remained too empty, too still.

'Come on,' Alistair said. They moved quickly, following the curve of the walkway as the street markers counted down.

They didn't see the Shi Fai until it was almost too late.

There were three of them, huddled together in the doorway of an abandoned electronics store.

'Well, that explains the smell,' Eve muttered as she automatically ground to a halt. 'What are they doing here, Alistair?'

The two of them pressed themselves back against the wall, keeping the Shi Fai in view, letting the shadows hide them. Alistair leaned forward, then quickly moved back.

'I don't know,' he said. 'They came to the *Europa* all the time, but it's close to jump gate 62, and that leads to their space. There's no reason for them to be here. It doesn't make any sense.'

'Well, I for one have no intention of asking them to explain themselves,' Eve told him. She started to move, but she wasn't looking where she was going and accidentally kicked a broken cleaning droid. It skidded across the walkway. One of the Shi Fai turned and glanced in their direction. 'Uh oh.'

'We should probably leave now,' Alistair said.

The two of them backed away, keeping their gazes locked onto the Shi Fai until they had put enough distance between them to turn and run. They didn't bother with the elevators this time. Instead, they found an old float cart tucked behind a broken food stall. Alistair pulled a universal starter chip from somewhere in his jacket and managed to get it going. He climbed on first, and Eve took the seat behind him, carefully positioning her body as far away from his as she could manage.

They scooted straight up, away from the Shi Fai, and he flew them around the centre of the station and through the vents to the upper level. They dumped the float cart next to the open vent and walked quickly away from it.

The doorway to Darkos's workshop lay just ahead of them. Eve could tell just by looking at it that Darkos had been the top dog of the *Articus*. Not only was the door gold, there were two scary looking security droids posted in front of it.

'I wonder what he was trying to compensate for,' Alistair said.

Eve smiled even though she didn't feel like it. 'Oh, I think we all know the answer to that question.'

About three metres from the doorway, she stopped.

'Eve?' Alistair asked.

'I don't know if I can do this,' she said. 'I don't know if I can face him.'

'Then don't.'

But she had to. And with Shi Fai on the station, they needed to be on the other side of those doors. She took a few more short, difficult steps. And then the droids stepped aside and the flashy door slid open, and the choice was taken away from her, because he was there.

Eve held her ground, but only because Alistair was right behind her.

'You!' the man said. 'It's you, you fucking bitch!'

'Bryant,' came a warning voice from behind him, and Jinn stepped out on to walkway. Her blades were out.

Jinn's arrival gave Eve the boost she needed. 'Yes,' she said. 'It's me.' She walked slowly, carefully, up to the man and stood close enough that he could touch her, if he really wanted to.

He didn't look like the man she had seen on the *Europa* anymore. It made a sour taste rise up into the back of her throat to see first-hand and close up exactly what her touch could do. No, she hadn't killed him, but in some ways this was no better. The kiss of her fingers against the back of his neck, and he'd been reduced to this.

But she held his gaze. She would not look away. She was a pirate, and she was Type Two. And she would not turn away from what she had done, no matter how much it hurt to look at it.

'I heard you wanted to see me. So here I am.'

He looked her up and down, almost in disbelief. A shaky hand came up and all but touched her face, but he stopped himself just in time. She refused to shy away from the contact. Let him do it if he wanted to. From the look of him, it would be doing him a favour.

'We saw Shi Fai down on the lower level,' Alistair said.

'Shi Fai? Here?'

'Yes.'

'Then we'd better go back inside,' Jinn said.

Bryant stared at Eve for a few seconds longer, then he turned and stumbled back inside the workshop. Jinn followed him, and Eve and Alistair followed her. The door slid closed behind them, the droids remaining on guard outside.

CHAPTER
8

If asked, Ferona would have said that dealing with alien races was more difficult than dealing with humans. She'd have stuck to that story, publicly anyway, because it suited her for other people to believe it. But it wasn't entirely true.

President Vexler was causing trouble. Again.

He had decided to bring forward his press tour of the newly built Type One facility. The decision had been made without consulting anyone, and it was only thanks to Lucinda that Ferona had been able to alter her plans and make sure she was there with him.

Fortunately, the medical centre that had been built to replace the *A2* was running at full capacity. As she walked through the clean, lemon-scented waiting room with a smugly prancing Vexler at her side, Ferona couldn't help feeling a sense of accomplishment and more than a little pride. She had to give credit to the others who had worked on the project – the team who had built this place in a matter of weeks and of course Weston, who had been responsible for the reformulation of the serums, making them both cheaper and more effective.

This was no rotting freighter, and the men sitting here didn't need to be drugged or restrained. They were volunteers, each and every one of them. They were all dressed in oversized jumpsuits that were rolled up at the ankle and wrist in preparation for the growth spurts they would experience once the second dose of serum had been administered.

There were three different serums in total, each changing a different aspect of their bodies. The first would boost their immune systems and healing rate in preparation for the second, which caused a rapid and painful growth of bone and tissue. Those who survived it would then be given the third and worst of the serums, the one which caused changes in brain chemistry. Their aggression levels would rise overnight. They would crave violence, and if it didn't come to them they would actively seek it out.

The men didn't really understand this, of course. But they had signed the consent forms and the information had all been there, hidden in very small print and very complicated language that she doubted any of them had the education to fully understand. But it didn't really matter. None of them would be coming home. It was a shame, she thought, but it was simply the way things had to be.

She shook hands with some of them and made meaningless small talk as they smiled and tried to pretend that they weren't nervous. Vexler talked about the ship-building programme that was already underway, preparing transports for the long journey to Spes, and made sure that the cameras always got his good side.

When they moved out of the waiting room the site manager showed them to a pair of eight seater cars that would take them around the rest of the facility. It was too big to cover on foot. Eleven journalists trailed along behind them, cameras hovering at shoulder height.

She had worked hard to persuade Vexler to bring the media here. He had wanted to go to the Type Two facility on the moon, as it was closer and more convenient. It wasn't yet common knowledge that the women were poisonous to the touch, and imagining Vexler ignorantly shaking hands with one of the women and then dropping dead at her feet brought Ferona out in a cold sweat. People were prepared to accept overgrown, overmuscled men, but toxic women were a step too far. Yet this particular trip had been necessary. They needed to show the public and the other ministers that the Second Species were safe, and do so in a controlled fashion.

It was all very exciting for the select group of journalists who had been invited. They stood in the way, pushing and shoving as they tried to get their shot and making it very difficult to be nice to them.

'Please stay in the car,' ordered the security droid. 'Please do not touch anything. We cannot be held responsible for any injuries sustained by failing to follow these instructions. We thank you for your cooperation.'

The next room was full of uniformed, masked workers, preparing the vials of serum that would be used in the first phase of treatment.

'Funny, isn't it?' one of the women said as she sat next to Ferona.

'What is?'

'That the human body can be changed so drastically by a little bottle of brown goo. I thought it would be more impressive.'

Ferona looked at her. 'Genetic modification is a very straightforward, safe procedure,' she told her. 'What did you expect?'

'I don't know,' she said. 'Something more surgical and terrifying. Though I suppose this is still quite overwhelming. Would you let them inject you with it?'

Ferona smiled. 'Everything has been rigorously tested,' she said. 'The treatment is life-changing.'

The woman held onto the rail on the side of the cart as it started to move. 'I've heard that half the volunteers don't survive the procedure. Is that true?'

Ferona could feel the heavy stares of the other journalists that sat on the cart with them. They, too, had heard those rumours. 'No procedure is without its dangers. We make sure all the volunteers are fully informed of this.'

'So what is the survival rate?'

She tried to ignore the little camera pinned to the woman's lapel, knowing that she was recording everything that was said. Self-important little bugger. 'The survival rate is extremely high,' Ferona said. 'As it is with all genetic modification procedures. But all those who enter the programme are aware of the risks.'

'What about the risk to the rest of us?'

'What do you mean?'

'Humans modified with alien DNA are no longer human. Especially not those modified with Sittan DNA. We all know what the Sittan are like.'

'The Second Species pose no threat to the rest of the human population.'

'Humans First think they do.'

'Humans First are mistaken,' Ferona replied. 'The Second Species are an opportunity, a chance to change the future of the human race. For the better.' She leaned forward a little, her gaze locked on the woman. 'How can something that will help all of us be wrong?' The woman sat back and pouted. That obviously wasn't the answer she'd been looking for.

The cart trundled along the yellow line painted into the floor, moving through twin sets of double doors before coming to a halt. This was the second treatment area where the second dose of serum was administered. The men were generally put under for a couple of days while it took effect. Gaining thirty kilos of bone and muscle in forty-eight hours was a brutal business.

The bodies in the beds were sleeping and calm. Monitors positioned by each one measured heart rate and basic brain activity, and robotic arms reached out to wipe away sweat. The occasional cracking of expanding joints made the scene even more eerie. Ferona found herself holding her breath, and those around her were equally silent.

There were so many. Ferona had known the number, but to see them laid out like this, in row after row of horizontal med-ibeds, made a figure on a page into a chest-tightening reality. The contents of this room constituted a single shipment. There was time for two more to be sent to Sittan before the Senate gathered to vote.

One of the journalists whistled. 'That's a lot of men,' he said. A couple of the others turned their heads, nodding their agreement.

'This is the second stage of the serum,' Vexler said. 'Patients are sedated, which makes the procedure very easy for them. The layout of this facility also allows us to modify multiple patients at once, which of course means that we can limit costs.'

'How much is this costing exactly?' asked one of the journalists.

'Ah . . . ' said Vexler. His gaze snapped to Ferona.

'The serums cost three hundred credits,' Ferona said. She didn't add that it was three hundred credits per serum, or that everything else was extra. 'Of course, this is a small price to pay when you consider what is at stake. Our latest reports show that the temperature at the poles has fallen by another two degrees.' It was widely known and accepted that a fall in temperature there was always followed by a fall everywhere else.

'We have to get to Spes,' she told them. 'We don't have time to wait. And we have to cross alien-controlled space to get there – space controlled by the Sittan and the Shi Fai. These men,' she gestured to the nearest bed, 'are the difference between a safe future for our race and extinction.

'As you can see,' she continued brightly, 'the patients are in no pain, and the procedure is very straightforward.' Being Dome-raised, the majority here would have no experience of this sort of genetic modification, as it was usually experienced only by Underworlders who opted for colony jobs. The most anyone here could claim was a tweak to lighten hair colour or lengthen their eyelashes. Genetic mistakes were corrected at the embryonic stage. Once that had been done, there was little need for anything more extensive.

She couldn't let them linger here, though she understood the fascination. The growth rate was so rapid that you could almost see it happening. An arm you had looked at only a few minutes before would seem bigger when your gaze strayed back to it. A bed that had been too large would suddenly look too small. But not all bodies were able to withstand such brutal changes. If they remained here long enough, she could guarantee that at least one patient would die.

'What's happening?' someone asked, pointing to something on the other side of the window. Ferona could see a screen that had started to flash, and the slow movement of a couple of medical droids towards the bed.

'All part of the procedure,' Vexler said cheerily. 'As you can see, we are using the top of the range XLR 350 medical droid, produced by Health Robotics. Come, let's go and take a look at one.'

Ferona exhaled slowly as Vexler steered them all onto the cars, which zipped them away from the treatment room, along a corridor and through to a hospitality suite complete with a fully laden buffet table and comfortable chairs. Screens hung on the walls, each playing a film advertising various Medipro services. And there, in the middle of the space, were two of the medidroids, elegant, flashy.

Vexler got to work. He had the journalists eating out of his hand in a matter of minutes as he showed off the new toys that he'd had specially created for the Second Species project. They'd been quite unnecessary – the procedure wasn't complicated. There was a current cheap model of droid that was more than capable of handling it. But that hadn't been enough for Vexler.

Although Ferona didn't regret her involvement in the removal of the previous vice president from office, she hadn't really appreciated how hard Mikhal Dubnik had worked to keep Vexler in line. She had always assumed that Vexler was merely vain and foolish. She hadn't realised that he was impulsive and capricious, dangerous traits in a man who had so much power. What made it worse was that she had to keep him on side, for now. He had a lot of support. She could not afford to make an enemy of him, and that was why, against her better judgement, she had allowed him to think that he was in charge of this visit.

At least playing with his robots was keeping him quiet for now. They were almost finished. All she had to do was wait for the journalists to finish eating their way through the buffet and then they'd leave, well fed and, hopefully, satisfied enough to present a positive picture of the facility. Vexler would see a bump in his approval rating, so he'd be happy, and it should be sufficient exposure for the Second Species programme to keep the public happy until the Senate cast their votes. After that, no one would care what happened to the people involved.

The doors at the far side of the hospitality room swung open and a group of people walked in. Had they come to clear the table? She hoped so. That would put a welcome end to proceedings. Having the journalists and Vexler inside the facility was making her twitchy. She wanted this to be over. It had all gone so well. Time to get everyone on the ship home before something went wrong.

Two of them had on the white uniform worn by all staff at the facility. As for the others . . . Before she could stop herself, Ferona backed up. She backed up until she was pressed against the wall at the far side of the room and stood there frozen and unmoving.

They were so *large*. Biceps strained against sleeves, shoulder bumped shoulder as they stood close together in the centre of the room. The jumpsuits that had been too big in the waiting room now fitted perfectly, and, in some cases, were verging on too small.

She hadn't realised quite how size would translate into power, how much space they would take up. They had hands that could crush both of hers without even trying. By the void, she hoped the security here was good. It would have to be. There was far more Sittan in them than she had realised, even without the third dose of serum.

A shiver ran down her spine when she made the mistake of locking gazes with one of them. What were they doing here? She hadn't ordered this. She had arranged for all the Type Ones to be viewed from the safety of the other side of the glass. Who ...

Vexler. It had to be, given that he was over there grinning like an idiot.

Ferona took a deep breath, and thought about wrapping her hands around his neck and strangling him. She would have to keep a far closer eye on him after today. The only solution was to have one of his assistants somehow removed from their job and replaced with a Type Three. Lucinda had been able to monitor him to some extent, but Ferona needed someone who could be with him all the time.

Vexler clapped his hands together, smiled, and walked up to one of the Second Species. He held out his hand. The youth stared down at him, his expression confused. Then he slowly reached out and took Vexler's hand. Vexler was by no means a small man, but the Type One towered over him. 'Wonderful to meet you,' Vexler said. 'Wonderful to meet all of you.' He let go of the youth's hand, and moved along the group, shaking hands with each of them as the cameras recorded every moment.

'Are they safe?' asked one of the journalists, as if the men were some sort of wild animal.

'Of course they're safe,' said Vexler now, beaming into the nearest camera, never one to miss an opportunity to take credit for someone else's work. 'Look at them. Isn't science wonderful?'

The Type One male said nothing.

'Completely wonderful!' cried one of the journalists, a woman with a thin face and hair coiled ridiculously high. She moved closer to the Type Ones and was daring enough to touch one. She petted him lightly at first, and then, when he didn't react, cranked that up to a full-on grope.

Stop it! Ferona thought desperately. You have no idea what you're doing!

'But look at them,' said another of the journalists, his voice almost shaking with terror. 'Just look at them.'

'Yes,' Vexler said. 'Aren't they magnificent?'

'Are we supposed to share Spes with creatures like this? What's to stop them taking over once we get there? Normal humans won't stand a chance against them. Maybe Humans First are right.'

'Well ...' Vexler began. He looked at Ferona, which was always his signal for her to take over. He was bloody useless. Absolutely bloody useless. He had engineered this situation, and now he expected her to get them out of it. How had Lucinda missed this? How had she not known?

Ferona forced herself to walk forward, closer to the Type Ones. Sweat slithered down her spine. 'Spes is a chance for humankind to start again,' she said, her tongue dry and thick. 'A chance for us to learn from the mistakes of the past, while making the most of all the things we have got right.'

'They're clearly dangerous!'

'So is a man armed with a blaster,' Vexler pointed out.

'Exactly! Which is why they are controlled! How are you going to control this?'

'We don't need to,' Ferona told him. 'It's perfectly safe. These are people, not weapons. They are just like you and me.' She inhaled deeply, and forced herself to relax, to walk closer still.

'They're nothing like you and me!' the journalist squeaked.

'Of course they're not,' Vexler said. 'They are different. Dare I say magnificent? And none of us have been hurt, have we?'

'Not yet,' one of the other journalists muttered.

'And we won't be,' Vexler continued. 'I'll prove it to you. I had the idea earlier today, when I saw the men in the flesh. Vice President Blue,' he gave a nod in Ferona's direction, 'is going to add one of these men to her personal team, as am I. Over the next few weeks, they will work with us, and you will soon see that the Second Species are nothing to be afraid of. In fact, I suspect we'll all be begging to sign up for the programme ourselves by the end of it.' He laughed, and a couple of the others laughed with him, though it was quickly drowned out by the roar of questions that followed.

As for Ferona, she thought she might faint.

Vexler had manoeuvred her into this and she hadn't even seen it coming. The man was more than just a liability, he was dangerous. But she couldn't refuse, not here, not in front of these people. If she did, Humans First would have a field day, and that was trouble she just didn't need right now.

She walked slowly up to the largest of the Type Ones, a towering beast of a man with hard eyes and a jumpsuit straining at the seams, and felt almost sick with fear. But she controlled it. She prided herself on being an intelligent, resourceful woman, able to think on her feet, and she drew on all her years of experience now. She looked the man over.

Maybe something could be salvaged from this. Swain and Lucinda were useful, but they had their limitations. This man could keep Senator Hann at a safe distance. There would be no more nasty surprises waiting in her box at the Senate with him by her side.

A deep breath, and her mind was made up. She would go along with Vexler's plan.

But she would make him pay for it.

CHAPTER

9

3rd November 2207

The *Articus*. Repair Station, Sector Four, Neutral Space

Eve hadn't slept the night after her first meeting with Bryant, her mind too busy, her thoughts rushing along at a million miles an hour. Bryant hadn't just wanted to talk to her. He wanted more than that. He wanted a sample of her flesh, her blood. Not much, just a tiny amount, enough for testing. He'd said it like that made a difference, as if a drop wouldn't kill just as easily as a syringe full.

She'd told him she needed time. He had begged and pleaded, but she had stuck to her guns and Jinn had stepped in when Bryant had threatened to do something stupid. None of them wanted that. More than enough stupid had already been done. But she still didn't know what to do.

'Alistair,' she said quietly. He was closest to her and he looked across to where she sat. He raised a questioning eyebrow.

'I'm going for a walk,' Eve said. 'I need some space.' She kept her voice low. Jinn and Li were at the other side of the workshop, locked in discussion with Grudge. A 3D holographic map spiralled in front of them, showing the planet Sittan and the jump gates nearest to it. Alistair hadn't joined in, preferring instead to sit close to Eve and watch the newsfeed on his personal unit.

'All right,' Alistair said, turning off the unit and sliding it into his pocket. 'Want company?'

Eve thought about telling him to stay where he was, then decided against it. If she left Alistair behind, one of the others would insist on taking his place and she wasn't sure she could deal with either the anxious pressure of Jinn or the intimidating silence of Li. 'Yes.'

Alistair got to his feet. Grudge glanced over at them. Eve caught his gaze and nodded. He nodded back, and she saw him quietly pass the message on to the others. She stood up and started towards the exit. Alistair was already there waiting for her.

They slipped out onto the walkway. 'What are you thinking?' Alistair asked her.

Eve pulled a face at him. 'Like you don't already know.'

'I haven't been listening,' he said.

'That never made any difference.'

Alistair slipped his hands into his pockets, keeping his gaze fixed straight ahead. 'You don't have to do this,' he told her. 'You don't have to give him what he wants.'

'I know,' she said. 'But we need that generator. Not just for Dax, but for Jinn. This is how we do things. This is how we make it work. We do what we need to do to keep everyone together.'

'This isn't about the generator. Between Jinn and Li, I'm sure we can find a way to persuade him to hand it over.'

'No, it isn't,' she admitted. 'It's about me. When I first heard that he was still alive, I thought that maybe that meant I was okay. Maybe things had changed since we left Earth, and the toxin in my skin wasn't as potent as it used to be. But that's not true, is it? He's still alive because he's too much of a stubborn bastard to die. But it's coming, and he knows it. And I don't think I can live with myself if I don't at least try to help.'

'Then what's the problem?'

'My skin is toxic to humans. We all know that. I'm careful all the time to make sure I don't hurt anyone.' She held up a gloved hand. 'Gloves. Sleeves. Even the rinse from my chemicleanse goes through its own network of pipes so that it isn't recycled with everyone else's, just to be safe. Now I'm going to give someone I don't know samples of poison, and I can't really know how they're going to use them.'

'That's Bryant's problem, not yours. Once the samples have been taken, they belong to him. It's his responsibility.'

'Easy to say,' Eve pointed out.

'You aren't to blame for any of this.'

'I poisoned him!'

'Because he deserved it,' Alistair told her. 'He brought this on himself, Eve.'

She knew why she had poisoned him. She would do it again in a heartbeat to protect the others. But that did not push aside the deep-rooted guilt that had only got worse now that she had seen him again. She hated herself for it, and she hated Bryant for being so ill, such a present reminder of everything that was wrong with her.

There was no going back. Things moved in one direction only whether you wanted them to or not. So she kept on walking, a little less bothered by the mess that surrounded her now. Places like this wouldn't matter anymore anyway once people started moving to Spes. They would be abandoned, left floating in space as decaying relics of a stretch of human history that had finished. Why clean up a mess when you could just leave it behind?

'Are you sure you're okay with this?' Alistair asked her.

'I'm not sure I'm okay with any of it,' Eve told him. 'I can't change the past, I know that. But maybe I can change the future, or at least try to. I'm not doing it for him,' she said, turning her head and catching his gaze, wanting to make sure that he understood. 'I'm doing it for us. For you and me and Jinn and Dax. For the *Mutant*. As you said, once it's done, it's no longer my responsibility.'

'As long as you're sure.'

Eve shrugged. 'What's the worst thing that could happen?'

'I don't think you really want me to answer that question.' Then he stopped. 'Can you hear that?'

'Hear what?'

Alistair lifted a hand to his implant, switched it off, and concentrated for a moment. Then he turned it back on. 'Sounds like Shi Fai,' he said. 'Maybe we should go back.'

Eve wasn't ready for that. 'Look, we know they're here. We just need to be careful and make sure we keep our eyes open.' To make her point, she started to walk a little faster. 'It's a big station. I'm sure we can keep out of their way.'

They rounded the corner of the walkway as it wrapped round the square spike that formed the centre of the *Articus*. Nearly a kilometre long, it was wide enough to form a street a good hundred metres in length along each of its sides. There were lifts in the central spike, but neither of them bothered with them given the state of the ones they'd tried earlier.

Instead, they headed for the main walkway, but someone had dumped a broken scoot bike across the bottom of the steps that led up to the next level and helpfully set it on fire.

'Well, that's unfortunate,' Alistair said as a fuel cell exploded, sending pieces of shrapnel flying up into the air.

'Where are the emergency service droids?' Eve said, looking around. 'They should be here to sort this out.'

'Trashed along with everything else, presumably.'

'We can't just leave it!'

The fire was already starting to spread. Bits of discarded rubbish were catching the flame, and the smell of scorched plastic quickly filled the air. Eve covered her face with her hand and tried not to cough as she looked around for something she could use to put the fire out.

'Here!' Alistair called, ducking into one of the abandoned units at the side of the street. From the look of the signage outside, it had been a shoe store before it was abandoned, though it had been thoroughly looted. Eve ran over to it. Alistair was already at the back of the store, pulling open the cupboards behind the counter. In one of them an extinguisher had been missed, probably because it was one of the cheap little palm-sized models and whoever had been in here had been more interested in helping themselves to a pair of free boots.

He tossed it to Eve and she ran out of the store with it, pulling the pin as she went. Instantly the chemicals inside the handle were mixed together and the device began to expand, a thin Plastex bag quickly filling with fluid.

Eve threw it at the burning scoot bike. The bag bounced towards the fire, stopping a couple of metres away. It wasn't close enough. It wouldn't get hot enough to burst and put out the fire.

'Oh, come on!' she yelled, holding her hood over her mouth as she ran to where the bag lay, a little useless blob. She kicked it towards the fire. It rolled along, taking its time, then sat within licking distance of the flames.

The bag burst. Relief washed over her just as the wave of liquid washed over the scoot bike, reducing it to a smouldering skeleton in a matter of seconds. Eve put her hands on her hips and exhaled, then let out a nervous laugh. That had been more excitement than she'd really needed. She turned, expecting to see Alistair right behind her, expecting to see him in the same state of jittery shock.

Instead, she saw a group of Shi Fai. Not one or two, but a dozen, maybe more. The smell of the burning plastic had overridden their musty stink. She hadn't heard them because she'd been too distracted by everything else, totally focused on the fire. They were coming around the opposite corner, moving in and out of the empty stores just as she and Alistair had done.

'Dammit!' Eve patted the blaster at her thigh and felt a little better, then started to back up. She caught sight of Alistair coming out of the store with a second extinguisher in his hand, and gestured in the direction of the Shi Fai, who were only a hundred or so metres away now.

'Oh,' he said. 'We should leave.'

'You think?'

They turned and started to walk briskly in the other direction, but they didn't get far. Another group of Shi Fai was approaching from the same direction. They were trapped. 'I knew this was a bad idea,' Alistair muttered.

Eve said nothing. There was no point arguing with him. She activated her comm. instead. 'Jinn? It's Eve. We've got ourselves into a bit of a tricky situation. Could do with some backup. Yes. Shi Fai. Sooner rather than later would be good.'

She kept her gaze fixed on the approaching aliens, her shoulders stiff as she sensed the ones approaching from behind.

'Let me deal with this,' Alistair said.

Eve worked hard to suppress her shudder when one of them stepped forward. The creature looked her over. 'You are green,' it said, the words translated by the little square device hung around its neck.

'We don't want any trouble,' Alistair told it. He moved his jacket a little, showing the blaster tucked underneath.

'Why is this Type Two female with you?'

'That's none of your concern.'

'You are mistaken. It is our concern. She is Type Two. She belongs to us.'

The Shi Fai reached for Eve, and she jerked out of reach and pulled her own blaster in response. She charged it and levelled it at the alien's face. 'Touch me and I'll blow your head off,' she told it, suddenly very afraid. Humans and Shi Fai had never had a particularly comfortable relationship, and there were all those rumours about them snatching women, but she had never really believed it, not until now. A white, rubbery hand closed over her arm. Foul breath hit her face and made her cry out in disgust. She fired her blaster, but the shot missed and dinged off the wall, then the weapon was pulled from her grasp.

'Let her go!' Alistair shouted.

'No,' the alien said. 'She belongs to us.'

There was a scuffle, and somehow Alistair ended up lying on the floor, eyes glazed, blood oozing from a cut on the back of his head. The one who had hit him tucked a thick club back into its belt.

Eve was grabbed and her hands pulled behind her back. She fought against them, but there were too many and they were too strong. Her wrists were quickly bound and she was pulled along the walkway. Only one of them had a translator, so she had no way to understand what they said to each other. When she refused to walk, they hit her with those long sticks, and that much she could understand. They took her to a docking bay on the far side of the station.

The docking gates were open, but instead of the shine of Plastex walkways she saw dark, snaking tunnels leading into the pit of their ships. And there were not just Shi Fai, but other creatures that she'd never seen before.

They sat in pairs at the entrance to the loading ramp of each vessel. Pale skin covered their muscled frames, folded and fleshy as if it didn't fit properly. And they had two heads, one stacked on top of the other, both with large, gaping mouths that displayed huge, square teeth. On the upper head they ran vertically, but on the lower one they had been turned through 180 degrees and meshed into a horizontal weapon. She saw one of them stretch out its upper head, its neck extending, telescoping up almost to the roof.

Eve fought even harder, but it didn't help. They simply picked her up and carried her along the long, sticky tunnel and into the belly of the Shi Fai ship.

CHAPTER
10

3rd November 2207

The *Articus*. Repair Station, Sector Four, Neutral Space

Jinn found Alistair on the walkway. He'd been coshed on the head, and blood stained the back of his jacket. His blaster was still in his hand. 'They took her,' he said dully. 'There was nothing I could do. There were so many. They smelled bad.'

Jinn and Li hauled him to his feet. He wobbled there for a moment, and Jinn grabbed his arm and slung it round her shoulders. He leaned on her. She could feel him sobbing. She couldn't even begin to think about Eve, or what had happened here. They'd left Darkos's workshop and got here as quickly as they could, but it hadn't been quick enough.

'I need to check the docking bay,' she said to Li as Bryant appeared, having finally caught up with them. 'Get Alistair back to the workshop. Grudge will take care of him.'

'What about you?' Li asked. 'What if there are more of them?'

Jinn snapped out her blades. 'It wouldn't be the first time I've dealt with them.' She gestured to Bryant. 'Looks like I've got backup, anyway.'

'Him?'

'It's better than nothing.'

Li acknowledged this with a nod, and started off with Alistair as Jinn broke into a run, taking the stairs up to the next level and the docking bays. The faint musty smell of Shi Fai filled the air. Most of the docking bays were empty, but one was still occupied, and she ran towards it, pulling out her blaster.

A couple of Shi Fai stood at the entrance to the spacewalk. Her finger hit the trigger before she even realised that she'd done it, and the first one collapsed with its head blown clean off. The second took a little more work, but three shots and it went down.

The door at the entrance started to close. Jinn charged at it, jumping over the bodies, but she was too late. She pressed herself against the Plastex in time to see the spacewalk detach and collapse back into the Shi Fai ship. She punched the door with her fist, howling in frustration. It didn't help.

And then, spent, she turned, pressed her back against the door, and sank to the floor, breathing hard. The two bodies were only a couple of metres away.

Bryant staggered up to her, eyes wild. 'Where is she?'

'Gone.'

'What do you mean, gone?'

'Shi Fai took her. The Shi Fai that you let move in down here when you holed up in Darkos's workshop and decided to leave everyone else on the station to fend for themselves.'

'You can't blame me for this!'

'Why not?'

'Because it's not my fault!' he screeched. 'This can't fucking be happening to me.' He spun away from her, babbling loudly. 'Why me? Why? What the fuck did I do to deserve this?'

'Bryant,' Jinn said sharply. When he didn't respond, she yelled his name again. 'Bryant!'

He turned around, glaring at her with bloodshot eyes. 'What?'

'Shut up!'

'Why, so you can yell at me some more?'

Jinn charged at him. One hand in the front of his jacket, a blade against his throat, she shook him, hard, and then got right in his face. In a small, rational part of her mind she knew that Bryant wasn't truly to blame for this, it only felt like he was, but that was enough to make her want to hurt him. 'Be quiet,' she said. 'I need to think.'

She shoved him away and started to pace. Dax on Sittan, Eve taken by the Shi Fai. Two different planets in completely different directions. She had one ship. And she couldn't split herself in two.

'Did you have those the whole time we worked together?' Bryant asked her as she continued to pace, trying to figure out what she was going to do. He gestured to her blades.

'Yes.'

'Huh,' Bryant replied. 'If I had known, I might have treated you differently.'

'What, you'd have been nicer to me?'

'No,' he said. 'But I'd have shot you with lot more anaesthetic before I dumped you on the *A2*.'

Jinn stared at him. 'Dax is on Sittan,' she told him. 'Eve is most likely on her way to Shi Fai. I've got one ship which isn't bloody working. I don't have time to talk about what you might or might not have done.'

'Why are you so worried about them?'

'Because they're my friends!' she said.

'They're Underworld scum with freak modifications.'

She moved so quickly that she surprised even herself. Her blade stopped only centimetres from his chest.

'Go on,' he said, leaning forward a little. 'Do it.'

Oh, she wanted to. How she wanted to. But she wasn't that person. 'No.' She willed in her blade.

'I bet you're just loving this, aren't you? All those years we worked together, and you never liked me.'

'As I recall, the feeling was mutual.'

But now, after all that had happened, she barely felt anything at all. He was disgusting and pathetic but none of her old anger remained. She didn't have the energy for it anymore. 'I want that grav generator, Bryant. It won't cost you anything. A few hours,

I'll have it fitted, and I'll be gone. We'll never have to see each other again.'

'And what about me?'

'What about you?'

'Am I just supposed to give you the generator and then stay here waiting to die?'

She had changed. Bryant, clearly, had not. 'You could always leave,' she told him. 'I assume you've got a ship, given that you got here in the first place.'

'It won't fly,' he said. 'Fucking thing is a mess.'

'You're on a repair station. Get it fixed.'

Bryant's shoulders slumped a little. The corner of his left eye was twitching. 'I can't.'

'Why not?'

'Because it's got a chunk of Sittan tech growing on the main drive.'

Jinn stopped pacing. She turned to look at him. 'What?'

'My pleasure yacht, which used to belong to Darkos and now belongs to me, has a chunk of Sittan tech growing on the main drive and is therefore completely useless. What part of that didn't you get?'

'Does it have jump capability?'

'Of course it does.'

'All right,' Jinn said. 'Take me to it. I bet that I can make it fly.'

Half an hour. She told herself she could give him half an hour. She contacted Grudge and Li, asked them to start ripping out the old generator. 'I was only doing my job, you know,' Bryant said, as she marched down towards the docking level and he danced alongside her.

'Of course you were.'

'It wasn't my fault. I had my orders, and I followed them.'

'So that's it? You get to deny all responsibility, because someone else told you to do it? I was your partner, Bryant. You betrayed me. We were a team. We worked together for years, and you dumped me on that black hole without a moment's hesitation.'

'You've got fucking blades in your hands,' he said, 'and you can't tell me they're just for decoration. That much Tellurium is illegal, which makes you a criminal. So don't tell me I did the wrong thing.'

Jinn couldn't even bring herself to look at him. She kept her gaze fixed straight ahead. This was definitely the more expensive end of the station. The bays were widely spaced, and there were hydroponic trees and long, comfortable couches and a fabulous bar. There were signs that the same crowd that had worked over the rest of the station had been here – the lighting had been stripped from the bar, and dark shadows on the floor showed where several of the couches had been removed. And the trees were dead, the hydroponic systems missing. But they hadn't taken everything. Jinn could see that one of the bays was occupied, an armed droid standing watch at the entrance.

Another droid rushed up to them, its polished exterior coated with a thick layer of oily dust. 'How may I serve you?'

'By leaving us alone,' Jinn told it.

The droid scurried away.

'Which one is it?' she asked Bryant.

'Over there.' He gestured with one bony hand.

Jinn followed him as he stumbled over to the central docking gate. The guard droid stepped aside. Then Bryant headed up the walkway that led to the ship. Jinn followed him. She willed out her blades. Better to be safe than sorry.

The airlock hissed, the door of the ship opened and they stepped inside. It was, as Bryant had told her, a pleasure yacht. Everything was pale, light, and airy. Layers of creamy truesilk and marble veneer covered the steel and Plastex that were left visible in most vessels. Chandeliers hung from the ceiling, and thick carpet covered the floor. It looked more like a Dome apartment than something designed to travel in space.

Then Jinn saw the holding cages. Her stomach turned over.
A dozen compartments ran the length of a side room, no higher
than her shoulder, and uncomfortably narrow. Clear Plastex
doors allowed their occupants absolutely no privacy, not even
when using the small sanitation units at the rear of each one. A
couple contained blankets. The rest were empty. 'This is where
you found the boys.'

'Yes,' Bryant told her.

They didn't speak of it after that. They made their way down
to the lower half of the ship, and engineering. 'What is that
smell?' Jinn covered her face with her hand and grimaced. The
vessel had clearly been on standby for weeks, with neither the air
filtration system nor the recycling units operating. She hadn't
expected it to be fresh, but this was something else. There was
something putrid and rotten down here.

'Unfortunately, there were a couple of Darkos's clients on
board the ship when I found it,' Bryant informed her. 'We had
an argument. They lost.'

'Obviously.' Well, decaying bodies stuffed in an inactive recycling unit would certainly account for the stench. She knew what
Bryant had done, and why he had done it. And even though the
man standing before her was still junkie Bryant, she felt a little
less disgusted by him.

She climbed down into the engineering section of the ship. It
was a quiet, narrow space, not much more than a corridor that
allowed access to the main components of the engine. Most of
it could be fixed by droids. The main computer would tell them
whatever needed to be repaired. It made these ships easy to
maintain. Jinn saw a couple of small engineering bots no bigger
than her hand on standby in one corner.

She moved the length of the corridor, examining the visible
components of the phase drive. It all looked okay. She climbed
up the ladder, back to where Bryant stood waiting. 'All right,' she
said. 'It stinks, but I can't see anything obviously wrong with it.
Show me the main drive.'

'This way.'

Jinn followed him, trying not to breathe too deeply. The smell really was awful. They moved to the control deck, which was compact and well appointed, just as she'd expected, though it was functional rather than luxurious. There were dark splashes across the floor, the ceiling, and the seats.

People had died here.

Even after everything she had seen and done, Jinn still felt a little sick.

'Here,' Bryant said. He knelt down at the side of the pilot's station and tugged at the panel, but it wouldn't come loose.

Jinn crouched down beside him. 'Let me,' she said. Using her blades, she cut the panel free. It dropped to the floor. She pushed it away. Bryant produced a torch from somewhere and handed it to her. Jinn swept the beam over the opening. She saw thick bundles of wiring, and circuit boards that shone with newness.

And there, right in the middle, was a dark, familiar lump. It was bigger than she remembered, clinging onto the power core with long, thin tendrils that hugged the electrical wires. Bryant had implanted this on Theon. And then Grudge had removed it and attached it to the ship of a customer who refused to pay his bill.

It was obvious now that customer had been Darkos. So Bryant had tracked the tech to the ship. He'd been looking for Dax but instead he had found the boys and their owners. He had killed the men, and then he had killed Darkos and holed up in his yard.

She sat back on her heels and considered her options. If she looked at Bryant closely enough, she could see the lines that cut in deeply around the sides of his mouth, and that the expensive fall of his coat didn't hide the gaunt lines of his body.

The phase drives on the yacht were new and powerful. They would do the job. Everything else looked to have been well maintained. It was even fully fuelled. She could see no reason why it wouldn't fly, even with the tech attached to it. 'What's wrong with it?'

'This,' Bryant said and flopped into the pilot's chair. He played around with the controls mounted in the arm of the seat. The main computer came on, lighting up the screens in front of him, but the drive refused to fire.

'Let me try,' Jinn told him, getting to her feet.

'I know how to start up a ship!'

She folded her arms and glared at him.

He glared back. But he was the first to fold. He heaved himself out of the chair and leaned back against the front console as she pushed away the seat arm controls and pulled the ports forward. She pressed her hands over them. A brief second, and she was in. She could hear the chatter of the system in her head shortly before the drives ignited. She let them run for a minute or so, and then powered down. 'Works for me.'

'Well, it doesn't fucking work for me.'

'What do you want, Bryant?'

'Ten million credits and my own personal harem.'

'I'm being serious. What do you really want?'

He sank slowly into the comm. seat. His hands were shaking as he set them in his lap. 'I want to get better,' he admitted. 'I thought . . . when I saw her, I thought maybe there was a chance. The last medic I saw told me that if I could get a sample of whatever I'd been poisoned with, they might be able to engineer an antidote.'

Jinn pressed her head against the back of the seat. She was still plugged in. She could hear not just the onboard computer, but the strange burble of the Sittan tech as it sucked energy from the wires. A plan was beginning to form in her head. She would have to run it past Alistair and Li, and quickly.

There was much to hate about Bryant, she couldn't deny that. But there was also a part of him that wasn't corrupt, that wasn't self-serving and rotten, the part that had taken those boys from this ship and found them, if not a good place, then at the very least a safe place to go. He deserved a chance.

'I think I might have a way you can get it.'

'How?'

'You're going to go to Faidal.'

'Don't be fucking ridiculous!' But he was watching her now. She could feel his interest. 'I don't have a ship.'

'You'll be using mine.'

That shut him up.

'You and Alistair will go to Faidal and find Eve. I'll take this ship and go to Sittan.'

'I'm not taking that skinny freak with me. I'll go on my own.'

'First off, I am not letting you take the *Mutant* anywhere unsupervised. Second, you don't know how to run that ship, and he does. You can't run it alone anyway. You can trust him.'

He lowered his head. 'I don't fucking trust anyone.'

'Well, you have to,' Jinn said. 'If this is going to work, you have to work with the people around you. You don't get to be a lone wolf any longer.'

'What about the boys?'

'Give Grudge the codes for Darkos's place,' she said, thinking quickly. 'He'll take care of them.'

'He's a Bug.'

'Yes,' Jinn said. 'But not a Euphoria addict. Let's face it, Bryant. You'll be doing them a favour.'

Bryant flinched.

But the next morning he was ready to go. 'You're in charge,' he told Davyd. 'If any of the others get out of line, it's on you. Grudge will keep you safe.'

Bryant walked over to Jinn. Before they could leave, the boy rushed over to Bryant and hugged him hard. Bryant froze, then his arms went around the boy. 'Come back,' the boy said.

'I intend to,' Bryant told him. Then he pushed the boy away. 'Let's go.'

CHAPTER

11

4th November 2207

> Vessel: The *Mutant*. Battleship/carrier hybrid
> Destination: Jump gate 199
> Cargo: None
> Crew: 4
> Droids: 7

They would make the first part of the trip together, with Bryant's yacht hidden in the belly of the *Mutant*. It was too small to carry enough fuel to make the entire trip on its own. The Sittan nanotech was in place, pulsing, growing, breathing, linking Jinn to Sittan, and so to Dax. Grudge had taken a look at it and agreed with her initial assessment. Somehow, using a process they didn't understand, the tech was spreading.

Jinn placed her hands over the control ports and plugged into the *Mutant*.

'Everyone ready?' she asked.

'Yes,' Bryant said. 'Go.'

'Shut up, Bryant,' Li said. He looked at Jinn. 'We're set.'

'I already said that,' Bryant grumbled. 'Honestly, what is it with you and these Underworld men?'

Alistair turned his head. He sat uncomfortably in Eve's old seat, the comm. headset in his hand. 'Do you want him to punch you in the face? Because he will.'

'Gladly,' Li agreed.

'All of you shut up.' Jinn turned to Li. 'Coordinates?'

'Programming them now.' His fingers flew as he uploaded the data. Jinn turned on her retinal screen. 'Strap in,' she said. 'It's going to be a rough flight.'

It was a long way to Sittan space. They were going to spend most of it locked in the roaring twists of a jump. She couldn't allow downtime between jumps, either. It was going to be tough, physically and mentally.

But she would deal with those problems when she had to, and not before. Jinn picked up the first jump gate on her retinal screen before it became visible on the huge viewscreen that stretched across the front of the control deck, the gate itself a vast floating oval designed to mark the otherwise invisible entrance to the jump. Not all gates had one of these. The less frequently used ones, those that didn't come out anywhere useful and didn't carry much traffic, were marked by nothing more than the flash of an onboard computer.

They passed through the first three jumps without seeing another ship. Jinn began to relax. The new grav generator was working perfectly, Bryant had stopped talking, and they were finally on their way.

She set the autopilot for the five day flight through straight space when they exited the third jump, and used the time to eat and wash and sleep. By the time they reached the fourth gate, she was more than ready.

It was busy.

Jinn slowed the ship, dropping the push of the phase drive, let them drift, then switched off her retinal implant so she could watch the chaos onscreen.

'I've never seen agents here before,' Alistair said.

Neither had Jinn, but she could count five Security Service ships alongside two large cargo ships.

'It's a delivery,' she said as realisation struck. 'See those cargo ships? I bet they're full of Type One males.'

'Want us to help you board one?' Bryant asked. 'You know, given that you're into that type of thing.'

Jinn could sense the broad, strong figure of Li shifting in his seat at her side. She gestured to him to remain where he was. 'You're an agent,' she said to Bryant. She gestured to the viewscreen. 'How do we get past this?'

'Was an agent,' Bryant corrected her. 'Hack into their comms.'

Jinn shook her head. 'Eve is the comm. specialist,' she said. 'I don't know how to do it.'

'What about you?' Bryant turned to Alistair.

Alistair shook his head.

'And you?' he asked Li.

The big man flexed his arms.

'I see,' Bryant replied. He fixed his gaze back on Jinn. 'My access codes may still work,' he said. 'But it's risky.'

'Try it,' Jinn ordered him. She retracted her tech, disconnecting from the computer.

'If you insist,' he replied. He settled himself more comfortably in the captain's chair and turned his attention to the control panel located close to his right hand. 'Access Channel Alpha seven two four,' he ordered the main computer.

'Acknowledged.'

Bryant reeled off his access code, and Jinn held her breath. This was either going to help them or get them killed. She wished Dax was here, now, wished it more than anything. And Eve. And Theon, too. The loss of the droid burned inside her, a physical pain. She had let the team break.

And now she had to put it back together.

'We're in,' Alistair said. He held the comm. smartware against his ear, his eyes bright. 'I can hear them.'

'Have they detected us?'

Alistair listened a little longer. 'Yes, but they don't know who we are. They haven't identified the ship.'

'They will,' Bryant warned her. 'All they have to do is look out of the window. Dax couldn't have built a bigger monument to his dick if he tried.'

'They're hailing us,' Alistair said. 'What do I do?'

'Accept it,' Jinn said.

The voice boomed over the internal speaker a moment later, 'Unknown ship, this gate is now restricted access. Identify yourselves and confirm your travel codes, please.'

On the viewscreen, she could see one of the Security Service ships break away from the group and start heading in their direction. As it moved closer it was obvious where modifications had been made. Atomic cannons had been added, and there were three fully loaded gun decks. It looked like it was going to war. Who were they expecting to meet? Pirates? Yes, she thought to herself. That's exactly what they were expecting.

'I think we might be in trouble,' said Bryant.

'It's so helpful when you state the obvious.'

'Jinn,' Alistair said. There was a note of urgency in his voice. 'They're running an ident scan.'

'Blast it.' On the viewscreen ahead, Jinn could see the other Security Service vessels starting to move. 'We *are* in trouble.'

'So what's new?' Li asked.

'He is.' She jerked her head in Bryant's direction.

'Don't look at me!' Bryant fidgeted in his seat.

'You used to be an agent, remember? Deal with this.'

'Deal with it how?'

She disconnected from the system. 'I am going through that gate,' she said, 'which gives you about thirty seconds to figure that out.'

'Weapons lock,' the onboard computer informed them. 'Do you wish to activate defences?'

'Yes,' she replied.

'Go.' It was Alistair who spoke up. 'Get to the yacht,' he told her. 'Now. We'll deal with this.'

Jinn nodded at him. 'Come on,' she said to Li. She sprinted to the rear of the control deck, then stopped. She turned back to face the others, a weight pressing down on her as if the gravity had suddenly doubled. 'You will find her,' she said to Alistair. 'I know you will.'

She turned her gaze on Bryant. 'And you. Try not to screw this up.'

There was no time for anything else. There was no time for doubt, for regret, or for an emotional goodbye. Jinn sprinted her way to the cargo hold, heart pounding, fear thickening her blood as she focused on what she had to do. She would get one shot at this, if fate was on her side and she timed it right.

A droid pulled the ladder into position as she sprinted towards the yacht. It clicked onto the side of vessel and Jinn climbed it quickly, boarding via the small hatch that led straight to the small control deck. She took a seat, plugged in, powered up. Li squeezed himself into the second seat. The phase drive hummed as her mind made connection with the system. The holding arm disconnected before she could instruct it to, and Alistair's voice echoed through the air. 'Good luck, Captain,' he said.

'If Bryant gives you any crap,' Jinn told him, 'you have my permission to shoot him.'

'Trust me, I will. Inputting coordinates now.' The coordinates she would need when she reached the other side of the jump. If she reached the other side. Jinn ruthlessly shoved that thought away.

Free from the holding arm, the yacht hovered in the middle of the hold. Jinn turned on her retinal screen as the autoharness rolled around her body, locking her into the seat. Then the jaws of the *Mutant* started to open.

The back of her throat burned. The *Mutant* was her home. After so many hours plugged into it, it had become a part of her in a way that none of the other ships she'd worked on ever had. Leaving it was far harder than she had anticipated.

'Stay in one piece,' she whispered, as the jaws parted further and she set the yacht in motion. 'And keep them safe.'

And then she powered up the phase drive and flew the yacht out into space. The gate lay ahead, and she aimed straight at it. There was no time for hesitation, no time for second thoughts.

One of the huge cargo ships was moving towards the gate. Two of the Security Service vessels were still with it. They weren't taking any chances. Dammit, if Alistair couldn't draw them away she didn't know how she was going to get through. The yacht was small, and although it was armed its defences would be nothing against the fire power of a Security Service gunship.

Then the *Mutant* opened fire on the Security Service ships. There were no direct hits, but the shots came close, skimming over the surface of a couple of them. She heard Bryant over the comm. 'Get to the gate!' He fired again.

The Second Species part of her kicked in. Adrenaline pumped through her veins, making her focus sharp, her will absolute. The gate was all that mattered now. Through her retinal screen, she could see the cargo ship still approaching it, see the gate start to spin and flash as the darkness in its centre shimmered and fluxed. It was open. It would only stay that way for a few seconds.

Jinn revved the phase drives to maximum. The yacht shot towards the gate. It was small enough to avoid detection by the huge cargo ship.

The retinal screen gave her a 360-degree view of the outside. She could see the *Mutant*; see the wide arc that Bryant flew it in as he drew the fire of the Security Service vessels. Small patches of red light appeared around the hull, fading almost as quickly as they had appeared as the shields of the pirate vessel absorbed the energy from hit after hit after hit. They wouldn't be able to withstand much more, and suddenly she had a new concern. The real, visceral fear that the *Mutant* might not survive this. Without tech, Bryant couldn't handle the ship the way she could. It wasn't just powerful, it was big and unwieldy and he didn't know it the way she did.

But she was out of time. With one last desperate glance at the *Mutant,* Jinn entered the jump gate. For a second the yacht hung motionless, then it was swallowed into the rush of brightly coloured light. Time meant nothing while she was here. Neither did speed. It was impossible to tell whether she was moving, or whether the universe was moving around her. She pushed the yacht through the narrow confines of the jump, her brain sensing the minute alterations in colour that kept her on course. Hit the edge of the jump tunnel, and the ship would instantly disintegrate. Surviving a jump took more than just skill as a pilot. It took nerve. It took the willingness to face death.

A strange darkness shimmered alongside her, not part of the jump, not part of the yacht. It took her a moment to identify it as the cargo ship. Its edges blurred, no longer harsh, but indefinable, dark bleeding into the light.

She easily matched it for speed. She had to more than match it. If the cargo ship exited the jump first, she risked being burned up in its wake. Through the next twist, a drop into the next turn, she pushed the yacht to the limit, forcing every bit of power she could out of the phase drive. The smell of burning Plastex made her eyes water as the onboard computer fought her will. 'Come on,' she hissed as she finally edged ahead of the much bigger cargo ship. A little more. She only needed a little more. If she could get ahead enough, she could push her way through at the next turn.

Six months ago Jinn would have been physically unable to make this jump. She would have been a bleeding, unconscious heap on the floor. But not now. Now she was Second Species. She was beyond human. And she could do this.

She edged ahead as they hit the turn. She flipped the yacht sideways, using the pull of the cargo ship to take her through the tight curve. And as they exited the curve, side by side, matched for speed, they got too close.

Metal crunched against metal. The yacht bounced sharply sideways, skimming the edge of the tunnel. The phase drive died. Through her connection to the onboard computer, she could sense the system fighting her control. She'd pushed too hard, too much. A rapid assessment of the contact indicated that the impact had damaged the right side of the yacht. Jinn swore loudly. Another broken ship was the last thing she needed. Bastards.

She was losing speed now, and with it her control of the yacht. On her retinal screen, she could see the cargo ship starting to pull ahead, the swirling wake of its functioning phase drive visible against the hot colours of the jump. She couldn't outrun it, not now.

But she could run with it.

'Hold on tight,' she said to Li.

'Trust me, I am,' came the reply. 'What are you going to do?'

'We're hitching a ride.'

Jinn gritted her teeth and fired the emergency boosters. They couldn't give her forward momentum, but they gave her enough control to shift the yacht to the right, cutting the gap between the two vessels. It wasn't close enough. And the other ship was moving even further ahead. It was now or never. She got this right or she died trying.

Another blast from the boosters. A sharp jerk to the right. Contact made. The yacht hit the side of the other vessel, and the instant that it did Jinn activated the electrostatic charge that was normally used for clearing parasites from the hull. With a little alteration, it quickly turned the skin of the yacht into an electromagnet.

The yacht stuck to the outside of the cargo ship like a leech.

In a few short minutes they'd be exiting the jump. The cargo ship took a sharp line through the jump tunnel. It wouldn't make for a pleasant trip for those on board, but she guessed that the Second Species cargo could handle it.

'Power levels at thirty-seven per cent,' the onboard computer informed her.

'How much longer until we exit the jump?'

'Estimated time remaining, two minutes eight seconds.'

'How long until the phase drive comes back online?'

'Phase drive will remain off line until temperature reaches safe operating level,' the computer said. 'This will take approximately nine minutes fifteen seconds.'

Through her connection to the system, Jinn could read everything the computer wasn't telling her. The temperature was dropping, but it wasn't dropping fast enough, and running the electromagnetic charge through the hull was only slowing it down further. 'We're overheating,' she told Li.

'Turn off life-support systems,' he said. 'Divert all cooling systems to the phase drive.'

Jinn did as he suggested. Then she unplugged from the control deck and shrugged out of her jacket. It was about to get bloody hot in here. Almost instantly, the temperature soared, and within seconds she was sweating. It trickled down the back of her neck, in between her breasts, as even the air she inhaled became hot enough to burn. But she didn't have time to dwell on it. They were at the end of the jump.

'Gate exit's coming up,' Li said.

It was now or never.

'Shut off the hull charge,' Jinn ordered the onboard computer.

The jolt she felt almost immediately told her that it had switched off. She was no longer connected to the other ship, but floating alongside it. If she didn't get the phase drive powered up, and quickly, they'd be smoke.

Time to see if her efforts to cool the phase drive had worked. Jinn pressed her hands back against the ports, connected with the vessel, and mentally linked to the phase drive.

The system refused to power up. The failsafe mechanism had kicked in. Even connected as she was, she couldn't override it. The system had been designed to protect the phase drive at all costs because without it, a ship was stranded. But there might be a back way. Closing her eyes, Jinn pushed her way deeper into the system, deeper.

And disconnected the main computer.

The phase drive powered up almost instantly. She heard the roar of it, felt the power, and without the buffer of the main computer she could sense the heat almost as if the drive was a living, breathing thing.

She'd never been connected to a ship this way before. It was unnerving and new, and she didn't know the rhythm of it. But there was no time to learn. They were at the end of the jump now, the colours widening, spreading, and as she activated her retinal screen she saw the edges of the gate, a ring of sharp black against the blurring light. She had to reach it before the other ship did.

'Come on,' she yelled, as the gate grew closer, as the jump pulled at the ship, desperate to cling onto it.

And then they were in the gate.

And she was ahead.

The phase drive screamed and Jinn screamed along with it, and they were flung out into the darkness of space. The yacht went into a spin as she lost control of it, as her entire body shook.

But they had survived.

Jinn fought for air that wasn't there before she remembered that she'd turned off the life support. She'd turned off everything.

'All systems back online!' Li yelled, but to no avail.

'I switched off the onboard computer,' Jinn told him breathlessly. 'I need to turn it back on.' She pushed her way back into the system, searching for the way to reboot the system. It wasn't easy to find, but she did it. Her breathing remained fast even when the oxygen levels started to come back up and the temperature started to fall and she pulled the yacht out of the spin.

On her retinal screen she could see the full panorama of space. Behind her, the gate and its marker. Ahead of her, empty space, and beyond that, Sittan. And Dax.

She flew on.

CHAPTER
12

The 10th day of the fifth turn

The Palace, Fire City, Sittan

It was days since Dax had been taken from the arena. The guards had brought him to the palace, and, exhausted and wounded from the fight, he had placidly let them. He regretted it now. They had pushed him down long, high-ceilinged corridors lit by sconces affixed to the walls, weaving their way through the maze of the palace until he had found himself in a room up in one of the towers.

He had stumbled to the centre of the room, the guards had stepped back, and before he could react bars had shot up from the floor and down from the ceiling, caging him. The space was generous enough. They fed him regularly, and a pool sunk into the floor allowed him to bathe and cool down. But that was it. Days of sitting and waiting for something to happen had left him edgy and restless. There was too much energy locked up inside his body. He needed to move, to break something, to hurt someone, only there was nothing to break and no one to hurt but himself.

He'd tried to smash the bars. That hadn't worked. He'd pounded his fists to a pulp against them, only to leave the bars without so much as a hairline crack. The guards ignored him, refusing to answer his questions. His frustration built. His mind raced until he could only sleep in snatches, waking anxious and shaking and paranoid.

Why had the empress brought him here? What did she want? He'd been modified to fight in the cages, to kill, and he didn't understand why he had been taken away from all that.

A shadow fell over him, and he shifted enough to see a tall, muscular figure standing at the edge of the cage. Dax didn't bother to get up. He remained where he was, stretched out on the floor, half hidden in shadow. He had been watching the Mountain. It was as dead now as it had been when he'd arrived.

'Get up,' said the figure.

'I won't.'

'Get up,' the figure repeated, 'or I will come in there and make you.'

Now this, this was interesting. Slowly, casually, Dax pushed himself into a sitting position. He made a great show of stretching out his arms, his shoulders, and used the time it took to assess his visitor.

Male. Dressed in white, which meant he was a slave. Tall, though that was nothing unusual. They all were. But there were kill tattoos on his bare shoulders and scars on his face, the thick, ugly kind that hadn't been put there on purpose. He met Dax's gaze. There was no arrogant challenge in his expression, merely calculation. He would hurt Dax only if he needed to.

Dax got to his feet. The potential for violence had his blood pumping. He felt suddenly awake, his vision clearer, the miserable fog of earlier already starting to lift. His fingers flexed.

The bars dropped.

Dax moved first. He charged at the Sittan male, who made no attempt to get out of his way. They collided hard. Flesh slammed against flesh. Bone crunched. And Dax found himself on the floor with a strongly muscled arm wrapped like a ring of stone around his neck. He struggled for air, his feet thudding against the polished stone floor.

'I have no desire to hurt you,' the male said. 'If I deliver you marked, she will punish me, and I have no wish for that to happen.' His voice was calm even as his arm tightened around Dax's neck. Dax locked his fists together and slammed his elbow into the male's side, once, twice, three times. The arm didn't slacken. And as quickly as it had risen, the hunger for violence began to abate. He knew when to ease back and when to wait, and this was one of those times.

'You stink,' the Sittan said, his scarred face creasing in disgust. He released Dax and dropped a bundle of clothes on the floor next to him. 'You are to bathe and dress.'

Dax got up carefully. He kept his breathing even, but he also kept his focus on the male as he dunked himself into the bathing pool and then climbed out and pulled on the white trousers the male had tossed down for him. 'Where are you taking me?'

He was curious now. He hadn't realised how utterly bored he was.

'She wishes to see you.'

'Why?'

'I did not ask. You will not address her directly,' the Sittan male told him. 'You will avert your eyes.' He beckoned to Dax, who strolled out of the confines of the open cage. 'You will show respect for our ruler and our ways. Is that clear?'

The male turned and started to walk and Dax followed him. The Sittan was a little taller, but they were otherwise of a similar size, and he kept pace with him easily. Too much time spent inactive meant he had energy to burn. His muscles ached with it.

But he controlled himself. He wondered what the empress wanted with him. Perhaps she would send him back to the arena. He hoped so. He wanted to fight so badly that he took a swing at the wall just for the fun of it. The pain was deeply satisfying.

'Do that again, and I will have to restrain you,' the male said.

Dax merely snarled at him.

They passed other small open rooms similar to the one he had been held in. All manner of creatures were caged inside them.

There were huge, hairy beasts that threw themselves against the bars, and monstrous glittering reptiles that lay still and watched them pass. The Sittan male walked past them all, not giving any of them a second glance.

'Who are you?' Dax asked him, as the sound of the animals faded into the background and they made their way along a cool, dark corridor.

'My name is Chal Gri.'

'You fought in the arena.'

'That is correct.'

'I thought males who won in the arena were given to females.'

'They are.'

'So why are you here?'

'Because the empress is my female.'

It didn't make sense to Dax. 'But you're a slave. Why do you let the females control you that way?' he asked. 'You're bigger, stronger. You should have just as much power as them.'

'Power has nothing to do with strength, or size. But I wouldn't expect a human to understand that. Your species thinks in the narrowest of terms.'

There was no time for Dax to ask what those were, because they had reached the end of the tunnel. They were in the empress's bathing quarters and there she was, lounging in a plunge pool big enough to hold fifty. The Sittan male kept his gaze locked to the floor. 'I have brought you the human, Empress.'

'So I see.'

'Do you require anything else?'

'No. You may go.'

The Sittan male did as he was told, leaving Dax alone with the empress. Despite having been told not to look at her, not to speak, he found himself unable to obey. He could not take his eyes off her. She was so strange, so alien. The skin on her body was smooth, almost humanlike apart from its colour, a deep cobalt blue, but her hands and feet were scaly and clawed. She wore jewellery, lots of it, around her neck and on her fingers and toes, gleaming dark rubies dripping from silver mounts. She looked him over, those cold yellow eyes flicking over his body. 'Humans are very strange,' she said, as she swam to the side of the pool. 'So hairy and pale.'

Water dripped from her naked form as she walked up the steps at the edge. She took her time about it. Her shape was ... interesting.

Her wet footprints patterned the stone floor as she strolled over to a large chest at the side of the room and selected a robe, pulling it on over her damp body. She turned back to him. 'All the others have died,' she said. 'All of them except you. Why do you think that is?'

'I don't know.'

'You're not taller,' she said. 'Not bigger. Not stronger. You're not young, either. Why are you different?'

She moved closer, close enough for him to smell her, and he suddenly found it hard to breathe.

'I know what you stole from us, Caspian Dax. I know every cargo you took, every crate of kerask and bubble sack of dark rubies. I thought to myself, this male needs to be taught a lesson. I asked for you specifically, did you know that?'

He hadn't.

'But then you came to my arena,' she continued. 'And I had never seen anyone fight the way you do. Not even the Sittan males have your apathy. They at least care if they win.'

'I care about winning,' Dax told her. 'I just don't care if I die.'

She stalked away from him suddenly, her clawed feet tapping on the hard stone floor, to where several heavy chains hung from the ceiling. The empress ran her fingers through them, then grasped one and gave it a quick, sharp tug. A cage rattled down, landing close to Dax.

Something was moving inside it.

The empress unlocked the lid, lowered an arm inside, and lifted something out. It looked like a snake, but it had legs, lots of thin little legs that dug into her flesh. She stroked the foul little creature, crooning to it as it coiled itself around her arm. One end of it arced up into the air and flicked from side to side.

The other fixed on Dax with a dozen blood-red eyes.

'What in the void is that?' he whispered.

She held it closer. 'Do you like it?'

The head lifted, undulating towards him.

Dax took a step back. The creature smelled like rotten meat. 'No.'

The empress laughed. She arranged herself on her massive day bed and selected something from a bowl of jelly-like treats set within easy reach. She chewed loudly. The creature, whatever it was, climbed to her shoulder and sat with its tail curled around her neck. She seemed to take great delight in it, stroking it, feeding it pieces of jelly. 'This is a Vreen,' she said. 'Very rare. They normally live out on the Obsidian Sea. There used to be more, when the Mountain was awake. Now there are less than a dozen left. It took nineteen males to retrieve this one.' She leaned forward. 'Could you catch one for me?'

'I don't know.' Dax kept his gaze on the creature. 'What would I get if I did?'

'What do you want?'

'I want to go back to the arena.'

'No,' she said.

Dax shrugged. 'Then I won't catch one for you.'

She swung her feet up onto the bed, setting her weight on her hip. The Vreen rubbed itself against her face. 'No matter,' she said. 'I have this one.' She looked him over. 'Are you hungry?'

'A little,' Dax admitted. He glanced at the bowl of jellies. They were pretty, fruity colours, and after weeks of nothing but Silver Rice, he wanted them. His mouth watered.

She reached up and pulled on another chain, this one thinner than the one that had pulled down the Vreen. A bell sounded somewhere far off. Within a few seconds, he heard the sound of approaching feet and a group of male slaves walked in, each carrying a large tray hoisted high above their shoulders. The platters were set in front of the empress. Shimmering dark liquid rose up from the floor and held them in her reach.

The males were accompanied by red-suited females, the empress's guard. The males were dismissed. The females remained.

'Come,' the empress said. 'Eat.'

Dax hesitated, but only for a moment. He had been locked up in his cell for too many days, and he was starving. He picked up a huge bowl of krent and tipped it down his throat, barely bothering to stop and chew. After that, a plate of dillies. He almost picked up the kerask, then stopped himself. He'd intercepted hundreds of shipments of the juicy orange fruit as they made their way from Faidal to Sittan. Sold on to an outpost near Darta Four, it had always made a tidy profit provided he could move before it went bad.

Finally, his hunger began to abate. He wiped his mouth with the back of his hand, suddenly all too aware of the empress and the guards. He tossed the empty bowl back onto the floating platter. They were all watching him, too many pairs of Sittan eyes trained upon him. His muscles tensed. This wasn't the arena, but it was a small, enclosed space, and there were too many of them.

The guards moved closer. One of them had a spear in her hand, and for that reason and that reason only, Dax controlled the urge to lash out. This was not a wise place to be under the effects of whatever they dipped those spear tips in.

'Dax,' the empress said, her tone full of reproach. 'They aren't going to hurt you.'

'Then what are they doing?' He flinched as one of the guards moved closer still and began to pull at the ties that held up his trousers. The room suddenly seemed considerably hotter, and he was starting to sweat.

'Taking care of you,' the empress told him. 'I suggest you let them.'

His arms were pulled to his sides, and he was stripped naked and pushed over to the large bathing pool at the side of the room from which the empress herself had only recently stepped. The water was blissfully cool when they dunked him into it, and it was clean, unlike the filth he'd been forced to bathe in before. It soothed his skin and his senses as it licked over his body. The guards pulled him to his feet and began to clean him. Their hands were quick and skilful. Tight muscles were relaxed. Old scars were massaged and softened. His hair was cut close to his scalp, and the rest of him was shaved bare.

His skin dried quickly in the heat of the room. The females dressed him again, though this time the breeches were close fitting, identical to the ones he had worn in the arena in everything but colour. They were the white of the slaves. It made him feel uneasy. But he didn't complain, because he didn't want this, whatever it was, to stop.

The empress rose to her feet and came to stand in front of him. She looked him over. 'Yes,' she said thoughtfully. 'That is much better. Tell me, Dax. What would you like to do now?'

'That depends on what is on offer.'

She tipped her head back and laughed. It was throaty and sensual, and he felt it right in the pit of his stomach. 'Perhaps a little entertainment,' she said. She walked to the wall at the far side of the room and pressed a hand against it. It shimmered and disappeared, revealing a bigger space beyond. In it was a fighting circle, a scaled down replica of the arena floor, and in the centre of that circle was a small group of men.

'It isn't Karakai, I'm afraid.' She sounded almost apologetic. 'But I hope it will suffice.'

'I don't understand,' Dax said.

'It's for you,' the empress told him. 'I know how difficult it must have been for you, locked up in your room, and the last thing I want is for you to be unhappy.' She gestured to the group. 'Go on.'

Dax felt his heart start to pound. He wanted this even more than the food.

He walked into the circle and began.

CHAPTER
13

When Ferona had agreed to take the Type One male as a body-guard, she had intended to use him only for public appearances and trips off-planet. But he had turned up at her front door an hour after she got home, told her his name was Victor, and refused to leave.

Even now, he was in the corner, shoulders straight, hands behind his back, staring out of the window as she attempted to enjoy lunch at her favourite restaurant. She'd taken her usual private room. Vexler had invited himself along, and that had completely ruined her appetite. She was still furious with him for forcing her into this. Lucinda had told her she hadn't known what he'd intended to do, which meant that Vexler really had thought it up on the spur of the moment when they reached the facility.

A man willing to make major decisions on a whim was not fit to be president. But this was not the right time to do something about it.

And that had put Ferona in a very, very bad mood.

Not even her favourite chateaubriand could change that, or her favourite red wine, or the dramatic feathered cape she had chosen specially for the occasion. Vexler sat opposite, picking his way through a very expensive piece of fresh salmon. He was as calm as she was tense. His own Type One stood in front of the doors, getting in the way every time the serving staff attempted to enter. Given the size of the room, Ferona knew that neither of them could overhear the conversation, but their very presence was enough to annoy.

Part of the reason for this was that they were proving to have been a good idea, and she did not like the fact that that idea had been Vexler's. She stabbed her meat with the tip of the silver steak knife and wished it was a delicate part of his anatomy.

'You seem tense, Ferona.'

'Do I?'

Vexler set down his cutlery. 'Is something bothering you?'

'Not at all,' she told him. She set down her own knife and fork and picked up her glass, taking a delicate sip instead of the large swig that she wanted.

'Good,' he said. He sipped at his own drink. 'I have to say, these creations of yours really are marvellous. We should have added them to our team months ago.'

But they hadn't. And for good reason. Although Victor had so far been incredibly well-behaved, Ferona found that she was constantly aware of him, noticing every move he made, waiting for something to go wrong. It was exhausting. The man was modified with Sittan DNA. It wasn't a question of if he would make a mistake, but when. She didn't understand why Vexler couldn't see that, and her patience with him snapped.

'I disagree,' she told him. 'These aren't toys, Vexler. This is serious. I am not comfortable with this at all.'

Vexler sat back in his seat. 'Well,' he said. 'I have to say I'm a little surprised. I expected more of you, Ferona. I can't believe that you don't see their potential.'

Oh, she saw plenty of potential. That was the problem. 'I don't understand what you mean.'

'Humans First.'

'What about them?'

'They're a problem.'

A serving droid moved in and took away his now empty plate. It returned a moment later with a steaming cloth in a gilded basket. Vexler took it and carefully cleaned his hands.

'I'm aware of that. But not a major problem. No one takes them seriously.'

'We should be taking them seriously.'

Ferona gave up on her steak and pushed her plate to one side. Almost immediately, the droid scooted in and took it away. What a waste. She had been looking forward to this meal for days, and it had been thoroughly spoiled. 'I fail to see why.'

'People are listening to them.' Vexler set his hands on the table and leaned forward. 'I do not want anything to get in the way of our journey to Spes, and I know you feel the same way.'

'Nothing is going to get in the way. Our approval ratings are up.'

'But they're not up enough,' Vexler said. 'And Humans First have a lot of followers.'

If Vexler had decided the group was a problem, then it was a problem. Not least because Vexler could all too easily make them one. As far as Ferona was concerned, they would soon disappear if deprived of attention. But Vexler couldn't be trusted not to feed the beast.

'We need to crush them at grassroots level,' he continued. 'Find out who they are, where they are meeting, and put a stop to it.'

'That could work in their favour,' she pointed out. 'It's not illegal to have an opinion.'

'Sometimes I think that it should be.'

Ferona busied herself pulling up the table-top menu. She scrolled through it, selected a dessert. She didn't usually allow herself one, but if she had to sit here and listen to Vexler she deserved something pleasurable as a reward. A pistachio cake with real chocolate ganache would do very nicely.

The droid brought the dessert. Ferona picked up the tiny

fork, cut a tiny piece, and let it melt on her tongue before she spoke. 'Any move to stop them from meeting will be seen as government interference. These are Dome-raised people, Vexler, not Underworlders. They won't stand for it. We'd have lawsuits coming out of our ears before we even got in the door.'

'But there has to be a way to stop them.'

'Of course there is,' Ferona said. 'Give them the rope and then wait for them to hang themselves with it.'

He sat back in his seat and folded his arms. 'I'd prefer a more direct approach.'

Sometimes Ferona wondered how on Earth Vexler had managed to become president. The man was completely lacking in any of the necessary skills. 'If you want to deal with Humans First, which in my opinion is completely unnecessary at this point, then get them to air their views publicly. Give them an opportunity to show just how out of touch their ideas are. A press conference would be the ideal situation.'

'A press conference. Yes. That would work.' Vexler looked very pleased with the idea. 'I'll get my people working on it straight away. We'll need a venue, of course, and a strong media presence. And agents. It should be possible to make some arrests afterwards. The public will want to see that.'

'Actually, I think I should be the one to take questions, don't you? I am our representative in the Senate after all. People will want to hear how things are progressing there. It will look far better if Humans First gate-crash a legitimate gathering. If we invite them to talk openly, the public will believe that we think they have something important to say. We need to be careful here, Vexler. The last thing we want is for this to look like a set up.'

'I suppose you are right.' There was no mistaking his tone of disappointment, but Ferona didn't let it sway her. Who knew what other bright ideas Vexler might come up with if he was allowed to take charge.

She was going to handle this her way. At least then she could be sure it would be done properly.

CHAPTER

14

13th November 2207

> Vessel: The *Mutant*. Battleship/carrier hybrid
> Destination: Faidal
> Cargo: None
> Crew: 2
> Droids: 7

Bryant watched as Alistair unfastened his restraints and got out of his seat. The Underworlder paced the length of the control deck with his skinny shoulders hunched and his hands gripping the back of his neck.

'That went well,' Bryant said, slumping back in his seat, his guts cramping. No way was he going to admit that the jump had been rocky, or how much it had frightened him.

Alistair stopped pacing. He lifted his head and fixed a sharp, tight-jawed gaze on Bryant. 'You think that went well?' he asked quietly.

Bryant nodded. 'We're here. We got through. What else do you want?'

'What else do I ... Where do I even begin?' He began to pace again. Bryant wished he wouldn't. It was annoying. 'I want Eve back, unharmed. Same goes for the others. I want a universe in which everyone has an equal shot at a decent life, not just rich bastards who've never done anything for anyone and think they're entitled to do whatever they like just because Mummy and Daddy had money. And I want to be on this ship with anyone but you.'

'Good luck with that,' Bryant told him. His hands were starting to sweat inside his smartware gloves and he longed to pull them off, but they weren't yet far enough from the gate that he could programme the autopilot and take a break. At least they didn't need to jump again for a while. He wasn't entirely sure that he was going to be able to when it came to it, but this didn't seem like the best time to break that particular piece of news to his new crewmate.

Flying the pirate ship wasn't easy. He had the basic controls worked out. It wasn't that different from the other ships he'd flown, and he considered himself an excellent pilot. He had competed in amateur skimmer races as a teenager. He'd seriously considered turning pro before deciding that he wanted to go to the academy and learn how to be an agent instead, partly because, although being a pro racer would get him sex and speed, it wouldn't get him the violence he secretly craved.

But the *Mutant* was something else. He'd never flown anything this big, and the computer system it used wasn't quite what he was accustomed to. Plus his brain hurt, a sure sign that he was going to crash if he didn't get a hit soon.

Bugger it. They were going in a straight line, in roughly the right direction, and there was nothing in front of or behind them. It wouldn't matter if he took a break for a bit. Pulling off the smartware gloves, he tossed them down on the instrument panel in front of him, wiped his hands on his trousers and disconnected the eyepiece.

He ran the tip of his tongue over his upper lip, found it dry and cracked, and reached into the inside pocket of his jacket where he'd slipped a little disposable drug gun.

Arm or neck? In the end, he lifted his shirt and jabbed himself in the belly. Although he'd lost weight, lost bulk, his gut had gone soft, and the end of the gun left a red indent in the flab.

The rush was instant, a hot wave of relief that gushed through his body, and he tipped his head back and closed his eyes. He opened them to find Alistair pulling the spent gun from his tightly curled fingers.

'Do not shoot up in the chair,' Alistair told him. 'If you need to do that, you go to the medical bay where the medidroid can help you.'

'It's only temporary,' Bryant said defensively. 'I'll be able to stop as soon as I find an antidote for whatever that green bitch poisoned me with.'

'Her name is Eve.'

'Whatever.' The Euphoria was kicking in already, a comforting warmth in the pit of his stomach, and as the pain subsided, he found himself inexplicably thinking about her. 'What is she like?' he asked, as he leaned back in his seat and propped his feet up on the dash.

'Stubborn,' Alistair said. He exhaled softly. 'Angry.'

'What's she got to be angry about?'

Alistair shook his head. 'You really are an ignorant fucker.'

There was no humour in his words, only disgust. 'So why is she angry? Seems like she's had a pretty cushy life.' He looked around the control deck of the *Mutant*. It was as big as his apartment back home. 'Living with this. Doing whatever she wanted, whenever she wanted. Stealing instead of working. Thinking the law was for other people.'

'Because she grew up in a nightmare,' Alistair said. 'And when she tried to escape it, she found that what awaited her was even worse.'

Bryant gestured at the huge control deck, the thousands of credits worth of the latest tech, the comfortable seats. Even the air tasted sweet. 'This doesn't look like a nightmare to me.'

'That's because you're a Dome brat,' Alistair told him. 'All you lot ever see is how much it cost. That's all you care about. What's it worth. What will it make other people think of me. Does my bank balance look big in this. I spent twenty years of my life selling cruiser upgrades to spoilt bastards like you, all so you could impress people you didn't even like.'

'What else are we supposed to do with all our money?'

Alistair ignored that. 'She couldn't have physical contact,' he said. 'Not with anyone. There she was, eighteen years old, full of hope and optimism, thinking she might finally be able to get out of the crappy little hole she grew up in and make something half decent for herself, and they changed her DNA so that she couldn't touch anyone without hurting them.'

'So?'

'What do you mean, so?'

'She had all this,' Bryant said. 'Not bad, for a thief. A lot better than prison, which is where she should have been.' And had she been in prison, she wouldn't have been on the *Europa*. Wouldn't have been able to poison him.

'She was a thief because she had to be,' Alistair said. 'What's your excuse?'

'I'm not a thief,' Bryant said smugly. He pressed his shoulders back into the chair. He felt soft and relaxed as the Euphoria hummed pleasantly through his system.

Alistair got to his feet. 'I'm not playing this game with you,' he said, and started to make his way off the control deck.

But Bryant wasn't ready to let it go. If he was going to have to spend the next few weeks with this miserable self-righteous prick, they were going to have to get a few things straight. 'I don't like you!' he yelled.

Getting up seemed like a good idea until he actually did it. His legs weren't quite steady, and he weaved a little as he chased after Alistair who walked like he had a steel pole shoved up his arse. Alistair stopped and then slowly turned. Bryant held himself up with a shoulder against the wall. The metal pressed hard against the bone.

'I don't like you either,' Alistair told him. He sounded weary. What the fuck did he have to feel weary for?

'Look here, you. I'm the one dying. I deserve a little sympathy. I deserve a little *respect*.'

Alistair looked him over, and, even through the Euphoria, Bryant didn't like the way he did it. It made him feel unclean. He wiped his hand against the front of his jacket, his palm still sweating from the smartware glove, or the damn heat in here, or something. He was Dome raised, genetically superior. He was an agent. He had been an agent. Alistair had no right to make him feel this way.

'You want to know what she's like? She's kind,' Alistair said. 'She tries to hide it, but she cares about other people. She cares what they think. She spent her whole life afraid she would hurt someone. And then she did.'

The hum of the engines filled the moment of silence that followed.

'And then the Shi Fai took her. And they did it because of me,' Alistair continued. 'Because I wasn't able to protect her. I'm not like the others, like Dax or Li or Jinn.' He lifted a hand then, gently touched the skin behind his ear.

His blue eyes danced over Bryant's face, and then he touched that same place again. 'You're afraid,' he said.

'No I'm not,' Bryant blustered.

'You can't lie to me,' Alistair told him. 'I know what it's like inside your head.'

Bryant swallowed. His throat was tight, sore, and Alistair's words made him punchy. He felt the fist form, felt his fingers curl into his palm, felt the muscles in his arm grow tense. 'No you don't,' he said. 'You don't have a fucking clue.' And he swung.

Alistair ducked.

Bryant's fist ploughed into the wall. Agony sang up his arm. He laughed until the pain got the better of the Euphoria and then he dropped to the floor, howling.

Alistair crouched down beside him. 'You want to find her,'

he said. 'So do I. I can't do this on my own, Bryant, and neither can you.' He grabbed Bryant's jacket and hauled him to his feet, keeping them close, eye to eye. 'We've got one chance at this. Don't mess it up. Go to the medbay and let the droid help you.'

Then he let go. He didn't shove Bryant away, simply released his grip, then turned and walked away down the corridor, off into the belly of the ship somewhere. Bryant didn't follow. He told himself it was because he had more important things to do, but the truth was that he wasn't sure his legs would hold him, and he didn't want to get lost somewhere in the maze of corridors.

But deep down, he knew the truth, and he knew Alistair did, too.

He was afraid.

He wasn't afraid that he would fuck this up.

He was afraid that he already had.

CHAPTER
15

18 cycles before ripening

Vessel: Shi Fai transport vessel, name unknown
Location: Shi Fai-controlled space
Cargo: 89 units
Crew: 2 workers. 13 drones
Droids: N/A

Eve awoke to find herself tied to the wall inside a small holding pen. The walls were oily and soft, and they flexed when she leaned against them. The floor had the same rubbery texture. She hurt all over and her head was pounding so fiercely that she wanted to throw up. But there wasn't enough in her stomach to even give her that much relief.

It was her worst nightmare made real. She knew where she was, even through the fog that was clouding her mind. The air was warm and damp, and she could feel her cells adjusting to the comfort of it. She didn't want to adjust to it. She wanted to hate it, wanted it to hurt, wanted it to feel wrong. But it didn't. It was perfectly suited to her modifications, or, rather, her modifications made her perfectly suited to it. She forced herself into a sitting position, gritting her teeth at the heavy weight of whatever it was that connected her to the wall. It yanked on her neck as she moved. She froze in place, trying to catch her breath as she felt for it, fingers closing round what seemed like a soft, flexible rope. Her stunners were gone, both the one she kept at her waist and the one she'd had concealed in an ankle holster. At least she still had her clothes.

She struggled to her feet, the weight of the rope pulling heavily at her shoulders, but she wasn't tall enough to see over the walls. She stood there for as long as she could manage until the screaming of her shoulder muscles had her sinking to the floor.

She was alone on board a Shi Fai ship. She was a prisoner. And she knew now what awaited her. Rape. Pain. Torture. The stories: they were all true. They had to be. Her skin crawled at the thought of it, and her thoughts hit the edge of panic and threatened to go further.

The far side of the pen opened with a rustle of movement. Eve pushed herself further back into the corner, hoping the dim light would hide her, knowing that it almost certainly wouldn't. If she could see well in the semi-darkness it followed that the Shi Fai would also have that ability.

One of them entered. It stared down at her with those three central eyes, its mouth opening and a bundle of fleshy tentacles pushing out to taste the air. She didn't want to look at it, but she didn't dare to look away. She pulled her knees close to her chest, hugging them tightly, trying to protect her vulnerable body.

It moved closer. Its putrid smell crowded her nostrils. Close up, she could see that its skin was flaking in places. It didn't look healthy. But, then, what did she know? This might be how they always looked.

A round silver disc hung on a thin chain around its neck. Eve recognised it as a portable translation device, though she hadn't seen one quite like it before. The more modern ones were small enough to fit inside a user's ear. She had one herself, back in her quarters on the *Mutant*, although she rarely used it. It was human technology, which meant that humans had given it to the Shi Fai, presumably all part of the service.

She stared at the creature, refusing to look away, refusing to show fear.

The situation was bad, but she wasn't dead, not yet, and she'd spent a long time in the company of Caspian Dax. She drew on that now. Dax had always said that there was a time to fight and a time to be smart. The trick was knowing the difference. 'I'm thirsty,' she told it. 'I need water.'

It looked at her, tentacles flexing and tapping against each other. Then it left the pen, giving her a view of what lay beyond. From what she could see, the rest of the ship was made from the same soft, dark material. All around her, the ship flexed like a living, breathing thing. The alien walked over to the wall. It placed a hand flush against it. The wall shivered and then moved, revealing a small storage area. Eve saw shiny packets that were all at once familiar. Silver Rice. Something else that had to have been supplied by humans. By the government.

For the first time, she fully understood what the Second Species programme really meant. The Shi Fai were being given food, translators, medical supplies, and, by the look of the bag that was tossed down by her feet, purified water. Everything they would need to keep their human pets alive. This had been years in the planning. It hadn't happened overnight.

Eve reached for the bag, bit down on the valve and tipped in enough to wet her tongue. Her throat was parched and she wanted to down the lot, but she didn't know how long this was meant to last her. She set the bag down and forced herself to stand up.

'Why were you at the *Articus*?' she asked.

The translator hissed out a puff of greenish gas.

'That is not your concern.'

But Eve persisted. 'It's not on the way to your planet. None of the workshops there can repair a ship like this.'

It didn't respond, but Eve knew now that this was by choice, not because it didn't understand her. The Shi Fai were intelligent enough to have muscled their way onto the Senate. They traded with everyone, peddling fruit to the Sittan, Euphoria and Silver Rice plants to humans and grains to the Lodons, and they always made sure that the buyer wanted to buy just that little bit more than they wanted to sell.

'My head hurts,' Eve told it. 'I need medical assistance.'

It slowly turned back, angling its lumpy head to one side, and looked her over. Then it went back to the storage area. When it returned it was holding a small scanning device, the type that medics used. It scanned her, but it held the device awkwardly, as if it wasn't quite sure how to use it. She watched it carefully. The more she could learn about these creatures, the better.

'I need pain blockers,' she told it.

The alien returned the scanner to the small case and extracted a drug gun. It hesitated.

'Here,' Eve said. She held out her hand. 'I will do it myself.'

The creature handed over the gun. It was fully loaded. She didn't know yet whether to put that down to stupidity or ignorance. There was more than enough inside it for her to kill herself, and she was tempted. But she pressed the trigger against her thigh and shot a single dose of the drug into her system, enough to take the edge off, and no more.

Then she handed it back to the alien. It was set back inside the case, no doubt another present from Earth's government.

'Why did you take me?' she asked, as it closed the case and picked it up. 'Aren't the government giving you all the women you want?'

'We have the right to take what is ours,' it told her. 'You are green. Green women are ours.' And then it stepped out of the pen. The opening closed up, the two sides of the panel spreading, knitting together until she could no longer see the join.

Eve closed her eyes. She could sense the ship all around her, the slow, slumberous pulse of it. As she leaned back against the wall, it seemed to cocoon her, soft against the sore bones of her back, moulding to her shape.

She wanted to sleep. She wanted to lie down and go to sleep and never wake up, which was why she forced herself to move away from the wall. It was why she forced her eyes to stay open, and forced her muscles to ignore the rope that pulled at her throat. But she knew one thing that she hadn't known before: as long as she remained on this ship she would be all right. The Shi Fai had water and they had food. They also had medical supplies, which suggested that they intended to keep her alive and healthy, for the time being at least.

She sat down slowly, crossing her legs and lacing her fingers together, listening to the sounds of the ship. The squeals of the Shi Fai. The low, soft murmur of the ship itself. It was all familiar to her now. She only heard it in the moments when she decided to listen.

Then she heard something else. Something that was not the Shi Fai, or the ship. Keeping a tight grip on the rope, she climbed up onto the bunk on the far side of the pen. It took her a couple of attempts. It was soft under her feet, not steady, and she had to work to keep her balance. But it put her up high enough that she could see over the side.

Sitting in the pen next to hers was another prisoner. There was one major difference between her and the other female, however.

The other prisoner was blue. She was Sittan.

'Hey,' Eve whispered. 'Hey.' Her Universal tongue was a bit rusty, but she could remember enough.

The Sittan rolled over, sat up, her head jerking up as she looked for whoever was talking to her.

'Are you okay?' Eve asked.

'I do not talk to humans,' the female spat.

In the corner of her pen, Eve could see a few packets of Silver Rice, all unopened. 'How long have you been on this ship?'

'I . . . I don't know.'

'Where did they take you from?'

'*Nava Four.*'

A Sittan trading post not far from the *Articus*. This was getting stranger and stranger.

'Are there others on board?'

'I don't know. And I don't care.' And then she jerked up. 'They're coming!' she said. She dropped back into her crouch, tucking herself into the far corner of the pen. Eve dropped down from the bunk just in time.

The wall of her pen split open. Two Shi Fai waited outside. One of them tossed a few packets of Silver Rice in her direction. 'You will eat,' it said. Then the wall was sealed again. Eve held her breath and listened as they moved through all the pens. She counted twenty at least.

Eve sank to her knees, pulled the packets closer. She picked up one, split it, and began to eat. The contents were foul, but she needed to keep herself together. She needed to think. She forced the paste down, rinsed her mouth with water. Then she climbed back up on her bunk and looked down at the Sittan female. She was still in the same place, untouched packets at her feet.

'You need to eat.'

'I won't,' the female told her. 'I'd rather starve to death than keep myself alive for them.'

Eve assessed her, considering. 'It won't make any difference,' she said. 'Eventually, they'll force-feed you. They won't let you die.'

'Then that's what they'll have to do,' the female replied. She huddled back in her corner. 'I'm not going to help them.'

Neither was she, Eve decided. But that didn't mean she wasn't prepared to help herself.

CHAPTER

16

16th day of the fifth turn

The Palace, Fire City, Sittan

Dax had begun to enjoy his time in the palace. He wasn't sure yet quite how he felt about that, but it was better than being in his cage under the arena. He had plenty to eat and cool water to bathe in. Nothing scuttled out of the cracks in the walls and bit him while he tried to sleep. He lay on his front on a soft, waist-high table, breathing slowly in and out as a slave massaged oil into a wound on his shoulder.

He had killed four men that morning. One of them had even managed to put up a half-decent fight. Dax had considered sparing him, but the empress had wanted the man dead, so he had broken him instead.

The empress lay on her day bed now, one clawed hand hanging lazily over its side, rings gleaming in the light from the fire pit. Her robe was open, revealing much of her naked body.

The Mountain stood silently in the distance.

'It still hasn't erupted,' Dax said.

'No.' She sat up and began to pick at the various plates of food crammed together on the low table in front of her. 'Hungry?' she asked, crunching loudly on a handful of Bacc crystals.

133

'No,' Dax said. He moved to sit up, and the male slave quietly stepped back, though he never took his gaze off Dax. The slave was afraid of him. They all were.

Dax, that soft female voice whispered inside his head. *You're a slave too.*

He refused to listen to it. He didn't care. If it was a choice between this and the life he'd had in the holding centre under the arena, he would take this every time.

But he discreetly looked around him anyway. High ceiling, smooth walls, smooth floor. The furniture was all low and heavy, though there wasn't much of it. Three open archways led out. There were guards at every single one, armed with spears and long blades that hung from hip to ankle. It was different from what he remembered of Earth. That had been much colder. He remembered being hungry a lot. More than anything, he remembered wanting to leave.

He got to his feet, strolled slowly over to the pool and lowered himself into the cooling water. A moment later the empress rose from her day bed, dropped her robe and joined him. She floated on the surface of the water. He could see her naked body just below it. He pretended not to look, but he didn't put much effort into it.

'Why hasn't it erupted?' he asked her.

The inner lid flicked lazily over her yellow eyes. He could tell that she didn't like the question. She swam a little closer, and he tensed. 'Because it is unsatisfied,' she purred at him.

'You make it sound like it's alive.'

'That's because it is.'

'How can a Mountain be alive?'

'The same way that you and I are alive. It feels. It breathes.' She rose a little higher out of the water. 'It hungers.'

'Then bring me more men. Let me do what I was sent here to do.'

'It will not be enough!' she screamed. 'No matter how many you kill, it will not be enough!' She picked up a pot of scented oil

134

from the edge of the pool and hurled it towards the balcony. It caught the floor at the edge and bounced off into the air, falling out of sight, leaving a trail of sharp green splatters in its wake.

She shook her head and smiled, baring those needle-sharp teeth at him. 'Forgive me.' Then she climbed out of the water. She walked over to the edge and stood with her back to him, staring out at the Mountain. She muttered something in Sittan, words that he did not understand, though their furious, frustrated undertone was clear. Then she turned around. He dropped his gaze, but it was too late. He had seen, and his body had reacted.

The empress noticed. It was there in the curve of her mouth, in the glint in her eyes, in the way she took her time pulling on the robe that one of the guards brought over. They were never alone. The guards were always present.

Dax found himself wishing they weren't. The thought disturbed him. He didn't know what she would do if he tried to touch her, and he was afraid to find out. But it was growing increasingly difficult not to want to.

The empress walked over to him. She stroked a hand over his face, along the tattoos on his shoulder. He stood rigid. 'Tell me,' she said. 'What is it like on your planet?'

'Cold.'

The empress shivered. 'I'm not sure I have ever experienced that.'

She took his wrist and led him over to the balcony. There were soft throws on the floor there, and the two of them lay down, facing the world outside, and the Mountain. From there Dax could see right out across the city. It was beautiful. Lights twinkled across the buildings as their occupants prepared for suns down. The Mountain itself was bathed in the fading glow of evening, highlighting its sharp sides and wide, flat summit.

'Everything is white,' he told her. 'If you look outside, that's all you see. Endless white. Not like this.' He gestured to the city. 'Earth used to be blue. They called it the blue planet, because from space you could see so much of the ocean. Now it's frozen.'

'I heard that humans caused it to be so.'

'We did,' Dax said. 'We dug up a type of fuel from the ground, and when we burned it, it released gases that destroyed the atmosphere. The planet started to heat up. We argued about it rather than doing something while we still could. When it was obvious that it was too late, our scientists tried to fix the problem anyway. It didn't work.'

'And now you have to leave.'

Dax shrugged. 'Or we stay and face extinction.'

'Your senator believes I should let humans cross through Sittan space so that you can reach your new planet.'

'Will you?'

'Perhaps,' the empress said. 'Though I have to admit I am not inclined to grant such mercy to a species that has already destroyed one planet. What do humans have to offer the galaxy that it does not already possess?'

'We have technology.'

'So do all of us.'

'But our technology is different.'

'Genetic engineering.' The empress sighed. 'Yes. I am aware of it, and what you use it for. It created you, after all. And there is no denying that you are quite unique, Caspian Dax.' She rolled onto her stomach, propped her chin in her hands and looked at him. The inner lid flicked lazily across her eyes and then back again.

Dax wanted to please her. He wanted to keep her as she was now, relaxed and contented. He didn't want to see another flash of the anger he had seen earlier. 'Is that why you brought me here? Because I am unique?'

'Dax,' she said, smiling. 'I brought you here because you are fascinating.'

'Didn't you find any of the other men fascinating?'

She bent her knees. Her feet, which were surprisingly small, were black-soled. Rings circled her toes, and there was more decoration around her ankles. It jingled as she swung her feet back and forth. 'Definitely not.'

'Oh.' Dax turned his attention back to the world outside. He couldn't look at her, because, when he did, he wanted her, and that was dangerous. The guards were still standing at the edge of the room, each armed with one of those spears.

'Humans do have positive qualities,' he said. 'They're intelligent. Tenacious.'

'Destructive.'

Dax inclined his head in agreement. 'Yes. But we also create. Cities. Ships. Civilisations. Like you.' He, too, rolled onto his front. Maintaining eye contact with her was easier than it should have been. 'Imagine being the one who saved an entire species.'

Her lips pursed, and he could see she was considering this.

'Imagine how powerful you would be. The debt that would be owed would be beyond imagining. Your standing in the Senate would be transformed. Whatever you proposed, Earth's senators would support you. They would have no choice.'

She liked what he was saying. He could see it in her eyes. 'Yes,' she said. 'Yes.' Her forked tongue flickered out. Dax tracked the movement.

'Maybe I will vote in favour,' she said. Then she got to her feet, so swiftly that it took him by surprise. He got up, too. She was already through the archway, moving into her private quarters.

Dax made to follow her. The guards stopped him.

He walked away, back to the balcony, the sleeping city and the dead Mountain.

Dax, whispered the soft voice inside his head. *What about me?*

He ignored it.

CHAPTER
17

16th day of the fifth turn

The Sand Seas, Sittan

By the time they landed the little piece of tech had expanded to cover half the control deck of the yacht. It was creepy. Jinn did her best to avoid looking at it, finding the strange pulsing of the oily surface deeply unnerving.

She felt like it was watching her even though she knew that to be impossible. It wasn't like it had eyes. But her skin prickled just the same.

'This stuff creeps me out,' she said to Li.

'You'll get used to it,' he said, though she noticed that he kept his distance from it as he buckled on an assortment of guns and knives, strapping them to his upper thighs and waist. He had an expandable pack which he filled with bagged water and vac-sealed items from the Autochef. He handed her a large cup of Soylate and programmed something for himself, then sat on the edge of the comm. seat, right ankle resting on left knee. 'Drink,' he said. 'It's hot as the sun here. It's vital to keep hydrated.'

He had already been outside the yacht to check their landing site, reporting back that they were in an area about ten kilometres outside the capital city, close to the base of one of the volcanoes that dominated the landscape of Sittan.

'What if someone sees the ship?' Jinn asked him.

'They won't.'

'But . . . '

'No one comes this far out into the desert.'

He tossed her an empty pack and told her to fill it. She drained the Soylate, which burned the back of her throat, and added bagged water plus some basic medical supplies. The blaster she strapped to her hip was a reassuring weight, though it didn't seem like much compared to what Li was carrying. Still, she had her blades, and she hadn't come here looking for trouble.

All she wanted to do was find Dax and leave, preferably without having face-to-face contact with any of the Sittan.

'Ready?' she asked Li.

He nodded and together they moved to the side of the small control deck where a little maintenance hatch in the floor dropped open. A hot blast of air hit her face, making her gasp, but her pulse calmed down when she realised that she could breathe. She dropped the three metres down to the ground with ease, keeping in a crouching position as Li dropped down next to her. There was no shout of alarm, no sound of footsteps. The only thing she could hear was the swirl of the wind that tugged at her hair and her clothing.

They walked for a good thirty minutes before the heat became too much and they were forced to stop. They tucked themselves in next to a small, rocky outcrop which gave them some shelter from the wind at least. Jinn leaned her back against it and looked at the ship.

Half of it had disappeared.

She shot to her feet, her heart racing. 'There's something wrong with the ship.'

Li shaded his eyes with his hand. 'Huh,' he said, sounding surprised. 'The tech must have made its way outside. I've never seen it expand like that before.'

When she concentrated, she could just see about see the out-line of the missing half. The Sittan tech hadn't just spread on the control deck; it had spread over the hull, too, matching perfectly with the jut of the volcano behind it.

'Whatever that stuff is,' Li said, 'it comes from that volcano.'

'The tech is lava?'

'Sort of,' he said. 'But not like the lava that used to erupt from the volcanoes on Earth. It's more than just molten rock. It has some degree of sentience. It's intelligent. It makes decisions. It learns.'

'Sounds like pretty amazing stuff.'

Li nodded. 'The Sittan certainly think so. They sacrifice their firstborn males for it. They believe that their blood will feed it, that as long as they keep killing their boys the Mountain will keep right on giving.'

'What on Earth makes them think that?'

'What on Sittan, you mean? My understanding is that the first eruption occurred during a particularly vicious civil war. The Sittan put two and two together and made five. But the volcano stopped erupting a few years ago.'

'That's hardly surprising. Volcanoes don't keep going forever. And they do not erupt because people kill each other.'

'No,' Li agreed. 'And that's the problem. My understanding is that they tried to mine under the volcano and dig the tech out, but all they found was rock. It's as dry as the rest of the desert. So they went back to killing in the hope it would wake up. It's my guess that's what the Type Ones are for.'

'What do you mean?'

'The empress is running out of Sittan males to sacrifice, and she's getting desperate. And the last thing you want is a desperate Sittan female.'

'Li?'

'What is it?'

'What do you think Dax will be like if I find him?'

'I don't know,' he said. 'He's more Sittan now than you or I.'

'But the men on board the *A2* were not like the Sittan. Not exactly.'

'No.' He rested his forearms against his knees. 'The Sittan have the aggression, but they have control over it.'

But that didn't mean Dax would. Now that she was here, on planet, it was harder to convince herself that Dax would have been able to overcome the effects of the third serum. 'If Dax is like the men we saw on the *A2*, I'll have to kill him.'

'I know,' Li said. 'Though knowing Dax, he'd probably survive it. Come on.'

He was on his feet and Jinn followed him, slinging her pack onto her back. Sweat dripped into her eyes and made them sting. Her feet squeaked and slipped inside her boots, but she kept her mind focused on Dax and that helped her keep moving. He had to have found a way to resist the effects of the serum. She would believe that until Dax proved otherwise.

She was thankful for Li, who at the very least seemed to know where he was going. He set a strong pace. They were in sight of the city within a couple of hours. By then she had run out of water and was trying not to panic.

All the buildings were white, sitting low to the ground, except for the one in the very centre. That was dark, made from what looked like polished black glass, and it speared high into the air, sharp and angular and completely different from its surroundings.

'That's the palace,' Li said.

In some ways, it reminded Jinn of the Domes, dominating the landscape, bigger, greedier than everything around it. To her left, the land sloped away and down, and at the bottom there was another unusual building. It was huge and circular and she instantly knew what it was. Her heart caught in her chest.

'That's the arena.'

'Yes,' Li told her.

Jinn glanced across at him. He was staring down at it with his arms folded. A vein stood out on his forehead, his jaw tight as if he was clamping his teeth together hard. 'How bad was it?'

'Bad,' he said. One hand slipped to his shoulder and rested there for a moment. 'Very bad.'

Jinn reached out and took his other hand and squeezed it. His fingers were still for a moment before squeezing back. When she let go, he pulled a little crystal from his pocket, shaped like a pyramid and the same colour as an amethyst. He balanced it against the palm of his hand. It glowed gently, and then unfolded. Li caught hold of the edges and held it steady. 'We're here,' he said, altering the position of the map so she could see. 'This is the arena here. When I left, they were building something underneath it. No one was entirely sure what it was, but knowing what we know now I'd bet it was living quarters for the Second Species humans. See the tunnels here? They're new, and it looks like they lead to the port at Sangoon.'

Jinn slowly shook her head. 'How long?' she asked him. 'How long were they planning this, without any of us knowing?'

'Years,' Li said. 'Has to be.'

'We were stupid,' she said.

'Not really,' Li told her. 'How could we have predicted this?'

She knew he was right, but it didn't make her feel any better. 'How do we get in?'

'The main entrance is here,' Li said. He flicked the map again, turning it to show the gates for the arena. 'I'd imagine the entrance to the living quarters is inside somewhere. The Sittan won't want humans getting outside of the arena. Which is why we'll be going in the back door.' He gestured to the map again.

'That looks like a pipe,' Jinn said.

'That's because it is.'

'What sort of pipe?'

'Best not to worry about that.'

'I'm not going to like this, am I?'

'Probably not.'

*

She didn't like it. It was viciously hot, and it was just dark enough that she couldn't quite see the things that brushed against her as they walked along it. But it took them where they needed to be, and they got there without being caught.

The arena was huge. Jinn hadn't been able to fully appreciate the size of it from a distance. She stood at the edge, simply trying to take it in. The floor was made from dark sand that was clumped together in places. The air inside was perfectly still, the high rise of seating trapping it and forming a giant cooking pot. At one side was a wide terrace with white flags hanging in elegant folds from high obsidian spikes. Lives had been lost here, thousands of them, and she could feel the weight of every single one.

Li crouched beside her, picked up some of the sand and let it fall through his fingers. Then he stood, shaded his eyes with his hand and cast his gaze around the arena. 'Fighters are brought up from under the terrace,' he said, pointing to it. 'The bodies are loaded into carts and taken up a trail to the top of the Mountain before being thrown in.'

'How many times did you fight here?'

'Enough,' he said.

There was something about knowing that so much death had occurred here that made Jinn want to cry. She knew death was inevitable. It was the end result of being alive. But it shouldn't be like this, brutal and violent and early.

'Why?' she asked. 'Why do the males do this? Why don't they refuse?'

'It's considered to be a great honour,' Li said.

'Is that why you came here? For honour?'

'No. I came here for money.'

'You couldn't think of an easier way to earn?'

'No,' he said. He rose to his feet and brushed off his hands. 'Come on.'

He started towards the terrace and Jinn followed him. She wanted to ask him what had happened, why he hadn't stayed with Dax and the others after they had escaped from the clinic back on Earth, how he had ended up on this alien planet killing for a living. But his demeanour didn't invite questions, and Jinn decided he was entitled to his privacy.

'It moves back to let the fighters into the arena,' Li said as he came to a halt a couple of metres away from the terrace. 'Before the fight, all of us were kept in holding cages over there.' He gestured to the edge of the arena. Jinn lifted a hand and shaded her eyes. She could see what looked like a line of prison cells complete with bars.

'We would be in there, sometimes for hours. Then guards would come to fetch us. We'd be brought under here, the terrace would roll back, then it's twenty steps to the top. The terrace moves back into position, the empress gives the signal and you fight until you're the only one standing.'

'And the empress sits there? Right in the middle of it all?'

'Gives her the best view.'

'She sounds lovely.'

Li huffed out a laugh. 'If we're going to find a way into whatever they were building underneath this place, my guess would be that we'll find it here.'

'Agreed.' But how to move the terrace? It was made from some sort of polished white stone that twinkled in the light, cut as a single vast piece that must have weighed thousands of kilos. They certainly weren't going to be able to push it out of the way, though Li gave it a quick try.

Jinn climbed up onto the platform, moving lightly on her soft boots. Each footstep left a dusting of dark sand, marring the pristine surface. It didn't matter. By the time anyone saw it, they would be well away from here, Dax with them.

She hoped he was all right. Just let him be all right. Let him be . . . still human.

The huge throne in the centre of the platform had to belong to the empress. It was exquisitely carved, a mixture of glossy onyx and the same strange substance that was on the transporter. It seemed to whisper as she moved closer to it. Instinct made her want to move away.

She circled it slowly. She didn't believe in gods and magic, only in science and technology. There had to be a lever or a button or something here that would activate the terrace. Willing out a blade, Jinn poked at various parts of the throne. Nothing. She took a step back, took another look. There was a smooth area at the base, as if a foot had rubbed against it.

Nerves spiked as she stretched out her own foot and pressed down on it.

The terrace moved so smoothly it was like it was gliding over ice.

Jinn moved quickly to the edge of the terrace and jumped down onto the sand. Li stood with his hands on his hips, looking down into the space that had opened up. A muscle was twitching in his cheek.

'You don't have to do this if you don't want to,' Jinn told him.

'It's fine,' he said, and started down the steps. She quickly caught up with him, and they made their way down twenty steps, and then some more. The first few were soft on the edges, as if worn by decades of feet, but then they changed and became sharper. She could feel the change through the soles of her boots.

'This is new,' Li said, as twenty steps became a hundred.

They had found what they were looking for. She knew that even before they reached the bottom and saw them, the Type One males, seated at long tables in a vast hall. More of them shuffled along in a queue that led to a serving hatch, where bowls were shoved out at regular intervals.

Jinn moved into the shadows at the edge of the steps. 'So many,' she whispered, as Li slid in alongside her.

'Too many,' he replied.

'I wonder how they keep them so calm.'

'Probably something in the food or the water. Can you see Dax?'

She scanned the hall. If he was there, he wasn't obvious. There

JANE O'REILLY

were just too many huge, dark-haired men. Once or twice she thought she saw him, but when the man turned around she realised she'd been wrong. 'No,' she finally admitted. 'No, I can't.'

Disappointment rode her hard. Now that she was here, now that she saw the true scale of it, there was no escaping the fact that she'd come here with little more than hope. She didn't know the planet, she didn't know the Sittan and the odds had always been very much against her.

Jinn turned, putting her back against the wall, and blinked back the tears that dared to wet her eyes. Then she dropped down into a crouch. This was crazy. She was never going to find him. She should never have come here.

A shadow moved over her.

Jinn looked up to see a young male looking down at them. He looked confused. 'Hello,' he said. His accent marked him out as having come from London, and the sense of familiarity was oddly comforting. 'What are you doing here?'

Definitely drugged. Jinn swallowed down the burn in her throat and wiped at her face with the back of her hand. Then she got slowly to her feet, keeping her Tellurium hot in her hands. She could have her blades out in a heartbeat if she needed them.

'I'm looking for a friend of mine,' she said carefully. 'You might know him. His name is Dax.' It was a gamble. He could call others. He could turn violent in the blink of an eye. She couldn't trust him. But she had nothing to lose.

'He's not here,' the man said. He blinked rapidly, swatting at his face as if something was tickling him. 'They took him to the palace.' The muscles in his arms and his bare abdomen bunched and flexed as he giggled.

'The palace?'

The man nodded vigorously. 'He was bad so they took him away. Bad Dax. Bad.'

'Yes,' Jinn said. 'Bad Dax.' She started to back up slowly, moving away from him. 'Well, thank you for telling me. We'll be going now.'

'Oh, no,' the man said. 'You can't leave. It's not allowed.' He slapped at something on his back, then scratched his head, a mad skitter of fingertips over his scalp. The giggling had gone, replaced by an undeniable slide towards violence. 'You're a woman. We don't have women here,' he said. 'No women. All men. Don't like men.'

The drugs were good, Jinn decided.

But they weren't that good.

She eased her way back, flexed her fingers just a little, sensing the ready weight of Tellurium in her hands, and willed him not to do it.

He lunged at her. Her blades were out in a flash and he staggered back, howling, clutching his shoulder, blood seeping between his fingers. 'Fucking bitch! I'll fucking kill you!'

Li swung one of his big fists, connecting with the side of the man's head. He dropped like a stone, mouth hanging open, eyes rolling back in his head. 'Useless,' Li said. 'He won't last five minutes in the arena.'

Jinn stared down at the prone figure of the man. She could feel the tension in her muscles, the fierce pounding of her heart. 'Can you teach me how to do that?'

'I could.' Li eyed her blades. 'But I'm not sure I need to. Come on.' He grabbed her hand and pulled her back up the stairs. But the terrace had rolled back into place. They were sealed in.

'How do we move it back?'

'I don't think we can,' he said. 'I'm pretty sure it only opens from the outside.'

'But there must be another way out,' Jinn said. 'You said they brought you in through tunnels.'

'Let's see what we can find.'

They kept close together, and this time they didn't stop halfway down the stairs. Once in the mess hall, she followed Li's lead. They fell in line with the others, taking a bowl, taking the food. No one seemed to notice that they weren't supposed to be there. They were all too interested in the food.

The contents of her bowl were all too recognisable. Silver Rice. She glanced around, saw one man lick out his bowl and then start to chew on his spoon. Presumably the bowls were also edible, nothing wasted. It was all very tidy and efficient.

Li turned, followed the line towards the tables. Jinn hesitated. It was only a moment, but it was enough. The man behind her walked straight into her. She felt the wet slide of his food down her back.

'You made me spill!' the man whined.

'Get more,' she told him.

'Don't want more,' he replied, pulling at her arm. 'Have to wait again. Don't want to wait. Hungry.'

'Here,' Jinn said, shoving her bowl at him. Out of the corner of her eye, she could see one of the tables emptying. The men leaving it were walking through a gap in the wall that had been invisible when they had first walked in.

She tried not to run, but it was difficult.

They marched out in a line, Li a few steps ahead of her. The sound of their footfalls was regulated, loud, mechanical, the march of robots. They didn't speak to each other, didn't communicate. Had this been done to Dax? Had he been reduced to a drone, like this?

Jinn wouldn't think about that. She couldn't think of him as less than whole, as less than the man she had known. She followed the others, put one foot in front of the other, breathing only a little, trying to make herself small and invisible when she felt anything but. Both her hair and her gender marked her out as other, and that was something she simply could not be here.

At least there were no Sittan guards. There were just the walls, the solid roof and the floor beneath their feet and the prisoners who seemed not to care. In fact, they cared so little that they weren't even held in cells. There were open cubicles, some occupied, some empty. The prisoners filtered off, flopping down onto their bunks. They didn't bother to speak to each other.

Nor did they try to use the little shuttle carts that hung

suspended from a ceiling track down one side. As Jinn watched, a cart sped along the rail, bumping into the others as it came to a stop. The side folded down and two dozen men climbed out. They had the same dazed look on their faces, but their clothes were clean.

New recruits.

At the other end of the track, the empty carts began to move, slowly but surely, swinging their way into a tunnel. They were going out. And so was she. There seemed to be no point in stealth. She walked boldly up and climbed into one. Li joined her a few seconds later. They swung their way into the tunnel. No one tried to stop them.

When she looked at Li, his expression was grim. 'So,' she said, refusing to look back. 'How do we get into the palace?'

'I don't know,' Li said. 'But I know someone who might.'

CHAPTER

18

16th day of the fifth turn

Dukian Quarter, Fire City, Sittan

The house that Li took Jinn to was in the middle of the town, a good thirty-minute hike from the arena and uphill all the way. The three suns rose high overhead. It was hot enough to make the surface of the road sticky against the soles of her boots.

'Where is everyone?' she asked Li.

'Inside,' he said. 'No one comes out at this time. The heat is a killer.'

'You're not kidding,' she muttered, draining the last few drops of water from her bag. She scrunched it up and stuffed it into her backpack. Sweat dripped off her chin. She leaned against the side of the building, immediately recoiling as the stone cooked her skin. Li rapped his knuckles against the door in a quick, anxious rhythm. The seconds while they waited for someone to answer were excruciatingly long, stretching for far too many hot, burning breaths.

Eventually, it slid open just a little. 'What?'

'It's me,' Li said. 'Can I come in?'

The door slid fully open. A blue arm shot out, grabbed Li by the shirt and hauled him inside.

150

'Bloody supernova!' Jinn yelped. She made a grab for him, but it was too late. He was already inside. Her blades snapped out and she lunged through the doorway. Her eyes took a moment to adjust to the light, which was far dimmer in here than it was outside. The cool air was delicious after the heat outside and she drank in great gulps of it.

She saw Li pinned up against the wall by a Sittan male. He was about the same height as Jinn, leanly muscled and delicately blue, dressed only in some sort of lightweight material wrapped around his hips and dropping to his ankles. It looked like it would come away with one good tug.

Li had his hands pressed flat against the wall, despite the forearm pressed up against his throat. They talked for several minutes in low, harsh tones, then Li lifted his hand, ran the back of his fingers over the Sittan's cheek.

Jinn dropped her gaze and edged back towards the door.

'Wait.'

The order came from the Sittan male, and he snapped it out in the Universal tongue instead of the Sittan the two of them had been using before. Jinn decided to obey him, or, rather, her legs did, as they wouldn't seem to move. She didn't know enough about the Sittan to accurately guess his age, though she suspected he was young. He was smaller than the other Sittan males she'd seen, and it was clear that Li could have flattened him if he'd wanted to.

'Who is she?' the Sittan asked Li.

'A friend of mine.'

The arm jerked harder against his throat. 'A friend,' Li said again.

'But she is female.'

'Humans don't limit friendships based on gender.'

'Then how does your breeding system work?'

Li raised an eyebrow. 'I'm not here to discuss the human courtship system, Merion.'

The Sittan glared at him for a few seconds longer, then

dropped his arm, though he didn't step back. 'It's been a long time, Jozeph.'

'I know. And I'm sorry.'

'I suppose you want to see Ritte.'

Li looked at Merion for a long time before he finally responded. 'Yes.'

Ritte turned out to be older and female, with mottled blue skin and an unexpectedly soft voice. She embraced Li with the affection of a mother, touched his face, touched his hands, and pulled him to sit with her on the floor of the elaborately decorated room in the centre of the house. It was cool and semi-dark with huge cushions scattered low on the floor. Oil burned in sconces mounted high on the walls.

Jinn sat on one of the cushions, legs crossed. Li sat next to her. Merion set out platters of strange alien fruit and dark meat, and pitchers of a lukewarm liquid that tasted faintly of lemons on the low table in the middle of the room, then took the seat on the other side of Li. Ritte took the remaining empty space. Jinn was so hungry that she chewed her way through all of it. Merion made no effort to speak to her, though he stared as if she was an exhibit in a zoo. 'What?' she asked him eventually, after swallowing one more mouthful than her stomach could really hold. 'What is it?'

'Your hair is strange,' he said. 'I don't like it.'

Jinn didn't quite know what to say to that.

'The others, their hair is dark,' he continued. 'Black, like the ash from the Mountain. I did not know that it could also be the white of the sand seas. And you are female. I have never seen a female before.'

'You've never been off planet?'

'Of course not,' he snarled. 'I . . .'

'Merion.'

Ritte spoke softly, but it was enough. Merion got to his feet and busied himself with the trays of food and the heavy pitchers. Li took the goblet that Merion held out, and it didn't escape Jinn's notice that Merion held onto it for just a second too long. This time, when he sat down, Merion settled himself closer to Jinn. He offered her a plate of fruit. 'Try the green one.'

Reluctantly, she did. It had a crisp, pleasant texture, and exploded with painful heat on her tongue. She kept her face muscles in check, but skewered the next piece with her blade, satisfied when Merion shuffled a little further away. Ritte and Li were engrossed in conversation, paying no attention to the two of them.

'How do you know Li?' she asked him, toying with the remaining piece of fruit.

'My mother hired him.'

'To do what?'

'To fight in the arena so I wouldn't have to.'

This was so unexpected that Jinn popped the rest of the fruit into her mouth without thinking. The second slice burned even hotter than the first, and she coughed. 'How in the void does that work?'

'She met him on the *Carter*,' Merion said. 'It's a trading post near gate 52.'

'I know where it is. I've been there.'

'She gave him rubysticks, he went into the arena and fought instead of me. He won all my fights and then he left.'

'How long was he here for?'

'I believe in human terms it was four years.'

Jinn thought that over. She wasn't sure she could survive here for a day, never mind four years. Li had to be even tougher than she'd thought.

'Jozeph told me you are here to find your male,' Merion said.

'Yes,' she said, still distracted by the burn of the fruit on her tongue, and thoughts about Li.

'He is your son?'

'No,' Jinn told him. 'Lover.'

'Why would a female bother to hunt down a lover? Surely you can simply find yourself a replacement.'

'I don't want a replacement.'

But Merion wasn't listening. He was watching Li, who had risen to his feet and was stretching out the muscles in his back.

'How much do you know about our planet?' Ritte asked Jinn.

'Not much,' she admitted. 'I know that you have an empress rather than a government. I know that our government has given you thousands of genetically altered men who are being forced to kill each other for reasons I don't fully understand.'

'You make us sound . . . primitive.'

'I . . .'

'It is quite all right,' Ritte told her. 'We are primitive. We have learned nothing from our contact with other races. We continue to do things as we have always done them. We ignore logic, reason, science.' Spikes flicked up across her scalp, her neck, rippled for a moment, and then disappeared.

Merion was on his feet now, too, filling a series of small pots of oil and lighting each one in turn. They filled the air with a heavy fragrance. 'My mother and I believe that it is time for us to leave the old ways behind. Unfortunately, not everyone else agrees with us.'

'The Mountain hasn't erupted in years,' Ritte pointed out. 'We need to accept that those days are over and move on. Find new ways to progress. We could flourish instead of killing our sons in the vain hope of resurrecting something we didn't even understand in the first place.'

'Can you tell me about the Mountain?' Jinn asked.

'When it erupts, it produces a substance we call Virena,' Merion told her. 'Only the females can control it.'

'Only *some* of the females,' Ritte interjected. 'And some of us have better control than others. The empress has the most control. That's what gives her power. But it has destroyed our society. We can't progress because we're too busy trying to make something that is broken work again, and for what?'

'We're Sittan,' Merion pointed out. 'Killing is what we do.'

Ritte just stared at him. 'You refused to kill the cherak that flew into the storeroom yesterday afternoon.'

'That's different.'

'No, it is not.'

Jinn could see that Li was trying not to smile.

'Excuse me while I refill this,' Merion said, lifting the jug a little. He was gripping it so tightly that his claws scratched the side. He strode out of the room.

'He has changed,' Li said in a low voice.

'He is very alone,' Ritte told him. 'Most of his friends are now dead. He is something of an outcast. It is good that you've come back, Jozeph.'

'Is it? I couldn't tell.'

'I could. Things are changing. The remaining Virena is old now, and the empress is starting to panic.' She turned her attention to Jinn. 'That's why the humans have been brought here. She is running out of Sittan males to sacrifice, and the Mountain must have blood.' Her smile, when it came, was harsh. 'She's losing her hold over us, and she knows it.'

'You don't seem too upset about that,' Jinn noted.

'I'm not,' Ritte told her. 'We've been living this way for too long. Trapped in the same old patterns, refusing to break them even though they aren't working. If this is what it takes to force change, then so be it.'

'It's a shame that forcing change requires the deaths of thousands of human males,' Jinn said quietly.

'Yes,' Ritte agreed. 'I see we understand each other.'

'We need to get into the palace,' Li said. 'The man we are looking for has been taken there.'

'Ah,' Ritte replied. 'You seek *that* man.'

'What do you mean, *that* man?'

'He fought in the arena,' Ritte told her. 'Killed the best Sittan males, and caught the attention of the empress. She had him taken to the palace after his last fight. Rumour has it that she has taken a special interest in him.' She lifted her cup, sipped at it slowly. 'Getting to him will not be easy. The palace is well guarded. The empress is very protective of her position. And of her possessions.'

'He isn't her possession,' Jinn snapped back.

'Unfortunately, he is. And she won't like it if you try to take him back.'

'I can't just leave him.'

'I appreciate that,' Ritte said. 'I simply wish to make sure that you fully understand what you are attempting to do.'

'But you can get me into the palace?'

'Yes,' Ritte said. 'You came at a good time. There is a Ba-Rat taking place three days from now.'

'A what?'

'A Ba-Rat,' Li said. 'Once a year, the best of our young females challenge the empress and try to overthrow her. When they fail, they are either killed or swear an oath and become her personal guard. Getting into the palace is the first stage.'

'It won't be easy,' Ritte told her. 'The females are strong, and they're smart, and they've spent their entire lives training for this. Even so, most of them will not be able to pass through the gates.'

'Why not?'

'The Virena guards the palace. Some of the females can connect with it. Others, it actively dislikes. We do not understand why. It does not respond at all to the males.'

'It responds to me,' Jinn said.

Ritte looked surprised.

'We have some on our ship,' Li told Ritte. 'It's a long story. I will tell it to you some time.'

'It kept trying to touch me,' Jinn told her. 'When I got too close to it, it would move.'

'Interesting,' Ritte said. 'I wonder . . .'

She tugged on a braided cord around her neck, and pulled up what looked like a large, polished stone. Jinn watched in astonishment as the stone floated up and hung motionless in the air. The surface swirled, metallic shades of purple and green dancing across it. Ritte pulled the cord free. A soft humming filled Jinn's ears. It was coming from Ritte. With a slight change to the sound, the stone settled into the palm of her outstretched hand, quivering slightly.

'Hold out your hand,' Ritte said to Jinn.

'Why?'

'Call it curiosity,' Ritte said.

Jinn hadn't realised Merion had come back into the room until he spoke. 'This is not for her!' he snapped out. 'She is human!'

'Be quiet, Merion.'

The Sittan male stormed from the room. Li got to his feet and followed him.

Ritte dropped the tech into Jinn's hand.

At first, nothing happened. Then it started to feel hot, not enough to burn, but enough for Jinn to decide that she didn't like it. Thread-like strands shot out from the droplet and wrapped themselves around her hand, her fingers and the Tellurium band at her wrist. Jinn shook her hand, but it clung tightly and she panicked a little. 'Get it off me!'

Ritte hummed a single pure note and the tech instantly unwrapped itself from Jinn's hand, pulling back into a drop-let and floating back over to Ritte. 'Interesting,' she said once again.

'That's not the word I would choose,' Jinn replied, rubbing her hand. Red lines had been marked into her flesh where the Virena had clung a little too tightly. She focused, sensed the weight of Tellurium in her hand, felt a little better. 'What is this stuff? Li tried to explain it to me, but I didn't really understand it.'

'To understand it, you have to understand our history.' Ritte settled herself more comfortably into position. 'The Sittan race is a relatively young one. We evolved quickly. We came out of the desert only ten thousand years ago, and began to build our cities, our technology. We are a very intelligent species, and things pro-gressed quickly. But we are also violent, and we soon learned that we did not work well together.'

'You're not the only species that has that problem.'

'So I understand,' Ritte said. 'And, as inevitably happens in these situations, war broke out and we spent rather a long time killing each other. By the end, only a few remained. Our cities were in ruins. We had nothing left. And then one day, the Mountain erupted.'

'That stuff?' Jinn asked, pointing to Ritte's hand.

Ritte nodded. 'At first, our ancestors were afraid of it. It burned their homes, scorched the land, filled the air with smoke. They thought it was a punishment for what they had done, as they had routinely dumped the bodies of their enemies into the Mountain. But then it began to build. You saw the palace, at the centre of the city?'

'Yes.'

'That was the first of its creations, and only a small part of what it can do. It powers our ships, our weapons. And it protects us. Without it we would be planet-bound and vulnerable.'

'How . . . ?'

'We still don't know,' Ritte said. 'All attempts at research were shut down.'

'By whom?'

'By the empresses,' Ritte told her. 'The current one isn't the first – ten females have ruled over us in the past thousand years.'

'Why would they stop research? Don't they want to know what it is, or how it works?'

'No.'

'Why not?'

'Because the Virena likes them the most. They can control it. Whoever controls the Virena controls the rest of us. And they have no intention of giving that up.'

CHAPTER

19

Ferona had always enjoyed a good press conference. She liked the opportunity to dress up, to answer the questions posed by journalists who would ask whatever she wanted in exchange for the odd little treat – meals at the best restaurants the Domes had to offer, rare books, bottles of imported Lodon liquor. She was particularly enjoying this one, knowing as she did that it would put an end to the nuisance of Humans First.

She had also decided that it was time to put an end to the nuisance that was President Vexler. Their meeting the other day had given her the push she needed. The man was utterly incompetent. All the work to get the human race to Spes had been done by her. It was only right that she should be rewarded for it.

'Vice President Blue, you were recently at the Senate. Can you tell us how that went?'

Ferona flicked her attention to the man in the front row, fixing on a confident, welcoming smile as she did so. 'It went very well. Our relations with our alien neighbours grow ever stronger. We remain a strong, vital part of the Senate.'

'Is it true that you have agreed a trade deal with the Minons?'

'We are in the process of negotiating such a deal,' Ferona replied.

'To what end?'

The questions came thick and fast, and she answered them with easy confidence. It wasn't difficult given that she already knew exactly what was going to be asked, and had Swain muttering cues through the tiny earpiece that she wore. And then the conversation swung around to the Second Species programme, just as she had intended.

'What do the Sittan think about the destruction of the *A2*?'

'The Sittan empress understands that there was an incident, and that alternative arrangements have been made. The loss of the *A2* has had no impact on the Sittan. They continue to be very pleased with the Second Species that have been sent to them.'

'Do you honestly believe that the Senate will vote in our favour?'

That question came from a woman at the back. Ferona couldn't quite make her out until she stepped forward. She was tall and thin, crowded in at the rear with the others who weren't influential enough to bag a position that came with a chair.

White blonde hair curled around a sharp chin. She wore black from head to foot, trousers and a high-collared jacket. She fiddled with a chunky gold cuff as she spoke and her eyes didn't quite meet Ferona's gaze.

At last. This was what Ferona had been waiting for.

'Absolutely,' Ferona said. 'At this moment in time, I have no reason to believe otherwise.'

Ferona didn't recognise the woman. She was Dome-raised, the eyes and hair indicated that much. The fit of the suit suggested that it was off the peg, relatively cheap, though she had good skin and good jewellery, so there was money somewhere. Given her age she was probably a journalism student at one of the universities, all of which had their own media channels, and all of which were breeding grounds for groups like Humans First.

'And afterwards? What happens then? Will we really be taking the Second Species to Bpcs?'

The more important journalists were shifting in their seats, turning to get a look at the woman, the noise level in the room rising and falling in a tight wave of curiosity.

'Where else would they go?' Ferona replied, pretending to be confused.

'That's not our problem,' the woman said. 'They're not human. Spes is for humans.'

And with that the room fell completely silent as the rest of them caught on. The media hacks in the front row certainly looked happy. This was something interesting, something that they could put on their video and net channels.

'Well?' the woman asked. 'Are we really expected to share our new home with these people? Half-alien monsters? They could kill us all, and you know it. We won't be safe with them there. How could we be? I don't know which I'm more terrified of, the men or the women.'

It was even better than she could have hoped. 'The Second Species are a unique and special group of people,' Ferona began, carefully, slowly. 'We owe them our thanks. Without their contribution, we wouldn't be preparing for a move to Spes.'

'You don't know that!'

The voice came from elsewhere in the audience. Ferona couldn't pinpoint the speaker. 'Yes, I do,' she said. She lifted a finger to her ear and deactivated the earpiece, cutting Swain off mid-flow. She didn't need his help to deal with these idiots. 'I've spent more time with the Sittan and the Shi Fai than anyone else in this room. I know how they think, how they operate. Without the Second Species, they'd happily have left us here to die.'

'You still haven't answered the question! Are we really expected to share Spes with those monsters?'

'They are not monsters.'

'You would say that. But we all know it's a lie. That's all you people do. Lie. We never hear the truth about anything. You tried to cover up the Second Species programme for months. It only became public because those pirates found your facility on Colony Seven and uploaded video of it.'

Ferona started to feel a little annoyed. Yes, it was true that Caspian Dax and her daughter had done those things. It was true that she had kept the Second Species project a secret. But it had been necessary at the time. 'I think you fail to see the bigger picture.'

'Hardly. The bigger picture is that you have lied about everything, and now you want us to share a planet with creatures modified with alien DNA when we have no idea what effect it will have in the future. What if they start to breed? Produce children? What then? This is nothing more than a science experiment on a massive scale.'

'All humans have the right to live in a clean, safe place,' Ferona said. 'That is a fundamental human right. The Global Government was founded on that belief. All humans have the right to a place to live, food to eat and meaningful work to do. Everything that I have done has been to that end. And I believe that it has been the right thing to do. In a few more days, the Senate will vote on whether or not to let our ships cross alien-controlled space. And when they do, it will be because of the Second Species programme.'

She paused, letting those words sink in, wondering how many of them were smart enough to read between the lines, to know that it was what she didn't say that was important. She had said humans. She hadn't said that Second Species were humans.

At the side of the room a man got to his feet. He was tall, strong enough in the shoulders, she supposed, though a little skinny in the legs. He was older than the woman who had spoken first, but his expression was just as keen.

'Spes is our opportunity to start again,' he said. 'An opportunity that we have no choice but to take. We are all agreed on that. It is also an opportunity for us to show our alien neighbours that we are not some weak, pathetic race that they can dominate. Humans First believe . . .'

'Oh, shut up!' bellowed someone from the other side.

A faint titter rippled around the room.

'Everyone,' Ferona said, her voice echoing softly around the room. 'Let's hear what the man has to say.'

She quickly scanned the crowd, looking for others. There would be more than just the two of them. She spotted at least two more that she was sure of. Excellent. It had worked. Once she knew what she was looking for, they were easy to see. They thought they had bested her. They would soon find out that they were wrong.

'We do not want the Second Species on Spes,' the man said. 'They are a threat to all of us. And we will do whatever it takes to prevent them from joining us. They aren't human. They have no right to live among humans. They're dangerous. What happens when they decide to enslave us? We'll be living in dirty cities, forced to work for them while they live a life of luxury, and we'll have no bloody choice because we won't be able to fight back.'

The audience fell silent, and Ferona knew they were waiting for her to respond. 'Spes is for all of us,' she said again. *Go on*, she willed him. *Keep talking. Show the world your true colours.*

'Exactly,' the man responded. 'All of *us*. They are not us. Those people gave up the right to call themselves humans the day they agreed to have alien DNA injected into their cells.' His lip curled in disgust. 'You should be thrown out of office for what you've done.'

'Do you really think this is the time to start arguing about what makes us human? We are days away from a vote in the Galactic Senate that will change the very future of our species. We have ships to build. Fuel to source. The degree of organisation required to pull this off is on a scale never seen before. And we aren't there yet. There is still so much work to be done. And we cannot risk doing anything, *anything* which might give the Senate reason to vote no.'

She moved away from the lectern, walked in front of it. The heavy skirts of her dress swirled around her ankles as she moved, and she kicked at the suddenly annoying weight of it. The lights blazed down on her, and on their audience. She was hot and tired and she had been carrying the weight of idiots like this for too long.

'Let me make something very clear,' Ferona said. 'We are one small planet among many. We need the cooperation of our alien neighbours, now and in the future. The alternative does not bear thinking about. We must . . .'

'Screw the Senate!' shouted a voice from the audience. 'Why are we pandering to alien scum? We don't need their permission! If we want to cross their space, we can bloody well just cross it! We've got ships. Weapons. What are we waiting for?'

And the repercussions of such action would be felt long after they made it to Spes. Human history had made that perfectly clear, over and over again.

'We will not go to war with our neighbours.' Ferona aimed those words at every single person in the room. 'I will not risk the future of the human race with war.'

Because it would be a war that they could not possibly win. If war could get them to Spes, they would be fighting right now, and the Second Species programme would never have been created. As a senator, Ferona knew just how big the divide between humans and other races like the Sittan really was. Humans didn't have the ships, the weapons, the technology. They would be crushed.

'Our *neighbours* need to know that we won't be pushed around. That they don't control us.'

'This is not about control,' Ferona replied. She could feel her voice booming around the room, a little too high and a little too loud. 'This is about *cooperation*. It's about finding a way for us to co-exist.'

'Of course it's about control,' the man called out. 'We don't like the Second Species, we don't trust them and we don't want them. They should never have been created, and we'll do whatever it takes to stop you from creating more. That's why Humans

First destroyed the *A2* – because the Second Species are too dangerous to be allowed to live!'

'Humans First did not destroy the *A2*,' Ferona snapped at him. 'They can barely even wipe their own noses. The men on board escaped from their cages and the self-destruct activated, just as it was supposed to. Did you really think I would create creatures like that, *killing machines*, and not take steps to make sure the rest of us were safe?'

It was as if a bomb had been dropped. Later, she would replay that moment, those words, over and over in her mind and wonder just what had driven her to say them. Years spent measuring every word, completely in control of herself, destroyed in a second, all because of a spoilt young man in a cheap black suit.

But for now there was nothing she could do except scramble back to the lectern, jam her thumb against the button, and numbly watch as the doors rolled open and security agents swarmed in.

CHAPTER
20

15 cycles to ripening

> Vessel: Shi Fai transport vessel, name unknown
> Location: Shi Fai-controlled space
> Cargo: 84 units
> Crew: 2 workers. 13 drones
> Droids: N/A

The longer Eve spent on board the Shi Fai vessel, the harder it got to keep track of the days. But she persisted. It gave her a sense of meaning, of control, of reality. It made her feel that she hadn't completely surrendered to her fate. It had been a surprise to discover how badly she wanted to live.

But she'd survived in this body for a long, long time. She was no longer afraid of it and the pain and shock of the initial transformation had long since passed. Her green skin was no longer alien to her. If she was honest, she found it hard to remember ever being any different.

Each time the Shi Fai guard opened the wall of her pen and tossed in a packet of Silver Rice, she took the opportunity to study them. She assessed their bodies for potential weak spots and tried to learn their anatomy. They all wore translation devices and at first she'd tried to converse with them, but she'd soon realised it was pointless. They didn't want to talk to her. Nor had she managed to make any further contact with any of the other prisoners, though she could sometimes hear them quietly sobbing when the rest of the ship was quiet.

She hoped Alistair and the others were coming for her. She had to believe that they were coming for her. So she forced herself to eat the Silver Rice and she stopped struggling against the chains that bound her hands and feet. Closer examination had revealed that they were organic, some sort of vine that tightened if she moved too much, digging tiny barbs into her flesh. She suspected the barbs were coated with some sort of sedative, because the wounds made her drift.

And so it went. She ate, listened, waited, drifted.

Then on the fifth day, something changed.

She could sense activity outside her pen, which was odd, because by her reckoning it wasn't feeding time. Footsteps pounded and the entire ship seemed to vibrate with life and an energy that hadn't been there before.

The landing was smooth, almost like they were skimming across water. She felt the pull of planet-bound gravity. The air seemed to taste different. No more pleasant, but different. When the wall of her pen opened, she was ready.

'Up,' came the order. The Shi Fai who stood before her held a stunner, no doubt another present from Earth's generous government.

Slowly, carefully, Eve got to her feet. The chains uncoiled themselves from her body and she rubbed her wrists. Scar tissue had formed where they had cut her, and it was sore and rough to the touch.

She could sense the creature watching her. The feeling made her skin crawl. Her gaze fell on the stunner it held. Jinn had fought these creatures off. She'd injured one of them, Eve recalled. Cut off its hand.

Her gaze drifted back to its face.

As soon as the opportunity presented itself, she was going to take her own pound of flesh.

'Out,' it ordered her.

'Talkative, aren't we?' she said, as she approached the opening of the pen.

'You are to remain quiet,' it replied.

All around, she could see other pens opening, other women emerging. There were a couple of Bugs, and the Sittan female Eve had spoken to. There was even a Dome female, her long pale hair a matted mess.

What were the Shi Fai doing with these women? She could understand why they had taken her. She was Type Two, after all. But there was no reason for them to have taken unaltered women, and definitely not a Sittan.

'Where are you taking us?' she asked, as the guard who had opened her pen bound her hands together with what felt like thin leather string. A collar was tightened around her neck, and a lead attached to it. The guard tugged her forwards. She had no choice but to obey.

'You are being taken to the Dar'ish,' it said.

'Dar'ish?' The translation unit didn't seem to have a match for the word, and the guard either couldn't or wouldn't explain further.

They were marched in single file along the narrow ramp, then down onto the surface. There had to be hundreds of ships here, lined up in neat rows that fanned out from a central point, like spokes on a wheel. Most of the ships were much bigger than the one Eve had been brought in on, and hundreds of women were pouring out of them. The majority of them were green, like her. She searched for others who weren't, but there were too many and there was too much else for her to think about.

The ground beneath her feet was hard and dark, not rock, but some sort of close-packed dirt, and further out, beyond the ships, huge trees speared up into the sky. She had never seen anything like it. She stumbled as she stared up at them. It was hot and damp, and smelled earthy and pungent and good.

The guards led them along a straight path, each woman controlled by the collar around her neck. Eventually the path started to rise. With so much greenery, the atmosphere had to be oxygen-rich, and she'd take small blessings where she could find them. At least she wouldn't suffocate here.

Progress was slow. Her guard kept a constant pull on her collar and a constant pressure on her neck. She could see that a couple of the other women were fighting against their collars and as much as she wished they wouldn't, she couldn't blame them for it. Her grip on her own fear was tenuous. She knew they were fighting because their instincts had taken over and they didn't know what else to do.

The path became a bridge, crossing over a deep ravine. It was a straight drop down. Eve leaned over the edge to see just how far. Her handler pulled so hard on her leash that her throat felt like it was going to collapse under the pressure. She grabbed the leathery strap, tugged it back, desperately trying to loosen the collar before she choked. Her handler kept its grip, staring at her with those strange, glassy eyes.

Then one of the other women jumped. Eve saw only the flash of movement as the woman went over the side of the bridge. Her leash hung loose for a moment, then jerked tight. The handler on the other end hung onto the strap. It caught tight on the edge of the pathway. A knife was pulled, and the leash hanging over the edge of the pathway was cut. The other end whipped out of sight. There was the sound of breaking branches, then a sudden thud.

There was no scream.

The Shi Fai started to move, dragging them further along the path. Eve saw the glances the other women exchanged, and knew what they were thinking. She saw the looks directed at the edge of the path as they all wondered if they were brave enough to take that same step.

Eve already knew that she was not. If she was, she would have done it years ago. And that was why she kept walking. It was why she kept her head down but all her senses alert as they were led further along the walkway. At the end, it widened further, and she saw what the trees and vines had been hiding. Behind the wall of green was a building, strangely shaped, as if it was made from droplets of melted rock that had fallen on top of each other and been left to harden. But it wasn't rock, at least not any type she'd ever encountered. It was an ugly brownish yellow, slightly shiny, semi-opaque.

It had to be some sort of organic material, but she had no idea what sort, if it was plant or animal or some sort of by-product. Maybe it was neither. Maybe it was some sort of life form that humans didn't know about. There were definitely plenty of those on this planet, and she'd been on it for less than an hour.

At the entrance to the building, women were being funnelled inside. More Shi Fai armed with stunners lined the edge of the path, ensuring the women went where they were supposed to go. Any who were too slow were stunned and dragged inside.

Eve found herself being pushed towards the entrance, gathered up by the surge of other women. There was a moment of excitement when a couple of Shi Fai pushed their way through the crowd, but all they did was grab the Sittan female and pull her to the side. Then she was taken away and Eve quickly lost sight of her. More women pushed in behind her. She had to either move further inside the building or risk being trampled.

And then the entrance closed up behind them, trapping them. At first, the new recruits stood clumped together in the centre. All of them were silent, anxious, looking around at their new home.

'What in the void is this place?' a tall, skinny woman said, low enough for Eve to hear. 'I thought we were supposed to be coming here to work on the farms. That's what I was told when I signed up.'

'I don't know,' Eve said. 'I didn't sign up. I was snatched from the *Articus*.'

The woman looked her over. 'But you're Type Two. Didn't you come from the medical centre on the moon?'

'It's complicated,' Eve said. The ceiling curved high overhead, arching up into a central point that had to be a hundred metres above their heads. Pillars speared up to it. Their waxy feet spread in solid puddles on the floor. It was vast and bizarre and felt deeply unsafe. They were so exposed. There was nowhere to hide.

And as she looked at her surroundings, she wished she'd been the one who'd jumped.

CHAPTER
21

Bryant had been hoping to do a little better than a crash-landing in the jungle, but after so many weeks in space it was all he had left in him. They had left the *Mutant* in orbit around the planet and used the little transporter to make the final leg of the journey down to the surface.

'Damage report,' Alistair ordered the onboard computer.

'Hull integrity at forty-eight per cent. Drive function normal. Power supply at seventy-two per cent.'

'So I pranged the hull. It could be worse,' Bryant said defensively. He stretched out the stiffness in his shoulders, decided to wait a few minutes before he attempted walking. Over the past couple of days, concealing the extent of his pain had become Bryant's main focus and he didn't want Alistair to know how badly his legs were hurting.

Leaving the *Articus* and coming here had seemed like a good idea until he'd actually had to do it. Now he was beginning to have quite a few regrets, the least of which was leaving behind his padded couch and the comfort of knowing that he had an almost endless supply of Euphoria.

172

Alistair flicked through a couple of screens on his console and then rubbed his hands over his face. 'I can't say that was the most fun I've ever had.'

'Come on,' Bryant said, breathing carefully through a stab of pain in his guts. 'Seriously. It wasn't that bad.'

'You're a crap pilot.'

'Noted.' Bryant tugged off his smartware gloves and tossed them down on the console. 'You can fly us out of here when we leave.'

Alistair picked up the gloves and hooked them neatly onto the side of the pilot's chair. 'If we leave.'

Bryant couldn't bring himself to respond to that. 'What's the plan?'

'The plan was to get here,' Alistair said. 'We've done that. We have no plan for after that.'

'Well, that's unfortunate. What do we know about this swamp?'

'Not a lot,' Alistair replied. 'Humans haven't spent a lot of time here. In fact, humans have basically spent no time here. The Shi Fai haven't exactly invited us to visit.'

'But we know some stuff about them. They breathe oxygen, they prefer a wet environment. They're farmers. Their entire planet is a biofactory.' Bryant paused, trying to remember what he'd read about them at school. They'd been neither interesting nor relevant. He'd been more interested in the girl with the big tits who had sat two seats across from him. He couldn't for the life of him remember her name. It didn't seem important anymore, which was funny really, given how important she'd been at the time. But then things changed.

'They can't speak the Universal tongue,' Alistair said, 'because their physiology doesn't allow them to form the words. They show up in neutral space now and again, mostly trading exotic seeds in exchange for scrap metal, and they stink. They gave us Silver Rice and the plant which Euphoria is made from, among others. But they mainly trade with the Lodons.'

'I don't remember that from the learning programmes.'

'I wouldn't know,' Alistair said shortly. 'I didn't have access to the learning programmes. But they used to come to the *Europa* sometimes. Occasionally women used to disappear.' He turned to his console. His fingers flew over the controls as he pulled up information on the planet. 'Everyone thought the Shi Fai had taken them.'

'Those are just rumours,' Bryant said. 'There was never any real evidence. The government would have intervened if there were.'

'All that means is that they looked the other way,' Alistair said. 'They aren't turning women green and sending them here to talk. The modifications interfere with their body chemistry. It's not much of a stretch to figure that it was done to make the women immune to the Shi Fai.'

'Good,' Bryant said.

'You think what was done to Eve was a good thing?'

'If she's immune to them, that means she's still alive.' He pushed himself to his feet, gripping the arm of the chair for a moment. Then he leaned in over the console and programmed a scan of the local area. A ten-kilometre radius should do to start with.

The computer got to work, the screen flashing as it built him a map of their surroundings. A similar scan carried out on board the *Mutant* had been less helpful than either of them had cared to admit – there were so many life forms down here that it had been difficult to know where to begin. They had chosen an area that appeared to have several spots that contained less organic material, Alistair's reasoning being that these could be clearings for roads or ports.

Alistair transferred the map to his wrist comm. 'All right,' he said. 'Let's see what's outside.'

Bryant followed slowly. With each step that he took, the bones in his joints grated against each other. He'd been stuck in this decaying body for so long now that he felt like he should be used to it, but he wasn't. Probably because every morning, after he'd got over the surprise of finding himself still alive, he found himself in a body that wasn't quite the same one he'd gone to sleep in.

They walked down to the cargo bay, via the weapons lockup, where Bryant armed himself with two blasters and a knife. He ignored the stunners, but he slipped a sonic grenade into his pocket just in case. He didn't wait for Alistair to finish picking his weapons. He grabbed himself a regulator and hobbled to the rear of the loading bay. 'Computer, lower ramp.'

'Affirmative.'

Bryant slapped the regulator over his face, pressing the edges tight against his skin as he took his first look at an alien planet. The noise got to him first. High-pitched squeals and short stabbing howls. Low, rumbling sounds that stopped and started, overlaid with clicks and taps and chirrups. His heart was pounding fiercely, and there was a definite trembling in his hands. Something scuttled across the ground by his feet and darted up and over his boot, dozens of sharp little legs scratching at the leather. He yelled and jumped back, kicking it away. It flew into the bushes and landed with an unexpected thud. If he hadn't had agent training, if he didn't have that to fall back on, he'd have run screaming straight back into the transporter and refused to come out. 'I fucking *hate* insects.'

'When I was a kid, my bedroom was full of them,' Alistair said. He was still standing at the edge of the transporter. 'Living in the cracks in the walls. They'd come out at night and bite you.'

'Didn't you have exterminators in your city?'

'Exterminators cost money,' Alistair told him. 'Didn't have any.'

'You must have got basic living credits.'

'Yes,' Alistair said, as he stepped off the ramp and looked around. 'But our rent was eighty credits a week. There wasn't exactly a lot left over. The air is safe, by the way.'

Bryant peeled off the regulator. 'No one in the Domes gets

handouts,' he said. 'You want anything there, you work for it. Nothing to stop people in the Underworld Cities doing the same.'

'I was just a kid,' Alistair said. 'What sort of work should I have done? The kind those boys were doing before you found them?'

Bryant had a sudden flash of Davyd thirty years from now that nearly knocked him over. He blinked, and it was just Alistair again, the same annoying know-it-all Bryant had been dealing with for the past three days. 'Don't talk about those boys,' Bryant told him. 'Not now, not ever. Understand me?'

'All right,' Alistair said. 'I'm sorry. I didn't think.'

There was clear liquid falling from the sky. Bryant held out his hand, caught some in his palm. 'Looks like water.'

'It's rain,' Alistair said. 'It used to happen on Earth, before it got too cold.' He unclipped a portable water bag from his belt, opened it up and caught some of the rain inside it.

'Is it clean?'

Alistair checked the test strip on the side of the bag. 'By Earth standards, yes.'

Bryant lifted his hand to his mouth and licked it. It tasted all right. 'At least we won't die of thirst.'

'Thirst is the least of our problems,' Alistair replied. He pointed at the transporter. 'Look at the state of that.'

The wet ground sucked at Bryant's boots, making progress infuriatingly slow, but he could move fast enough to see the damage. A huge dent marked the side of the hull and there was visible cracking along one side of it.

'It's not my fault,' Bryant told him.

'I never said it was.'

'Look, it was a difficult landing.'

'I know.'

'You think you're better than me. Well, you're not. I'm sick.' Bryant coughed, spat. 'And if you'd taken better care of that green bitch, the Shi Fai wouldn't have been able to snatch her, and we wouldn't be here in the first place.' And he wouldn't have had to leave the boys, or the Euphoria.

Bryant suddenly found himself flat on his back with a blaster in his face.

'She wouldn't want me to,' Alistair told him. 'That's the only reason I'm not going to do it. But let me make one thing clear. If you ever, ever, call her that again, I will kill you. I won't hesitate. I'll just shoot you right in the head. Understand? Her name is Eve. Use it.' He stepped away, shoved the blaster back in its holster.

Awkwardly, painfully, Bryant got to his feet. Mud clung to his clothes. Sweat dripped from the end of his nose, his chin. For a long moment, he stared at Alistair, and Alistair stared back at him. Hate boiled in the air between them.

'I don't fucking like you,' Bryant told him.

'I don't like you either. But we don't know nearly enough about this place, and we're going to have to help each other out, because I don't think that the wildlife is going to be friendly.'

Bryant looked around them. They'd only been on this planet for a short space of time, and already he wanted to leave. 'If it slithers, crawls, or tries to eat me, I'm going to shoot it.'

Alistair smiled, a tight, painful little thing. 'I see you are not one of those people who believe that we should try to make friends with our alien neighbours.'

'I used to be an agent, remember?' Bryant said. 'The first thing they teach you in training is to shoot first and ask questions later.'

'Did they teach you how to find your way out of an alien swamp?'

'No,' Bryant said. He was beginning to think they hadn't taught him anything useful. He shielded his eyes and tipped his head back as a new sound caught his attention. A ship was flying low overhead, the engines making a heavy rumble that silenced the jungle. It was wide-bottomed with three pairs of stubby wings and made a dark shadow against the pale sky. Looked like the scan they'd done on the *Mutant* while still in orbit hadn't been that far out after all.

'I think our alien friends just showed us the way,' Alistair said. 'Come on.'

They started to walk. Soon, the soft ground gave way to knee-deep water. It pooled in troughs, each maybe five metres long and a metre wide. The strips of hard ground that separated them were too narrow to walk on. They had no choice but to go through the water.

There were things moving in it. Bryant opted not to look too closely at what they were. It was enough to know, when they broke the surface, that they were brown and glossy with no apparent head.

He lowered his blaster and fired several shots into the water. There was a crackle and a hiss, and whatever had been moving stopped. He felt a little better so he fired again, just to be on the safe side.

After an hour of wading through the water they finally reached the end of the troughs. Now they faced tall, wiry plants, row upon row of them. Alistair pulled his blade and began to cut through the stringy shoots that grew between the trunks of the plants and knotted them together in an impenetrable block. Hand-sized flowers in shades of blue and red and purple were dotted around the coronas of each plant.

Bryant followed him. Winged creatures buzzed against his face.

'There's too much bloody wildlife on this planet,' Bryant grumbled. 'And too much of it wants to eat me.' He swatted at more of the little fluttering insects but it only made them angry, and soon he had a line of stinging bites across the side of his face.

'I thought agents were supposed to be tough,' Alistair said as he slashed his way further forward.

Bryant blinked as perspiration dripped into his eyes. His tracking equipment indicated that there was something up ahead, but he had no idea what. 'I'm not an agent,' he said. 'Try to remember that. Don't make me come over there and smack you in the head.'

Neither of them spoke much after that. They were too busy

trying to force their way forward. Jagged branches tore at Bryant's jacket and dug into his skin. The welts burned and bled, and soon Bryant needed a hit. But he hadn't brought enough shots. He knew that now. The thought of running out frightened him so much that he didn't dare use one even though he wanted to.

Alistair glanced back at him, and Bryant could tell from the look on his face that the change was obvious. But the other man said nothing. Instead, he turned back to the gap he'd cut in the undergrowth and disappeared through it.

Just beyond the edge of the jungle was a low wall built out of a strange, waxy substance. Beyond it was what appeared to be an enormous field, stretching out as far as the eye could see. It was full of what he supposed were trees, planted in straight rows a couple of metres apart. The trunks were pale and lifeless. The bark was cracked. Branches speared up from each one, sometimes three, sometimes four, reaching up to the sky like arms, and from each branch hung a dried out pod the size of his head. A couple were open but whatever had been inside them had gone.

'What is this place?'

'I don't know,' Alistair said. 'They're farmers, so I suppose it's some sort of crop.'

'What sort of crop grows in pods this big?' Bryant asked, reaching up and poking one. 'I could wear it as a helmet.'

'I have absolutely no idea.' Alistair rubbed the surface of one that hadn't yet split. It coated his palm with a dusty purple substance, and he cleaned it off on his trouser leg. 'It's very strange. I heard stories back on the *Europa* that they grow their ships like fruit on trees, but I didn't believe it. Looking at this, though, anything seems possible.'

'Ships don't grow on trees. That's ridiculous.'

Alistair shrugged. 'Maybe. But at this point nothing would surprise me.'

'I suppose we could pull down one of the closed ones and take a look.'

'No,' Alistair told him. 'We're not doing that. It could be poisonous.'

'What are you, a coward?'

Bryant pulled out his blaster, took aim and shot down one of the closed pods. It hit the ground with a thump. The dry exterior cracked. He tucked the blaster away, then kicked the pod until it split open completely.

There was something inside it.

He crouched down and took a closer look. It wasn't a seed or a fruit, not of the kind he recognised, anyway, but some sort of creature. It was small and desiccated. He could make out bones, possibly a skull and legs. The skull had three eye sockets.

'What is it?' Alistair asked him.

'You don't want to know,' Bryant said. 'Nothing that we need to worry about, anyway.' He opened his pack, pulled out a water bag and drank from it. 'Let's keep moving.'

CHAPTER

22

18th day of the fifth turn

The Palace, Fire City, Sittan

It was two days since Dax had last seen the empress. He had been left alone, trapped inside his room, too afraid to leave despite the fact that he had seen no sign of the guards. He felt a little ashamed by it, but every time he got close to the open archways that led out of his room, anxiety would swamp him and he would retreat back inside.

He sat at the edge of the balcony, feet hanging over the edge, watching the city below. It was mid-afternoon and he could see the movement of the Sittan who lived there, striding along the streets, pushing floating carts, stopping to talk, to trade.

In comparison, he felt dreadfully alone.

He thought about going back to the arena. At least there, he would have the company of others, and he would be able to work off some of his unspent aggression. He was sure he could find his way there, if he tried. But if he did that she would be angry with him.

He didn't want to let her down. He was afraid to feel the heavy weight of her disappointment. So he stayed where he was, waiting, hoping for the empress to return. There were three ruby filled timers on the wall. He used them to track the passing of the hours.

She swept into the room when the second one was almost empty.

Dax scrambled to his feet. He smoothed down his hair, close-cropped as it was, then stood with his hands loose at his sides, uncertain what to do next. He dropped his gaze. He didn't speak, in case that was wrong and made her leave.

'Dax,' she said. 'Whatever are you doing over there?'

She sashayed over to where he stood. He could barely breathe, wanting so badly for her to stay. 'Nothing,' he said. 'I was just . . . where have you been?'

Her yellow eyes flashed, and he immediately regretted his words. His face flushed and he dropped his gaze to the ground once again.

'Oh,' she crooned. 'Did you miss me? Is that it?'

Dax nodded.

'Poor Dax,' the empress said. She sounded almost amused. She turned away from him, long robes sweeping out behind her, and made her way over to the day bed in the corner. She stretched out on it.

Dax remained where he was, nervous and uncertain.

With a ring of the bell at the side of the bed, she summoned slaves and guards, and suddenly the room was flooded with people. All of them ignored Dax. His stomach rumbled at the sight of the food.

He still didn't move. He didn't dare.

Finally, the slaves retired to a discreet distance, and the guards took their places at the edge of the room. The empress beckoned him forward. He went without hesitation. 'Sit,' she ordered him, and he did that, too, without so much as a word. He stole glances at the platters of fruit, smoked meats, roasted insects. But he didn't reach for any of it.

The empress watched him as she deftly sliced open a Kerask and sucked on the juice. She licked her lips. They were stained a dark violet today. Silver rings decorated her ears and her nose, and swirling patterns had been painted across her face. She looked wild and alien. He felt pale and ugly in comparison, and sank a little lower, wrapping his arms around himself to hide the bulk of his body.

Finally, she tossed the fruit aside. A slave came forward and cleaned her hands before slipping away just as quietly. Then she linked her jewelled fingers together and looked down at him. 'Are you hungry?'

She must have known that he was. He hadn't eaten in two days. 'Yes.'

'Oh! Why didn't you say? You must eat. Please. Help yourself.'

He tried not to rush, but it was difficult. He swallowed the pieces of smoked meat, barely chewing or tasting them. He could feel her watching him the entire time. Desperate not to appear rough and uncivilised, he stopped when he was still hungry and stiffly moved away from the table. He wanted to ask her where she had been, why she had left him alone for so long. He didn't dare.

The empress stretched her arms over her head. She yawned. Then she got to her feet. 'It's a shame I can't stay longer,' she said. 'But I'm afraid that I have things to do.'

'I could help you,' Dax told her. 'Let me come with you. I can ...'

He was forced to take a step back as Grenla and another of the more senior guards came forward. They weren't carrying their spears. Their uniforms were gone, replaced by close-fitting tunics, still in that same shade of scarlet. Their upper arms were decorated with twisting spirals of the strange black substance that Dax had seen in the empress's quarters. It flexed and shimmered as he looked at it.

The empress got to her feet and stood patiently as the two guards undressed her. Dax forced himself to avert his eyes. His heart was pounding fiercely as his awareness of her grew. The guards washed and oiled her body, hands rubbing over flesh.

The empress made little sounds of pleasure. 'I'm afraid that's not possible,' she said. 'You will have to stay here.'

Robes were fastened around her. They were different from the ones she usually wore, still in her favourite shade of black, but decorated with intricate scarlet embroidery. A belt was wrapped around her waist and a heavy blade slung through it. Another guard came over with a large oval tray. On it sat numerous pieces of jewellery, and, one by one, they were given to the empress. Rings for hands and feet. Cuffs for wrists and ankles. Chains that looped around her face and head. When it was done, she looked breathtaking.

'Why?' Who was she dressing that way for? Was it a male? Chal Gri, perhaps?

'Today is the Ba-Rat. Today, the strongest of our young females will break into the palace, and they will challenge me. It is something that happens every fifteen turns. You need not concern yourself with it.'

'When you say they will challenge you, do you mean they will try to fight you?'

'What else would they do?' She moved closer to him, smiling a little, and traced a claw gently down the side of his face. 'We are a violent race, Dax. This is how we settle things. And surely you did not believe that our males are the only ones capable of fighting. We females are just as strong, just as skilled. If anything, we enjoy it more. They will come, they will try to take the Virena from me, and they will fail. This is how it has been for the past one hundred rounds, and how it will continue to be. I will not give up my crown easily.'

'But you said the females are younger.'

'Yes.'

'Then they will be quicker. Stronger.'

'No. The young know nothing. They have not had time to fully develop their bodies or their skills. It is their main weakness. But it does not stop them from trying, just as I did when I killed Empress Mie. Only the strongest female can be empress. Mie was old and weak. She tried to fight me. I cut her down.' One of the guards moved in with a large silvered mirror. The empress took a moment to admire her reflection.

Dax was afraid. If the empress had earned her position in the palace by killing her predecessor, then that meant that she, too, could be killed. A new empress might not want him. He might be returned to the arena, a place he was suddenly sure that he did not want to go. He had food here, a comfortable bed. Although the cravings for violence were still there, the empress had made sure they were sated. She brought him males to fight, trapping them in the courtyard in the centre of the palace and letting Dax do what he would with them. He didn't want to go back to his cage.

'I will fight them for you,' he told her. 'Let me do it.'

The empress's eyes widened in delight. 'You would defend me?'

'Of course.' Even as he said the words, he heard the voice inside his head. *No.* He shook it off.

'There will be no need,' the empress told him. She held up a hand. The cuff around her wrist shimmered, then swam up to pool in her palm. 'I am neither old nor weak. None of them will be able to defeat me. Though I do so enjoy it when they try.' Then she flicked her gaze back to him. 'Stay here. Eat. Swim. Relax. And later, I will show you just how powerful an empress can be.'

CHAPTER

23

The Ba-Rat was to be held later that day, when the temperature had dropped a little, so they remained in the cool comfort of the house. Li and Merion stretched out in the chilled waters of the bathing pool. Jinn left them to it. She was too tense to relax, and every time she went anywhere near Li, Merion would scowl and show his teeth.

She wasn't afraid of him particularly, but she couldn't see that there was anything to gain by rising to the challenge he was so desperately trying to present to her. She wasn't interested in Li, and Li was obviously interested in Merion. Only Merion seemed to doubt that.

She found Ritte in another part of the house, in a surprisingly large room filled with endless piles of stiff yellow paper. 'Can I come in?'

'Of course,' Ritte said. 'Come. Sit.' She picked up the sheet she'd been looking at and tucked it back on a shelf.

The smell of dust and sand was heavy in the air, and the few lines of light that filtered in through the cracks in the ceiling provided just enough illumination to view the papers. They were not blank as she had first assumed, but had an intricate pattern pressed into the surface. 'What is all this?' Jinn asked.

'My library,' Ritte said. 'A way to preserve knowledge. Memories can be stored in the Virena but that allows the empress to access them, and some things are best kept private.'

'She can read your minds?'

'No,' Ritte said. 'Only our memories. Which means that things can all too easily be wiped from history. This is my way of ensuring that doesn't happen. Now. The Ba-Rat.' She settled herself a little more comfortably and motioned for Jinn to take a seat on a soft cushion opposite.

'Every year, the strongest of our daughters break into the palace and seek out the empress. One of them will challenge her. If they succeed, and the empress is killed, that female takes her place, and the others form her guard. I was a guard myself, before Merion.'

'You worked inside the palace?'

Ritte nodded. 'I can tell you how it was when I was last there. But things may have changed since then. And if you find him, she will not give him up willingly, this man you seek.'

'If I know Dax, she won't have a choice,' Jinn said.

'I saw the human fight in the arena,' Merion said. He was standing in the doorway, still wet from the bath. 'He was not as good as Jozeph.'

'No one is as good as Jozeph.' Ritte laughed. 'Why do you think I paid him so much?'

'You saw him?' Jinn got to her feet. 'Was he all right?'

'He won his fight,' Merion replied.

Jinn realised that her heart was racing and made herself sit back down. 'Good,' she said. She didn't press him for more. She didn't ask if Dax had still seemed human. That was too much, too frightening.

'Merion will take you to the palace,' Ritte said. 'You will leave at suns down. You will have to go alone. Jozeph cannot be seen out on the street. It is too dangerous.' She led Jinn into another room on the other side of the house. 'Here,' she said, lifting something from a large trunk on the floor. 'This is for you.'

It turned out to be a set of soft Sittan clothes. They were deep crimson-red and covered Jinn completely, hiding her face and her hair with an anonymous mask. She willed out her blades and struck out with them, testing the leather. It moved with her like a second skin. Ritte moved into her line of sight, and for the next minute or so the two of them sparred, trading punches and kicks.

'You fight well,' Ritte said. 'For a human.'

'I'm not human,' Jinn told her. 'I'm Second Species.'

By the time they left, the temperature had dropped considerably, and the streets were crowded. Jinn kept her head down, kept moving, certain that she would be recognised as non-Sittan. Something in the way she moved, the way she smelled, would give her away, she was sure of it.

But although she drew the odd glance, no one tried to stop her.

She walked a little faster. Someone bumped into her and snarled something in Sittan.

Merion snarled something back, then grabbed hold of Jinn's arm. 'Be careful!' he berated her.

'I'm doing my best!'

'Do better. If I get caught here with you . . .'

'You won't.'

She couldn't blame him for being afraid. He had good reason to be. The palace was only a hundred or so metres ahead of them now, and the crowd was thick. There was plenty of pushing and shoving and aggression in every fierce word. From what Jinn could see, females outnumbered the males three to one. A significant minority were dressed the same as her, in head-to-foot red with their faces covered.

At the end of the street, the crowd spilled out along the high wall that circled the edge of the palace grounds. Some climbed up onto the boulders that lay along the side of the road and sat at the top, presumably to get a better view. All the red-suited females moved forward, away from the crowd. Merion fell back and disappeared.

Jinn was on her own.

But Dax was behind that wall, somewhere inside the huge building that speared up into the sky, and if she wanted to find him that was where she had to go.

The females had gathered together in a group in front of gates that were too high to be easily climbed and too big to be easily opened, though that didn't stop them from trying. Jinn approached the group as slowly as she dared, watching as one of the females had a go at climbing those gates. At first, it looked as though she might make it over, but about a metre from the top she suddenly stopped. Her body went rigid. A sound escaped her, a furious howl, and then she dropped from the gate, hitting the ground with a bang. She didn't move.

The other red-dressed females stepped away from her and looked at each other. They put a little more distance between themselves and the gate.

Jinn remained where she was, hovering at the back of the group. Another female braved the wall, and another had a second go at the gate. Neither of them made it over. It was possible to climb almost to the top, but then the material would crumble, and what had been a solid hand or foothold would suddenly become nothing more than dust.

If the Sittan females couldn't make it, what hope did she have?

Three more tried and failed.

Another female walked up to the gate. She didn't try to climb it. Instead, she stretched out a clawed hand and pressed it against the surface of the gate. At first, nothing seemed to happen. The excitement level of the crowd started to level out.

Then the female's arm began to turn black.

It spread across the red. The female's arm began to sink

through the gate. It wasn't made of obsidian at all, Jinn realised. The entire thing was made from the Virena. And by the looks of it, it liked this female. It washed over her in a wave, and when the surface of the gate settled she was gone.

Two more females were able to pass through. Another pressed her hand against the surface only to fall back shrieking. The rejected females were hauled away by people in the crowd. A chant rose up, a song of Sittan words that all of them seemed to know. Soon voices swelled up into the air, making the hair on the back of Jinn's neck stand on end. Ritte had told her that only at this time could the empress be challenged, and also that many on Sittan wanted to see the end of their current ruler. No wonder excitement prickled through the crowd. Another female made her way through, and another, and the crowd began to buzz.

Jinn was shoved forward, only catching her balance at the last moment. She could sense the Virena pulsing inside the gate. The piece on the transporter had been attracted to her. So had Ritte's amulet, and Ritte had been positive that Jinn would be able to pass through the gate. Jinn flexed her fingers, feeling the heat of the Tellurium in her hands. She could hear the Virena singing to her, just as it had on board the yacht.

She took a step closer. And another. The Virena reached for her.

She closed her eyes and leaned against the gate. The Virena stroked her as she moved through, and she fell out of the other side. Her knees hit the paved surface of a huge courtyard. Dark rubies set into the ground shimmered in the light from a fire contained within a vast crucible that sat in the very centre of the space. Large reptiles stalked around it, forked tongues tasting the air. They were at least three metres long, with thick, heavy bodies and ridged skin that glowed violet. They ignored her, too busy feasting on what remained of one of the females who had come through the gate earlier.

Jinn scrambled to her feet and willed out her blades. Quickly, she sighted the remaining females, easily spotted in their red clothes. She jumped over one of the reptiles, dodged another. The entrance to the palace lay ahead, at the end of a wide, beckoning bridge.

One of the other females finished with her lizard and slotted her blades back into the holder on her back. She motioned to Jinn, and to the other remaining females. The others moved towards her, and Jinn quickly realised that she would have to do the same. She followed the others, copied their movements.

A quick conversation in Sittan that she couldn't understand and they were off, running together along the length of the bridge. One of the females fell out of sight right in front of Jinn. She leapt over the hole that had appeared in the surface of the bridge and kept on running. First flesh-eating reptiles and now booby traps. At the entrance, they huddled again for another short conversation. One of the females had clearly taken charge, and Jinn could only assume that she would be the one to try and kill the empress.

Well, that was fine by her. All she cared about was getting inside the building. When they moved, she moved with them, keeping her hands by her sides and her blades ready. They set a fast pace but Jinn was ready for it.

The lower sections of the palace passed her by in a blur. They lost two more, one to a burst of some sort of liquid from the wall just inside the entrance and the other to one of the other females. An argument broke out as they took a moment to catch their breath hiding in the shadows of a vast hall on the ground floor, and the taller of the two females cut down the smaller.

Jinn held her ground and her nerve. She had to somehow slip away from the group. This was not the time to let herself feel any emotion, let alone risk it showing. The palace was just as dark and terrifying on the inside as it had been on the outside. She stuck with them as they negotiated their way up to the next level. They moved with speed and stealth. Two more traps were avoided and only one more female was lost.

The further they ventured into the palace, the more Jinn

began to understand what this really was. It wasn't a game. This was real. These females were here for one reason and one reason only, and the empress, holed up in this building somewhere, would defend herself to the last. She couldn't even begin to imagine what that female would do to a human woman. If she was caught . . .

She wouldn't get caught. It was not an option.

The group continued their march. The lead female held out her hands, one at each side of her body, and, with a flick of her wrists, black droplets began to rise from the floor and pool in her hands. Jinn watched the flow of shimmering liquid with a sense of fear and wonder. She'd never seen anything like it, had never imagined even for a moment that something like that could be real. It was as close to magic as she'd ever seen.

Looking right and left, she slowed her pace a little, dropping to the back of the group in the hope that she could slip away into the shadows without being noticed.

But it was not to be.

Because behind them, forming a dense line, were the palace guards.

There were so many. Far more than the small group that had made it into the palace. They, too, were all dressed in red, but their clothing was heavier and more ornate, decorated with dark studs in swirling patterns. Cloaks fell from shoulder to hip, and blades hung from hip to ankle. It made the females that surrounded Jinn suddenly seem small and out of place, and she supposed that was the point.

Her small group switched position. Suddenly, instead of moving forward, they were back to back, their blades drawn. The guards slowly, confidently formed a ring around them.

Jinn willed out her blades as all the others unsheathed their own weapons. Bloody supernova, why hadn't she played dead down on one of the lower floors? Because she'd been afraid one of the others would notice she was only playing, that was why. But she hadn't been nearly afraid enough.

The air was thick with tension. She saw one of the guards lick her lips and smile. Spikes shot out across her head and in a sharp line across each cheek. She yelled something, and all the other guards began to bang the tips of their swords against the hard floor, ringing out a heavy beat that matched Jinn's pulse.

One of the females from Jinn's group rushed out of her place, charging towards the guards. She took two of them on and cut them both down, whirling around, her blades moving so fast through the air that Jinn could barely see them. She challenged a third, and the challenge was accepted. Jinn quickly realised that the guards would not all attack at once. There were rules to this, after all. The invaders were at least being given a fair chance.

The guard cut down the female with a rapid swing of her sword.

And then the next female moved forward. She, too, challenged a guard. But this female was stronger and more skilled, and the two of them fought long and hard, blades smashing together, feet fighting for a grip on the polished floor. At first it looked like the guard was going to win, but the female was too desperate to let that happen. The moment of death was sudden and it was quick.

The victorious female stepped back, her arms trembling with exhaustion. Her chest rose and fell as she pulled in air and let it out, and still the guards kept up their constant drumming. Sweat rolled down Jinn's back as she looked around her, trying to find a way out, knowing there wasn't one. All she could do was survive this minute by minute, and hope that a chance would present itself. She couldn't even think about Dax right now.

Another guard stepped forward and the female fought hard, but it wasn't enough. It was never going to be enough. Jinn knew that even before the killing blow landed. The female fell slowly, her body crumpling to the floor, her death less brutal but no less final than the one that had ended the first challenger.

The group moved a little closer, the loss of those two making

Jinn feel even more vulnerable. She felt an odd sense of camaraderie with the others, and almost considered challenging one of the guards herself. But she was saved from what would undoubtedly have been an utterly stupid move on her part by the arrival of someone new.

She wore white, draped elegantly around her lithe body. Heavy jewellery decorated her hands, her wrists, her neck. The guards all dropped to their knees, the pace of the drumming picking up until it was a constant thundering.

And the female who had led them into this place, the one who had given the orders to the others, pulled off her mask and stepped forward. She pulled the blades from her back and dropped them to the floor before kicking them away.

The new female smiled, a wicked, chilling thing. She held up a hand. Black liquid spilled from the ceiling and fell into her hand. It swirled and danced around her, snapping into a series of different shapes, all of which looked potentially lethal.

Jinn caught her breath as she realised that this must be the empress.

Which meant that this would be the final fight.

She felt the empress's gaze touch her, and found herself unable to look away, staring into hard yellow eyes. She felt sure that the empress could see through her disguise and sense the human beneath. But the empress moved on. She spoke to the others, more words in Sittan that Jinn could not interpret, though the very sound of them sent a shiver down her spine.

When Ritte had talked about the empress, she had given Jinn the impression that this was an evil, dangerous female who needed to be removed from power as quickly as possible. She hadn't said anything about how this female had gained power in the first place. But Jinn could see it now. The empress was magnificent. Her body was tough, her face angular. Spikes rushed out across her head in an elaborate pattern, each one tinted a delicate lavender blue. The empress wasn't like the other females. There was something about her, an aura of power that came not from her size, but from her sheer presence.

She was beautiful, something Jinn had not expected. It quickly became apparent that she was also a highly skilled fighter. No one breathed. No one moved. Everything was balanced as if on a knife edge. The empress had astonishing control of the Virena. It flowed around her like air, creating a shield, a blade, a spear at will, but the challenger was young and she was fast and she wanted the victory. She wanted it so badly that Jinn could almost smell her desire, mixed with the pungent scent of Sittan blood and the perfumed air of the palace itself. The very walls seemed to move closer as the two females fought on, crashing into the guards, into each other. There was plenty of blood flowing thick and dark across the floor.

But far too much of it belonged to the challenger. Although the empress's white clothes were no longer pristine, her movements hadn't changed. The younger female had visibly slowed. Pieces of the Virena were falling away from her, no longer under her control, and with the loss of each one the empress struck out at her a little harder.

As the final piece of Virena fell away, the empress took a bold step forward, calling all those loose pieces into her possession. They built into a swirling black cloud that filled the space between the two females. The challenger fell to her knees.

An unexpected sorrow filled Jinn as that dark cloud surrounded the fallen female. It wrapped around her, and with one final, desperate cry, she gave up the fight. Her limp body was lifted high above all their heads, and it hung there, broken and lifeless.

The guards moved. The other females surrounding Jinn moved, too. One by one, they pulled off their masks and moved to kneel in front of the empress, heads bowed, blades tossed aside.

If Jinn was to get out of here, it was going to have to be now.

Seeing her chance, Jinn mixed herself in with the crowd, moving slowly back until she was pressed up against the wall.

There was a corridor to her left. She took one more look at the crowd, held her breath, and darted silently around the corner and started to run.

But she didn't get far.

Because she ran straight into the man she had come there to find.

CHAPTER
24

14 cycles to ripening

Somewhere in the Shinan Region, Faidal

Bryant was hot. He was also tired and slightly hysterical. If only they had a skimmer, something that would let them see the landscape from above the cover of trees. Why hadn't these creatures got ground-level transport? They'd invented space travel, so they weren't completely stupid. Surely they should have some sort of infrastructure. Transport. Houses. Something other than jungle and little flying buggers that bit.

For the next five steps, he told himself he could manage. For some reason, the thought of shooting up in front of Alistair made him uncomfortable. But after ten steps, it seemed the lesser of two evils so he pulled his pack open, found his drug gun and injected himself into the forearm, straight through the fabric. He tossed the spent gun into the undergrowth.

Alistair went to retrieve it.

'Leave it,' Bryant ordered him.

'No.'

Bryant shook his head in disbelief. 'Whatever,' he muttered to himself. The Euphoria acted quickly. The pain became a background hum. They pushed on for what felt like hours, though according to his wrist comm. it was little more than one. Sweat poured out of him until his jacket stuck to his back and his head was spinning with dehydration.

With every step, he hated Alistair more. Self-righteous, pathetic little twit. Bryant was so busy wallowing in his own self-pity that he didn't notice the danger that lay ahead until Alistair let out a yell and disappeared.

Bryant stopped. 'Alistair?'

No response.

He picked his way forward. It had been impossible to see from where they were, but about ten metres ahead there was a sudden steep drop. At the bottom of it was a pool of dirty water. It was impossible to tell the depth but it reflected the light well enough to suggest that it was a lot more than a puddle. Long green pipes ran down into it, protruding from the ground maybe half a metre below where he stood. It looked like some sort of irrigation system.

When Alistair popped up in the centre of the pool, spluttering and coughing, Bryant felt a bit disappointed. *Oh well*, he thought to himself. *There's still time.*

He carefully surveyed the clearing. There was no easy way down. In the end, he had no choice but to climb. He took his time about it, too, though he jumped the last metre. He sauntered around the edge of the pool, crouched down and held out a hand which Alistair took. Bryant heaved him out of the water.

The Underworlder stood there, dripping wet and filthy. 'Thanks,' he said. He rubbed his hands through his hair, flicking muck everywhere.

Bryant took a step back. 'I hope you've got a strong immune system.'

'So do I,' Alistair said, his hands going to his belt. He checked his weapons. Both of them refused to charge. He shook them, tried again, opened up the casings. Thick, sludgy water fell out.

'They're fucked,' Bryant told him.

'I can see that,' Alistair said. Bryant saw the man's gaze fall on his own weapons, both safely holstered on his belt. 'Can I . . . ?'

'No.' Something had caught his attention. On the other side of the pool, maybe fifteen metres away, a creature was approaching. He felt Alistair grab at his arm as the other man noticed it, and shook him off.

They both kept very still.

At least, Alistair did.

Bryant tried, but he quickly got bored of it. Keeping his eyes on the Shi Fai, he moved to the edge of the pool and climbed out. The creature jerked round. It had noticed them.

He ran straight at it before it could get away and tackled it to the ground. They rolled together for a moment until finally Bryant got the upper hand, mostly by poking the alien in the eyes. It tried to scramble away from him but Alistair was there, blocking its path. It twisted its head, staring from one to the other, and started to make a horrible squealing sound.

Bryant had never been this close to one before, and its anatomy was fascinating in a repulsive sort of way. Its skin was almost translucent with purple veins tracking underneath. It had three eyes arranged in a triangle in the middle of its face. Its mouth was circular, and he couldn't see any teeth, but four or five tentacles protruded out of it like dead white fingers.

The squealing got even louder. 'I can't understand a word you're saying!' Bryant yelled at it.

'I can,' Alistair said. He tapped the side of his neck. 'Universal translator. Had it fitted on the *Europa*.'

'What's it saying?'

'I can't make out all of it. It's frightened.'

'Can you talk to it?'

'No,' Alistair said. 'Not unless it has a chip, which seems unlikely. I don't think it's ever seen humans before.'

Bryant considered things for a moment. 'Is your comm. still working?' High-end comms were built to withstand almost anything, including mud, unlike blasters which apparently fell apart at the first sign of trouble.

Alistair checked it. 'Seems so.'

'Have you got a picture of Eve?'

'Yes.'

'Show it to this thing.'

Alistair knelt down awkwardly next to the Shi Fai. His fingers flicked over the touchscreen of his wrist comm., and then he unfastened it and dangled it in front of the creature's face. It flapped its arms around and squealed.

'What is it saying?'

'I believe it's the alien equivalent of fuck you.'

Reaching down, Bryant grabbed Alistair's comm. He shoved it right in the face of the terrified alien. 'Where is she?' he yelled.

The alien stopped squealing. It sucked in its tentacles, its entire face seeming to fold in on itself, and Bryant surrendered what little hold he had on his self-control. He kicked it. It let out a sound akin to a sob, but that only pissed him off more. They had been on this hideous planet for too long already, and all he had to show for it was a headache.

'Don't,' Alistair said to him, his voice heavy. He grabbed at Bryant, pushed him away from the creature. 'Leave it alone. It's more frightened of us than we are of it.' He moved back a little. The alien got to its feet and ran, heading back towards the little houses.

'What did you do that for?'

'Because we weren't going to get any more information from it and I didn't see any reason to hurt it. It was frightened of us, Bryant.'

'I don't care.'

'Well, I do.' Keeping his hand firm on Bryant's chest, Alistair gestured to a gap between the trees. 'Anyway. Before you so kindly kicked it in the ribs, it said we need to go that way. Ride the Chelnor.'

'What the fuck is a Chelnor?'

'I don't know,' Alistair told him. 'I guess we go that way, and we find out.' He took his comm. from Bryant and fastened it back round his wrist.

The pool was situated in the middle of a clearing and, as Bryant walked away from it, he saw shapes in the vegetation, low domes made from twisted, knotted leaves. After he'd spotted the first one, he started to see them all over.

There was movement to his left and to his right. Alistair grabbed him by the sleeve, dragged him off the path and into the bushes, keeping them both in a crouched position. The Shi Fai were on the move. Feet rushed past their hiding place, white and fleshy and oddly round, with thick, stone-like nails all around the edge. Bryant moved a little deeper into the undergrowth. They were heading in the direction of the pool. Presumably the one that Alistair had let go had gone straight to tell the others.

Blaster in hand, Bryant waited until the last pair of feet had passed them, counted to ten, shook off Alistair's grip and made a run for it. He kept low and moved close to the nearest of the domes, which he quickly realised were lumpy little houses.

Something blocked the path up ahead, something tall and spindly and dark. At first Bryant thought it was the trunk of an oddly shaped tree but then it moved. He looked up.

It was some sort of enormous insectoid creature with six angled, rigid, hair-lined legs. The body consisted of three separate segments with a saddle fastened around the central one. It reminded him of the ants that were used to clean the hydroponics gardens back in the Domes, but he'd never seen an ant this big.

If the Shi Fai used these creatures to get around, then so could he. He took a deep breath and sprinted between its back legs, grabbing at the long hairs that covered them.

It was dry and oddly cold against his palm as he swung himself up and started to climb, hand over hand, foot over foot. Damn thing had to be five metres tall. He reached the body, pulled himself into the saddle.

It lurched unsteadily on its spindly legs. Bryant kicked it and smacked it with his hand, but it did nothing. He didn't know how to ride the giant ant, how to persuade it to move, or even where he wanted it to go. He was used to spaceships and technology.

He didn't know what in the void to do with this. He kicked at it, smacked its hard back with his hand, and whacked it with the butt of his blaster. Bloody thing didn't shift, and a group of Shi Fai were heading in his direction now. Time to move. He punched the ant again. 'Come on!' There had to be some way to make it move. The saddle, which was made from some sort of squishy woven material, extended forward towards the neck of the creature. Bryant hadn't noticed at first, but there were splotches of colour on it, shimmering occasionally as the light caught them. He rubbed at one with his hand. The ant started to move. Bryant rubbed it harder and the ant picked up speed. He made a grab for the handle between his knees as the motion almost sent him sideways.

Dammit, he'd forgotten about Alistair. 'Alistair!' he yelled. 'Alistair!'

There was no reply. Oh well. There was nothing he could do about it now. It wasn't like Alistair had been of much use anyway. Clinging on with one hand, he actively started to poke at the patches of colour.

'Bryant,' came a voice from the rear. Bryant jerked round to see Alistair pulling himself up onto the ant's back. His face was flushed, and there was a cut on the side of his cheek. He half fell, half collapsed onto the back of the ant.

'Oh,' said Bryant. 'There you are. I thought you might be dead.'

Hands planted firmly on the ant's back, Alistair edged forward a little at a time until he was seated just behind Bryant. 'You really are a bastard,' he said. 'You were all set to leave me behind.'

'No I wasn't,' Bryant replied, though he knew full well that he was. 'I haven't got time to wait around for you. You already messed up once. I can't rescue you every time you get yourself in trouble.'

He almost lost his grip on the ant when Alistair punched him. It wasn't particularly hard or particularly well directed but it still hurt. 'Next time, I'll bloody well leave you behind,' Alistair told him.

'I didn't leave you behind,' Bryant protested. 'I just . . .'

The ant chose that moment to lurch hard to the left, and he stopped trying to talk and instead focused on not falling off. It was stamping through the village at a considerable pace now. A few Shi Fai were still chasing it, but most of them had given up.

'You left me behind,' Alistair said. 'I get that you're a self-absorbed prick, but that's not how this works, Bryant.'

'It works how I say it works.'

This time, there was a pause before Alistair replied. 'What is it with you Dome brats? Why can't you understand?'

'Understand what?'

'You can't go around only thinking about yourself.'

'It's how it works for me,' Bryant told him. He had the rhythm of the ant now and found he could easily stay on if he moved with the sway of its big, hard body. Wasn't the most comfortable experience he'd ever had, but it beat walking.

'So I see,' Alistair replied. 'And I can see that's working out really well for you.'

'It's got me this far.'

'And you're a mess.'

'I'm *dying*,' Bryant told him. 'I'm not taking Euphoria for fun. This isn't entertainment. I'm taking it because I can't put one foot in front of the other without it. Do you have any idea what it's like to be in that much pain? *Do you?*'

'No,' Alistair said finally, and turned away. 'But it's not an excuse. It doesn't mean you're not responsible for your screw-ups.'

'At least my screw-ups can be fixed,' Bryant muttered to himself.

'Can they?' Alistair asked him.

'Why else do you think I'm here?'

'I don't know,' Alistair said. 'It's not for Eve, I know that much.'

'Of course it's for her!'

'No, it's not. You don't care what she's going through, what they're doing to her. This planet, these creatures ... human women don't belong here. What the government is doing, it's wrong.'

'The women volunteer.'

'Because they don't know what they're getting themselves into.'

'You expect me to feel sorry for them?'

'I expect you to feel something!'

'I'll tell you how I feel,' Bryant said, as the ant lifted its head, mandibles clicking. 'I feel bloody well pissed off. She *poisoned* me.'

'You deserved it,' Alistair told him. 'And she suffered for it. She thought she hid it, how she was feeling, but she couldn't, not from me. It nearly destroyed her. Do you know, you were the only person she'd touched since she'd been changed?'

'I'd feel bad for her,' Bryant said, 'but I'm a little busy right now. I'm stuck on top of a fucking giant ant heading fuck only knows where with a sanctimonious bore who doesn't know one end of a blaster from the other.'

Alistair didn't bother to reply. The ant, or Chelnor, or whatever it was, continued to walk. For the next few hours, they clung on in silence as it swayed its way through the jungle, and as the last hit of Euphoria started to wear off Bryant could feel panic rising.

He clung to the back of the ant as it carried him forwards, drifting in and out of consciousness as the pain exploded inside him and became a constant burning roar. Eventually, the ant stopped moving. Bryant opened his eyes to find himself at the edge of another settlement. The buildings here were fresh waxy yellow structures that gleamed with moisture. His ant had stopped next to one of them, though he didn't understand why until he saw it drop its head into a trough and realised that it had stopped to feed. Shi Fai wandered around the edge of the buildings, moving in orderly lines. They looked like clones, all identical, all walking in unison. It was creepy.

And then he saw the women. Collars made of some sort of dark, twisted material circled their necks, and they were being dragged along by the rope attached to those collars. All of them were silent, though he could see that one of them was weeping. Her hands were bound behind her back, giving her no way to protect herself when she stumbled and fell face first into the mud.

The Shi Fai holding her leash grabbed her by the hair and dragged her to her feet.

'This is it,' Alistair muttered. 'This is where they're keeping them.'

A surge of hope washed through Bryant. He rubbed a hand over his face, tried to stay calm, and realised that he was crying out with each exhalation of breath, the muscles in his chest hurting so much that he could barely get oxygen. Leaning to the side, Bryant let go of the Chelnor and let himself fall. He hit the ground with a thud.

He lay in a stinking heap of ant dung, closed his eyes and started to laugh.

CHAPTER
25

18th day of the fifth turn
The Palace, Fire City, Sittan

Dax stared into the face of the first human female he had seen in months. She was pale-haired and sharp-featured, with unnaturally bright blue eyes, and she was looking at him in a way that he didn't like at all.

'Who are you?' he snarled at her. 'What are you doing here?'

She wobbled a little, clutching her hood with both hands. She'd pulled it off as soon as she'd seen him. She licked her lips, and a panicked sheen of sweat sprang up on the surface of her skin. 'Oh, no,' she said. 'No. You don't remember?'

Her voice was like a knife in his brain.

He forced himself to look at her. She had a curving metal implant at her right temple, wrapping around the socket of her right eye. Dax grabbed her wrist and tugged back one of her sleeves. A thin metal band circled her wrist, a light flashing softly red.

'You shouldn't be here,' he said. It was the only thing he was truly sure of in that moment. He grabbed her neck with his other hand, lifting her so she was up on her toes. She scrabbled at the hand that held her throat, pulling fruitlessly at his fingers. It was the work of a moment to yank both hands behind her back and pin her wrists together. There was something familiar about her, but when Dax dug for the memory he found nothing. He didn't know her. And even if he had, it didn't matter. This was his life now, here in the palace, and the empress would be very pleased if she knew he'd caught this intruder.

There was only one thing to do with the female. He pushed her forward and kept pushing until she started to walk. He could smell the heat of her skin, and it filled his head with that same sense of familiarity. Her hair swung in a long plait down between her shoulder blades, falling almost to her wrists, and he had to make a conscious effort not to touch it.

He marched her along the corridor until they reached the hall beyond, where the empress stood surrounded by her senior guards. The guards immediately pulled free their swords when they saw the human female. Dax kept his grip tight. She wasn't going anywhere.

The empress stepped forward when she saw him approaching. 'What's this?'

'I found her running down that corridor,' Dax said. 'She is human.'

'I can see that,' the empress said. The spikes rippled across her head as she walked right up to the woman and looked her over.

'Who are you?' the empress asked, keeping her voice light, which Dax knew meant she was in a dangerous mood. He silenced the voice inside his head that wanted him to help the woman. 'And how did you get inside my palace?'

The woman kept her mouth obstinately shut. When the empress struck her across the face, she cried out, spat blood, but still refused to speak. The empress stared down at her. A forked tongue slid out and danced across her lower lip, and her eyelids flickered. She gestured to Dax, who released his grip on the woman and stepped away from her.

'You're female,' the empress said.

'Yes.'

A hand shot out, gripping the woman's face. Five lines appeared and began to bleed. Dax watched the blood trickle slowly over pale skin before finding its way over the empress's bony fingers, red stripes against the blue. The Sittan didn't bleed red.

Something about the colour made his heart pound.

'I asked you how you got into my palace.'

The woman's hands curled into fists, knuckles whitening. She was breathing loud, her chest heaving, her eyes huge and wild like those of a cornered animal. 'I heard you pay humans to fight in the arena,' she said. 'I need money. So I came.'

'Females don't fight,' the empress said, as if this was something that everyone should know. 'Only male blood can appease the Mountain. Female blood is far too valuable.'

'I can fight,' the woman said. 'I'm strong enough.'

The empress laughed. 'Don't be ridiculous.' She released her grip, striding back to her day bed and throwing herself down upon it. A servant immediately moved forward and began to clean the hand that had touched the woman with cloths and oil. 'Now,' she said. 'I will ask you again. And this time you will tell me the truth.' The servant with the oil bowed low and crept away. With a click of her fingers, the empress summoned one of her guards. The guard listened intently as the empress spoke to her in the harsh consonants of the Sittan language. Dax was only able to pick out the odd word, and those weren't enough to make sense of what the empress was saying.

Was this a dream? He wasn't sure.

He watched, muscles tensing, as the guard strode to the side of the room, scarlet cloak swirling around her ankles. Then the guard lifted a hand and swept it across the wall. Lights appeared in a concentric pattern and the surface rippled back, revealing the largest stash of weapons Dax had ever seen. There were long, thin blades that resembled needles, and axes with polished handles and circular blades. A double-ended hammer. Hooks of all different sizes. Something that looked like a bat with finger-thick spikes protruding from one end. The guard reached for something, brought it down, and walked over to him. Then she held it out.

It looked like a length of thin, coiled rope, finely woven and lightweight. 'Take it,' she ordered him.

It was soft, supple, heavier than he had expected. One end had been bound with plaited hide, forming a handle of sorts, and he wrapped his fingers around it. As he did so, the rest of the length uncoiled. It slithered silently to the floor.

Two guards moved in and seized the woman by the arms. They flung her to the floor, her knees smacking against it, though she didn't let out more than a small groan of complaint.

'Why are you here?' the empress asked her.

'I told you, I came here to fight.'

The empress cast a look at Dax. 'One lash,' she said.

Dax looked down at the length of rope in his hand. He tested the weight of it, giving it a gentle flick. It was perfectly balanced. He walked closer to the woman, then raised his hand and jerked his wrist forward. The end of the whip shot through the air. There was a snap as it made direct contact with the back of her suit. The fabric split as if it had been cut with a blade, revealing snow-white skin. A deep red line showed where the whip had caught her.

She hissed, but that was all.

'How did you get here?'

She shook her head. Loose strands of hair stuck to the back of her neck. 'Ship,' she said finally.

'Where is it?'

She didn't answer. Silence stretched. The empress looked at Dax. 'Again,' she said.

This time the whip cut into flesh, and the woman cried out. The sound seemed to bounce around inside his head like a sharp little dart. He tightened his grip.

'Again,' the empress said.

Dax raised the whip. He focused on the exposed skin of the woman's back, picked his target, and raised his hand. He saw her stiffen, muscles locking into place, just before the end of the lash kissed her flesh, the thousand shards of razor-sharp obsidian embedded in its final few centimetres making raw meat out of her back.

'Where did you get that suit?'

Dax lashed her again without waiting to be told. He had the rhythm of it now. But before he could finish, the guard on the woman's left crumpled to the ground. For a moment, he didn't know what had happened, and then several things happened at once. He heard the empress spit out a sting of harsh, Sittan words. He smelled death, dark and dirty and bitter, and he saw the flash of a blade, pure silver, in the hand of the woman.

He moved quickly, dropping the whip and grabbing the woman's wrist. He dug his thumb into the tendons and twisted. Her head jerked back and she cried out in pain, something she hadn't done when the lash had caught her. Her eyes were dark now and disturbingly familiar. He didn't like it.

The empress moved off the day bed, not with her earlier languid movements, but quickly, stealthily. She ignored Dax, her entire focus on the woman. She reached out, touched a claw to the blade. 'Who are you?' she asked.

Dax still had hold of her wrist, and he wrenched it harder when she did not reply. The blade wasn't in her grip, but protruded from the flesh. The metal band circling her wrist flashed red, flashed and flashed.

'Jinn,' she said. 'My name is Jinn.'

The word rang inside Dax's head, as clear as a bell. He knew that name. But he did not know this woman, and he would not allow himself to think otherwise. She had come here to hurt the empress, his empress, and that was all that mattered.

He took a step back and lashed her again, and again, until she fell to the floor, unconscious.

Then he dropped the whip to the floor and stepped back.

The empress was staring at Jinn.

She gestured to the guards. 'Take her to the west tower. Keep her alive. I'll question her again in the morning.'

CHAPTER

26

Ferona had always considered herself to be cool, calm, in control of any situation. It was one of the things that had enabled her to survive the trial by media that was part and parcel of politics. But in the space of a few fatal seconds, she had single-handedly managed to destroy everything she had worked to achieve. It had been a stupid mistake, perhaps the most stupid of her career.

Did you think I would create killing machines, and not take steps to make sure the rest of us were safe?

If only she could turn back time and stop herself before she had blurted out those fateful words, then she wouldn't be stuck in a damp, smelly, cramped apartment in Lower London. It belonged to Lucinda's parents and was, as Lucinda had delicately put it, 'in need of maintenance'.

The sanitation unit didn't work properly. There was no chem-icleanse unit to speak of. The bed was a nasty fold-down thing, and the sole entertainment screen was cracked from corner to corner.

But no one knew she was here.

And for that reason, and that reason alone, Ferona remained

locked inside this claustrophobic little box. She missed her apartment. She missed her clothes, her flowers, her lovely soft bed and attentive house droids. But she had been afraid to go back, knowing the media would be camped out on her doorstep.

She moved that thought to the bottom of her list of problems. Her stomach was grumbling. She had food; a box of assorted dehydrated meals, any of which could quickly be prepped by the ancient little hydramax sitting on the greasy worktop in what passed for the kitchen, but she didn't want mushy, old-tasting food. She wanted something fresh – peaches and cream, or crusty French bread with ripe tomatoes, or even just an apple, green and crisp and tart on the tongue. She could have all and any of those things if she was at home instead of this stinking hole.

Ferona kicked the door of the nearest cupboard, adding another dent to the ones already there. She activated her wrist comm. and put a call through to Vexler's personal number. His image popped up above the tiny screen.

'Ferona,' he said. 'Where are you?'

'Can we meet?'

'Of course. Why don't you come to my office?'

'No,' Ferona replied. 'Not your office. Somewhere else.'

'Where do you suggest?'

Ferona imagined Vexler in this tiny apartment and shuddered. 'Somewhere outside the Dome. Let's keep this off-grid, shall we?'

'Canary Wharf,' he said. 'One hour.'

The call ended and the screen went blank.

Ferona felt even worse than she had before. Of all the places he could have suggested, Canary Wharf was at the bottom of her list. She considered not going, but one look at her surroundings soon knocked that idea out of her mind. She was stagnating, sitting down here with the cracked entertainment screen and the occasional call from Swain or Lucinda her only contact with the outside world. This wasn't how she did things. It was time to take action.

She washed her face in the chipped sink and pulled on all the clothes she had. Canary Wharf was an area outside of the Dome, once a bustling place full of highly paid workers and modern offices, now abandoned and derelict, disintegrating next to the frozen river. At least there they were guaranteed some privacy.

Ferona pulled on a padded coat, tugged up the hood and left the tiny apartment. She knocked on the door of the one opposite. It opened a crack and Victor looked down at her.

'I'm going out,' she told him. 'Stay here.'

'All right.'

The door closed. She would have preferred to take him with her but he was just too large and too obvious. Ferona marched along the rusty walkway that led up to the surface. It was busy enough to make her pull the hood closer round her face and hunch her shoulders, but no one gave her a second glance. It was so dirty down here, and everyone was so pasty and miserable looking.

It was almost a relief to feel the cold air touch her face as she angled into the tunnel that led to the surface. There was rubbish everywhere – bits of tangled wire, packaging, a solitary shoe. When she reached the surface, that relief quickly gave way to misery. It was unbelievably cold. The wind bit through the padded fabric of her coat. She shoved her hands into her pockets, but it made no difference.

The whiteness hurt her eyes.

It took her thirty minutes to walk to Canary Wharf, during which time she considered all the ways in which she could destroy Humans First, both politically and personally, and then all the ways in which Victor could end their miserable little lives. She played that press conference over and over in her mind. It was as if they had known exactly which questions to ask, which words to use, how to apply pressure in exactly the right way to make her snap.

Vexler hadn't come to the Wharf on foot. He sat inside a warm, comfortable land roller, his skinny behind nestled into a padded seat as he sipped warm brandy from a double-handled mug.

The door of the roller rose up as she approached. 'Ferona,' Vexler said.

'President.'

'You look . . . tired.'

'Hmm,' Ferona replied. 'Perhaps you would look tired if you had spent the past two days in an apartment in the lower city.'

And if he had any shame, he would have. He was the President. He was supposed to take responsibility when things went wrong.

'You should have come straight to me,' Vexler said. 'Your decision to hide has put me in a very difficult position.'

Ferona took a moment to step up into the roller. She chose the seat opposite Vexler. He didn't offer her a drink, although the in-car Autochef was switched on, lights flashing away merrily. 'Did it?'

'I risked a lot to come here,' he said. 'You can't even begin to imagine the trouble you've caused. You gave Humans First everything they needed when you told them that the *A2* was destroyed by the men on board. They're using it as evidence that the Type One males are dangerous.'

'None of those things were my fault!'

'Ferona,' he said, shaking his head. 'You openly admitted that the destruction of the *A2* was an act of collective suicide. You told a press conference that the Second Species humans are dangerous after spending weeks insisting otherwise.'

Ferona stared at him, her teeth clamped together, vibrating with anger.

'You'll have to resign,' he continued. 'It's your only option.'

'I won't do that. Not now. There is too much at stake. Now more than ever we need stability in the Senate.'

Vexler shifted in his seat. 'This is politics, Ferona. Sometimes situations force our hand. Once you're out of office, all this will blow over.'

'I am not going to resign.'

'The others . . .'

'Who?'

'Collins. And Batista.'

'Collins has been after my job for years. And Batista has his own agenda. You must know by now he's got links to Humans First.'

Vexler looked away when she said that and became suddenly very interested in his drink. Ferona snatched the cup from his hand and threw it out into the snow. Vexler looked her full in the face, then, and what she saw in his eyes unnerved her. 'What?' she demanded. 'What are you not telling me?'

'Humans First have a lot of support,' Vexler told her. 'Far more than we realised. They have trebled their number of subscribers overnight.'

'So shut them down. That's what you wanted to do, isn't it?'

'I can't.'

'Why not?'

'Because I'm already sliding down in the ratings!'

'Screw the ratings.'

'Public opinion . . .'

'Changes more often than you change your bloody suit, and you know it. If you don't like the ratings, change the way the data are analysed. Make them show what you need them to show.'

'You make it all sound so simple,' he said, 'but the bottom line is that this isn't simple at all. You've led us head first into a political nightmare and now I have to somehow find a way out.' He pinched the bridge of his nose. 'How could you do this? How could you be so foolish?'

Pressure. Stress. A moment of madness. Ferona knew there was no way to excuse what she had done. It had been a mistake, nothing more and nothing less than that. But she couldn't stand to hear it from this man. 'Perhaps next time you'll give your own press conference rather than allowing a minister to do it for you.'

'Careful, Ferona.'

She closed her eyes for a moment and gathered herself. 'I

could give you the same advice. You brought Type One males on planet.'

'The public needed to know that they are harmless.'

'But they're not harmless!' Ferona shouted. 'The Sittan wouldn't be interested in them if they were!' She slammed her fist down on the empty seat next to her, and then somehow managed to calm herself.

Vexler coughed, rubbing his hands together as if warding off the chill, although it was warm inside the roller. 'Are you sure the Sittan and Shi Fai are on our side?'

Ferona was angry now, really angry. She hadn't walked two miles across the frozen streets of outer London in an ugly coat for this. 'Absolutely sure.'

'I will be the president who takes the human species to Spes,' Vexler said. 'I will not give that up.'

'I see no reason why you should,' Ferona lied. 'But we must do something about Humans First, and that means weeding out those ministers who support them. We need to make them go away, and quickly. Collins is a snake, but he's relatively harmless. Give him a promotion. Make him Chief of Urban Planning for the new developments on Spes. That'll keep him quiet. Batista is a nasty piece of work, but we can get him onside, I know it. We're almost there, Vexler. One last push is all it will take.'

Her mind raced as she worked through the possibilities, the best way to overhaul the government to make it work in her favour given the current situation. She would have to give an explanation for the *A2*, and the fact that she had covered up what had really happened. Perhaps some concessions would have to be made to Humans First. She could at least agree to meet with them for talks. She had underestimated their influence, which had been a mistake, but there was still time to correct it. Once the vote happened, and they had permission to cross Sittan and Shi Fai space, nothing else would matter. Humans First would be quickly forgotten.

'This can be fixed,' she told him. She could feel desperation building within, though she told herself it was merely anticipation and excitement as she thought of the job that lay ahead.

'Can it?'

Ferona just stared at him. She didn't know this man. Vexler was opportunistic and flighty. He wasn't like this.

'The wind is picking up,' he said. 'Looks like a storm is coming. Take care, Ferona.'

She angled round in her seat and then climbed slowly out of the roller. She didn't say goodbye. She didn't look back. Nor did she pull her coat more tightly around herself until the wind bit so sharply that she almost cried out.

The cats circled closer, tails in the air, voices raised in hungry, high-pitched cries. Ferona walked a little faster. There was indeed a storm coming in. The air was heavy with it.

And Ferona didn't know when it would hit.

CHAPTER
27

19th day of the fifth turn

The Palace, Fire City, Sittan

Jinn sat in the darkness in the back corner of the West Tower, shielding herself with the rough blanket that she'd pulled from the bunk carved into the wall on one side. The walls curved around her and up above her, the open side of the room blocked by horizontal bars made from more of that sharp obsidian that the Sittan seemed so fond of. It had certainly done a number on her back.

She didn't bother trying to hold in the whimper of pain as she moved, trying to get into a more comfortable position. Whenever she moved her arms it pulled the freshly healed skin across her back. It was still incredibly sore.

She tried to lie down. Her vision went black, the world shrinking down to just the pain before expanding again. With every beat of her heart, her back throbbed. Bang bang bang.

The bottom of the bars pulsed and buzzed. She willed out one of her blades, as much to distract herself from the pain as anything else, and stretched her hand slowly out towards the Virena. It jumped towards her, an eager black finger.

She only just managed to move back before it reached her.

Having seen how it had taken over the cruiser, the last thing she wanted to do was let it take hold of her body. She willed the blade back inside and curled her fingers into her palms before pulling her hands in against her chest.

All she'd been able to think about for the past few weeks was finding Dax. It had got her up in the morning, and it had been her last thought when she collapsed into her bunk at night. Hell, she had given the *Mutant* to Bryant of all people, such had been her desperation. Never had she been so fatally unprepared.

She had known there was a possibility that Dax might have changed. She had seen the people on the *A2*, those who had received the third and final dose of serum. But she had believed that he was different. She hadn't for a moment thought that Dax wouldn't remember her. That he would look like the Dax she had known, but that the similarity would end there. The man who had flogged her hadn't been Dax. He had been a stranger, trapped inside Dax's body. And now she was trapped, too, stuck in this hot stinking cage on this hot stinking planet.

It seemed all very inevitable, somehow, that she would end up alone like this. That her life would end this way.

But she wasn't dead yet.

She'd survived the *A2*, the vast prison ship. She'd survived a blaster shot to the gut that should by rights have killed her. She'd survived the modification programme.

She'd survived Caspian Dax, too.

And she would survive him again.

A hole opened in the wall, and something was shoved through it. From this distance she could see that it was a bowl of some sort of sloppy orange mush. It smelled like old fish. 'It can't be worse than Silver Rice,' she told herself, though she wasn't convinced. But she was hungry enough to try it.

It was slimy and cold and the taste was definitely off. She shovelled it in nonetheless, holding her breath, before she could chicken out. The aftertaste wasn't good. Shoving that thought from her mind, she set the bowl aside to eat the rest later as the pain in her back started to recede. Had the food been drugged? It couldn't make things any worse if it had.

But without the pain, there was nothing to stop her thoughts from shifting to Dax. She could remember the hard grip of his hands, the sound of his voice, so familiar and yet so wrong. And then there had been the burn of the lash on her back, and the sick disbelief that Dax would do this to her. She didn't hate him for it, but she hated the people who had done this to him. She folded her arms and rocked back and forth, unable to stop the rush of frustrated anger that swamped her.

Her private moment was rudely interrupted.

'Get up.'

The words were spoken in the Universal language, the accent awkward, as if the speaker didn't use that language very often. Jinn lifted her head, and outside the room saw four of the scarlet-cloaked guards. She willed out her blades full length and got slowly to her feet.

One of the guards moved closer, and the bars that kept Jinn on one side of the room sank down into a narrow trough cut into the floor.

'You are to come with us,' the guards said.

'And if I don't want to?'

'We will persuade you.'

Jinn considered this. The guards were all armed, she could see that, but then so was she. On the other hand it was four against one, and the pain from her back had softened, but she wasn't foolish enough to think it gone.

She walked slowly forward, keeping her blades by her sides, focusing on breathing, wondering what was going on. The Virena in the trench shivered when she moved across it, but it made no move to touch her this time.

The guard who had spoken grabbed her wrists, yanking them firmly behind her back, and held them there as cuffs were twisted into position. They tightened up instantly, cutting the circulation to her hands. 'Where are we going?' she asked casually, as the guard pushed her forward and they started to walk. Her question was ignored.

The guards picked up their pace, and Jinn stumbled along beside them. The heat and exhaustion had started to catch up with her. At the end of the tunnel they took a left. The floor sloped down before finally levelling off, and they trekked for what seemed like forever in the darkness before she felt the floor begin to rise beneath her feet.

She was shoved into a large room. A floor-length leather curtain blocked the opposite doorway from view, but the smell was different here, the air dusty, and she could hear the sound of feet and voices in the distance, though she couldn't make out any words.

'You are to bathe and dress,' the guard said, gesturing to the clothes that were draped over a stool. In the corner was a plunge pool, with dark liquid that she hoped was water lapping over the edge.

The cuffs melted away. Jinn started to undress. Her ripped jacket was the first to go, followed by her boots and trousers, leaving her standing there in nothing more than her thin undershirt and pants. She hesitated for a moment, then stripped those off, too.

The guard gestured to the pool. 'In,' she said.

Jinn moved to the edge. When she dipped her toes in the liquid it was cool and it didn't sting or burn, so she assumed it was safe. She held her breath and lowered herself in. The cold permeated her skin, a blessed relief. The liquid was faintly oily and it made the wounds on her back tingle.

She closed her eyes and dunked her head under the water, and then climbed out of the pool. Her skin dried almost instantly. Squeezing the excess water from her hair, she walked over to the trousers and picked them up. She shook them out and stepped into them. The leather of the trousers clung to her skin. They tied at the waist with a thick, pleated belt and ended at mid calf. There was a long length of cloth that she fastened around her upper body as best she could, trying to copy the way the guards wore theirs. Her arms, shoulders and feet were still uncomfortably bare.

Then the guards moved in, surrounding her, one of them carrying a whip that looked very much like the one that had been used on her the previous day. Jinn shivered at the sight of it. She didn't fight them when the leather curtain was pulled back and she was pushed through the opening. Steps led up, though to what she couldn't see. She turned, thinking to go back, but the curtain had been pulled across and familiar black bars now blocked the space.

She had no choice but to go where they wanted her to go. The steps rose steadily upwards, and, as she climbed them, she heard an increasing crescendo of voices joined together in unison, chanting the same phrase over and over. Jinn didn't need to understand the language to hear the excitement, the anticipation. It became a background roar as she reached the top of the steps and stumbled, falling to her hands and knees in the dirt.

She lifted her head.

She was in the arena.

It was a circle of sand and blood flanked by seating that rose so high she had to tilt her head back to see the top of it. Heat scorched the ground and her exposed skin as she staggered to her feet. The air quite shimmered with it. In the centre of the ring, a group of human males were fighting. Rivers of blood flowed over their bodies and coated the sand. These were individuals pushed beyond the edge of sanity. She saw one snap another's neck, then shove his body to the ground. The crowd roared out its pleasure.

Sourness rose in the back of her throat, and she had to work hard to swallow it down. But there was excitement, too, and she hadn't expected that. She hadn't had the third dose of Type One serum so in theory she should be no more inclined to fight than a normal human. But she could feel the urge in her body, in her bones. What was it Li had told her? That she'd be aggressive if she wanted to be?

Something landed on the ground next to her foot, a little flaming ball that burst open, spilling hot oil dangerously close to her toes. She leapt away in surprise. Another landed a little further out, and then one smacked her on the back of the leg. She twisted around. They were coming from the crowd. Where each one had landed, the oil was starting to burn, flames licking along the ground, jumping in her direction.

She had no choice but to move closer to the centre of the area.

Fight or die, that was her choice here. Fight or die.

So she willed out her blades and joined the fray.

The first one fell from a slice to the neck. He snarled at her as he went down, clutching what remained of his throat with a scarred hand that had only two fingers. She spun into the next, plunging her blades into his gut. It felt almost like she was watching someone else slash and jab at the others, as if she was trapped inside a body that someone else had control over.

As the third one fell, she realised she was glad of it. All she had to do was stay sane, stay calm, let her body and the Second Species modifications that had altered her DNA do what they had been designed to do.

She slashed out at another. Not since her early years as a freighter pilot had she been forced to work like this, but all the fights she'd survived then seemed to have prepared her for it. It was almost as if her body knew what to do without any conscious instruction from her brain.

But as she felled her fourth victim, she realised her mistake. The others were circling her. Pale eyes regarded her with violent hunger. They had stopped fighting each other. Now she was their sole interest.

She saw one of them drop his gaze to her chest, and knew he'd registered her as female. Holding her blades out, she dropped into a defensive crouch, slashing out at the air as she spun. But whichever way she turned, it meant giving her back to one of them.

Six remained.

Two charged.

The first caught her from behind, knocking her forward onto the burning sand. It cut into her skin, scorching her flesh. She pushed herself upright, but the man was on top of her almost immediately. He was huge, with a scarred, bleeding face and foul breath. Jinn bucked against him. He was too heavy. Her skin screamed as her bare torso pressed into the ground.

Ignoring the burn of the sand, she let her body go limp. When he moved, she was ready for him. She rolled, kicking up at him, and then buried her blades in his gut. Blood sprayed everywhere, hot and sticky, and she scrambled away from him, refusing to think about the shock on his face as his innards fell out of his body. Five to go.

They were wary of her now, she could sense it. Biding their time. She could feel all the hairs on the back of her neck stand up as blood pounded loud in her ears, and time itself seemed to slow down. The world began to move in slow motion as they circled each other, the crowd roaring, the ground beneath their feet sticky with spilled blood. The bodies created barriers, and for the next few minutes the remaining fighters made use of them.

She saw a couple of them glance at each other and knew she couldn't wait. She would have to take the fight to them before they brought it to her. Curving her hands into fists, she lunged at the nearest. The move took him by surprise. He dodged it, but a moment too late. Her blades scored his back as a large fist caught her on the shoulder.

The screaming pain in the joint told her he'd dislocated it, causing the arm to hang uselessly at her side, her blades pointing towards the ground, more of a hindrance than a weapon now. But she didn't have time to deal with the pain, to think about how she was going to fight with only one set of blades, because two of them were on her now, stinking, sweating, snarling, pounding her with fists like hammers. She cried out as the blows struck home, as one of them hauled her up by her hair and held her upright so the other could use her as a punch bag. She tasted blood as the blows fell, and for a moment she thought about death. She almost wished for it.

But she wasn't quite ready to give in, not yet, and she kicked out, twisting her body, landing a foot in her assailant's face. She scissored her legs, trapping his head between her thighs, then she locked her ankles together and began to squeeze. At the same time, she slashed back wildly at the one holding her up. She might only have one good arm, but it had a damn good blade at the end of it, a blade that met solid flesh and dug in.

She locked her thighs more tightly, choking the other. He thrashed, but she held on. She held on for herself, for Dax, for life itself, and when the thrashing stopped a few scant seconds later and, after the two of them dropped her, she sliced her way through the next three in a berserker rage. It wasn't just her Second Species modifications that drove her now, but anger. As she shoved herself upright, and faced down her final opponent, she realised that something had changed.

The crowd had stopped cheering.

The empress stood at the edge of the royal box, no longer reclining, no longer disinterested, but leaning forward with her hands planted on the edge of the barrier. Watching. Waiting.

'End it,' she said. Her voice echoed around the arena, just as it had before, and from somewhere the sound of drums began a steady, pulsing beat. Jinn didn't know what it meant, but she could feel it vibrating up through her body, matching the thump of her heart, and, when she turned her attention to the one remaining fighter, she knew that he felt it too.

He was younger than the others, still tall, but not as thickly built, as if he hadn't quite grown into his height yet. He was wearing the same knee-length breeches as she was, dark against his pale human skin.

She stared at him, suddenly uncertain. He was so young.

She started to lower her blades.

And then he went for her. He was bloody fast on his feet, light and quick, but Jinn was quicker. She dodged to the side as he rushed her, spinning away from the thrust of his fist. She only realised that was what he'd intended when his other arm slammed into her thigh.

Jinn stumbled back, her leg numb. Young he might be, but he certainly wasn't harmless. He kicked a body out of his way, sending it flying through the air. A demonstration intended to prove his strength. She could see from the look on his face that he was enjoying himself. She'd encountered people like him before, ones who lived to inflict pain. Their brains were wired differently. They couldn't be reasoned with. They couldn't be changed. They could only be stopped.

He went from relaxed to charging at her in an instant. He was almost upon her before she had a chance to react, using a speed that he'd kept hidden. But Jinn knew the fury of desperation and took the blow. She curved into it, letting her body feel the pain, letting him think that he'd won. He punched into her gut. His laughter rang through her ears, filling her head, the sound of a creature thrilled by its own insanity.

'I'm going to kill you,' he said.

'Not if I kill you first,' Jinn replied. Her wounds were already healing, but she was exhausted and the damage was considerable. She was a long way off full strength. But she wasn't dead yet. All she had to do was tempt him to take another run at her. To think she was weak. She let one hand fall down by her side and willed in her blades. She cradled her dislocated arm with the other and sank down to one knee. Her hair fell across her face in a dirty curtain wet with blood and sweat. She watched him through it.

She pulled in a lungful of the burning hot air, let it out.

And tensed as the boy charged her again. All she had to do was hold her position, hold her nerve. His fist met her face, a punch of shocking pain that loosened two of her teeth, but it brought him close, close enough for her to react.

A blade to his gut.

A blade to his throat.

And it was over.

Jinn rolled away from him, sprawled out flat on her back as the world spun around her. She barely had the energy to close her eyes against the suns. Somehow her heart kept beating as the crowd roared, a sound of thrilled fury.

A shadow drew over her. Jinn turned her head to the side. 'If you expect me to fight you,' she said, her thick tongue almost mangling the words, 'you're going to have to wait a minute.'

'I don't expect you to fight me.'

Dax.

She'd know that voice on any side of the galaxy. 'Good,' she said. 'Because I'm really not in the mood.'

He took hold of her, and she cried out in agony as he snapped her shoulder back into place. Then he lifted her. 'Where are you taking me?'

'The victor must be presented to the empress,' he said. 'You have to be marked.'

'Marked?'

'You took eight lives today,' he said. 'Now you must honour them.'

He carried her to the royal box. The last thing Jinn remembered was the yellow glare of the empress's eyes, and the sharp stab of the needle as her victories were tattooed into her flesh.

And the warm, strong feel of Dax's hands on her body.

CHAPTER
28

19th day of the fifth turn

The Palace, Fire City, Sittan

That night Jinn cried herself to sleep. She didn't know where Dax was, and even if she could get out of this room she had no idea if she could find him, or even if she wanted to. And she felt sick when she thought about what she had done. Every time she moved, the tender flesh of her shoulder reminded her of it. Something had changed inside her when she had stepped out into the arena. She had become someone she didn't recognise, and she felt horribly alone and ashamed.

But by the next morning she felt clearer. The bruises had already faded to a dirty yellow that she tried not to look at as she lowered herself into the chilled pool out on the balcony, and her shoulder no longer hurt.

She could see the Mountain in the distance.

It had changed.

A red plume rose from the very peak, turning grey at the edges.

Ignoring the lingering stiffness in her arms, Jinn pushed herself upright and climbed out of the tub. The balcony had a tall balustrade built from thick lengths of polished obsidian, and she swung her legs over it and sat facing the volcano.

229

The Mountain that had not erupted for a thousand years was smoking.

And Jinn did not think this was a positive sign.

It was a long way down to the ground below. All she had to do was lean forward a little. She'd never survive the fall. It would be easy. She flexed her fingers against the edge, gritted her teeth, and found that it wasn't easy after all.

Climbing back down wasn't easy, either. She swung one leg over, took a moment to catch her breath, and then brought the other round to meet it. As she straightened up, she saw Dax. He was standing at the edge of her room. Two red-cloaked guards flanked him.

Her heart started to pound. Why was he here? Was he going to beat her again? Slowly, she forced herself to walk towards him. She stopped just out of reach and took a good look at him.

His hair was short, cropped close to his head, and his skin was darker, presumably due to his time in the sun. He was dressed in Sittan clothes, not the expensive boots and tailored jacket of a successful pirate. Tattoos lined his shoulder. They were identical to hers in every respect.

But he had more.

He held up a pile of clothing. 'Put this on,' he told her, tossing it down at her feet.

Jinn picked it up. More leather. The Sittan were big on leather. She pulled on the trousers and vest, tightening the ties and knotting them in place. Her hair was a ratty mess, but she did her best to plait up the tangled strands so that they at least hung down her back and out of her face.

Dax looked her over. He nodded, as if what he saw pleased him.

'What's going on?'

'You are to follow me.'

He led her down to a courtyard in the centre of the palace. The two guards brought up the rear, jabbing at her with the blunt end of their spears if she moved too slowly. It was a huge space, open and circular, the air hot and still. Although open to the sky there was no mistaking the fact that it was still a cage.

'What are we doing here?'

'Training,' Dax told her. 'Run.'

'What?'

He gestured to the stone pathway that circled the perimeter of the courtyard, drew the shape of a circle with his index finger. 'I want to see you run.'

Jinn put her hands to her hips. 'Why?'

'Because I told you to. Now run.'

His eyes gleamed. She could sense his aggression building. He lunged at her.

She darted away, fast and light on her feet, then she broke into a sprint. She found the track and settled into it, keeping that same fast pace. Dax gave her a few seconds' head start, and then he began to chase her down. He kept pushing until they were side by side, running flat out round the track. Sweat dripped into her eyes, slithered down her back.

'You really don't know who I am, do you?' she asked, her voice strained. She turned her head and looked at him.

'Should I?'

She upped her pace. It hurt less than answering that question.

He chased her down. She almost got away.

Almost wasn't enough.

He made one final, desperate charge and caught her. One arm went around her waist as the other grabbed hold of her plaited hair and jerked her to a standstill. She kicked out at him, but he had her, and he wasn't about to let go. He pulled her to the floor, pinning her there with his weight.

'If I can catch you,' he said, 'the others will be able to catch you, too.'

'I killed all the ones who managed it yesterday.'

'And the Mountain responded.'

Jinn stared at him in disbelief. 'No, it didn't.'

'The empress believes that it did. And tomorrow she will want

231

you to kill a hundred,' he told her, pinning her hands at her sides. 'How will you manage then? You think you hurt now, it's nothing compared to how you're going to feel after that. You're not strong enough, you're not fast enough, and you don't know the rules.'

'I thought this place didn't have rules.' She shoved him off her, scrambled to her feet and willed out her blades. She found herself unable to trust this man who stood before her. She didn't know him. Why did the empress think she had caused the Mountain to erupt? It was co-incidence, that's all.

'There are always rules,' Dax told her. He kept lunging at her, and each time he did she danced away. 'Are you fighting to win, or fighting to survive?'

'I'm fighting because I'll die if I don't.'

'You're not fighting me.'

'You're not going to kill me,' she said.

'Are you sure about that?' He kicked sand up into her face. 'The men you fought yesterday were slow,' he said. 'The next ones might not be. That means you have to lose everything that might make you vulnerable. And you are vulnerable.'

'These blades say I'm not.'

He pushed her away, and they circled slowly, gazes fixed, adrenaline pumping. He was bigger than her, had the reach, the experience, but she had her blades. And her anger. He had been able to resist the effects of the third serum, that much was clear. Unlike the men she'd fought in the arena he had complete control of himself. But he wasn't the man that she'd known. 'You're doing this for her, aren't you? For the empress? She wants me to fight. She thinks that's why the Mountain has erupted.'

He didn't say anything, but a muscle flickered in his cheek.

'Why are you on her side?' Jinn persisted.

'I don't know what you mean.' He went for her again, and this time she wasn't fast enough. He kicked her legs out from under her, knocking her down with a forearm across her gut. He pinned her with a foot to her throat.

Jinn didn't move. He was breathing hard, sweat trickling down the sides of his face, big hands clenched.

'Again,' he said, stepping back.

This time she started to get the rhythm of it, of him. There was a familiar elegance to the way he moved, despite his size, and once she had it she had him. The fight became a dance. She willed in her blades and went at him with her fists, knowing that it wouldn't really hurt him. Each blow that landed was merely a mark of her frustration.

He retaliated in kind. Fresh bruises bloomed on her arms, her thighs, though he was careful not to hit her face. Her other opponents wouldn't be so kind. But then neither would she. Quickly, she learned how to defend, how to block, when to come in and when to move back. She learned her own weak spots. She learned how much pain she could take and still keep going.

And inside her, that tight little knot of frustration pulled ever tighter. She staggered back from him. *'Why don't you remember me?'*

He bent at the waist, chest heaving for breath. Then he barrelled forward, planting one huge shoulder in her belly. He shoved her back and over, and she hit the ground hard. The air was pushed out of her lungs and she curled up, desperate for breath, making a sound like a mewling kitten. Dax loomed over her, hands planted either side of her head, covering her in shade. 'Why should I remember you?' he asked. 'What makes you think you were anything to me?'

Jinn rolled slowly onto her back. His face was in shadow, making it impossible to see more than the vague details of his face. 'Because you were everything to me,' she whispered.

She could hear the thump of his heartbeat. It pounded in time with her own, matching the fierce rush of blood through her body.

'Your name is Caspian Dax,' she told him desperately. 'You grew up in Underworld London. You left Earth when you were eighteen. You've got your own ship. It's called the *Mutant*. You ...'

He clamped a hand down over her mouth before she could say any more. 'Stop it,' he told her fiercely. 'Just stop it.'

She struggled against his hold. It didn't work. He had her pinned. Panic started to rise in a way that it hadn't before. Her arms started to burn, then her wrists, her fingers. Before she could stop it, her blades were out and had scraped down the side of his body.

He reared up. 'I know you,' he said. His gaze was distant, as if he wasn't quite with her. Then it snapped back to the here and now, and she found herself at the mercy of those bright green eyes. 'You tried to kill me.'

She struggled against him, feet braced against the floor as she tried to buck his weight off her. Dax didn't move. She was strong, but she wasn't that strong. It didn't matter. She saw a glimmer of her Dax. It was enough.

'We were on a ship,' he said. 'I don't ... I can't ... I can't remember. Why can't I remember?'

'You were given the third dose of the Type One serum before you were sent here. It must affect memory.'

'No,' he said, shaking his head. 'You're wrong. It's you. You did this to me.' He leaned in closer then, so close that she could feel his breath against her face. 'Get out of my head,' he told her. Then he got to his feet and walked to the edge of the courtyard, pushing past the guards who stood there.

Jinn pushed herself into a sitting position and watched him go, trying to make sense of what had just happened. There was movement on one of the courtyard walls. She looked up to find the empress gazing down at her before slithering out of sight like the hideous reptile that she was.

Then the guards moved in.

29

12 cycles to ripening
Drang Fields, Faidal

When Eve had first been brought to the holding centre, she'd had plans to escape. She wasn't like the other women, she told herself. She wasn't just going to sit here and accept her fate. But all her big talk had led to nothing. The only way in or out was the entrance she'd been shoved through when she first arrived, and from down in what she'd christened the Pit there was no way to reach it.

She'd explored it as best she could. Some of the other women had formed tight-knit groups, defending their few scant metres of floor space, moving only to gather the packets of Silver Rice that were tossed down to them five times a day. Water trickled from tubes at the edge of the Pit, and everyone had a little wooden bottle to hold it in. It was so hot that Eve spent most of her time lying on the floor, listening to the gargle of her overfed stomach.

So far she'd managed to dodge the terrifying spider-like creatures that dropped from the ceiling every time a chime sounded. They had hairy bodies and strange arms that were some odd combination of metal and plant. They would spin themselves down on spidersilk as thick as her thumb, grab onto whichever women didn't move out of their way fast enough, and disappear up into the ceiling with them, spinning ropes of white silk around their bodies as they did so.

No one knew what happened to the women who were taken. Eve refused to think about it. She needed to focus on what was around her, not what lay ahead. Her skin wasn't a weapon here. All she had was her brain and her own two fists, which were pretty pathetic in comparison to those of some of the other women. Almost all of them had implants, meaning that they were colony workers. Unfortunately, the parts of those implants that might have been useful in this situation had been removed.

'Oi,' called a voice that had become all too familiar over the past few days.

It was Doran, a tall, bullish woman whom Eve had quickly learned to avoid.

The other woman walked right up to her and stood unpleasantly close. Eve didn't step back, despite the sour stink. 'What are you doing?'

'Nothing,' Eve replied. She folded her arms, refusing to let Doran see that she was shaking. The other woman was a Bug, one of the people who had undergone genetic modification and implants in order to work on one of the colonies, and then skipped out on their job before they had finished paying for them.

It took a certain attitude to be a Bug and Doran had it in spades. She was also built like a snow skimmer. She had a habit of pushing the other women into the path of the spiders and it had become something of a game.

She frightened Eve, and she knew it.

The sound of the chime rang through the Pit and immediately the scramble began. Doran turned on her heels and ran. It was hard to predict exactly where the spiders would drop but it was generally agreed that the edges of the Pit were the safest place to be. There was plenty of pushing and shoving and the sound of bare feet slapping against the hard floor in the few scant seconds that passed before the drop began. Some women didn't bother to move and they were picked off first. It bought a little time for the others, the ones who still had enough desire for survival left to run.

The spiders disappeared silently up into the ceiling, taking their prey with them. As the first few moved up, more dropped down, legs extended, ready to grab. The pushing grew worse. A few of the women started to scream. Panic spread like wildfire, infecting all but those already tucked away safely at the edge.

A spider dropped down less than a metre from Eve and found a victim. She caught a glimpse of the woman's face as those long legs closed around her before she was jerked up out of sight. Pure terror was written on her features.

Another spider dropped down in front of her, and she almost ran into it. It reached for her. She swerved out of its way. She crashed into a couple more women, jumped over one who had fallen, her feet slipping on empty Silver Rice packets. But she was almost there. Almost there. Just a few more metres and she'd be able to hide in the safety of the tiny caves that formed the perimeter.

Eve spotted a gap and headed towards it, but before she could get there a figure blocked her way. It was Doran. 'You're not coming in here,' she said, her voice sharp with authority.

'There's room,' Eve pointed out.

'Not for you,' Doran replied. 'Runt.'

'Come on,' Eve said. 'Don't do this, Doran.'

For a moment Eve thought the other woman was going to let her into the safety of the little cave. But she was wrong. A meaty hand came up and caught Eve hard on the shoulder, sending her tumbling to the ground, straight into the path of the still empty-handed spider.

There was nothing Eve could do. She locked gazes with Doran the very moment those thin spider legs closed round her. Doran shrugged and turned away.

Eve didn't scream. She couldn't. Her entire body seemed frozen, out of her control. The creature spun her until she was dizzy, and, when it stopped, she found herself up in the ceiling of the building, unable to move her arms and legs. The silk it had wrapped around her was cold. She felt strangely sleepy. But she worked to keep her eyes open, to keep focused.

The spider let go of her. She was suspended from the ceiling by a thin length of silk. All the other women were hanging in the same fashion, swinging gently in the cool silence. Eve tried to look down. The bodies of the spiders blocked her view. They formed a network underneath their captives, not quite a floor, but enough to close them off from the Pit.

It was eerie and weird, being suspended up there with all the other women. Eve closed her eyes. She thought of Dax and Jinn and wondered if Jinn had managed to find him yet. She hoped so. She thought of the *Mutant*, the ship that had been her home for so long, of her cabin, the first space that had ever been hers, and the foolish little plastic dolls she'd decorated it with. And she thought, finally, of Alistair.

She could see him, the little details, the shape of his hands and the exact fall of his hair, the way his forehead wrinkled when he was trying to do one of those impossible puzzles that he was so fond of. The way he always ate his dinner slowly, enjoying every mouthful.

She had been so angry with him.

She wondered if he knew that she loved him almost as desperately as she hated herself, but that the only way to survive what had been done to her had been to take it out on him. All she wanted now was the chance to tell him she was sorry.

She opened her eyes when she started to move. It was slow, at first, and then a little faster. It wasn't the spider moving her this time, but some sort of mechanism above her that softly hummed as it drew her along. She was carried through a narrow corridor, her feet a good metre above the ground, where the walls were thin and yellow and she was fairly sure the dim glow coming through them was from outside. At the end of the corridor, the tunnel turned left, and Eve found herself being carried through into a small room.

Two Shi Fai moved forward. One held her steady as the other cut her down, and then she was carried to a platform in the centre of the space. She lay there, frozen in place, staring up at the ceiling, imagining giant spiders plunging down.

But there were no giant spiders in here, just a medidroid that was almost an exact replica of the one that had modified her so long ago, back on Earth. The monitors and wires looked oddly out of place against the waxy yellow surface of the floor and walls, and that made them appear all the more frightening, all the more wrong.

The droid moved. There was a beep, and something pressed against her shoulder. Eve glanced down to see a drug gun fire against her skin. 'What the ... ' she began, but the rest of the words escaped her as the world seemed to shrink into nothing.

When she opened her eyes to find herself still alive, someone touched her face and the spout of a water bag was pressed against her mouth. She drank thirstily. 'Easy,' said a low, human voice. 'You're still weak from the procedure.'

'What did they do to me?'

'The same as they're doing to all of us,' the woman replied. 'Using you to incubate more Shi Fai.'

CHAPTER
30

20th day of the fifth turn

The Palace, Fire City, Sittan

'How did she do this?'

The empress had been asking Dax that question over and over for the past hour. 'I don't know,' he told her, as he had done a thousand times already.

The empress stalked away from him and out onto the balcony. She gripped the edge of the railing and stared at the Mountain. It was no longer just smoking. It was erupting. And the empress was convinced that Jinn was the cause.

Even at this distance, Dax could see the wide spread of lava as it flowed down the side of the rocky upthrust. It added a crackling, snapping roar to the background hum of the palace, as if it had just discovered its voice and wanted to make sure that everyone could hear it.

'How did a *human female* do this?' she asked him.

It was a question that had kept the empress awake throughout the night. Her pacing had kept Dax awake as well, though he doubted he would have slept anyway. His mind had raced constantly. Flashes of the human female interspersed with images of the empress had left him hot and hard and confused. He was trying to hide it, afraid that the empress would see and would punish him for it.

She turned away from the balcony and stalked back into the room. Her Vreen sat on her shoulder and she stroked it, nuzzling up against its ugly little face, but her gaze returned to the Mountain. 'It hasn't erupted like this in a hundred turns. I give it Sittan males. Human males. Nothing. And then a human female comes to the planet, to my planet. She fights in the arena, something no female of any species has ever done. And then this.'

'She didn't just fight,' Dax pointed out. 'She won.'

'Yes,' the empress agreed. 'Tell me, Dax. Are human females normally this strong?'

'I . . . ' What did he know of human females? Soft skin. Sweet mouths. Easily broken. He used droids. 'I don't think so.'

'There is something different about this one. Not just the metal on her face, or in her hands. It's almost as if . . . '

Her words drifted off. She crooned at the creature on her shoulder, then walked back over to her day bed and lowered the little lizard into its open cage. When she turned back to Dax, her expression was hard. 'Someone helped her get into the palace,' she told him. 'She did not do this on her own. I want to know who helped her. How did she get here? Where is her ship? Find out for me.'

'How?'

The empress walked over to the table that held her perfumes, her oils. She selected one and picked up the bottle. It was polished and ornate, silver inlaid with gold, with a stopper made from a finger-length dark ruby. She pulled it free and let a few drops of the oil fall to her wrist. Then she set the bottle gently down, lifted her wrist to her face and inhaled. The scent obviously pleased her, because she pulled down the top half of her robe and rubbed those drops of scented oil over her skin.

Then she sashayed over to Dax. She didn't bother to cover herself. The warmth of her skin had heated the oil and the scent drifted up to him, spicy and rich. His mouth watered a little. He licked his lips. His body felt hot and heavy. He wanted to touch her, and inside the tight restraint of the white slave breeches he regularly wore his cock responded.

'I'm sure you can think of a way,' the empress told him. She was right there, so close that all he would have to do was reach out, and he could have her. Clenching his fists, Dax concentrated on breathing, on trying to control the fierce rush of blood through his body. She wouldn't like it if he touched her. It wasn't allowed.

'What is it?' she asked.

'I . . . it's nothing.' But his gaze slipped momentarily down to the exposed flesh of her breasts. She noticed.

'Is it this?' She gestured to herself. 'Oh. I didn't realise.' And she smiled, feral and satisfied. 'How very rude of me.' She started to cover herself, but made no serious effort. And then she let go of her robe, reached out, and touched him.

Her claws scraped over his skin, making everywhere she touched feel hot and sensitive. When she pushed at his shoulder, he leaned back a little. Her gaze dropped to the bulge in his trousers and she smiled, flashing those sharp teeth. It made him feel both frightened and aroused.

He'd been a long time without physical contact, and he was starting to hunger for it. It wasn't just violence that he needed now, but something more.

Distracted, he watched as her hand moved lower.

'Today is the last day of the fifth turn, which means that we must honour the Mountain. The dead will be taken to the summit. You and the female will be left alone in the palace.'

She cupped him. He groaned. Her fingers began to massage his erection through the soft leather of his breeches.

'What do you want me to do?' Anything. Whatever she asked, he would do it.

She was playing with the ties that fastened his breeches. 'Tell her what she wants to hear. I'm sure you know how to do that.'

'I don't . . .'

The ties pulled free. 'Oh, I think you do,' the empress said. 'I heard the two of you down in the courtyard. Convince her that you want to leave Sittan. Get her to take you to her ship.'

The tips of her claws skated over the skin just inside the waistband. Dax flexed his hips, but her hand slid no lower. She leaned in, putting her mouth close to his ear, and whispered, 'I shall make it worth your while.'

Then she withdrew her hand and walked away, leaving Dax where he was, breathless, frustrated. For a split second he almost went after her, but she was already marching through the doorway that led into her sleeping quarters, and there were guards in the archway.

He closed his eyes and rubbed a hand over his face, his mind confused and his body hot. Jinn's arrival had changed everything. He felt like he should know her, but he didn't. She seemed to know him, though. Everything had been simple before she arrived. Now it was anything but.

But he knew one thing for certain.

He would do what the empress asked.

Because he wanted what she had offered.

CHAPTER
31

Jinn lay on the floor in her room, trying not to pass out from the heat. No matter how many times she doused herself with water from the pool in the corner, she never seemed to cool down.

She hated this planet and everything on it.

The Sittan were cruel. The environment was harsh, verging on unbearable. She was being forced to do things she could never forgive herself for in order to stay alive, and the food was shit.

The stripes on her shoulder ran down the length of her arm now. The smell of blood still lingered in her nostrils. She had seen Ritte and Merion in the crowd during her last trip to the arena, but she had been unable to reach out to them for help.

As Jinn was certain that all she had to look forward to was more of the same, she wasn't feeling particularly optimistic about the future. She had survived a lot of difficult situations, some of them of her own making, but she had always been able to find a way out.

Not this time.

She was trapped, Dax was a stranger and her plan to be the great hero who waltzed in and saved him had turned out to

244

have more holes in it than a ventilation filter. So now she was stuck trying to make a new plan while trapped in a cage in an alien palace.

Jinn was pretty sure that the empress wouldn't have her killed, not while she believed that Jinn was responsible for the fact that the Mountain had decided to erupt. As long as she won her fights in the arena she was safe, for now.

But it couldn't last forever.

Someone struck the bars of her cage, making them ring. Jinn jerked herself upright. She gripped the hard edge of the bunk as she searched the darkness. Movement caught her attention. She focused on it. Whoever it was took shape and form, as they came closer, and Jinn recognised the female instantly.

It was the empress.

Now this was unexpected. Jinn got to her feet, her hands tingling. Whatever the Sittan female wanted with her, she was sure it couldn't be good.

The empress sauntered closer and studied Jinn for a moment. 'Is it true that on your planet, men and women are considered equal?'

'Yes.'

'Then how do you control your males?'

'We don't,' Jinn told her. 'We expect them to control themselves.'

'But they can't, can they? No wonder your planet is in such a mess.' The empress lifted a hand and almost immediately the bars of the cage dropped down to the floor. Jinn didn't move, didn't flinch, but every muscle in her body was primed for attack.

Four huge Sittan males moved in to flank the empress. They towered over her. She turned to the nearest male, looked up at him. His spikes snapped out. Jinn could see him almost trembling. His fear was palpable. But he didn't move. The empress turned her attention back to Jinn. She smiled. It was a cold and cruel thing. 'They only breathe because I allow it,' she said.

She gestured to the implant at Jinn's temple, the ones around her wrists. 'You'll have to forgive me. My understanding of your backward technology is somewhat limited. This is all connected to your body, is that correct? The metal grows into your skin?'

'That's right.'

'What is it for?'

Jinn hesitated, then thought, why not? 'I needed it for my job. I was a pilot. With these, we can connect directly with the ship. It makes it easier to fly.'

'I like it,' the empress said. 'Give it to me.'

'I can't.'

'But I want it.'

'I can't just take it off. It would have to be surgically removed. Cut out.' Jinn kept her gaze fixed steadily on the empress. 'If you remove it, I won't be able to fight,' she pointed out. 'And if I can't fight, what happens to the Mountain then?'

The empress regarded her steadily. 'You are extremely arrogant, for a human.'

'I'm not human,' Jinn told her. 'I'm Second Species. Part human, part Sittan.'

'Indeed,' the empress said. 'Though I thought that all the Type Ones were male. So how did you come to be modified?'

Jinn hesitated. How much could she give away? 'My mother arranged it,' she said finally.

'I see. Why?'

'She wanted to improve me.'

'Did you need improvement?'

'Apparently so.'

The empress laughed. And then she slipped away into the darkness, leaving Jinn alone. Sometime later the guards came for her. Jinn was given food. She was given a pot of oil and instructed to rub it into her shoulder, where the kill tattoos stood out in stark contrast to her pale skin.

Then the guards left, and she was once again alone.

She dipped in the pool, then stretched out again on the floor.

Someone moved into the room. Jinn swung herself up into a sitting position, watching whoever it was as they moved closer.

Dax stood on the other side of the bars, hands at his sides, and stared at her. She could touch him, if she reached through the bars, but she chose not to.

'What do you want?'

'It is the day of offering,' he said. He moved a little closer and put a hand against one of the bars.

Jinn got slowly to her feet. She willed out the blades on her right hand but didn't move any closer to him. She had already learned that lesson. 'So?'

Dax glanced behind him, then back at her. 'The palace is empty.'

He moved to the side of the room and pulled a lever. The bars of the car dropped down, pooling into dark puddles. Jinn shot to her feet, blades out. 'What are you suggesting?'

'This is our chance. Come on.'

He led her through several corridors, each lit with burning torches. She didn't recognise any of them, and knew that she would never be able to find her way back through them. It didn't matter. She had no intention of ever returning to the palace. It quickly became apparent that Dax was right. The place was deserted.

Finally, they reached the courtyard that surrounded the palace. Dax dragged out a tub of krent tails and threw the pieces across the flagstones. The huge lizards crawled lazily towards it, and once they had settled in to feed he motioned for Jinn to follow him.

When they had passed across the courtyard and reached the gate, Jinn stopped him. 'Dax?' she asked, still uncertain. She knew she could pass through the gate with or without him. Was this the Dax she knew, or the one she had met when she first arrived, the one who had beaten her? Had something happened to make his memory return?

He didn't quite meet her gaze. 'I still don't know who you are,'

247

he admitted. 'But I have to get away from this place. You've got a ship, haven't you?'

'Yes.'

'Good,' he said. 'Can you take me to it?'

Jinn hesitated. He had beaten her so badly. But he wanted to get away from here, and that was enough for her. 'Of course.'

She put her hand against the gate, just as she had on her way in. It flexed a little, and heated up against her hand, but didn't suck her through. Instead, a smaller gate opened inside the big one, large enough for both her and Dax to pass through.

It silently closed behind them, and Jinn took a deep breath. But they weren't out of trouble yet. The first thing was to find her way back to Ritte's house. If she did that, she'd be able to find Li, and her way back to the ship.

She moved quickly. Dax kept pace with her easily. The city was just as empty as the palace had been, but it didn't feel safe, and she expected to find Sittan around every corner. At first the buildings were tall, like small replicas of the palace, though the further away they got the less ostentatious things became.

She recognised Ritte's house. The carving on the door and the wind chimes that hung beside it, were easy to spot. She had intended to call in and find Li, but now she was here, she hesitated. Dax was ... he wasn't himself. And from everything that Ritte had told her, she knew the Sittan female would be in trouble if the empress found out that she had helped Jinn.

Li could take care of himself. She knew that much.

So she kept on going. They edged further through the town, until the houses became smaller and less opulent. At the very edge of the town, the dwellings consisted of little more than small domes, each with a blackened fire pit at the side. They didn't have doors or windows, just a low archway to allow entrance and exit. There was a distinct air of poverty here, both in the cracked, faded buildings and the dry animal carcasses that littered the side of the road.

The ground started to slope up. The landscape was barren

and scorched, but Jinn recognised certain landmarks – tall hunks of obsidian in unusual shapes, burn marks that resembled clouds.

This was the way she and Li had come, she was sure of it.

'It's not much further,' she told Dax, suddenly aware of how hot she was, how desperately thirsty.

'Is it the *Mutant*?'

'No. I didn't bring the *Mutant*.'

'Too big,' he said, and then blinked, as if he'd surprised himself. 'Can't land on planet.'

Her legs suddenly felt a little less heavy, her head a little less fogged. 'You can remember?'

'I remember my ship. Class Seven long-haul carrier with advanced jump capabilities. One of a kind. Bunks fifty but could transport five times that. I have an Autochef in my quarters. Rare steak. I like rare steak.'

Jinn stumbled over her own feet. He reached out, steadied her.

'Yes,' she said, looking down at the hand that held her arm.

She was desperate to ask him if he remembered anything else, but there wasn't time. They needed to get to the ship before someone noticed that they were missing. But the suns were high, and she had to stop to catch her breath.

She spotted shade underneath an overhanging rock and went for it. It felt good to be out of the heat even if it was only for a couple of minutes. Dax tucked himself under there with her. 'How far is it to this ship of yours?'

'Not far. I hope.'

'Who else did you come with?'

For a moment, Jinn wondered if she could trust him, but she shook her doubts off. His memories were coming back. He'd already proved that. It wouldn't be long until he'd be able to remember everything. And then they'd be back to where they'd been, before he surrendered to her mother.

All she had to do was keep going until then.

'Jozeph Li,' she said. 'He escaped from the *A2* with me. He knows people here. That's how I got into the palace.'

'Which people?'

'What is this, an interrogation?'

'I have to . . . ' He got to his feet. 'We need to get moving.'

Jinn didn't disagree with that.

They trekked on for another half-kilometre. The landmarks were all correct, she was sure of it. The ship was here. She stood, trying not to look too hard, until finally she saw the outline. 'It's here,' she said.

Dax grabbed her hand. 'Good,' he said. He held her steady.

And then he started to pull her forward. Not towards the ship, but away. 'What are you doing?'

'I have to take you back to her,' he said.

'What? No!'

She tried to pull her hand free, but he was too strong. When she stumbled over the rocks, he picked her up and put her across his shoulders, gripping her wrists tightly so that she couldn't use her blades. 'Why are you doing this?'

'I have to,' he said. 'I'm sorry, Jinn. I don't have a choice.'

It was the first time he'd used her name.

That stayed with her as guards she hadn't realised were following them closed in.

CHAPTER
32

12 cycles to ripening

Drang Fields, Faidal

Bryant didn't know if he was happy to find himself alive or a little pissed that he was still on this stinking planet. He settled on pissed. It felt like the more comfortable of the two emotions. 'Where in the void am I?' he croaked as he tried to get into a sitting position. His head spun. The last thing he remembered was falling off the giant ant and landing in a pool of shit and thinking it just about summed up his life.

'We're inside the building.'

'How did we get inside the building?' He focused on the fuzzy figure of a man, and blinked until he became clear. It was Alistair.

'There are ventilation holes cut around the base,' Alistair said. 'I shoved you down one, and then I went down after you.'

'So we're in the basement.'

'Pretty much.'

'Excellent,' Bryant said. 'I must congratulate you on a job well done. We're . . . ' He looked around. 'What is this?'

'You must have hit your head harder than I thought,' Alistair said. 'Isn't it obvious?'

'No.'

Alistair got to his feet. His movements were stiff and jerky, and Bryant suspected that he wasn't the only one feeling the effects of the fall. Well, Alistair would just have to manage. He bloody well wasn't sharing his drugs. Speaking of which . . .

Bryant patted down his jacket. He found his little case. He pulled it out with shaking fingers and flipped it open. The gun was still there, together with the little vials of fluid, but one was empty. The case was damp where it had leaked. At least the others were still intact. Bryant loaded one into the gun. Straight in the thigh. He sagged back and let out a long, relieved sigh as the Euphoria took effect. He loaded another vial into the gun and slipped it into his trouser pocket, tucking the case back into his jacket ready for when he needed it.

Then he took a proper look at his surroundings. There were four huge tanks, each the size of a skimmer. From each one ran thick cables that twisted together, trailing along the floor and looping up into the ceiling. He couldn't tell if they were putting something into the tanks or taking something out. He climbed up beside one of the tanks. It was full of thick yellow goo.

'I think this is some sort of organic power generator,' Alistair said.

'They're using plants to make electricity?'

'Something like that.'

'I never thought of the Shi Fai as being that advanced.'

'They've got space travel,' Alistair said. 'They're not primitive.'

'The Lodons gave them the technology,' Bryant pointed out. 'Not one of their better decisions, if you ask me.'

'No one did.' Alistair was on his feet. 'We need to get up to the next level. I think there's a way through over there.'

Over there turned out to be in the centre of the space, where the cables twisted together, forming what looked like the trunk of a tree. They branched out from it higher up, each one disappearing up through the ceiling. Alistair wiped his hands on his filthy trousers then started to climb.

After a hard couple of minutes Alistair was no more than a few metres off the ground and Bryant was losing patience. He strode up to the trunk and started his own descent, kicking the toe of his boots in to get hold, determined to show Alistair how it should be done.

The surface of the cables was sandpaper-rough and bit into his hands, but he was high, so he didn't mind. He made it just beyond halfway. Then he settled himself on one of the branches, wiping the sweat and blood from his palms. Alistair had some-how managed to catch up with him.

Bryant pulled himself to his feet and carried on. Eventually, he was high enough to stretch up a hand and touch the ceiling. It was waxy and strange with a pungent odour that burned his sinuses when he breathed too deeply. The cables twined their way up through it, and around the thicker ones there was a gap.

Alistair was already pushing his way through. Bryant had no intention of being beaten by a bony Underworld twit, so he too forced his body through that narrow space between cable and wall. He kicked and pulled his way up then collapsed flat on his back, fighting to get his breath. Alistair was already on his feet.

This level was smaller than the one below, though not by much. The cables crawled across the floor, narrowing out until they climbed up the walls in a spindly mesh. Light seeped through the gaps. The whole place glowed. Everything was organic and Bryant didn't like it. He wanted the sharp angles of steel, the chemical taste of recycled air.

'Look,' Alistair said. He was leaning over a familiar looking transport crate. He held up his hand. In it was an even more familiar looking packet. 'Silver Rice. This must be what they're feeding the women.'

He tossed one to Bryant, who ripped it open and chewed it down hungrily. Never had the mix of salt and sweet tasted so good. He walked over to the crate and helped himself to another, stuffing a couple more into his pockets. Alistair did the same.

'If they're storing food here, they must have a way of getting it to the higher levels,' Alistair said.

'Over there.' Bryant walked over to the high-sided basket hooked up to cables that hung down through a hole in the roof. It was impossible to see what was up there, but if they were going to find out, this was the only way.

They climbed in together. Bryant elbowed Alistair out of the way, netting himself the bigger share of the space. He told himself he wasn't afraid, that he was totally prepared for whatever came next. He almost convinced himself, too, until the basket jerked into motion. It rose silently and quickly. A well-oiled machine couldn't have done any better.

The next level was empty and still. A gentle hum filled the air. It was deserted apart from a solitary Shi Fai. It stood a good twenty metres away from them, facing in the other direction. Alistair motioned to Bryant to stay down, stay quiet. Bryant pulled a face in return. Did Alistair think he was stupid? He knew how to move quietly. He took a couple of steps forward.

The creature tipped back its head and tested the air with its undulating tongue. Then it turned. For a few seconds, Bryant and the Shi Fai just looked at each other. It was different from the one he had seen in the village, not an adult as compared to a child, but as if it was at a different stage in its life cycle. Its face was more angular, the mouth wide instead of small and narrow. There were tendons growing out of the side of its head and twisting around the back. Its skin was almost translucent, and he could see the intricate network of dark veins running through the inside of its body. The three eyes were still the same, though. It made Bryant think of the field with the dead trees and the skeleton he had found inside that desiccated pod.

It shouted something, a high-pitched sound, and it charged at Bryant.

They both crashed to the floor. Bryant kicked and struggled, but the Shi Fai was heavy and it had landed on top. It peered down at him. A long tentacle extended from its mouth, like a pulsating white worm, and dragged across his skin, then it shrieked again, and gave off a strange smell. Bryant couldn't breathe under the weight of it.

If he couldn't get it off him soon, he was going to suffocate.

Then he remembered the drug gun in his pocket, the one he had loaded and put there so he could use it whenever he wanted. He shoved his hand down, felt the hard shape and somehow managed to pull it free.

He jammed the drug gun against the thing's flank and pressed the trigger. It fired with a beep, a sound that was almost a comfort to him as over the past few months it had come to mean the end of pain.

The Shi Fai went stiff. It exhaled, bathing his face in its sour breath. Those three black eyes stared down at him. He couldn't tell if it was dead or just high and decided he didn't care.

Between them, he and Alistair pushed the creature off.

'Come on,' Alistair said. 'There'll be more of them. There always are.'

The small chamber led through into a larger one, and from that ran multiple passages.

'We should split up,' Bryant said. 'We'll never be able to look everywhere otherwise.' He didn't wait for a reply. The drugs were already starting to wear off, and he didn't want Alistair to know. It was probably because this planet was so hot. He was sweating so much that the Euphoria was leaking out through his pores. He went straight down the nearest corridor, trying to ignore the twinge in his belly that signalled pain was on its way.

He had only one shot left. His felt for the gun in his pocket. He had no idea how long it would take to get back to the transporter, and then back to the *Mutant*. He hadn't thought to bring many shots with him. He hadn't thought he would need them. He hadn't thought at all.

'Eve!' he shouted. 'Eve!'

And then he heard something. A voice. A human voice,

shouting a human word. It was three pods along by his reckoning, and he ran to it. The shadow inside was moving. And yelling.

Bryant found himself no longer caring if it was Eve. If the person in that pod was female, and she was green, he was taking her and he was leaving.

CHAPTER
33

11 cycles until ripening

Drang Fields, Faidal

The first thing Eve heard was footsteps outside the little pod she'd been sealed into. They didn't sound right. The Shi Fai had a distinctive gait. She always knew when they were outside, when a packet of Silver Rice was about to be stuffed through the little hole that opened up in the top corner.

She sat up and listened. The footsteps grew closer. She told herself she was imagining it – how could she not be? She held her breath, so that not even that quiet sound would distract from what was going on outside.

Those footsteps were definitely new. 'Hello?' she called. 'Hello? Is someone there?'

The footsteps got louder, closer together. 'In here!' she shouted. 'I'm in here!'

Through the thin layer that sealed her in, she could see a dark shape. It was too skinny to be Shi Fai. Her heart started to race. She got to her feet, hitting her head on the low ceiling of her little pod.

'Get back,' came a muffled voice from the other side. 'I'm going to shoot the wall.'

257

Three blaster shots were fired in rapid succession. With the first, the wall started to crack. The second broke open a hole the size of her head, and she had just enough time to see dark eyes staring back at her before the third shattered it completely.

It crumbled to the floor in a sticky, lumpy mess.

Eve looked at the man who stood on the other side. He was tall and lean in an unhealthy way that had drawn the skin tight across his cheekbones and jaw. Those dark eyes were sunken and dull, and thin patches of dirty hair were plastered to his scalp with sweat. Bryant looked very different from the last time she had seen him, but she'd never forget that face.

'Bloody supernova,' he said, staring at her. 'Hit the target first time.' He leaned in and made a grab for her, jerking his hand back just before his fingertips could graze the bare skin of her arm. He rubbed a hand over his face and then over his head. 'Shit,' he said, more to himself than to her. 'Forgot about that.'

Then his gaze shot to her. 'Come on,' he said. 'We're leaving.'

Eve didn't need to be told twice. She clambered over the pile of debris. It left a gluey mess on the soles of her feet. The corridor was empty, but she doubted it would stay that way for long.

'This way,' he said.

She followed him, eager and terrified. 'Are there others? How many? Have you got ships? There are hundreds of other women here. We've got to ...'

But she didn't finish what she had been about to say, because they rounded the corner and she saw someone. Another man. It couldn't be.

It was.

She dodged Bryant and ran up to the other man, slamming to a halt centimetres before she slammed into him. 'Alistair!'

'Eve!'

She wanted so much to throw her arms around him, to press her body to his, to feel his gentleness and comfort and life. His serious expression creased into a smile, and what he couldn't do with his hands he did with his eyes. They rushed over her, and, as they did, his smile disappeared. 'What did they do to you?'

'It doesn't matter,' she told him. 'You came for me. You came.' She leaned in. She knew she shouldn't, but she couldn't help herself. She had missed him so much. She dared to rest her head against the front of his shirt just for a second.

'Of course I did.'

'I knew you would.'

'Did you?'

'Yes.' She shifted her head to look up at him, but Bryant was watching them, and it stopped her from saying all the things she wanted to say.

'Are you all right?' Alistair asked her.

Eve shook her head as she tried to work out an answer to that question. 'I don't know,' she said. 'Get me out of here, and I will be.' She refused to think of the thing growing in her belly, already a heavy weight, like a little ball of stone resting heavy against her bladder. If she could get away from here, get to a medical centre, it could be dealt with. There would be a way. There had to be. 'Where are the others?'

'There are no others,' Alistair said. 'Just us two.'

'What? Where's Dax? Jinn?'

'Still on Sittan, as far as we know. We've got a transporter,' he said. 'It's not far from here. We left the *Mutant* up in orbit.'

Her brain stumbled over it. A transporter. 'But the other women . . .'

'We didn't come here for the others,' Bryant said. 'We came here for you.'

Eve glared at him. 'And I'm grateful. But I won't just leave them behind.'

'How many are there?' Alistair asked her.

'I don't know,' Eve said. 'A thousand, maybe?'

He didn't say anything. He didn't have to. It was written all over his face.

'We can't leave them here!' she insisted. 'We can't let this carry on, Alistair. They're using women as incubators. Putting something inside them.' Her fingers curved into a fist and pressed against her lower belly. She moved it aside quickly. She didn't want Alistair to know what had been done to her.

'We can't save a thousand fucking women,' Bryant said. 'And I'd rather we didn't stand around here like a bunch of fussing old women discussing it. We need to get out of here before more Shi Fai turn up. I don't have enough Euphoria for all of them.'

He signalled to Alistair with a jerk of his head, then turned and started to march away, back along the tunnel. A bony, long-fingered hand went to the empty holster at his side and danced there for a moment, as if he expected the weapon to be there.

'He looks terrible.' She stared after him, seeing the way his thin body failed to fill his jacket, the places where his hair didn't cover his scalp, and the dark, discoloured patch on the back of his neck that she knew would match the shape of her hand. 'Why in the void is he here?'

'Because I couldn't fly the *Mutant* on my own,' Alistair told her. 'After you . . . Jinn and Li took Bryant's yacht and went to Sittan. We came here.'

Bryant had dragged himself halfway across the galaxy to find her. And from the looks of him, he was barely alive. But there wasn't time to let the sting of guilt settle in. She could hear the sound of feet moving along the tunnel, flat, rubbery, alien feet that slapped against the waxy surface. She wanted to help the other women, but she couldn't do that if the Shi Fai found them.

She grabbed Alistair's sleeve and pulled him into motion. Together, the two of them sprinted after Bryant. The walls sloped in, narrowing the tunnel as it spiralled higher and higher. More pods like the one she had been trapped inside lined the walls, though most of them were empty. They waited patiently, those little hollow spaces, and Bryant was using them to climb.

He gripped the edges to pull himself up, scrambling between the little pods. Eve darted forward and did the same. It was tricky. She had to stretch for each handhold, each foothold. She waited only long enough to make sure that Alistair was doing the same, and then put all her focus on the climb. Three pods up, she tucked herself inside one and took a minute or so to catch her breath. But she didn't dare linger for too long. The pale yellow walls closed around her, a claustrophobic cocoon that made even the weight of the air feel like too much.

She was getting out of here. Alistair had come for her. Her chest burned with the need to sob, but this wasn't the time to cry. So she forced herself to keep climbing instead, pushing everything else aside. It could wait until later. Getting out of here could not.

The roof itself was thinner than the walls, the lumpy material sheer enough to let in daylight. She saw Bryant hammer at it with his fist. A few slender flakes dropped down.

It wasn't enough.

He leaned back inside his pod and emerged a few seconds later with his trouser leg half up and a lethal looking blade in his hand. He gripped the hilt with both hands and hacked at the roof.

The first crack of true daylight made her heart pound hard in her chest. When a chunk hit the floor, and that crack became a jagged edged shape large enough to put a fist through, she started to believe. He hacked and hacked, and the pieces of falling material cascaded to the floor. Then the smell hit her. There were Shi Fai below, and they were angry. She'd learned how to read them now, what the different smells meant.

Eve didn't look down. Going that way was not an option. She was not going back to the Shi Fai, not now, not ever. She would rather throw herself off the roof. She crawled to the edge of the little pod she had hidden herself in and started to climb. She refused to think about the others, the women she was leaving behind. If she did, she wouldn't be able to move.

Only three more pods were between her and the roof. Her fingers dug in and her leg muscles tightened and cramped as she forced her body up. The hole Bryant had made was wide enough for him to get his shoulders into and she saw him disappear through it.

'Come on!' he yelled at her.

Eve reached, but it was too far. 'I can't reach!'

'For fuck's sake,' he yelled. He scrubbed a hand over his head, more hair coming out with the movement. Then he pulled off his shirt and wrapped it around his arm. He held it out to her. 'Grab on.'

Eve hesitated.

'Just fucking do it!'

So she did. She reached up and wrapped her fingers round his wrist, as he wrapped his bony digits around hers. He pulled her up. It took only seconds. She let go of him as quickly as she could.

Alistair was almost there. Almost there. 'Come on!' she shouted to him. She wanted to hold out her hand, as Bryant had offered a hand to her, but she knew that she couldn't. She wasn't strong enough, and she wouldn't risk Alistair touching her. All she could do was watch as he painfully made his way to the last pod, then reached for the edges of the hole.

He stretched out, gripped the edge, but he wasn't quite tall enough. He swung out, grabbing onto the edge with his other hand, and hung there for a moment. It seemed an age before he was able to heave himself up. Eve could do nothing more than scream at him to hurry.

One elbow planted firmly on the surface, then the other. Eve got to her feet, got hold of his shirt, and started to pull. She didn't know if she was helping or hindering him. She pulled as he struggled. When he made it up, he collapsed on the surface, just as she had done.

Bryant had rolled to his knees. He shuffled closer to the hole, close enough to spit in it. Then he opened his jacket with unsteady hands and pulled something out of his inside pocket. A palm-sized sonic grenade.

'What are you doing?' Eve asked him.

'This should be enough to break open the cells and let the other women out. Should give them a chance, if they're smart enough to find a ship and get away from here.'

'No, wait!' she shouted, but Bryant had already dropped the grenade. The boom shook the surface beneath their feet. It rippled through the air around them, and Eve closed her eyes as she felt it move through her body.

Bryant gave Alistair a push. He went flying down the side of the building.

'Your turn,' Bryant said to her.

Somewhere below them there was another bang.

Eve didn't wait any longer. She sat, leaned back and pushed herself into motion. Air rushed past her as she zoomed over the side of the building. She couldn't breathe, her bones hurting as she bounced over the uneven surface, her brain screaming at her to stop, that she didn't know what was at the bottom, that this was going to hurt, it was really going to hurt. She braced herself. There wasn't time to do anything else. She landed in water. It was dirty and thick with weeds and tree roots and she plunged deep down into it.

When she surfaced, coughing, she saw Alistair hunched over a tangle of roots, black water dripping from his hair, his breathing fast and loud. Eve kicked her way over to him. There were cuts on his face, his arms. 'Alistair?' she said, frightened. The bloody sonic grenade.

The sound that he made was something Eve knew would never leave her. It scraped its way through her body, leaving a trail of fear and hurt in its wake. But there was no time to think about it.

There was an almighty splash somewhere behind her. A few seconds later, Bryant surfaced, spluttering and swearing. Behind them, the dome had started to smoke. Within seconds, the smell of it was everywhere, bitter and acrid. Bryant coughed as he half walked, half swam over to her.

'We need to get moving,' she said, desperately keeping her gaze fixed on Alistair, willing him to get up, to move. 'How far is it to your yacht?'

'Too bloody far,' Bryant replied. He stood there, dripping, a hand curved round to protect his eyes from the light as he turned his head and stared at something in the distance.

'What are you looking at?' Eve asked him.

'Our way out of here,' he said. He splashed his way over to Alistair, looped an arm around his shoulders and hauled him to his feet. 'We'll take one of their ships.'

1st day of the sixth turn

The Sand Seas, Sittan

The ship wasn't familiar. It wasn't one that Dax had seen before, he was sure of that much, though he felt increasingly uncertain about everything else. The guards had seized Jinn and taken her back to the palace. She was there now, locked in her room.

Dax, however, was at the Sand Sea with the empress and the rest of her entourage. She had wanted to see the ship for herself. Tents had been set up, forming a small camp, providing shade from the scorching heat of the suns. He sat in the shelter of one of them and watched as the guards probed the ship.

So far, they had not been able to find a way on board. The Virena that covered the surface, blending into the background and rendering the ship virtually invisible, flexed and spat at them whenever they got too close. It was clearly making the guards nervous.

It therefore came as no surprise to Dax when the empress got to her feet, dismissing the guards with an irritated flick of her hand. She stood a couple of metres away from the ship for several minutes. Then she walked right up to it and placed a hand on the side. The surface shimmered violently, rippling through a myriad different colours. She sank her fingers into it and took hold.

She pulled the Virena away from the surface. It seemed reluctant at first, but she kept the tension on it. It came away in a thin strand that grew thicker and thicker as she wrapped it around her hand, until finally the whole lot came away in a rush. It spilled out of her hand and pooled at her feet, rubbing against her like a pet. The empress ignored it. She was too busy staring at the ship, and so was Dax.

He got to his feet and walked over to stand beside her.

'Do you recognise this?'

'It's a pleasure yacht,' he said. He walked the length of the ship and back again. It wasn't particularly large, so it didn't take very long. 'Bigger than a skimmer, capable of long-distance space travel. Expensive.'

'I want to see inside,' she told him.

'Here,' Dax said. He didn't have a key for the ship, but the emergency lock was easily located and broken. The side of the ship folded out, revealing a narrow stairway.

He went first. The interior lights switched on automatically. Dax felt confident that this was not a ship he had ever owned. Whatever he had done, whatever he had been before he came to Sittan, he was certain that he had not traded in flesh.

The empress had followed him onto the ship. She looked around, her eyes flickering, but said nothing. The control deck was next, and that did interest her. 'How does it work?'

'Pilot sits there,' Dax told her, gesturing to the seat in the middle. 'They plug into the onboard computer using Tellurium, a kind of metal implant that connects them directly to it.'

'The female has that,' the empress noted. 'She told me it was fused to her body and refused to give it up.'

'She couldn't give you it,' Dax said. 'It's part of her.'

The empress ran one clawed hand over the back of the chair, and then dropped down into it. She touched the controls, the keypads, opened up the screens. Dax couldn't tell what she thought of any of it. He felt more than a little overwhelmed. He thought of taking the controls, firing up the phase drive and leaving the planet, just flying as far away from it as he could. His head started to hurt when he thought about leaving, a sharp pain pressing against the back of his eyes. He would stay here, he decided, and the pain immediately began to recede. He followed the empress as she walked off the ship.

The Virena had formed a shimmering cloud, and it followed the empress as she returned to her tent. A couch had been placed under a wide awning. She stretched out on it. A pair of male slaves brought pitchers of chilled water and a bowl of the empress's favourite fruit, and she partook of both. Dax, too, was offered water, and he drank thirstily.

The empress was talking to the Virena in a low, soothing voice. The surface kept rippling, the colours changing, until they became more than just colours. Images began to appear, blurred at first, but growing more and more distinct.

He sat up a little straighter when he appeared in one of those images. 'What is this?'

'The Virena is showing me where it has been,' she said, and there was a note of amusement in her voice. 'It seems that it was attached to a ... what do you call it? A droid.'

Dax watched, unable to form words, as snatches of a life he didn't remember were played out in front of him. Jinn was there, and others, too. He felt he should know who they were, but he didn't, and he couldn't find the memories. When he searched for them, he found only blank spaces where they should have been. 'This isn't right,' he said. It was as if he was watching the life of a stranger, only that stranger looked exactly like him.

It wasn't clear exactly how the Virena had made its way to the ship. Some patches of time had been lost. One thing that was clear, however, was that Jinn had come here for him, and she had not come alone. Another male had been with her, one that the empress recognised. 'Jozeph Li,' she said, suddenly sitting upright. She exhaled sharply, her nostrils flaring.

'Do you know him?'

'He fought in the arena on behalf of a male named Merion. His mother, Ritte, was once a guard of mine. They live in the city.'

The empress gestured to her guards. Two of them hurried closer.

'Find Ritte Tas Nar,' the empress told them. 'Search her house. You are looking for a human male. Bring them both to me.'

The guards bowed then slipped away. They climbed onto small vehicles that looked a bit like scoot bikes, with wide seats and a single vertical handle at the front which allowed them to hold on and steer. But it didn't run on wheels or a hover platform. Instead the Virena boiled underneath it, providing momentum. They had quickly moved out of sight.

The rest of the guards began to pack up the tents, the food and the pool that had been erected just in case the empress felt the need to use it. Dax followed the empress back to her personal transport, a sharp-tipped, open-topped boat powered in a similar way to the scoot bikes. She operated it without having to use controls, the link between her mind and the Virena alive and powerful. Something had changed in her since the Mountain had started to erupt. She had become all at once brighter and sharper and palpably more powerful.

They sped back to the palace in silence. Dax was glad. He did not wish to talk.

All around them, the once dry rivers were full. The air smelled of hot rock. There was a definite change in the atmosphere, and most certainly a change in the empress herself. Gone was the desperation that had licked around the edges of everything she did and everything she said.

But Dax barely noticed any of it. His mind was full of what he had seen, the images that the Virena had showed them of his life before he came here. He couldn't remember any of it. He'd never felt more confused or more uncertain, and that frightened him.

He gripped the side of the boat tightly as they sped through the tunnel that led under the palace. It came to a stop in the centre of the large cave that served as a docking area for all the empress's transports.

In comparison to the human ship, the Sittan ones were considerably more elegant. Hulls curved and twisted in shapes that a human would never have dreamed up. They took up space abundantly and greedily. He could never fly a ship like this.

And yet he could fly that human ship. He could almost feel the shape of the controls under his hands. No. No. He wouldn't think about it. He didn't want to think about it. He wanted to stay here, to fight. He knew who he was here.

'Come,' the empress ordered him.

He obeyed. He stepped up onto the waiting transport circle and stood stiffly next to the empress as it carried them back to her quarters. But he could not stop his mind from wandering back to Jinn. He had known her. More than that, he had shared something with her. He was certain of it. A hollow space inside him had begun to ache.

When they reached the empress's chambers, they were empty. There was no sign of the guards. Dax remained in the doorway. He watched as the empress stripped out of her robes, dropping them where she stood and stepped down into the cooling waters of her private pool. She swam across it, her naked body just visible under the surface of the water, and then she stretched her arms out across the ledge. She looked at Dax. One jewelled hand rose from the water and beckoned to him.

He wanted her. He wanted Jinn. He wanted to leave this place, this hot, strange place that had not been built for humans. But he was afraid. So he walked to the edge of the pool and stood there, watching the empress as she bathed, the water blurring the edges of her body.

'Join me,' she invited him.

His mind wasn't sure, but his body responded and his hands went to the ties that held his breeches in place and loosened them. He stripped them off, removing the leather that bound his upper arm as well. He wound it up into a coil before dropping it at his feet.

The water was cool when he stepped into it. It drained the heat from his skin, but did nothing to calm the fire in his blood. He had been without for too long. He moved further into the pool, until the water reached mid-thigh. The empress stretched out in front of him. Her mouth curved into a wicked smile and the spikes rippled across her head and her shoulders. She was so exotic, so alien, so different from him and yet female, and it was that aspect of her that he craved so very badly.

Her legs parted as he moved closer still, allowing him to slide between them. Her skin was slightly rough against his. She made no move to come closer or to touch him. He didn't even know if he wanted her to. But he could not step away.

Breathing became difficult. Despite the coolness of the water, his skin burned. He felt slightly dizzy as the blood drained from his head and went thundering south.

Her smile got bigger.

'It is strange,' she said, 'that we can be so different and yet so much the same.'

'I am not like you,' Dax told her.

'Maybe not.' She leaned forward and steadily got to her feet. Water moved slowly down her body, winding its way along naked skin and curves, and Dax found himself shaking. His erection pressed hard against her belly. She encouraged it to. They were almost the same height, and that put her face very close to his. He could feel the heat of her breath against his cheek, smell the sweet scent of the fruit that she gorged herself on daily.

He put a hand on her breast. He could feel the fast beat of the heart in her chest, and the echoing beat of the second one located lower down, in her belly. His own pulse began to beat in time with hers. Her hips swayed, and he slid his hand down to feel their rhythm.

Need beat hot and hard within him. It had been so long. So long.

He closed his eyes, and, when he did, he saw Jinn. But the empress's hands were on him, stroking, squeezing, forcing a reaction from him that he was powerless to stop. He got harder at her touch, and he tipped his head back and groaned.

He was almost there. Almost there.

Sweat ran down his body. His muscles tightened. He dropped his head and opened his eyes. Yellow eyes stared back at him, gleaming with avarice and pleasure.

His stomach lurched, and he knocked her hands away. He staggered back to the edge of the pool. 'No,' he said, holding out a hand to keep her back. 'No.' He felt suddenly very self-conscious and disgusted with himself, and covered his genitals with his hand. He scrambled out of the water. His clothes were where he had left them, and he fought to get them on, all too aware that he might have just made a terrible mistake, but knowing there was no other choice he could have made. He didn't want her.

He wanted the human female.

'Dax.'

He stopped, turned to see the empress emerging from the water. He wanted to look away, but that felt too dangerous, so he forced himself to look at her. She didn't even try to cover herself. He wished she would. 'Where is the human?' he asked.

'That's no concern of yours.'

'I want her,' he said. He spun, trying to find a way out of the room. His head was pounding.

The empress hissed. 'No,' she said. She walked over to where he stood, her muscular body moving quickly and easily. She raised a hand, as if to strike him. Dax caught her wrist before she could follow through.

Her fingers flexed, claws moving mere centimetres from his face. She was astonishingly strong, becoming even stronger as black strands of Virena began to bind her body. Dax let go of her and pushed her away. He could feel the need for violence surging within him, and soon he would not be able to hold it down.

'How dare you refuse me,' she shrieked at him. She reached

for the chain that would bring down the little cage that held her pet and pulled it. The cage rattled straight down to the floor. She flipped open the lid and the Vreen crawled out, its little feet gripping the edges. It dropped to the floor, landing with a surprisingly heavy thump.

The empress said something in Sittan and the Vreen turned and fixed its gaze on Dax. By the time he realised the danger it was too late. The creature rushed towards him, tail up, grey tongue flickering.

Dax tried to back away, but the room was cluttered and he couldn't move far enough or quickly enough. The creature was on him. It scampered up his leg, clinging tightly, and when it reached his thigh it bit him. Sharp teeth dug in and sank deep. He shouted in shock and pain. He tried to pull it off. It refused to let go.

The empress laughed. He grabbed his head in his hands, trying to block out the sound. It felt like an eternity but it was only a few seconds later when he dropped to the floor, his legs no longer able to hold him up. The last thing he remembered was the empress leaning over him.

And Jinn.

CHAPTER

35

2nd December 2207

Apartment 12, Nobel Tower, Colony Seven, Earth-Controlled Space

There was only so much of Underworld London that Ferona could take. Returning to her apartment in the Dome had still been out of the question. She had sent Victor to look, and he had reported back to say there were still journalists and cameras camped outside her front door. She wasn't ready to answer their questions yet. She suspected she never would be.

So she had instructed Swain to arrange transport, and she had come here to her apartment on Colony Seven instead. Victor had made it all possible and she had been grateful for that. She had eaten decent food and she had slept. She had endured a dose of Rejuvinex administered by her beauty droid instead of her usual medical technician. It had helped erase some of the darkness under her eyes and the shocked pallor that had taken over her skin.

Now it was time to get to work. She knew that she no longer had Vexler's support. That was fine. Once the votes had been cast in the Senate she would no longer need it. But she had to do something about Humans First. Her motivation was no longer entirely political. This had become personal. She seated herself behind her desk and called Lucinda, who had remained on Earth with Vexler.

Lucinda looked fresh. Her hair had changed. Gone was the sleek length, replaced by a glossy crop. Ferona didn't like it. 'You're looking well.'

'As are you,' Lucinda replied.

With that lie out of the way, Ferona moved swiftly onto more important things. 'What is the situation there?'

'The same,' Lucinda said. She pursed deep pink lips that were most definitely fuller than the last time Ferona had seen her. Lucinda had always been attractive. It was part of the reason Ferona had chosen her. An attractive female assistant was extremely useful, especially one with Lucinda's other skills. But she'd never been prone to obvious cosmetic tweaks before. 'I hate to say this, Ferona, but I think you should seriously consider resigning.'

'*What?*'

'It's the sensible thing to do. You have to understand that you can't carry on.'

Ferona sat back in shock. Of everyone, Lucinda was the person she had trusted the most. She had given her everything. *Everything.* 'No,' she said. 'That is not going to happen. If I resign now, everything I have worked for will fall apart. The other senators must see that we have stability in government. I have to be the one to go to Kepler. Sending someone else would be absolutely out of the question.'

She ended the call before she could say something else, something she might regret. And although Lucinda couldn't hear her thoughts over the comm., she didn't want to spend another second communicating with her.

Something was not right. The feeling had been growing for a while, but she had ignored it. Now it throbbed at the back of her neck and refused to go away. She got to her feet and slipped through into her private dressing room. Victor was in the main living area, watching something on the screen, impeccably behaved as always.

An impeccably behaved, Underworld-raised Type One, given to her by Vexler. A press conference that had gone completely wrong, when her press conferences never went wrong, when she was always in control no matter how much pressure was applied.

'Lock the door,' Ferona ordered the apartment's computer. There was a hiss as it complied and the door was locked tight. She staggered over to the rose silk slipper chair that stood by the window and sank down on it heavily. She sat there for several minutes, staring at the door.

It couldn't be, could it? She was simply being paranoid.

And yet the thought nagged at her.

Lucinda had turned against her. She hadn't returned from Vexler's office, where Ferona had planted her in order to keep an eye on the president. When Ferona had requested that she leave in light of what happened, Lucinda had given some very convincing arguments against that and had remained.

Ferona thought about the expensive hair, and the lips, things her assistant could not have afforded on her current salary, and she was all of a sudden certain that she knew why. Lucinda was working for Vexler.

And then her thoughts returned to Victor. Impeccably behaved Victor, who had not put a foot wrong. The man was too good to be true.

Quickly, Ferona got to her feet. She stepped into her wardrober and waited as the machine quickly clothed her in plum trousers and tunic. She didn't bother with the beauty droid. She dialled up a coat, bag and shoes on the screen and waited impatiently as the system located them then delivered them to the rail. It took only a matter of moments to slip them on. She took off her wrist comm. and took a pile of high-value credit chips from the safe.

If her suspicions were correct, there was someone here on Colony Seven who would know. Weston. He had a house on the other side of the city, somewhere he could play with his inventions in relative privacy.

All that she had to do now was get past Victor. He had insisted on accompanying her everywhere she went, and she hadn't questioned it. That's what bodyguards did.

But this was one trip she had to make alone.

She ordered the computer to unlock the door. She gathered her courage, then walked up to the door and straight through when it slid open. 'I'm going out for a while,' she told Victor. 'To visit a friend. I don't need you to come with me.'

She kept on walking as she told him that. 'Computer, code orange.'

Her hasty exit took Victor by surprise, as she had hoped it would. Code orange closed the door before he could get to it. He was locked inside the apartment now and wouldn't be able to get out until she returned and deactivated the locks.

Ferona breathed a little sigh of relief as she walked to the elevator that would take her down to the lower level. She felt a little less comfortable when she was forced to take a cab, but the journey was fortunately short. She shoved a credit chip in the slot when the car stopped and the screen flashed up the fare.

'Have a nice day!' the automated system called before the cab wheeled away.

That seemed highly unlikely.

Weston lived in a row of cheap houses on the outskirts of the city. She didn't know why he didn't opt for something better. It wasn't like he couldn't afford it. She stepped carefully between discarded food wrappers and drink bags as she made it to his front door.

There was no comm. panel. She was reduced to hammering on the door. 'Weston!'

No response. She hammered again, and this time gave the door a kick for good measure. 'Weston! I need to talk to you.'

He answered. She could smell alcohol. 'Ferona!' His face stretched into a smile. 'How pleasant to see you. Would you like to come in!'

She was already through the door before he'd finished asking. 'Shut the door,' she told him. 'Quickly.'

'Is something wrong?'

The house was small. She had stepped straight into the living area. It was a monument to guns. From floor to ceiling, every inch of wall space was covered in them. She didn't even recognise half of them, though she was sure that many were antique and very valuable.

Ferona turned to face him, the hatchet faced little worm. 'Perhaps you would like to answer that question yourself.'

'I'm sure I . . .'

'He's Type Three, isn't he?'

'Who?'

'Don't play games with me, Weston.'

He walked over to the Autochef sitting on a little table at the side of the room, and ordered himself a drink. He knocked it back in a single swallow before he turned to face her. 'Yes,' he said. His eyes were bright. 'I'm surprised it took you so long to figure it out.'

'You're mixing the serums now?'

His face flushed as the alcohol hit. 'Actually, I've been mixing them for a while. Haven't had much success with the Type Two. But this combination of Types One and Three has real potential.'

'I didn't tell you to do this.'

'No,' he said. 'But you are not my only client.'

Ferona opened her mouth to ask who, then shut it again. Vexler. 'How did he find out about you?'

'I believe your assistant told him. Lovely girl. Very ambitious.' Lucinda.

Suddenly Ferona needed a drink. She walked straight over to the Autochef, repeated the last order, and snatched it up as soon as it appeared. It burned as it hit the back of her throat. It helped. 'Why?'

'They want you out. It's as simple as that. You're too powerful, and they don't like it.'

'You betrayed me.'

'Ferona,' Weston said patronisingly. 'This was a business arrangement. I was always available to the highest bidder. I thought you knew that.'

'So what is he? Victor, I mean.'

'One of the Type Three plants from the colonies. Engineered to change the hair and the eyes, of course. All we had to do was send him to the centre on Colony Four and they took care of the rest.'

And all Vexler had to do was offer him more credits. Ferona closed her eyes and fought down her rage. 'How much?' she said finally.

'How much for what?'

'How much to put me back in control.'

Weston smiled. His teeth were very yellow. 'I'm sure we can work something out.'

CHAPTER 36

3rd day of the sixth turn

Karakai Arena, Fire City, Sittan

Jinn had never thought when she came to Sittan that she would end up here, locked in a holding cage at the arena, waiting to be sent out to fight. She had thought sometimes that Dax might not be himself. But she hadn't expected to find him changed in the way that he had. The Dax she had known would never have betrayed her. He would never have allowed anyone to control him the way the empress seemed to. He would have wanted off this planet. He would have found a way off this planet.

When the guards came, she washed in the cool water of the plunge pool and dressed in the clothes they threw down for her. 'Who am I fighting today?' she asked them, more because she needed to talk to someone than because she wanted to know. In any case, they didn't answer.

Her skin was oiled, her hair plaited back away from her face. They held her arms out to the sides, stopping her from using her blades, though they couldn't stop her from willing the Tellurium in and out of her hands, forming different shapes. It put the guards on edge and she took pleasure in that. They left her alone as soon as she was dressed. She sat by the side of the pool, one hand playing in the water, and waited.

She didn't know what she was going to do next. She was no longer convinced that she was going to be able to get Dax away from here. In her darker moments, she no longer knew if she wanted to. Perhaps it would be better if she simply accepted that the Dax she knew was gone. He had died on board the *A2* the day his genes had been modified by that final dose of serum. All that remained was the flesh, the meat, and that was not the man she had loved so very desperately. Her eyes and her throat burned as she tried to make herself accept it. She had told Li that if Dax had become like the men on the *A2*, she would kill him, and she still believed that would be the right thing to do. But Dax was not like those men. He had done terrible things, yes, but he had also shown her flashes of kindness. He wasn't a mindless monster. There was still some human left in him. She tried to persuade herself it was enough.

When the chime that signalled the start of the fight rang through her cell, she got to her feet and positioned herself in front of the bars. They were formed of sharp-edged obsidian, only now tiny little drops of black Virena were moving over them, dancing across the polished surface. Jinn held up her hand. They danced nearer. She extended a blade and the Virena practically vibrated with delight. She let a couple of little drops run down the length of her blade. It was such a strange substance. She didn't understand why it responded to her.

The bars dropped away. She took a deep breath and walked out into the arena, deliberately choosing not to rush. The Mountain loomed over the arena, no longer a dark, silent presence, but one that was hot and bright and full of life. Whatever the empress had chosen for her, she would meet in her own way and on her own terms. That was the only way to deal with what time she had left. For Jinn was in no doubt that her time now was limited. The empress didn't need her any longer.

To Jinn's surprise, the arena was empty. There were no other fighters waiting for her. The stands were empty and silent, too, and only two of the three suns could be seen. Somehow, she had lost track of time. She turned, looking around her, and willed her blades out to full length. Something was not right here.

And then a cage opened up on the other side of the arena, and a man walked out.

It was Dax. She would know the lines of his body anywhere. His time here had made him leaner and harder, but nothing could change the height, the shoulders, the way she felt when he looked at her. It was just as it had been the first time she had met him, and he was just as much a stranger to her now as he had been then.

She did not move as he began to walk towards her. Let him cut the distance between them. Because if Jinn knew anything now, it was that this would be her final fight. Dax would be her final fight.

So this is how it ends.

He came within a couple of metres of her before he halted. He looked her over, and she did the same to him. Neither of them spoke. What was there to say? A little piece of her heart broke as she looked at him. She did not let it show on her face.

She was glad of that when the empress's platform lit up with a soft amber glow. The empress was there, reclining on her day bed, surrounded by her guards and several male slaves. She reached for a piece of fruit from the bowl that sat next to the bed and bit into it. Juice ran down her arm and dripped onto the platform. She tossed the half-finished piece aside. When she spoke, her voice rang loud and clear across the empty arena.

'Fight,' she said.

And that was it.

'And if I refuse?' Jinn asked.

The empress moved into a sitting position. She got to her feet and moved to the very edge of her platform. Slowly, it sank down to the floor of the arena, and she stepped off it, her feet leaving narrow imprints in the hot sand. A strange creature sat atop her left shoulder. It was an ugly little thing. Jinn didn't know what it was, but she was pretty sure that she didn't like it.

'This is my planet,' the empress told her. 'And you *will* do as I say.'

'Why?' she challenged the empress. 'What will you do to me if I don't?'

'Nothing,' the empress said. 'But I will do something to him.'

'Go ahead,' Jinn told her. She didn't look at Dax. 'I don't care.'

'All right.' The empress turned her head, and muttered something to the lizard on her shoulder.

'No,' Dax said suddenly. He started to back away. 'No. Not that.'

He looked at Jinn. He looked at the lizard. Then he looked back at Jinn. For a moment, she thought she saw something in his eyes, a flicker of the man she had known, but the next moment proved her wrong.

Because he went for her.

He came in fast. She barely had time to dodge the first blow and it caught her on the shoulder, knocking her back. She dodged the next one, trying to get away from him, but he was too quick for her and far too determined. He was going to make her fight, she realised, even if she didn't want to. And if she didn't fight him, he would hurt her. Or the empress would use that strange creature, whatever it was, to hurt Dax.

She had no choice. And so she used everything she had learned in the arena, everything that Dax had taught her, and fought back with everything she had. She kept her blades in despite the burning heat of the Tellurium in her arms. They had been told to fight, not to kill. But she couldn't help feeling a sick wave of fear that it would all too soon come to that. Now that she faced him here in the arena, Jinn knew for certain that she could not leave him as he was. The Dax she had known would not want to live like this.

She dodged a blow to the gut, caught him on the side of the head, right on the ear. A smack to the chin, an elbow to the stomach, then she spun away, wanting space to catch her breath and plan her next assault. He let her have it but only for the briefest of moments, and then kicked out at her. The move caught her in the thigh and she dropped to the ground, but the hit hadn't been nearly as hard as it should have been. The other men she had fought in the arena had hit her far harder.

Was he holding back?

No. She was imagining it. For the next few minutes, they fought hard, Jinn giving as good as she got. And then she took a chance and opened herself up to him. It was an easy shot, a blow to the ribs that would floor her. He took it, and it bloody well hurt, knocking the wind out of her, almost cracking a rib.

Jinn dropped into a roll to avoid the kick that he swung in her direction and came to her feet with all blades out. They clashed again and this time he knocked her to the ground. He pinned her down, lowered his face close to hers. She struggled. 'You can't win,' he told her. 'I can keep going all day. I'll keep going until you've had all the pain you can take. And then I'll give you a bit more. You'll be begging me to end it before I do.'

She slashed out at him with her blade. How could he be so cruel? He didn't move back quite far enough, and a thin cut opened up on his chest. He grabbed her arm, twisted it painfully and shoved her to the ground. He held her there. He lifted his head slightly and glanced across at the empress, then dropped his gaze back down to Jinn. He let go of her arm, grabbed her hair, pulled her head back. She cried out. 'She thinks we were lovers.'

'She's right.'

'She thinks there is still something between us.'

'She's wrong.'

'There could be, if you wanted.' He leered down at her. 'Right here, right now.' He made a grab for her breeches.

She kicked out at him, punching his hand from her throat, and scrambled away. He came straight back at her, as she'd expected he would. They grappled again, and this time Jinn got the upper hand. She didn't know if she truly earned it or if he let her have it, if this was just part of his play. But he was flat on his back and she was on top of him, knees planted firmly in the sand.

Her blades were out. The tips of them were pressed against his chest. 'Do it,' he said, snarling up at her. Jinn hesitated. She looked over at the empress, who was on her feet and watching them closely, and knew that there was no other way. Dax was gone. He would not want to live as what he had become.

'Just fucking do it!'

She drove her blades straight through his heart right before it registered how much that had sounded like the old Dax. Like *her* Dax. He reared up from the sand, gasping for air. 'Jinn,' he said, and she saw that what had been only a flicker before was now very much real and present. His eyes were bright, his expression aware.

'Dax?'

He grabbed her wrist and held it as the Tellurium rushed back inside her body and the blades withdrew. Blood poured from the wound. 'That creature she has, it's called a Vreen. It bit me. Something ... something in the venom ...'

What had she done? Jinn pressed her hands against his heart, trying to stem the flow of blood. 'Why did you ... what ...?'

'She has Li and a female Sittan,' he told her. 'They're trapped in the passages below the palace. When they take my body to the Mountain, she'll take them, too. She intends to sacrifice the pair of them. You've got to get them away from here.'

'No,' Jinn cried. 'No!' But she couldn't seem to hold the wound together. Her hand was wet. His colour was fading. Sweat beaded at his hairline, and his breathing was fast and panicked now.

'It's the only way. She will never let me leave the planet alive. Use the Virena. Take my body,' he said. 'Take ... take me home. Promise me, Jinn.'

'No! No! Dax, you've got to fight this! Keep breathing. Just ... no!'

And then the light in his eyes went out.

CHAPTER
37

11 cycles to ripening

Panpon Wilds, Faidal

They made it away from the holding centre and into the surrounding jungle before they were forced to stop. The sonic grenade that Bryant had detonated had had the desired effect. A plume of smoke rose high above the very tops of the trees, dirtying the sky, and even at this distance Eve could still hear the shouts of the other women as they made their escape.

But it wasn't freedom. They were still trapped on this planet. Many of the women would still have the Shi Fai embryos growing inside them. They didn't have food or access to medical treatment. She wasn't sure that what Bryant had done would make life any better for them.

At least they had hope, now. There was a chance. If they could get to the Shi Fai ships and steal one, there was a chance for all of them. They had stopped to rest tucked into a crevice under the roots of a huge, flat topped tree. It helped to keep out the worst of the rain which had begun crashing down through the canopy a scant few seconds after they had stopped to rest.

'We need to get moving,' Bryant said. He started to climb out and back up onto the path they had forced through the trees.

'Wait,' Eve said.

Because Bryant might be ready to go, but Alistair most certainly was not.

Bryant turned back.

'You're going to have to help him,' Eve said. She moved as close as she dared and looked at Alistair. He was curled up, hugging his knees, with his chin resting on top of them. His eyes were closed and his ears were bleeding. She had seen him hurt before. She knew what his modifications did to him, physically. But she had never seen him like this. It had never been worse than a terrible headache, painful and distressing. This was something else.

'Alistair?' she said gently.

One hand moved slightly. He opened his eyes just a crack, enough for her to see a thin gleam of blue. 'It hurts,' he said.

'Can you get up? Bryant is going to help you.'

'No.'

'Bryant,' Eve called, but even at that slight increase in volume, Alistair visibly flinched, and whimpered.

This was bad. This was really, really bad. 'You have to let him help you,' she told Alistair, feeling a sudden horrible wash of fear. 'Come on.'

'I can't,' Alistair said. His eyes opened a little wider, enough for her to see them properly, and in them she saw sadness. But she also saw something else. Calm acceptance.

'You have to!'

'I'm done, Eve.' He lifted a hand as if it weighed the same as a skimmer and pressed it to his temple. 'The sonic grenade . . .'

'I know. I know. Don't try to talk.' She moved position a little, trying to make room for Bryant to come down and get him. The space was tight. Roots dug against her spine, a sharp pressure.

'Are you coming, or what?'

'In a minute,' Eve snapped back at Bryant.

'I have to tell you something,' Alistair said. His face was completely white now, making the blood that ran from his ears look even darker.

'Don't,' she said.

'Don't what? Don't say that I love you?'

She shook her head. It was too much.

'Eve,' he said, and in that one word was everything. They both knew what was happening to him. Still, she wanted to deny it. But she found she couldn't deny him. His skin was clammy and cold but when his fingers closed around hers, he smiled. It devastated her.

'Get away from here,' he told her, holding tight. 'Take one of their ships. You can fly it, I know you can. Live your life, Eve. Live it for me.'

He closed his eyes again, and she didn't let go. She held on and held on, knowing the poison was seeping through his skin and into his body, knowing it was bringing the end faster and that was what he wanted, what he needed. He coughed, his body wracked with spasms, and he cried out. And then he went still.

It was over.

A single tear made its way down Eve's cheek. She wanted to scream, to rage, but she couldn't seem to find the emotion within her. She felt entirely blank. Slowly, carefully, she let go of his hand. She smoothed the hair back from his forehead and touched his cheek. She moved onto her knees, put her arms around him, and pressed her mouth to his skin.

Then she got hold of his arm and tried to pull him up and out of the crevice, but he was too heavy, and she was too hot and too exhausted to fight against his weight. She got him to the edge of the path and that was as far as she could manage.

'We need to go,' Bryant said. There was a new urgency to his voice. Eve was able to process that much at least.

'You'll have to help me.'

'There isn't time.'

She heard the crashing of trees being broken. A large branch fell, landing only a couple of metres away.

'We can't leave him here!'

Then she heard the echo of Alistair's voice. *Go*, he said. *Just go.*

So she did.

She couldn't think about the fact that she was leaving him behind. That she would never see him again. She could only put one foot in front of the other and follow Bryant as he pushed his way through the thick jungle. She didn't even know if he was moving in the right direction, or if he knew where he was going. The Shi Fai had ships and they were going to take one. That was the only thing in her head as she ran.

Branches caught on her clothes and tore at her skin as more shrubbery rained down around them, pelting them with sharp little needles of wood. But eventually they broke through the tree line.

The Shi Fai landing port lay ahead of them. There were ships lined up in perfect, neat rows. There were women, not many, but enough. Some of them had made it this far. And there were Shi Fai. But the women were desperate, the Shi Fai small in number. There was a chance and Eve took it. 'Come on!' she yelled to Bryant as they broke, running from the trees, heading out across the clearing.

She picked a ship and made for it. Nothing else mattered now but getting on board. She would kill a Shi Fai with her bare hands if she had to. Bryant went straight to the side of the ship, rubbing at a row of coloured patches. The side of the ship opened up. He climbed inside, Eve following. There was no time to try and get any of the other women on board with them. Eve could only hope that they would find a way onto some of the other ships.

But for now their priority had to be getting this one airborne. She looked around, trying to find something that resembled a pilot's chair, or controls, but saw neither. The walls were made from rectangular bricks with rounded edges. They were faintly translucent, and she could see through to the pale liquid within. It glowed softly and she could see little pink bubbles moving round inside it. A ring of pots sat on the floor in the centre of the ship. Each one contained a dark liquid. There was no other sign of anything that might possibly control the ship.

'How in the void are we supposed to fly this thing?' Bryant asked, running his hands over the walls, moving quickly from one end of the little ship to the other.

'Here,' Eve said. On instinct, she moved over to the pots and dipped her hands into two of them. The walls began to glow brighter. She looked around, saw that those few pink bubbles had turned into a full-on fizz. 'Put your hands in the pots.'

Bryant did as she said, sinking his hands in right up to the wrist. The walls glowed even brighter, and then became transparent. 'Now what?'

Now we go, Eve thought to herself.

And the ship started to rise.

'How are you doing that?' Bryant said.

'Think it,' she told him. 'Think about where you want to go. The ship is alive. We're connected to it somehow.'

He didn't argue, didn't call her a fool as she expected him to. He held still, bracing himself against one of the long, twined strands that connected ceiling and floor. It was terrifying, watching the world move under their feet as the ship shot upwards. All around them, Eve could see other ships moving.

Some of the women had made it.

But Alistair had not. And the further away they got, the more it hurt, until it was a vicious wound in her gut. She breathed through the pain of it as they broke atmosphere and everything around them went dark. More than anything, she didn't want Bryant to know how she was feeling.

They caught up with the *Mutant*, somehow, falling in alongside as it orbited the planet. Together, they brought the Shi Fai ship alongside, and Bryant activated his comm. and spoke to the onboard computer. The docking entrance for the *Mutant* opened. They flew the little ship inside. It hovered in the middle of the docking bay as the doors closed up behind them, sealing them in.

Bryant was the first to disembark. He jumped down to the floor of the hold, and a moment later the whole place was flooded with bright, artificial light. Eve wanted to step out into it. She wanted to climb down the ladder that Bryant had rolled up against the side of the still floating ship. But if she did that, it would be admitting that Alistair was really gone. This ship was her last connection to him. And she hadn't told him anything. She'd always been too afraid.

She didn't know how long she sat there in silent agony, unable to cry. She couldn't even bring herself to take her hands out of the pots. It wasn't until Bryant climbed back into the ship that she realised her legs were numb, her mouth dry, the heavy weight in her belly somehow even heavier. And it was that which brought her to the present. Everything else, everything she felt, everything she needed, would have to wait until that had been dealt with.

'You can't stay in here forever,' he pointed out.

Eve looked at him. 'I need medical attention,' she said.

'Why? Is something wrong?' There was enough terror in his voice to remind her that he had come to Faidal to find her for a reason. When she looked at him, she felt numb.

'They put something inside me,' she said. 'I need to get it out.'

She moved over to the ladder and slid down it. Bryant followed, though he took a little longer to get down it than she did. Her feet carried her automatically to the med bay. She programmed the droid, lay back on the medibed for the scan.

'What the fuck is that?' Bryant asked.

Eve didn't respond. She didn't look at the image. She simply lay there with her eyes closed as the droid took care of the thing growing inside her.

And then she wept.

CHAPTER

38

4th day of the sixth turn

The Palace, Fire City, Sittan

Dax's body lay cold and motionless on a waist-high table. Jinn had been given water, scented oils and clothing, and told to prepare him.

So she did as she had been told.

She carefully cleaned every centimetre of skin, dipping the rough cloth into the cool water and gently wiping him down. She rubbed the oil over the body that she knew so well, but which was at the same time different and strange. His time in the arena had made him bigger, stronger. The suns had darkened his skin. And the tattoos on his shoulder, matching her own, were new and unfamiliar. She traced the outline of each one with her finger. He had so many. He was still so beautiful to her.

And he was gone. She should have known that he was different when he walked into the arena. She had replayed those few minutes over and over in her mind, wondering if she could have seen it. Perhaps, had she not been so willing to be led by the act he had put on.

'Dax,' she said sadly, 'What have they done to us?'

'Nothing less than you deserved.'

It was the empress.

Jinn spun to find her watching.

'What do you want?'

'Only to see if he is ready,' the empress said. She came closer and walked around the table, examining Dax. Jinn didn't like it. She didn't like it at all. But she controlled the Tellurium that burned in her hands. She sensed that her blades would not help her now. The empress had brought with her a dozen guards, and they ringed the room, always watching from behind their scarlet veils.

'He's ready,' Jinn said. She pulled the ties tight on his breeches, but she didn't step back from his body. He was hers, even now, even in death, and staying close to him let her control her devastation.

'Good,' the empress said. 'Seize her.'

The guards were on Jinn before she could think to move. She tried to fight them, but there were too many and they were too strong. They bound her wrists with long leather straps and pushed her forward. The table that Dax lay on began to float. It followed her and together they moved her out of the huge chamber and along a passageway and out into the courtyard.

The empress was already seated in her carriage. Dax floated at the rear. Behind him, male slaves pushed three covered carts. More bodies for the Mountain, Jinn realised.

And behind them, two figures she recognised.

Ritte and Li.

She was shoved alongside them, and the procession got underway. They moved through the town, walking slowly along the winding streets as more and more Sittan came out of their houses to stare at them. Some joined in with the procession, the numbers increasing the further they walked, until a long tail of males and females and children stretched out behind them.

'What happened?' Li muttered to Jinn.

'She put us together in the arena. He ... he tricked me into thinking he was too far gone. And I killed him.'

Saying those words out loud made it all too painfully real. For the next few minutes, she couldn't speak. The grief was over-whelming. Li remained silent. She was grateful to him for that.

'But he wasn't,' he said finally.

'No. He wasn't.' Her legs felt like stone after that, and each step became almost impossible. Dax had asked her to get Li and the others away from here. To take his body. To take him home. She had no idea how she was supposed to do that.

'They found our ship,' Li said. 'The empress found the Virena on board. It told her you came here with me, and that led her to Ritte. She doesn't have Merion.'

'Where is he?'

'Gone,' Ritte said. 'My son is no fool. He knows how to take care of himself. We have planned for this.' She stood with her back straight, her gaze fixed straight ahead as they walked on towards the Mountain. Occasionally one of the guards would poke at Ritte with the tip of their spear, and she would flinch, her face twisting in pain, but she did not cry out.

Jinn felt horrible. 'I didn't mean to cause you any trouble.'

'Trouble was coming our way regardless,' Ritte said. 'All you did was speed up the process. I knew ... when I saw the Virena respond to you, I knew that you were something different. Something we had not seen before. And I wondered what that meant, why you had come. Now I know.'

'I came here for Dax.'

Ritte shook her head. 'You came here because you were meant to, Jinnifer Blue.'

Jinn didn't believe that. There was no such thing as fate, or destiny. There were only chances and mistakes, and she'd had both of those in her life.

But before she could respond, the whole procession slowed to a halt. They had reached the top of the Mountain. The empress's carriage floated further up out of the way, and she climbed down from it. Dax's body was carried forward. Every centimetre he moved further away from Jinn was too far.

The empress turned and addressed the crowd. 'Today will be

marked down in our history,' she said. 'It is a day of change, a day in which our future has been shown to us. There are those among you who have tried to change our ways, tried to persuade others to join you. Today you will learn how wrong you were.'

She gestured to the slaves. The first few carts were brought forward. The crowd began to sing, their voices lifting in a powerful chant as the remaining Type One bodies were thrown into the crater. The Mountain responded with a thunderous roar, jetting glossy black sprays high into the air. They fell like a fountain.

It was a fitting display for a funeral procession.

Finally, it settled. The crowd began to stir as Dax's body was brought forward.

When Jinn had first met him, he had seemed indestructible. Nothing could hurt him. Not even the arena on Sittan had been able to stop him. But she had. And she knew now that this could have ended in no other way. He had been right. The empress would never have let him leave the planet alive.

Beside her, Li shifted a little, pulling on the chains that linked all of them together, and Jinn felt the Virena that bound her wrists flex and stretch. Dax was almost at the edge of the crater. Any second now they would throw him in, and he would be gone. Dax's body was lifted high. The empress walked over to him. She reached out a hand to touch him.

Something exploded inside Jinn. She would not have that alien female be the last person to lay a hand on Dax. She snapped the chains that held her in place. She didn't know where the strength had come from. It didn't matter. She charged forward.

But she was too late.

Dax's body was already falling.

Jinn didn't hesitate. She didn't even stop to think about what she was doing. She ran straight to the edge of the crater and jumped. Wind whistled past her. She couldn't breathe. She could see Dax falling below her and reached for him.

'Dax!' she screamed.

When he hit the dark liquid below, he would be gone. She

would lose him. She would not let that happen. She reached for him harder.

And suddenly, he began to slow. The distance between them decreased, cutting down until it was nothing, until she had him. She wrapped her arms around his big body and held tight. If they were going to go, they would go together.

But it didn't happen. Instead, Jinn found them both floating on a gentle cloud of Virena. The wind was no longer rushing past. They hovered a metre above the surface. It was incredibly deep, incredibly clear. There was no sign of any of the other men who had been thrown in only a few minutes before. The cloud shifted, moving them into a horizontal position. It caressed Jinn's legs, her arms. How was this happening?

She thought back through everything, and she knew.

She was controlling the Virena. And if she was controlling it, that meant she had a way out. Dax had known it even before she had. But she would have to move quickly. Hearing the whispers of the Virena, she focused. She held Dax tighter.

And she flew the two of them up and out of the crater.

They landed directly in front of the empress. Her shock was palpable. 'What ... how ...' Her control of the Universal language slipped, and she switched to Sittan. The meaning was still clear.

Jinn lowered Dax carefully to the ground. Then she willed out her blades. 'You were right when you thought that the Mountain erupted because of me. But you didn't understand why, did you? You never stopped to wonder how I had managed to get inside the palace, what it meant. I can control the Virena.

'I am leaving this place,' she told the empress, 'and I am taking Dax and the others with me.'

'Never,' the empress told her. She threw off her cloak and held out her hands. Twin spheres of Virena gathered above her palms, and then formed into blades. 'You think you can control it? You have no idea what that even means. You will die here, Jinnifer Blue. I will kill you myself.'

CHAPTER

39

4th day of the sixth turn

Mountain's Heart, Sittan

So this was how it would end. Here, at the very heart of the Mountain, the birthplace of the Virena. The crowd fell back. So, too, did the guards. There was a change in the atmosphere. The singing had stopped. Everyone was silent. Only the hum of the Virena behind them could be heard.

Jinn landed gently. She stood with her hands at her side and willed out her blades. Her time in the arena, Dax, the Sittan DNA in her cells, all of these things had made her who she was. And she was not the woman she had been when she had first come to this planet. She was stronger. Harder. She could do things she wouldn't have thought possible. She wasn't of this world, but she had an affinity with it, an understanding, and finally everything was falling into place.

The empress swung her blades, wrists circling slowly. They were long and vicious-looking. Jinn couldn't help but admire them. She held up her hands, put her own lethal blades on display. Virena misted around her hands, and then threw itself at the Tellurium, coating silver with glistening black.

'How are you doing that?' The empress's muscles visibly tensed. 'You are human!'

'No,' Jinn told her. 'I told you before. I'm Second Species.'

Not human. Not Sittan, either.

And, right now, that meant everything.

Jinn charged the empress down. But the Sittan female was quick, and she dodged the move. The tips of Jinn's blades clashed with the empress's swords. The impact rang up her arms. It shivered its way through her body.

She wanted more.

So she took it.

They came together again, blades clashing, harder, harder, until she felt the impact in her very bones. But her blades didn't break. The Virena strengthened them, strengthened her. It fought with her. Strike after strike, she felt her power build.

Then the empress changed one of her blades into a rope. She spun it, threw it out, catching Jinn around the waist, and pulled her in. The blade came down, catching her hard against her upper arm, cutting deep. Jinn cried out in shock and pain.

The empress laughed. She struck again, but this time Jinn was ready for it and knocked the blade away. Her other hand came up and hit true. A cut to the hip, not deep, but enough to make the empress snarl in anger. And that anger fuelled her.

She rained down hit after hit on Jinn. She was incredibly strong, and, as Jinn knew from watching her fight the intruders at the Ba-Rat, incredibly skilled. The chances to attack were few and far between. Jinn soon found herself driven back by the force of the blows. Her heart was racing wildly. Her vision narrowed down to just the empress. The rage in the alien female's eyes was terrifying.

'The Virena belongs to me!' she spat. 'How dare you try and use it against me! This is my planet. No one can take that from me. You thought to ally yourself with traitors, with rebels. But I found them, and I will kill them as soon as I have finished with you. I will hunt them down and wipe them out. Ritte and her son are only the beginning.'

Jinn put up her arm to defend herself. The next blow hit her Tellurium bracelet. The metal cracked. It hung loose from her wrist, revealing the skin underneath. The holes where it had been fitted were open wounds. Blood welled from them before they could close up. Jinn pulled off the bracelet and threw it aside as she rolled away from the next blow, putting distance between herself and the empress this time.

The empress looked even more pleased with herself. She spun her swords, holding them up at an angle so that the crowd could see. 'You cannot defeat me,' she said. 'You might as well surrender.'

Not while there was still a chance for Ritte and Li and Merion. Her wrist ached fiercely, and, when she tried to will her blade out of that hand, it would not come.

But Jinn would not give in.

'I will never surrender to you.'

'Then you will die.'

They came together again and again, each hit fierce and determined. Neither was willing to give in. Jinn used the blades she had left, the power of a kick, a fist. The empress was more skilled, there was no denying that, but she wasn't desperate. She was too certain that she had already won.

Her sword glanced off the other bracelet on Jinn's other wrist. The empress lunged at her, sword raised high, and Jinn only just managed to move away. Her entire body was exhausted.

The empress struck again, and this time Jinn wasn't quite quick enough. The other bracelet smashed. Without them, the Tellurium wouldn't work. Jinn was defenceless.

The empress kicked her to the ground. She raised her sword high over her head and held it there, shouting at the crowd in Sittan. The hot dirt pressed against Jinn's cheek, and her vision blurred for a moment. *Help me.*

She didn't know who she was calling out to.

But she got a response.

The song of the V'rena filled her head, a whisper at first. It quickly became a shout. Jinn flexed her fingers. She could feel the weight of the Tellurium in her hands, but something was different about it. There was a tingle that hadn't been there before. She focused on it. It became a roar.

Her blades shot out, no longer silver, but black. Dark strands spooled out from them and wove back across her hands, wrapping around her forearms. It was a part of her in a way that her blades had never been. Not a prosthetic, but an extension of her very being.

She held up a hand, and the empress's blades dissolved. They melted away until there was nothing left. The empress screamed. She charged at Jinn, but ropes of Virena flew up from the crater and caught her. She struggled against them but there was nothing she could do.

Jinn looked at her. 'I am leaving,' she told her. 'And I am taking them with me. All of them.'

She walked over to where Dax lay on the ground and picked him up. She glanced across at Ritte and Li. The bonds that held them snapped, freeing them both. No one approached them. No one dared.

Ritte smiled at her.

And then she called forth a wave of Virena of her own. It ran across the ground towards her, and Ritte took it. She held it close and whispered something to it.

Moments later, a roar sounded in the distance. It grew closer and closer, louder and louder, until Jinn was certain that she knew what it was. She started to walk. The crowd parted to let her through. They stared at her in amazement, eyes wide, stepping back to keep their distance from her. Even the guards kept back.

Merion flew the ship over the crater. The ramp lowered. Jinn broke into a run. Ritte and Li followed her. Their footsteps hammered against the ramp as they sprinted up it, into the belly of the yacht, and safety.

She set Dax down. Li and Ritte went through to the control

deck, and, seconds later, the ship started to move. But Jinn didn't hear the roar of the phase drive or feel the jolt as they broke atmosphere. She knelt down beside the body of the man she loved, the man she had travelled across the galaxy to find. His eyes were closed. He didn't move.

He had known the Virena would respond to her. He had known she would try to kill him, and he had let her.

What else had he known?

She placed a hand on his chest. His skin was cold and dry to the touch, but the feel of him was so familiar. She couldn't believe he was truly gone. She could live with having him forget her, with having him become someone else. But she didn't know if she could live in this galaxy if he was no longer in it.

'Come on,' she said. 'Come on, Dax. You wouldn't have done this if you didn't think you could survive it.'

And then she felt it.

The slow and steady beat of his heart.

CHAPTER
40

Ferona contacted Vexler almost immediately after leaving Weston's house and told him that she had considered his suggestion and they needed to talk. Not over comm. link, but face to face.

Then she headed back to her apartment. Just before she stepped inside, she had slipped the little device that Weston had given her into her ear. She felt a pinch, and then nothing. He had promised her it would prevent Victor from being able to hear what she was thinking.

Shoulders straight, she walked through the door of her apartment. Victor got straight to his feet and looked down at her. There was annoyance in his flat grey eyes. Ferona pretended not to notice. 'We are returning to Earth tomorrow,' she told him. 'Please make the necessary preparations.'

There was no reason to think that he would not. After all, this was what Vexler wanted. She would have preferred to go immediately, but Weston needed time. So Ferona spent the night preparing. Her hair, face and nails were all polished and perfected. She watched her favourite film from beginning to end.

She drank a little champagne, and then took a sleeping shot. She woke exactly at six, feeling refreshed and ready.

They made the trip back to Earth on her private transport. Her pilot was a quiet, reliable woman who didn't bat an eyelid when Victor climbed on board and attempted to fit himself into one of the seats.

Ferona took her own seat and pulled on her privacy headset, giving a clear signal that she was not to be disturbed. She switched to a soothing panorama of a beautiful beach, warm water lapping at her toes, and let her mind wander.

She knew that Weston had no morals. He was genuinely driven only by credits. As long as she kept paying him enough, he wouldn't betray her. He seemed to be enjoying the game of it most of all. It was dangerous to let a man like Weston grow bored, and that had been her mistake. Vexler had offered him excitement.

Now Ferona was offering him the opportunity to do something that would outdo anything either she or Vexler had so far required of him. She wasn't entirely sure what he had planned yet. She had told him what she needed. He had promised to make it happen. Ferona had gone along with this even though it made her feel deeply uncomfortable to leave the finer details to a man who could not be trusted. But the less detail she knew, the better. She had to be able to deny everything, should it come to that.

They made it back to Earth in good time, landing at a small, private port some twenty kilometres from the Dome. Swain arrived thirty minutes later in a rented skimmer.

'I got your message,' he said. 'Are you sure this is what you want to do?'

'Stop worrying.' Ferona pulled on her favourite gloves, white suede lined with fox fur, then stepped out of the waiting room into the cold. Her breath frosted in the air.

'So you're really going through with it.'

'Yes,' she replied. 'It feels like the right decision.'

Swain nodded. 'I agree,' he said.

Even you, Ferona thought to herself. *All of you have lost faith in me. Well, you will soon learn.*

Swain drove the skimmer at a steady pace. He didn't seem to be in any rush. That suited Ferona. She took the time to enjoy the view. This might well be the last time she would see this. She wouldn't miss it. She was tired of this cold, dead planet. She was looking forward to a wonderful, bright future.

And then the Dome was in sight, and they were rolling up to it. Swain parked the skimmer on the landing pad and the three of them stepped out. They quickly got into the elevator that would take them to the upper level and Ferona's apartment as the skimmer fired up and set off for the garage on autopilot.

Swain fidgeted anxiously, looking small and uncomfortable next to the towering bulk of Victor. Ferona stood still. She left the two men waiting with her hostess droid as she went through to her dressing room to change. Something sombre and yet elegant was required. The black coat with the sharp shoulders and red silk lining would do perfectly. She paired it with boots and a hat made from a thousand tiny silk butterflies, and took a moment to admire her image on the holomirror.

She sent a message to Vexler to tell him that she was on her way and checked the time on her wrist comm. Everything was going according to schedule. A little shiver of nervousness worked its way down her spine regardless as she gathered herself together and prepared to leave. Maybe it would have been better to know what Weston had in mind.

No, she told herself firmly. It was better this way.

Her skimmer was back on the landing pad when she stepped out of the elevator. Everything now had become about putting one foot in front of the other, taking the next breath, and the next breath. She lived from minute to minute, hyperaware of her surroundings, her body. She'd used the route often, so the autopilot took control. Swain sat opposite her, repeatedly smoothing the fabric of his trousers. Occasionally he would catch her eye and smile, and she would force herself to smile back. Victor sat in the front, out of the way.

Finally the skimmer settled down outside the government building of the London Dome. The door opened, winging up, and, beyond it, Ferona saw the tall glass doors of the building that had replaced Westminster. She had worked her whole life to find a place in that building, to be able to step through those doors into the hallowed chambers beyond.

And the man who stood waiting for her on the steps wanted to take all that away. Lucinda stood by his side, and never had Ferona been more certain that her assistant was no longer working for her. There was something in the way she stood, in the expression on her face. Swain got out of the transport first. He fastened his jacket and moved towards the steps.

Victor came up behind her.

This was it. This was the moment.

'Ferona,' Vexler said. 'I am so glad that you have come to your senses. This really is the only way.'

'Indeed,' Ferona said.

She stood square onto Vexler and looked him right in the face. All the frustration and bitterness bubbled up, and she could not stop it from spilling out. 'I would like to say that I have enjoyed working with you. But that would be a lie. You are both incompetent and self-serving. You do not care about the people of this planet. All you care about is yourself.'

Then she took a step back.

It was not a moment too soon.

There were two explosions. One was her skimmer. It caught both Victor and Swain. The other came from somewhere to the right. Vexler took the brunt of it. He dropped to the ground, motionless. Ferona was thrown off her feet by the force of it, and lay there, heart pounding, ears ringing. She looked up to see Lucinda staring at her, eyes wide and horrified. 'You,' Lucinda managed. There was blood running from her ears, dirt in her hair. Her perfect white suit was scorched and torn. But she was alive. 'You did this.'

Then she sank to the ground, her head in her hands.

The medics arrived then. Ferona didn't remember much after that. Her injuries were checked over and found to be superficial. She was given meds for pain, meds for shock. Her cuts were sealed. Then she was sent on her way.

Victor and Swain were both dead. Lucinda was taken to hospital but checked herself out shortly before Ferona was discharged. Vexler remained in hospital, in a coma. No one knew whether or not he would come out of it.

And, less than an hour later, a video emerged on social media in which Humans First claimed responsibility for the blast. Public opinion quickly turned against them.

As vice president, Ferona stepped up to take Vexler's place, temporarily. There were three days left before she would go to Kepler and witness the vote that would change the future of humankind.

She was ready.

CHAPTER

41

30th December 2207

The *Articus*, Sector Four, Neutral Space

Somehow, they had all managed to make it back to the *Articus*. There had been relief and there had also been tears. The group that had been broken had been put back together, but it would never be the same as it had before. None of them would. The absence of Alistair and Theon created a huge wound that Dax wasn't sure could ever be healed.

He was desperately worried about Eve. She sat apart from the others, silent and seemingly devoid of all emotion, wrapped in a soft silver blanket. He wanted to fix everything that had happened to her. But he couldn't. He couldn't fix any of it. Not himself, not Jinn, not Eve, not Bryant. He didn't even know what the future held for them. What happened in the next few minutes could make or break the human race.

Grudge dimmed the lights as he powered up the screen that he had wired up to his power system. He and the boys had found it out on one of the walkways, one of the few left unbroken here on the *Articus*. They had taken it down from its position high on the wall and dragged it in here. Now, instead of showing advertisements, it was showing the newsfeed. All across the galaxy, he imagined, humans were sat in front of screens like this, feeling just as anxious, just as unsure as he did.

The news presenters were almost beside themselves, talking incessantly as they tried to fill the time. Politicians old and new were interviewed and sound bites edited and repeated over and over.

President Vexler was still in hospital, in a coma, after Humans First had set off a bomb outside the government offices in London. Somehow Ferona Blue had managed to survive the attack. A livid purple scar decorated the side of her face. Her hair had been carefully styled to show it off to full effect. She was dressed in her senatorial robes and the camera panned to follow her as she walked across the Senate, greeting all other senators. It wouldn't be long now.

At the sight of the Sittan empress, Dax found it a little difficult to breathe. He couldn't bring himself to look at Jinn. She sat across from him. He could feel the distance between them like a gaping wound, and knew that he had put it there. What else could he expect? He should have found a way to communicate with her, to let her know what he intended instead of tricking her into doing what she had done. He could still remember the feeling of her blades entering his chest and piercing his heart.

His time on Sittan had left him unsure and ashamed. He had hurt Jinn. Every time he went to sleep, he heard the crack of the whip as it cut into the flesh of her back, ruining her beautiful skin. He had lost himself on that planet. He wanted to believe that it wasn't his fault. But that would be a lie.

He had made his choices. And they had been poor.

Li sat with Ritte and Merion. They were watching the screen just as carefully. Li had his hands wrapped around Merion's. There was at least that to be grateful for. The boys, too, were gathered close around Bryant, who was curled up in a float chair. He didn't have long left. The medical centre was working on an antidote but so far they'd come up with nothing. The oldest of the boys, Davyd, kept wiping Bryant's face with a cloth, and it stirred a pang of deep sadness inside Dax.

It shouldn't be this way.

'We have just heard that the vote is about to begin,' the announcer said. Everyone sat up a little. No one spoke. They all watched as, one by one, the senators stepped up to cast their votes. A black stone for yes, a white stone for no. They fell down a long, twisting chute, and piled up in a large bowl in the centre of the meeting hall.

Black after black fell.

They were almost there. Finally, Dax found the courage to look across at Jinn. The silver Tellurium bands that had wrapped round her wrists were gone, replaced by a beautiful pattern of spiralling black. The implant at her temple was still in place, and still as it had always been.

But she was more than she had been before.

She leaned forward, hands pressed against her cheeks.

I love you, desperately, Dax thought, but he could not say it out loud. He had to content himself with the fact that she was here, and he was too. Maybe one day they would find their way back to what had been. He was determined to cling to that hope, to do everything he could to bring her back to him, but he knew in the end that it would be Jinn's choice. If she couldn't forgive him for what he had done, what he had become, then he would have to live with that.

Dax turned his attention back to the screen. The Sittan empress had stepped up to the chute, stones in her hand. She looked down at them both. Surely she would pick the black, as all the other senators had done. But even before her vote was cast, Dax knew what was coming.

She slowly and very deliberately tossed down the white stone.

'No,' Jinn said. 'No!'

'What happened?' asked one of the boys.

'Be quiet,' Davyd told him. He moved in a little closer to Bryant. On the other side of him, Grudge reached out and took his hand.

The empress stepped down from the chute, but she didn't return to her seat. Instead, she walked across to the centre of the floor. 'Permission to speak,' she said.

'Permission granted.'

She stepped onto the speaker's platform. It rose up to waist height, then lifted her into the centre of the space. She gripped the edge with her clawed hands. Dax felt chilled.

'Members of the Senate,' she began. 'I'm sure you have all noticed that I have cast a white stone. I am sure you are all wondering why. It falls to me to tell you of an incident which occurred on my planet a few turns ago. As you are all aware, we were given a gift by the people of Earth. The Second Species humans. Type One males. They came to our planet, and we were grateful for them. We wanted nothing more than to create harmony with our human neighbours.'

'Liar,' Ritte hissed.

'One particular man became very important to me. His name was Caspian Dax. I took him into my palace. Into my home. After all, Senator Blue had given him to me. He was mine.' She looked around at the others. 'A human female travelled through Sittan-controlled space without permission. She landed on our planet, and she came to the palace, to my home. My home! And she took this man.'

The camera panned to Ferona. She had gone white. She sat in her seat, and it was obvious that her whole body was shaking.

Lights started to flash as other senators requested their own turn to speak. The next to get to his feet was the Shi Fai senator, Hann. 'Humans came to our planet also,' he said. 'They caused much destruction.'

The empress nodded.

The Lodon senator, Alaran, got to his feet. 'Senator Blue. Please respond to this.'

Slowly, slowly, Ferona stood. She gripped the edge of her lectern with white-knuckled hands. The scar stood out even more clearly on her face. Her eyes were huge and dark. She swallowed.

'I . . . I have heard nothing of this,' she said. 'I call for an immediate recess of the Senate. I require time to consider my response.'

'There is no time!' the Sittan empress said. 'If you have nothing to say, Senator Blue, then retake your seat.'

She stood straighter, looking tall and elegant and completely in control, in total contrast to Ferona, who looked as if the world was falling apart around her.

'There will be no vote,' the empress said. 'The human female who came to our planet violated the laws of the Senate. She came without permission, without permits. She came in a ship which had not been quarantined and in so doing could have brought any of a number of potentially devastating diseases with her. And in taking the male, she stole from us. This has left me with only one option.

'As of now, Sittan is at war with Earth.'

Jinn reached out and took Dax's hand. 'What have we done?' she whispered.

He didn't move, terrified that if he did, she would let go. Her touch grounded him in a moment when everything was wrong. 'The only thing we could.'

And this time, no matter what happened, Dax was certain of one thing.

There would be no surrender.

ACKNOWLEDGEMENTS

This book was a tricky one. Nothing about it was easy from beginning to end, and I would like to thank my agent Ella Diamond Kahn for her support and patience, and my editor Anna Boatman for all the work she did on this book. Anna, I know I put you through the mill with this one and I hope it was worth it – thank you for your help and your insight, and for taking a book that was quite frankly a bit rubbish and making it into something great. Everything you did was very much appreciated.

During the writing of this book, I was undergoing treatment for severe endometriosis. Some of that treatment was at UCLH in London, where I had surgeries in November 2016 and March 2017. It is hard for me to explain just how ill I was – often in terrible pain, anxious, frightened, not knowing from one day to the next if the pain was going to get the better of me, if I would have to go to A&E for help. The surgery I had in March 2017, although difficult and drastic, changed my life. I would like to thank the endometriosis team at UCLH, in particular Ertan Saridogan, Oliver O'Donovan and Sarah Parker for their skill, care and kindness. I am almost 12 months out from that surgery now, and I am pain free. I took my daughter to Paris for her 13th birthday. You made that possible.

I would like to thank my writer friends – Jessica, Julia and Maggie – and all my Twitter friends, people I have met in real

JANE O'REILLY

life and people I haven't, who have been unstintingly kind. Sometimes the internet can be a scary place, but sometimes it can be brilliant, and we mustn't forget that.

Finally I would like to thank my family. My mother-in-law Linda, who has helped us so much when things were difficult. My kids, Caroline and Matthew, for being funny and fantastic and continuing to be the best people I know. Caroline, keep smashing the patriarchy, and Matthew, you just keep being you.

And last of all, my husband Patrick. You told me not to put anything embarrassing, so I will say only this: I chose well.

AUTHOR LETTER

A huge thank you for choosing to read *Deep Blue*.

If you enjoyed the book, it would be fantastic if you could write a review. I'd love to know what you thought about Dax and Jinn, the empress, or Ferona and her endless scheming. Reviews also help new readers to discover a book, and there's nothing better than spreading the book love!

Want to know more? Wondering what will happen to Dax and Jinn now that they are back together but their world is about to fall apart? I love to hear from readers, and you can find me on Twitter as @janeoreilly, on Facebook, or on Goodreads. You can also find out more at my website, www.janeoreilly.co.uk

Thank you,

Jane